G000146466

Across the
Sapphire Seas

Across the Sapphire Seas

Heather Graves

PIATKUS

Copyright © 1997 by Heather Graves

First published in Great Britain in 1997 by
Judy Piatkus (Publishers) Ltd of
5 Windmill Street, London W1

**The moral right of the author
has been asserted**

*A catalogue record for this book is available
from the British Library*

ISBN 0-7499-0399-6

Set in 11/12 pt Times by
RefineCatch Limited, Bungay, Suffolk
Printed and bound in Great Britain by
Butler & Tanner Ltd, Frome & London

For – The cabbie, the clairvoyant and the lady who loves ballroom dancing . . .

Prologue

'Mama? Pa?' Pink in the face because she had run all the way
home to share her good news, Niamh slammed the back door
and ran through the kitchen on her way to the saloon of the
Silver Star, blowing Sally a kiss on the way. She almost can-
noned into her mother who was coming to see what the noise
was about and to forestall her daughter's entry into the largely
male stronghold of the saloon. 'Mama, I've decided. I know
now what I want to be!'

Janet raised her eyes heavenwards, aware that Niamh's
enthusiasms, like those of most fifteen-year-old girls, seemed
to change every day. 'Now then Niamh,' she said, herding her
back to the kitchen. 'How many times must I tell you – don't
behave like a hoyden. You know your papa doesn't like to see
children in the bar.'

You mean *you* don't, Niamh thought, knowing full well that
her father was too easygoing to care who came in and out of
his bar. 'But never mind that now, Mama, listen to me. There
was a lady at school today – a lady from London. She's old
now but she was a nurse at the Crimea – with Florence
Nightingale. She told us all about it. Oh Mama, she was thrill-
ing. She said well-trained nurses are as valuable as rare jewels –
an honour to the profession. You should've heard her, she was
an inspiration to us all. So that's what I'll be. A Nightingale
nurse, just like her.'

Janet placed her hands on her hips and took a deep breath,
preparing to do battle. 'But Niamh, you don't have to *be* anything. We haven't scrimped and saved to send you to that good
school in order to let you sacrifice yourself—'

'But it won't *be* a sacrifice, Mama. It's what I *want*.'

'We can't always do as we want, Niamh.' Janet's lips settled into a determined line. 'You've a foolish, romantic notion of what nursing will be. A fold of the bedclothes, maybe? A cool hand on the fevered brow? Well, it's not like that at all. It's a dirty business and most nurses are drunken old women, no better than they should be.'

'No better than they should be? What's that? You're always saying it and I don't know what it means. And Miss Nightingale's nurses aren't drunken old women – they're ladies.'

'Maybe. But Niamh, can you see yourself on your knees, scrubbing floors at some filthy hospital or asylum—'

'Nightingale nurses don't do that!'

'No? You think you'll be allowed to pick and choose? Sick people don't lie there suffering in silence, you know. They vomit and – and do other unpleasant things. How will you feel about changing a person's soiled sheets?'

'I'd do it willingly if I was asked. Miss Liggins was saying' – Niamh's face took on the glow of adulation as she spoke of her headmistress, reflecting the hero-worship she inspired in all of her girls – 'there's a new lying-in hospital to be opened soon. That's why the lady from London is here – to train nurses the Nightingale way. She says there'll be many opportunities for us girls, and then asked for volunteers. I was the first to put my name down. I'll be joining them next year after I leave school.'

'Niamh! How could you do such a thing without asking your papa or me?'

'Because this is *my* life, Mama. Not Papa's or yours. I know what I want to do.'

The sound of raised voices brought Niamh's father from the bar. 'Land sakes, you two,' he said, running his hands through his sandy red hair. 'What's all the shoutin' for?'

'You talk to her, Tully, I can't. Maybe you can make her see sense.' Janet sniffed. 'Meanwhile I shall be having a word with Rosamond Liggins. I didn't send Niamh to her fancy school for this. I sent her for one reason only – to learn the manners of a lady and make a good marriage. I don't expect to find her turned into a hospital skivvy the moment my back is turned.'

'It's not behind your back, Mama. I'm telling you now.'

'And I'm telling *you* – no!'

'Leave it now, Janet.' Tully spoke gently. As always he was the calming influence in these arguments which arose all too frequently of late. 'And Niamh, that's quite enough. We'll talk about it again later, when you can discuss it calmly without goin' off your head.'

'No, Papa.' Niamh wouldn't give way. 'I want this settled right now. I've always been interested in healing, as you know. I'd be a doctor, if I could.'

'A woman doctor,' Janet sneered. 'Who ever heard of such a thing.'

'One day, Mama, women will do everything men do. Miss Liggins says so. All it takes is time.'

'You wait till I see your precious Miss Liggins,' Janet muttered. 'Filling your head with such nonsense.'

'But I'll settle for being a nurse if only you'll let me. Oh Mama, please! Aunt Maggi will pay. She offered – she said she'd pay for me to have training in anything I liked.'

Tully smiled. He put an arm round his daughter's shoulders and gave them a shake, trying to get her to relax. 'For piano lessons, darlin'. Not somethin' like this.'

'But, Papa, why not?' She was getting plaintive, seeing her dream slipping away. 'Aunt Maggi won't mind. I'm sure she'd be just as proud of a nurse as a piano-player. What else am I going to do when I leave Miss Liggins? Serve with you and Mama behind the bar?'

'Maybe. When you're old enough an' have sense enough to be useful.' He was trying to make her smile. 'Oh Niamh, you've the whole of your life ahead of you. You're just fifteen years old. Enjoy yourself. Spend some time with Maggi up at the property an' with the Maitlands at The Oaks. You don't have to make up your mind now.'

'But I have. And you did what you wanted when you weren't much older than me. You went to sea.'

'Yes, an' a fine mistake that turned out to be.' Tully's expression clouded. 'I should've listened to me sister – she was right all along.'

'You're changing the subject.' Janet watched the exchange, anxious to get back to the original argument. 'If you don't

3

know what's expected of you, young lady, maybe it's time you did. We sent you to that school to give you a better start in life than we had – your father and I.'

'Yes, yes, Mama – I know.' Niamh closed her eyes against these arguments which were all-too familiar. 'And if I'm not living up to your expectations, I'm sorry. But this is what I want to do.'

'Then you can put it out of your mind because it's not going to happen. I won't allow it.'

Tully groaned, powerless to stop his wife from handling the situation so badly.

'I want to be a nurse!' The girl burst into noisy tears as she ran for the stairs, heading for the refuge of her own room. 'And if you stop me, I'll never forgive you, never. Not for the rest of my life!'

Chapter One

It was a quiet evening at the Silver Star. Most of them were, just lately. Or so it seemed to Tully as he stood polishing glasses behind the bar, remembering the rowdy, spendthrift days of the gold rushes. Rough and ready days, when you couldn't tell from a man's appearance if his pockets were empty or if he had money enough to shout the bar. Days when the diggers came storming in from the gold fields, bringing life and energy to the city, literally with money to burn. Brave days. Golden days. Gone now . . . and the city of Melbourne was becoming grown-up and respectable, Tully McDiarmit along with it.

Twenty years ago he used to pay five other people to work behind the bar which left him free to strum the piano, entertaining the customers. He wouldn't have had a moment to glance at himself in the mirror opposite, let alone study his reflection as he stood in front of the antique barrels containing brandy and gin. They had been there since the days of his father-in-law. Recently, he had added another containing Scotch whisky, made fashionable by the Queen.

What had he accomplished during this time? Not a great deal. Sometimes he had the feeling that Melbourne had prospered, forging ahead while he had been left behind, his customers drifting away to more modern entertainments, more fashionable bars. Perhaps he should have made some changes and moved with the times. But he liked the old-fashioned frontier atmosphere as did the customers who remained. Modernise and the old place might lose its character. He had kept the same mirrors his father-in-law had brought out from England. Expensive bevelled mirrors which ran the length of

5

the room on either side, doubling the illumination of the new gas-lights, giving the illusion of space and allowing a long narrow room to seem twice as wide.

He lit a taper from one of the lamps and touched it to a cigarette, breathing deeply and blowing out a column of smoke. He looked at himself. He hadn't changed so much. His sandy hair was no less abundant, if peppered with grey. Only the metal-rimmed spectacles were new, giving a studious look to what had been a dreamy, musician's face.

Tonight his customers were few. Two regulars, playing cards at a table in the corner and a couple of middle-aged men who'd been to the races, lounging at the bar.

He heard his daughter laughing in the kitchen, sharing a joke with Sally, and he smiled at the old woman's delighted cackle in return. *Niamh.* The one good thing to come out of his marriage to Janet Napier. One bright star in a wasted life. Two more regulars came in and he greeted them by name. Years of practice and he had it down to a fine art; welcoming but never familiar. He ushered them to an empty table and brought them two beers. Then he returned to the business of taking stock of his life – his achievements and his failures, recalling his sister's words. *You are so young – too young to be wed. Oh Tully, don't you see what you've done? You've tied yourself to this woman in marriage and business as well. You'll never be free of her now for the rest of your life.* Unfortunately, Maggi had been right. At seventeen, he had married smiling, happy-go-lucky Jinks Napier only to have her turn into Janet McDiarmit overnight; a disappointed, discontented woman who resented the whole world and everyone in it.

For Janet, who had no female relatives to support her, childbearing had been a horrifying experience which left her nervous and debilitated. While he himself, caught between his wife's needs and the demands of the business, was too inexperienced, too young to understand.

For the past twenty years, since Niamh was born, Janet had refused him his conjugal rights. Conjugal rights. Such stiff formal words to describe what had been so joyous between them before. At first it had been hard for him to accept that the physical side of his marriage was over. At first he reasoned with her, then tried to insist.

6

'Jinks, listen to me. The longer we leave it, the worse it's going to get. I can't live like this any more. It's been over three months since the baby was born . . .'

'You have to be patient,' she said, sitting high on the pillows and rocking herself as she hugged her knees. 'The midwife told me it's not unusual to wait six months—'

'Six weeks, not six months! Darlin', I miss you. I miss *us*. I'll be careful – I won't get you pregnant again.'

Tearful and trembling, she tried to accommodate him but when she shrank from his touch, it unmanned him. And after a while he just didn't try any more. He could have left her but he didn't. So, apart from a few unsatisfactory visits to prostitutes, usually at the instigation of his friends, he stayed faithful to Janet in body as well as in mind. He kept himself busy and accepted the fact that sex was no longer a part of his life.

As if conjured by his thoughts, his wife swept into the saloon, dressed for the evening, making an occasion of her entrance as she did every night. She flicked imaginary dust from her skirts and patted the smooth, dark coil of her hair worn high on the crown of her head. With no curls to soften it, she wore it in the style of a Spanish dancer, pulled severely away from her face. Of late it was darker than ever and he suspected she was dyeing it to hide the increasing grey. But, having kept her figure, Janet at forty-six was still exotic enough to turn a few heads, the purple smudges beneath her eyes suggesting a passion alien to her nature; a passion she didn't feel. As usual, she wore black, although tonight, in honour of his birthday, her skirt was a rustling silk taffeta shot through with gold.

He would have complimented her on her appearance but, before he could do so, Niamh staged a dramatic entrance from the kitchen.

'Ta – tarahh!' She sang the fanfare before starting across the room, carrying an enormous cake decorated with rough white icing and flickering candles set in the midst of bright green sugar shamrocks and ribbons.

'Happy birthday, dear Papa – happy birthday to you!' She finished the song, set the cake on the counter in front of him and gave him a smacking kiss on the cheek.

'Half your luck, Tulls! Many happies!' The regulars raised their glasses, well aware that it was usual for a hotel-keeper to

7

celebrate his birthday by shouting the bar.

'Happy birthday.' His wife brushed his cheek with lips as dry as dead leaves. It would have been so easy to turn and kiss her on the lips but he decided against it, reluctant to feel her shiver of distaste. So he kissed toothless old Sally instead. Sally who had come waddling in behind Niamh to witness the cutting of the cake. Sally who had been both mother and grandmother to the little girl his wife had largely ignored. Janet took an interest in her daughter only when she was grown. It was a tribute to the girl's good nature that she bore no malice towards her mother for this early neglect.

'Hollis is coming to see you later, Papa,' Niamh whispered as they bent together over the cake. 'There's something he has to ask you.'

'Oh, an' how's that?' he said, deliberately keeping it light. 'I thought it was the custom to ask for a girl's hand on her *own* birthday, not her papa's?'

'Now Papa, be nice to him. You know he'll be nervous.'

'I'm always nice,' he teased. Then, suddenly serious: 'You are sure about this, princess?'

'Yes, Papa.' She hugged him. 'I can't remember when I didn't love Holly. I must have loved him all of my life.'

'Exactly. Like the brother you never had,' he muttered, too softly for her to hear.

'All we're asking is to be betrothed. We won't be getting married for ages yet. Now blow out your candles, Papa, before the wax drips all over the cake.'

He breathed in and closed his eyes in the time-honoured manner of making a wish, blowing out the candles to a round of applause, leaving a smell of wax and smoke in the air.

'What did you wish for, Papa?'

'Happiness, darlin', as always – especially yours.'

She looked at him, shaking her head. 'Oh Papa,' she said. 'Why do you never ask anything for yourself?'

'Because I've had all I was due for and more. More than you'll ever know, girl.' Still in a sober mood, he started cutting the cake, filling plates for Niamh to pass to the customers. It was amazing how quickly the word had spread that it was his birthday and he was shouting the bar.

*

8

'I don't know why you're so against it,' Janet tackled him when they had filled all the hands reaching for glasses of free ale and Niamh was out of earshot, offering cake. 'Hollis Maitland is a very good catch.'

'So is our girl,' Tully said mildly. 'And I'm in no hurry to part with her. Forget the obvious advantage, will you, an' look at the man himself.'

'What about him? He's the Maitlands' only heir – he'll inherit the practice when Harley retires.'

'I know. Everything's come to him so easily.'

'And why not? It's a family business, not so different from our own. Would you call Niamh spoiled and indulged because one day she'll inherit the Silver Star?'

'It isn't the same.'

'It is. And if Niamh *has* to marry, it may as well—'

'Be to the highest bidder?' He knew what she would say. 'The man with the most to offer in money and goods?'

'Yes – and why not! '

'Niamh's happiness is more important to me than her husband's wealth.'

Janet made an impatient sound in her throat. 'You always were a soft-hearted Irish fool. If I'd only known at her age what I know now—'

'You wouldn't have married me.' Once more he finished the sentence for her.

'I didn't say that. You think she's a child but she's twenty this year. Another year and she'll be on the shelf.'

Tully laughed shortly, increasing her irritation. 'Rot! There's a chronic shortage of women in this town, remember?'

'There must be.' She resorted to dry humour. 'Or else why are you still here with me?'

'Ah, Janet. Let's not dig up the past to throw at each other. Not tonight.'

'And why not? Birthdays are milestones, husband. Time to take stock. Time for the past to catch up with you.'

His eyes widened momentarily behind his spectacles. Unwittingly, she had reminded him of a visit earlier that day. Albert Smith had called in, bringing with him a young man he had taken on as foreman at the foundry. They were buying drinks to seal the bargain, celebrating the event.

9

Fresh off the boat from England, the young man had the clear suntan that only comes from an ocean voyage and was still wearing his English clothes, too heavy for an Australian spring. He hadn't been here long enough to discover the comfort of crimea shirts and moleskins – the practical working clothes which had come into favour on the gold fields and had subsequently been adopted as the uniform of the working man.

'Judah Burden,' he introduced himself, shaking Tully by the hand. 'My friends call me Judd.'

Burden. Not that common a name but disturbingly familiar to Tully. He looked at the man more closely this time, old memories stirring as he thought of Jem Burden, the man who had befriended him when he was young, encouraging him to kick over the traces and join the crew of the *Sally Lee*. He hadn't thought of Jem or the *Sally* in years. Could this be a relative maybe? Certainly, he was tall and broad-shouldered enough, the voice uncannily the same; the distinctive vowels, the good-humoured growl of a man from the West of England. But there the similarities came to an end.

Jem's features had been nondescript, homely, while this Burden was both handsome and confident. He hadn't been hiding behind the door when the good looks were handed out! Tall and well-built, he had a thick head of dark brown hair which he wore a little longer than the current fashion and he had those bold, dark eyes so appealing to women. He was cleanshaven too, which was perhaps a good thing. Facial hair would have made him look villainous; something of a pirate. Unconsciously, he presented a challenge to others less favoured, making them want to spoil his good looks by punching his lights out.

Tully wanted to punch him too, his fatherly instincts alerted, when he saw Judd assessing his daughter through half-closed eyes, watching her covertly as she moved about the room. A man for the ladies all right. Fortunately, Niamh ignored him, being used to such frank appraisals from the other side of the bar.

To take his mind off his irritation, he turned to Albert, encouraging him to talk about the foundry.

'Too right!' Albert said, clapping Judd on the shoulder. 'My

lucky day when this one called in asking for work. He's no
ordinary smith, you know. He's a craftsman skilled in working
wrought iron.'

'Oh, yes?' Tully tried to look interested and attentive. It was
easier to listen to Albert than make conversation himself.
And, looking at Judd, he remembered that other man by the
name of Burden and the violence of the storm which had
wrecked the *Sally Lee*. The masts had been first to go,
probably struck by lightning, followed by the cracking and
groaning of the ship's timbers as they sprang apart one by one.
It was years ago but he could remember it, as if it were yesterday. The rage of the storm and the ominous calm which had
followed it. The emptiness of the tropical waters and the heat
which robbed them of energy and breath. The sun hanging
overhead at midday, scorching them without mercy; a malignant ball of fire in a cloudless sky. Only the three of them had
survived. Jem Burden, himself and Pieface, the dog, adrift in a
leaky boat. Even at night, when darkness brought some relief,
they didn't dare sleep in case the boat filled up with water and
sank, leaving them floundering in those deep, shark-infested
waters.

He returned to the present with a slight bump as if his soul
had temporarily left his body and now returned. *Time for the
past to catch up with you*, Janet said. Earlier it had been Judd
who unsettled him. Now it was his wife, jogging his memory
and his conscience, reminding him of times he would rather
forget.

In the kitchen, Niamh leaned back against Hollis, twisting the
solitaire diamond, new and surprisingly heavy on the third
finger of her left hand.

'Oh Holly, it's lovely,' she breathed, 'but you shouldn't. A
small token would have been quite enough.'

'I didn't want to give you a small token. I wanted you to
have this.' He rocked her in his arms, kissing her temple and
pushing back a lock of fair hair which had fallen from her coil.
'Plenty more where that came from. I'll be a full partner in the
firm in less than two years. Then I'll make those whinnying old
conservatives sit up and take notice. I'll show them how real
money is to be made.'

11

She twisted around to look up at him. 'Take it slowly, Holly. You're only just out of college – a junior yet . . .'

'Oh, stop it,' he said. 'You sound just like Pa.'

'And you should be saving your money, not spending it all on me.'

'Time somebody did,' he said, plucking at the sleeve of the severe, high-collared dress. 'My neat little church mouse, always dressed in brown. You wait an' see. When we're married I'll make you queen of this town. Your father won't be able to look down his nose at me then.'

'Be patient with him, Holly. I'm sure there isn't a father alive who thinks any man good enough for his daughter. And Pa's not himself today, not at all. I didn't realise he'd take his fortieth so much to heart.'

'He is a bit distracted. Didn't even bother to put me through the *"What are your prospects?"* routine.'

'Because he knows!' Niamh grinned. 'Mama reminds him a dozen times every day.'

'At least *she's* pleased.'

'More than Aunt Lilias, anyway. What did she say?'

'Oh, you know Mother . . .' Hollis avoided her gaze.

'Holly?' She peered into his face, suddenly anxious. 'You have told her?'

'As a matter of fact, I didn't.' He pulled at one of his sideburns, looking shamefaced. 'I took the coward's way out and left it to Pa.'

In a salon very different from the kitchen of the Silver Star, Lilias Maitland was appraising herself in the ormolu mirror above the fireplace, delighted with both her own appearance and that of her home. Recently redecorated in the colours she thought were the last word in London and Paris, she was preparing to reopen The Oaks to Melbourne society, planning a dazzling evening of music and dance which even the Governor of Victoria might attend. George Phipps, Marquis of Normanby. What a coup that would be!

Her reflection smiled back, assuring her she'd lost none of her looks although she was old enough to be a grandmother. Just. Maybe the skin was drawn a little more tightly over her cheekbones these days and her hair which had once been a rich, dark brown, was now a blonde secret between herself and her hairdresser, but the sparkle in her blue eyes was still there. She had lost none of her confidence and was pleased with husband and household, both trained to her ways.

The thought of becoming a grandmother made her think of Hollis and the reflection looked less pleased. She stroked away an incipient frown with her middle finger and smiled at her husband who had just come into the room. He looked around, nodding his approval of the newly refurbished room.

'I say!' he said. 'This is rather splendid, isn't it? And you were right about the curtains, after all. I was afraid the dark blue might be cold.'

'I'm always right about colour.' She kissed him briefly, wondering if this were the right time to bring up the subject of Hollis and the McDiarmit girl.

Below stairs, Ellen, the housekeeper, flinched at the sound of raised voices. So rare was it for the Maitlands to argue, it didn't occur to them to do so behind closed doors.

'Oo-er, hark at that,' whispered Mavis, the scullion, listening open-mouthed. 'Goin' at it hammer an' tongs, they are!'

'All right, Mavis.' Ellen began to shove her towards the back door. 'I need a bunch of fresh carrots for supper and you can pick us a few salad greens for tomorrow.'

'But Ellen, it's dark outside an' there's spiders out there. I won't be able to see!'

'The spiders won't hurt you but I will if you don't move. Out! Before I box your ears till they burn.'

Mavis knew this was no idle threat and lunged for the door. Ellen followed, closing it firmly behind her.

Upstairs, Lilias was glaring at her husband, tears standing in her eyes.

'But Harley, how could you? How *could* you give your consent without discussing it with me first?'

'Our son is old enough to do as he pleases, Lil. He doesn't need our consent. To ask it at all is a courtesy. He's of age and soon he'll be a full partner in the firm.'

'Who will need a wife who can uphold certain standards – entertain the Governor and his lady, if necessary.'

'I'm sure Niamh's up to it. She's no fool, my dear.'

'No, indeed. I certainly underestimated her.'

'Oh come, my love. It's not a surprise. They've been sweet-hearts ever since they stood up and held hands together when they were small. You used to say it was charming.'

'I thought they'd grow out of it. Holly's so naïve – he's had no experience of women and no chance to compare. He's been far too busy studying to meet other girls.'

'He doesn't want other girls: he's happy with Niamh. And I have to say I approve. She's an intelligent girl.'

'Far too intelligent for her own good. Remember when she was fifteen and she wanted to be a Nightingale nurse?'

'How can I forget, when *I* was the one roped in to talk her out of it – to my lasting shame. Persuading her to put her parents' wishes before her own.'

'A pity. If she'd been allowed to follow her calling, we wouldn't be facing this situation now.'

'That's not what you said at the time.'

'Maybe not. But how was I to know she'd grow up with her hooks so firmly in Holly?'

'Oh?' Harley raised quizzical eyebrows. 'I'd say it was the other way around.'

'I didn't want him married straight out of law school. I wanted him to travel – go on a tour of Europe maybe . . .'

'And come back with an heiress in tow? A horse-faced woman with a trunk full of Waterford crystal and Rockingham for the table?'

'Precisely.'

'Then I'd say he's had a lucky escape. Niamh will be an asset to any man. And if Hollis is safely married, he'll devote his energies to the business instead of staying up late with his cronies to go boozing and chasing girls.'

'Men! That's all you ever care about, isn't it – business. Well, I'm warning you, Harley Maitland, I'm not finished with this. Not by a long chalk.'

Exasperated, Harley ran his hands through his thinning hair. 'Lilias, please. We don't want a family upset over this. Niamh is Maggi's niece, remember?'

'Can I forget? It's because of these claustrophobic family relationships that Hollis is caught in this coil.'

14

The front door opened and closed with a bang, announcing their son's return.

'Now that's enough.' Harley raised a warning finger to his lips. 'Not a word to Hollis of any of this. And for heaven's sake, Lil, try to cheer up and smile. It's the boy's wedding we're talking about, not his funeral.'

Dan MacGregor ran up the steps of the verandah with the mail he had collected from the Post Office at Beechworth and flung the bundle into his mother's lap. Maggi, who had learned to read only late in life, flung it back.

'Sort out the bills, Danny, and put them aside. Then you can read me the letters before you go out.'

'Oh Ma, do I have to?' Danny was itching to catch up with Dermot, his twin, who was already away catching yabbies, the big freshwater crayfish infesting the dam. Holiday times like these were precious to the two boys, who delighted in being free from the rigours of boarding school. The pleasures of fishing weighed heavily against the chore of reading letters to his mother. 'There's only one, anyway. Can't you try and read it yourself or wait until Pa comes in?'

'Who's it from?' Maggi's eyes sparkled. Always hungry for news of her relatives in the city, she took a childish delight in receiving mail.

'Only Uncle Tulls,' Danny said reluctantly, knowing he wouldn't be allowed to escape without reading it.

'Then what are you waiting for? Read it at once.'

Sighing, Danny leaned against one of the supports of the verandah, hoping it wouldn't take long. Much as he expected, it contained news of his cousin, Niamh. News which produced a whoop of delight from his mother and which he was at a loss to understand. What was so wonderful about getting married? Why did women have to make such a fuss?

His mother was smiling, eyes filling with tears as she clasped her hands under her chin; a working woman's hands, calloused and chapped from grooming and riding her horses. But it was a task she loved, refusing to delegate it to anyone else. Her stockhorses and hunters were prized the length and breadth of Victoria, and she could never breed enough to keep up with the demand. The extra money she earned was a bonus

15

during the lean years when the price of wool was down, her income helping to keep the twins at the boarding school they pretended to despise. Like many a person lacking in formal education, Maggi revered it above all things, determined her boys should have the best that money could buy. At fourteen they weren't old enough to be grateful for this.

Daniel loved his mother dearly. She wasn't set in her ways and boring like the mothers of most of his friends, and never tried to make out that she was a lady. She was just Mama and there was nobody like her; no one in all the world. Because her face was mobile and expressive, it was marked with crow's feet around the eyes, and her smile showed the deeper lines unavoidable in a climate which drained the skin of moisture, leaving it chapped in winter, tanned like a brown leaf in summer. But the daily exercise on horseback allowed her to keep a trim figure and she moved with a lighter step than most women her age. There were times when Dan wished she could have been slightly more conventional, or that he and his twin had inherited their father's fair hair instead of their mother's vibrant red curls but, in general, the joys of having Maggi MacGregor as his mother outweighed the disadvantages. Sometimes, from across the room, she could look like a girl, her hair the same startling red as his own and with only the occasional strand of grey.

'What kept you?' Dermot asked him when Danny finally joined him at the dam, having crossed several paddocks to do so. The sides of the dam were of clay, the water murky, the colour of milky coffee. It was hard to believe any creature could live in it at all, let alone something good enough to eat.

'Is that all you've caught?' Dan ignored the question, crouching to examine the bucket of water in which two big brown yabbies were patiently searching for a way out.

'I threw the little ones back.' Dermot tied another piece of meat to a string and cast it into the water, crowing with delight when another yabby latched almost immediately on to the bait. He whisked it expertly out of the water and on to the bank. The creature let go of the meat at once and scrabbled, trying to get back into the water before being caught and thrust into the bucket along with its fellows.

'Give us a go,' Dan said, grabbing a piece of meat and a

16

string for himself. 'Wanna hear the latest? Niamh's getting married to Hollis. Ma's gone all soppy about it.'

Dermot removed his scarf and simpered, tying it woman-like around his head. 'Here comes the bride!' he carolled, taking a few mincing steps. Dan giggled and soon both boys were rolling on the ground, howling with laughter at themselves.

Over the dinner table Maggi repeated the news to her husband, Callum. Her eyes bright with sentiment, she sighed: 'Isn't it lovely, Cal? Like a fairytale comin' true.'

'Is it?' Unsmiling, Callum set down his knife and fork to consider this news, remembering the quiet, independent spirit that was Niamh. Born and bred in the city, she had been nervous of horses, unused to the large heads suddenly swinging towards her, but she didn't refuse when Maggi insisted she must learn to ride. It was Callum himself who had come to her rescue suggesting a compromise, offering to teach her to drive a pony and trap. Her gratitude and relief had been patent but she had never complained. Then he thought about Hollis, also his nephew, his sister's child. Like his father before him, Hollis was blest with ability and a will to succeed but there the similarities came to an end. Certainly, he would make a good lawyer but he was charming and selfish like Lilias, his mother, lacking his father's instinctive kindness and compassion for human frailty. No, Holly wasn't the husband Callum would have chosen for Niamh, not at all.

'Oh Callum, don't look so solemn. It's wonderful news!' Maggi rejoiced. 'A wedding and a strengthening of family ties. And it'll give us an excuse to go to Melbourne for once. High time I had a new dress. I might even stage a comeback at the Queen's—'

'Oh Mama, no!' Her twins groaned in unison. Maggi's career in the music halls as 'The Southern Songbird' provided the boys at school with yet another excuse to tease them.

'Depends on the time of year. I can't just drop everything and leave. The shearing has to come first,' Callum said slowly. As usual he was the calming influence over the volatile Irish element in his family. A typical son of the country, he was a man of few words but when he did have something to say, his family listened. 'Besides, it's too soon to get excited about it. They've not even set the date.'

17

Chapter Two

Armed with a note from Albert, recommending him to some relatives who would provide him with lodgings not far from the foundry, Judd packed and left the crowded boarding house in Melbourne for the last time. Too thrifty to spend the last of his resources on a cab, he rode to Richmond on the upper level of a horse-drawn bus. He thought he would be warm enough in the sunshine but he had not yet learned that in Melbourne winter is slow to relinquish its grip. Perfect as it was for sight-seeing, giving him a first-class view of the growing city, the biting winds made his ears sting and his eyes water.

While some of the buildings rivalled the grandeur of any city in Europe, Melbourne appeared to retain a village atmosphere. Most people who lived and worked there seemed to have at least a nodding acquaintance as they greeted each other on the streets.

There was no conductor on the bus and it fell to the driver to look after everything, including the horses. He had to give change as well as open and shut the door by means of a strap tied to his foot. As the journey was long, the horses slow and they kept stopping to let passengers on and off, Judd had plenty of time to look around, mull over the past and consider the new way of life that lay ahead.

Alone, after the death of his mother, he had come to Australia in search of an uncle who had disappeared some twenty odd years ago, together with an inheritance his mother told him was his due. Not that his expectations were high. He held out little hope of finding either his uncle or the inheritance. But, by leaving England at this time, he could sidestep two young women who were closing in on him, each one hoping to be his wife. Both were named Jenny, one as dark as the other was fair. He loved them a little but not enough to marry and it was easier to bow out of the situation rather than choose.

At twenty-seven he was old enough to know his own virtues and vices, one of which was a weakness for pretty women. He liked them not only for their bodies but their minds, and made friends of his lovers. This was the secret of his success. But Judd wasn't ready for marriage. Not yet. Why should he tie himself down to one woman when there was always a new challenge around the next corner – a new pair of eyes to light up his life?

Beautiful eyes made him think of that girl at the Silver Star. There was a challenge, indeed. She was more like a candidate for the nunnery than a barmaid, with those long tight sleeves down to her wrists and that crisp white collar fastened right up to her throat. If anyone had asked him what he found so intriguing, so attractive about her, he couldn't have said. Her features were even but a little too neat, her mouth too small to be sensual. But she had the most beautiful eyes; brown eyes, the colour of rich sherry, as long-lashed and expressive as those of a fawn. One glance and he was in thrall.

Judd, you are a prize idiot! He laughed at himself. Here's a city bursting with pretty women and you start daydreaming about this girl and falling in love.

To exorcise his vision of Niamh, he turned his attention to the womenfolk of Melbourne, looking them over with a practised eye. Taller than their English counterparts, they were generally better dressed, unafraid to wear rich fabrics and bright colours; silks and satins were out on the streets even at this early hour. Willowy Australian girls who strode about like young men, too busy to allow themselves to be hampered by their long skirts. Strong girls who would take to a life in the bush without flinching, kill snakes to protect their babies and think nothing of helping a man to build a house. He couldn't imagine any one of them feeling faint or needing smelling salts to revive her. Their eyes sparkled with good humour and merriment as they called out to each other, laughing without inhibition. He smiled and waved to them and they waved back, happy to do so because they had safety in numbers and he was aboard a moving omnibus.

The well-dressed citizens of Melbourne reflected the buoyancy of the economy and the air of excitement which surrounded a city still coming to terms with its wealth and prestige. In the spring of 1878 Melbourne had everything of the best the modern world could provide, her wealth founded on gold discovered in the surrounding countryside several decades before. Gold which had brought fortune-hunters from all over the world. Even after several decades, money and people were still pouring in and the city was in the midst of a building boom.

And if, by international standards, Melbourne was small, it lacked nothing in the way of amenities. There were theatres to rival any in London, as well as dance-halls and saloons. Exclusive boutiques and shops for the wealthy co-existed with markets for the poor. Every kind of horse-drawn transport was out on the wide streets which ran between buildings three and four storeys high. Only the stink from the gutters was an unpleasant surprise. Progressive in so many ways, the city fathers had been slow to spend money on sanitation and the disposal of waste. Cesspits reeked and gutters overflowed with all manner of garbage and filth which encouraged the breeding of flies. And flies there were in their thousands, some capable of inflicting a nasty bite.

An hour later, Judd was drinking tea with Daisy and Matthew Bradley, tucking into a plate of delicious home-made scones. He had fallen in love with their home as soon as he saw it – a solid weatherboard house which had started life as a simple cottage. The pair of straggling rose trees on either side of the door weren't a patch on his mother's roses in England, but they bloomed, just as bravely – a reminder of home.

Beyond the kitchen was a mass of haphazard extensions, built to accommodate a family grown-up and gone. Shabby but comfortable, the house came with a large portion of land at the rear, marked out to grow vegetables and surrounded by currant bushes for the making of jam.

'Second-generation, that's me,' Daisy told him with pride. 'My mother come out with the first fleet.' Matthew groaned, having heard the story too many times before. Ignoring him,

20

Daisy pushed the plate of scones towards Judd. 'Have another one, Mr Burden. Looks like the first one never touched the sides.'

Judd accepted, reminding himself to eat more slowly. It was a long time since he'd tasted such delicious, home-cooked food.

Fair-haired and well into her forties, Daisy put him in mind of a plump domestic hen. Her husband, Matthew, obviously older, went by the odd nickname of Cabbage Tree. He had to be nearly sixty but he moved like a younger man, free of arthritis or any stiffening of the joints.

'I don't walk with the bullocks meself any more,' he sighed. 'The boys like to work on their own now, without any tellin' from me. But the game's not as tough as it used to be.' He sniffed as if this were cause for regret. 'They have it easy. Highways to the country towns. Proper bridges over the creeks. Hoo, shoulda been here in the early days. High old times we had then.'

Now it was Daisy's turn to groan as Matthew launched into his own reminiscences. Tales of coaxing bullocks to swim over swollen creeks and rescuing folk left destitute after bush-rangers had robbed them of everything, even their clothes.

At the end of the afternoon, Judd felt as if he had known the Bradleys for ever.

'An' I'll be a grandma soon,' Daisy nodded, eyes sparkling as she spoke of the subject nearest her heart; the married daughter about to give birth to her first child.

'Put a sock in it, Daise,' Cabbage Tree wriggled in his seat. 'That's women's talk. Judd don't wanna hear that.'

But he wanted to hear about everything. It was good to sit at a kitchen table and be part of a family again. The Bradleys were proud parents whose world revolved about these happily married children and their achievements. Daisy's smile faltered only when she mentioned their youngest, Carl.

'Don't talk to me about Carl!' Matthew's normally good-natured expression hardened into a scowl. 'Bloody little mongrel. Ah well, I s'pose every family has to have its black sheep – always one rotten apple in every barrel.'

'Oh, Matthew.' Daisy's soft blue eyes filled with tears. 'You've never understood him. You don't even try.'

'Oh yes, I do. I understand him only too well.' Her husband

narrowed his eyes. 'That's the trouble, ennit?' He lurched to his feet and headed towards the back door. 'Ah, well. No peace for the wicked. Garden's not gonna weed itself.' He nodded to Judd. 'Be seein' you, lad. Fix up the details with Daise if you're goin' to stay.'

Daisy showed him the room they were offering, which was on the other side of the house. Sparsely furnished, it was newly painted, airy and he was relieved to see that the bed was generously large. After being cramped in a bunk at sea and a crowded dormitory in town, this was luxury indeed.

'Will it do you, then?' Daisy said, plumping the pillows. 'Will you stay?'

Judd nodded. 'Oh yes, Mrs Bradley. Yes, please.'

'Then if you're stoppin', you'd better call me Daise.' She smiled, offering her hand to shake on it, surprised when Judd turned it over and brushed it with his lips instead.

'Well, I'll be—' A man spoke up behind them, making them both start. 'Takin' a boyfriend, Ma? What's Dad going to say?' Judd looked up to see a tall, rangy young man lounging in the doorway, regarding them.

'Oh, hush with your nonsense, Carl!' A flush rose from Daisy's neck and she glanced at Judd, wondering how he would take her son's teasing. 'An' never mind about me, you young monkey. Where'd you get to last night? We was worried sick when you never come in.'

On meeting the son, Judd gained some insight into the reason for the father's bitterness. Carl might have been Matthew forty years earlier – a living reminder of the passage of time. At eighteen, Carl looked older than his years, for there was a toughness in his bearing, a glint of steel that was missing from his father's honest, straightforward gaze. Judd had come across young men like this one before. Reckless fellows who lived for the moment. They made good soldiers but turned naturally to crime during times of peace. Carl had odd eyes, one amber and one green, merciless as those of a jungle cat. He looked as if he had recently been in a fight; the dark swelling on his cheekbone confirmed it.

He hugged Daisy, grinning and showing a mouth full of strong white teeth. A panther no more, he was simply a boy coming home to his mother, tired and in need of a wash.

22

'God, an' ye stink,' she scolded, pushing him away. 'An' what's happened to that shirt? Clean on only yesterday.'

'Aw, don't go on, Ma!' Carl winced, looking pained.

'Been fightin', haven't you?' She peered at him. 'What's happened to your face?'

'It's nothing, Ma.' He gave her a quick buss on the cheek. 'You should see the other bloke.' To change the subject, he winked at Judd, bringing him into the conversation. 'Who's this, then? Aren't you goin' to introduce me?'

'This here's Judd Burden,' Daisy said. 'Goin' to work for yer Uncle Albert. He'll be lodgin' with us for a while.'

'Good-oh.' Carl offered his hand and Judd clasped it, finding it shaking slightly, hot and feverish in his own. Maybe he didn't feel so well as he'd have his mother believe. Forestalling any more queries, he delved in the pocket of his waistcoat to bring out a small gold brooch in the form of a heart, set with seed pearls. Daisy swooped on it with small squeals of delight.

'Ooh, Carl! It must've cost a small fortune!'

Carl shook his head and the two of them left Judd to unpack and acquaint himself with his surroundings. Having done so, he lay on the bed and gazed at the ceiling for some time, grateful to the fates that had guided him here.

As the three-piece orchestra struck up, making the potted palms quiver, Niamh looked around the crowded café, very conscious of being observed. She had been here with Hollis before, but this was the first time since their engagement. Suddenly, everyone seemed to know who she was; the girl who was marrying Hollis. Women studied her critically, hiding their smiles behind their hands. She could read their minds as clearly as if they had spoken aloud. Who was she, this nobody who had secured the most eligible bachelor in Melbourne? What could he see in this shy, ordinary girl?

Hollis was speaking and she had to lean across the table to hear him over the clatter of teacups and the musicians struggling with Mozart.

'Darling, I hope you don't mind but I've asked Buffy Trescott to be my best man. I know he's a bore but he'll be cut to the quick, if I don't.'

23

'Of course I don't mind, Holly. The choice is yours. But I do think . . .' She faltered, realising she had lost his attention; he was waving to an acquaintance on the other side the room.

He turned back to her, the long-range smile still on his face. 'A Christmas wedding, I thought.'

'Oh? This year or next?'

'This year, of course.' A slight frown marred the smooth planes of his face. 'Who will you ask to be flower girls?'

'Oh . . .' She thought for a moment. 'Ellie, of course.' She smiled and he nodded. His cousin, Elinor Maitland, was a favourite with both of them. 'And Sukie.'

'Sukie who?'

'You know, Sukie Smith – Albert's daughter. You must remember her – she's my best friend.'

'Vaguely.' Hollis frowned. He remembered meeting Sukie only once; a girl who might have been beautiful had it not been for the cruel, disabling squint that left her partially blind. '*That* Sukie. Won't she be rather out of her depth?'

'No more than I'll be.' Niamh looked around the room, realising to her dismay that she was becoming a celebrity, a curiosity. 'I'm out of my depth in here. Holly, isn't it a bit soon to be planning the wedding? We've only just got engaged. I'd rather wait, at least till your mother—'

'Don't take any notice of Mother. She'll rattle her chains for a bit but she'll come around.'

'I'm not so sure.' Niamh paused, preferring not to tell him exactly what his mother had called her. *Gold digger* and *beastly little opportunist* came quickly to mind. 'She said we should think it over. We could be too closely related.'

'That's nonsense. We aren't in the least bit close. You're the niece of her brother's wife; we're related by marriage – not blood. She's grasping at straws, Niamh.'

'But she still isn't pleased.'

Hollis sighed. 'No one can come up to her exacting stand-ards. She'd like it no better if I came home and told her I was marrying a princess of the blood royal.'

Niamh smiled at last, amused by the thought of her Aunt Lilias turning her nose up at a princess, tiara and all. 'But we should respect her feelings, Holly. It isn't the end of the world if we have to wait.'

'Just what *did* she say to you?' He sat back in his chair, regarding her. By nature impatient, he hated delay. 'A lot more than you're telling me, I'm sure. Damn the woman. Damn her for her meddling interference and for upsetting you this way.'

'Stop it, Holly. It's bad luck to curse your own mother. I really don't mind. I'm happy to wait.'

Irritated, he raised his voice. 'Well, I'm not.'

'Don't shout. People are looking at us.'

'Let them. I'm tired of putting it off. First it was: *Wait because you're too young Hollis. Wait and finish your studies, Hollis.* Well, my studies are over now and I've waited long enough.'

'Holly, be reasonable. How can we get married when we have nowhere to live?'

He stared at her. 'We'll be living at home, of course – where else?'

'I don't think so, Holly. The Oaks is your mother's home and she's mistress there. I'd much rather wait till we can afford a home of our own. A rented cottage would do.'

'Love in a hovel? How quaint!' Holly was genuinely amused. 'There's really no need. If you want a house, you shall have one. I'll have a word with Pa.'

'No, Holly. We should be responsible for our own home. You can't expect your father to provide for us.'

'Why not?' he said, staring back at her. 'I could make enough money to pay for a house twice over, if only he'd let me.' He took her hand, leaning across the table. 'But these are trifles, darling. Small obstacles. Now, how about a kiss? Let's give these nosy old biddies something to talk about.'

She closed her eyes obediently as he pressed his lips to her own. A theatrical kiss, given solely for the benefit of the onlookers, light, respectful and totally lacking in passion. As she kissed him, Niamh felt like a traitor as somebody else came to mind – the dark-eyed handsome stranger who was going to work for Sukie's father. She had been as aware of him as he was of her as she went through the motions of serving her customers, collecting glasses and pulling beer.

Abruptly, Holly stopped kissing her. He was staring at her, head on one side, an injured expression in his cool, green eyes.

25

'A penny for them, Niamh?' he said, making light of it. 'You were miles away.'

'I'm sorry, Holly. So I was,' she said, biting her lip as she searched for a reasonable explanation. Fortunately, she didn't have to find one. A round of applause started at the next table and spread until the little orchestra joined in, limping through a few bars of the *Wedding March*.

Somebody shouted 'Speech!' and Hollis stood up to acknowledge the applause, enjoying the attention. He thanked all present for their good wishes and drew Niamh to her feet, introducing her as his wife-to-be. This was the cue for a small girl to present Niamh with such a huge bunch of tiger-lilies and roses, she could hardly hold them. She hid her face in the flowers to conceal her blushes, breathing in the scent of the expensive, hot-house blooms. So this was the future. This was what marriage to a Maitland was going to be like. She would be in the public eye . . . but living in Hollis's shadow for the rest of her life.

Chapter Three

The hours were long at the foundry and during those first few days even Judd, who liked to boast of his strength and endurance, found the work unusually tiring. By nightfall, his limbs would be shaking with fatigue and he was ready to drop. He used to think of himself as a tireless worker but these Australian men were made of sterner stuff, able to withstand the heat of the furnaces as they worked on like automatons, sweat pouring from their bodies like water. His own body had not learned to sweat so freely and he sweltered, plagued with heat rashes, all the harder to bear because as summer progressed, the weather became hotter each day.

He had grown soft during those weeks of inactivity while he was at sea. He found the heat of the furnaces oppressive to the point of being unbearable, all too aware of the meaningful glances exchanged between his co-workers who smirked, waiting for him to collapse from exhaustion. He would have to toughen up if he wanted to survive at the foundry and also hang on to his job.

Although he was essentially fair-minded, Albert Smith required a lot more of his workers than to turn up for work each day and depart on time. Opposed to the progressive ideas of the unionists, including the concept of an eight-hour working day, he expected his men to arrive before time in the morning, poised and ready to start on the dot of eight-thirty. At the same time he frowned at the clock-watchers who threw down their tools the moment the clock struck six at the other end of the day. No job in progress was ever abandoned, even if it meant putting in more time to complete it and for little or no

27

extra pay. It was his golden rule that every morning the work of the foundry should start anew. Anyone who didn't see eye to eye with his policy didn't last long. Judd employed several promising young men, only to have them fired by Albert for watching the clock. But he worked hard himself and didn't care that each night he returned to his lodgings exhausted, his hair singed, his face throbbing and scorched from the heat of the furnaces.

Carl was already seated at the kitchen table when he arrived home one evening, worn out and later than usual.

'Whooee, look at you!' The younger man pushed his hat to the back of his head, grinning at Judd whose limbs were still shaking with the effort of getting himself home. 'Wanna watch yourself, Judd. Don't let Uncle Albert work you into the ground or you'll be an old man before your time. I've worked for that slave-driver meself an' I know. Lasted all of two days, till I blew me stack an' told him where he could stick his buckets of molten metal.'

'Carl!' Daisy shot him a warning look.

'Well, it's true, Mum,' he shrugged. All the same he waited until Daisy turned her back before lowering his voice to speak to Judd. 'There's easier ways to make money than workin', *if* you get my drift.' He tapped the side of his nose and winked. 'We'll have a chat some time – when you're fed up o' bein' a work-horse for bloody old Albert.'

Judd nodded and smiled, certain that Carl was involved in something shady. Not that he was averse to working outside the law if need be, but he resented being given advice from someone almost ten years his junior.

Fortunately, Albert was delighted with him and said so, holding him up as an example and offering him a wage rise in front of the other hands. Judd knew this wouldn't add to his popularity and wished his employer had been more discreet. The men gathered to smoke and air their resentments, grumbling amongst themselves.

'Boss gone soft in the head or what?' One man spoke loudly enough for Judd to hear. 'Four years I bin here an' I don't get no pay rise. 'Course the Pommie don' mind workin' all hours God sends – he has no folks to go home to at the end o' the day.'

'Nah. The ole man has to think o' the future, as we all do.'
Another man took a swig from a mug of scalding tea as his
face streamed with sweat, shining and red as an over-ripe
apple. 'An' I'll say this much for the Pommie – he knows his
craft. He knows about iron, even if he can't stand up to the
heat o' the furnaces.'

'Trust you to stick up for him, takin' his part.'

'I reckon the ole man wants him for Sukie,' another man
sniggered loudly, wheezing with suppressed laughter. 'Wants
him to take his ugly, squinty-eyed daughter off his hands.'

Judd glared at this. He liked Albert's daughter very much;
Sukie didn't deserve to be the butt of their crude humour.
Sukie was trim of figure and blest with an abundance of rich,
taffy-coloured hair. Unfortunately, any other claims to beauty
were marred by a pair of wickedly crossed eyes. They seriously
affected her vision and meant she had to hold something right
up to her face if she wanted to see it clearly. Spectacles didn't
help. Sometimes the men treated her as if she were deaf as well
as half-blind, but she didn't bear them a grudge. Instead, she
made up big enamel jugs full of freshly squeezed lemon juice
in the hot weather, keeping it ice-cold and reviving to offer the
men who had to stand at the furnaces. Work that became even
more exacting as the sun rose early, glaring down on them
from a harsh cobalt-blue sky with not even a breath of wind to
give any relief as the temperature soared.

Mid-morning and afternoon she distributed mugs of strong
tea and plates piled high with the nourishing oatmeal biscuits
she baked herself.

Judd accepted his wage rise with a clear conscience, knowing he deserved it. He was the experienced craftsman while the
others were largely unskilled.

He thought back to that first morning and of Albert who
had done his best to keep a straight face and conceal his
excitement as Judd demonstrated the full extent of his skills,
hammering a piece of iron into elegant, ribbon-like patterns in
the manner of French Art Nouveau.

'Where in the world did you learn to do that, son?' he whispered, turning the finished article in his hands.

'From my stepfather.' Judd's mouth took a wry twist. He
didn't care to talk about the man who had forced his way into

29

the comfortable life he shared with his mother and made his life and hers a misery before he deserted them to return to his native France. 'I hated him. The only thing I could respect him for was his craft. And his motive for teaching me was selfish, as well. He only wanted me to make more money for him.'

'The French decorative arts,' Albert nodded, more interested in Judd's skills than how he obtained them. While any willing worker could be taught to make moulds and cast iron, only a craftsman like Judd was capable of adding the finishing touches which would turn them into works of art.

Judd, on the other hand, had just as much to learn about the process of casting iron. The combination of skills would benefit both of them so that neither would feel exploited. Under Albert's expert tuition and guidance, Judd learned even more. Firstly, that the skill was in the creation of the mould rather than in the more spectacular process of pouring the molten metal. An initial pattern was carved from a piece of wood and from this template a special casting would be made in iron or bronze, providing an 'original' from which all future moulds would be made. He was quick to master the technique of pouring a mould of the desired shape and allowing it to cool.

As foreman, it was his responsibility to see that the originals remained intact, repairing any damage so that the pattern could be kept for ever and used again and again.

In addition to the work which he now enjoyed, he liked living in Melbourne. Far from being a country town on the fringes of civilisation, it was developing into an elegant city, becoming the trendsetter of architectural style on this side of the world.

Christmas came and went – a hot Christmas, curiously unreal to Judd. He would have been happy to dine on cold cuts and salad but Daisy Bradley wouldn't hear of it, lighting the stove as usual and slaving over it until she could set before them the traditional Christmas meats of roast fowl and ham, followed by a hot plum pudding, christened with rum sauce.

February was hotter still, but at the end of March the hot weather vanished almost overnight, giving way to a gusty autumn. Work at the foundry seemed easier in the cooler weather and Judd had energy enough to go out, although he was slow to make friends; other men were resentful of his good looks and jealous of the sparkle he brought to their women's eyes. Now and then he took a girl out for companionship but he guarded against involvement and never asked her twice. He grew closer to the Bradleys than anyone else, particularly when he and Matthew discovered a common interest in freshwater fishing. They spent many a lazy Sunday afternoon dangling a line as they sat in the shade of the trees lining the upper reaches of the Yarra.

Autumn was followed by a mild, wet winter which started in June. Morning after morning of grey skies when the rain seemed to fall before dawn, setting in for the day. Other mornings began clear and frosty, making Judd shiver and hasten into his clothes. These colder mornings were followed by days of bright sunshine in which there was little warmth. When the wind was unusually bitter, Daisy told him it was because snow was falling on the ranges to the north-east.

But Judd found the winter invigorating; a time when he could work without the added pressure of heat. Best of all he liked strolling through town, admiring the 'iron lace' on the terraces and verandahs of the new buildings. It made him feel as if he were making a visible contribution to the beauty of the city he had adopted as home.

Well-paid and secure, he could have moved away from Richmond or rented a house of his own but he was happy enough where he was. Daisy pampered him shamelessly, keeping a pot of stew on the stove to give him a hot meal no matter what time he came in.

Except for one night in the middle of winter when he had been living and working in Melbourne for some seven months. As soon as he opened the door he sensed that something was wrong. There was no welcoming smell of good food, no laughter or song from Daisy and the house was unusually cool. The fires had gone out.

Daisy sat at the kitchen table, weeping, her head on her arms, while Matthew paced the room like a caged lion, his teeth clamped on an old clay pipe.

Judd glanced at Daisy and back to Matthew, eyebrows raised in query.

'Carl of course, the little mongrel – who else?' Matthew

31

snapped. 'The only one of our kids to bring us to grief.' He paused, gesturing with his pipe at his Daisy who was too distraught to look up. 'If I've told her once, I must've told her a thousand times – she ruined him when he was small. Let 'im grow up expectin' too much out o' life. Bound to end in tears.'

'It isn't Carl's fault!' Daisy raised her head to glare at her husband through reddened, tear-washed eyes. 'He's easily led. It's the company he keeps.'

'Ho well.' Matthew threw up his hands. 'You can kid yourself, if you like, Daise. But if you asked me, I'd say our Carl was bad news for everyone else! Should've been born with flamin' red horns an' a tail. Then we'd have known what we was dealin' with an' recognised the little bugger for what he was.'

'Matthew, don't. He's our son!'

'Born be hanged – a throwback to your blasted—'

'Just don't say it! You've been harkin' back to my mother, holdin' her up against me these thirty years.' Daisy broke into noisy tears and could speak only with difficulty between sobs. 'Look to yourself, Matthew Bradley. If you'd have been home more often, more of a f-father to him, he wouldn't have turned out this way.'

'Dammit all woman, I had a living to earn. Did the other boys grow up wild an' out of control?' Matthew was working himself up into a rage. 'He's a wrong'un, is Carl. A throwback to bastard convict stock, like I said.'

'But what's happened? What has he done?' Judd wanted to break the cycle of pointless argument and stop them blaming each other.

'What hasn't he done?' Matthew scowled, grinding his teeth on the pipe. 'Nineteen years of age an' he's served on the road gangs already. Gettin' to be a hardened criminal, that's what he is.'

'He's still my boy – my boy!' Daisy rocked herself in her misery, breathless from sobbing, tears dripping from her cheeks and her nose. 'He acts without thinkin' – he told me. He's high-spirited an' that's how he gets caught up in these pranks.'

'High spirits? Pranks, woman?' Matthew's temper finally

snapped. 'Armed robbery won't be dismissed as boyish high spirits an' pranks!'

Unfortunately, Matthew was right. Daisy had to sit in the public gallery weeping into a handkerchief too small to contain her sorrow as her youngest child was sentenced to gaol with hard labour for two more years. Fortunately for Carl, he wasn't the man with the guns or his punishment would have been more severe.

Life in the Bradley household was quiet after that, the atmosphere pervaded with gloom. Daisy sighed about the place like a woman bereaved and Matthew brooded, hiding behind his newspaper, refusing to speak to anyone. Judd's offer to hire a boat and go fishing was met with a curt refusal. Thinking it unfair to desert the Bradleys in their hour of misfortune but uncomfortable with their misery, Judd began working longer hours at the foundry. And often Sukie would ask him to dine with them afterwards, giving rise to further ribald comment and speculation among his fellows. Ignoring their jealousy, Judd spent many a congenial evening with Albert and Sukie who lived in a comfortable villa not far away from the foundry, overlooking the Yarra and the open parklands beyond.

Albert liked to share his memories of earlier days, filling the gaps in Judd's knowledge of Melbourne's history and in particular the establishment of the foundry.

'It was my father started the business soon after the Gold Rush,' he would begin, settling himself in his chair and looking forward to an evening of reminiscence.

'Oh, Pa.' Sukie tried to prevent it. 'Judd doesn't want to hear them again, your tales of the old days.'

'It's all right.' Judd smiled at her, encouraging the older man by pouring him another glass of ale from the bottle on the table. 'Go on, Albert.'

'I remember goin' out to the fields with my father an' mother when I was no more'n a lad.' Speaking of his parents made Albert lapse into an accent reminiscent of his native Hampshire. 'Lots of people left their womenfolk and children behind, but not my Dad. He said we should stand or fall together. An' we were lucky too, although the old folks had a bit of a barney when we came back. My mother said our fortune was made – why not take it an' go home? Our Dad wouldn't go. Said there was more'n enough opportunity, staring him in the face right here. So he started the foundry an' never looked back. But my mother couldn't ever settle, poor soul. Pined and died of homesickness, or so we think. Never did get back to England, not even to visit.'

'Poor Nan,' Sukie whispered, earning herself a sharp look from her father who raised his voice to add emphasis to his words.

'It was the right decision. Father knew best. The business prospered, building has boomed an' no sign of an end to it yet. Here in the city and out in the bush, there's squatters an' merchants spending fortunes, trying to outdo one another with bigger and better homes. Mansions with ballrooms, conservatories, balconies and verandahs all needing iron lace . . .' Albert's eyes gleamed. 'This is God's own country, me girl, no doubt about it. And the one thing we have in abundance is space. An architect can build as high and wide as he likes – let his imagination soar.'

Sukie smiled at her father, shaking her head. 'Oh Pa. Who else could get so worked up over a bit of cast iron.'

'A bit of cast iron? Where's your soul, girl? There's art in all this. We're creating the antiques of the future, Judd Burden and I. Creating iron lace unique to Australia, depicting the flora and fauna of the Australian bush.'

Sukie smiled. While Albert masterminded the foundry, it was she who kept her eye on the purse-strings, remembering to send out accounts when Albert would have let matters slide. Sukie spent almost as much time at the foundry as he did and worked equally hard. She dealt with initial enquiries, smoothed over customer complaints and acted as her father's right hand. All this on top of the other womanly duties of keeping house.

So Judd was annoyed when he caught the men mocking her squint and calling her 'dopey' behind her back. Ashamed of their behaviour, he tried to make up for it by being extra kind and considerate to her himself.

'Just how old are you, Sukie?' he asked her at the close of another long and arduous day. 'It's not right for a young girl to be working herself to a shadow. Don't you ever go out?'

'Oh, I'm not all that young. I'll be twenty-one come September.' Sukie blushed scarlet, embarrassed that he should be interested enough to ask. 'And as for going out – who'd ever bother to ask me, and where should I go?'

'These are your best years. You should be having fun while you're still young and—'

'Pretty?' She finished the sentence for him with a smile and a shrug. 'I'm not that much of a fool, Judd. The kindest critic wouldn't say I was pretty with eyes like these.' And as usual when she remembered her disability, her eyes rolled up, the lids fluttering, out of control.

'You could come out with me,' he said on impulse. 'It is Saturday, after all, and the foundry closes at one.'

She blushed to the roots of her hair. It was obviously so important to her that he wondered whether he ought to have asked her at all. It was clear that the prospect of such an outing meant much more to her than it did to him. 'Oh, I'd like to, Judd, but I can't. Not possibly. I have to catch up on the chores I've neglected all week.' She counted them out on her fingers. 'There's the beds to be changed, the house to be swept and then there's the washing and ironing to be done . . .'

He could have taken the opportunity to accept her refusal but some impulse drove him on. 'You can do that tomorrow, can't you? Tomorrow's another day.'

'Do my housework on a Sunday?' She smiled. 'What would the neighbours say?'

'Nothing. If they're so religious, they should be on their knees with their eyes closed and won't see you.'

Sukie laughed. It started as a throaty chuckle that set Judd's spine tingling, surprising him by provoking a stab of desire, gone as quickly as it appeared. 'Let's do it, then! Let's go out on the town.'

The evening wasn't a success. Away from the foundry and her home where Albert was there to keep the ball of conversation rolling, Sukie was shy and over-anxious to please. Judd couldn't get her to relax and just be herself. If they'd gone to a theatre or a music hall it might have been easier, but he knew she wouldn't be able to see the stage; the actors would appear to her as a blur.

So they ate oysters from a stall set up outside the Eastern

35

Market and made brief visits to several cafés and saloons, ending up at the Silver Star. That too, was a mistake. Judd fell silent, feeling left out, as Sukie relaxed at last, laughing with Niamh and enthusing over the plans for the wedding due to take place at the end of the year. Misinterpreting the reason for his silence, Sukie tackled him about it in the cab riding home.

'You didn't like her, did you?'

'Who?' Judd said, pretending not to know who she meant.

'My friend, Niamh, of course.'

'Niamh?' He shrugged. 'I've no opinion of her at all. Why should I?'

'You don't have to lie to me, Judd. Sometimes I see things with more than my eyes. I could feel you, almost vibrating with irritation the whole of the time we were there. And I was surprised. Most people get on very well with Niamh. Most people love her.'

So do I. The words sprang to his lips but remained unsaid. He shrugged again, pretending to have no interest in pursuing the conversation and turning aside to look out at the winter's night. It had come on to rain now, somehow matching his mood.

Seeing Niamh again, he wondered how he had been able to put her from his mind so completely. An instinct for self-preservation, perhaps? He didn't care to feel strongly for anyone but the attraction was still there. She couldn't know it, of course, but she held his heart right there in those capable little hands. Or maybe she did know. And that's why she shied away from him, excluding him from her conversation with Sukie, careful never to glance his way. And in her shoes, he thought gloomily, he would have done the same. It was the only sensible thing to do. Whatever the alchemy of attraction, whatever might have been, he was way too late. Wedding plans had been made and she was wearing a diamond big enough to pin on a Maharajah's toque. The very sight of it, the very ostentation angered him, making him want to snatch it from her hand and throw it as far as he could. But of course he did no such thing.

Seeing him lost in dark thoughts and not in the mood for small talk, Sukie yawned delicately and snuggled into the rug the cabbie provided. They rode to Richmond in silence apart from the rhythmic clanking of harness, the rumble of wheels and the measured trot of the horse.

Outside the darkened house where Albert lay sleeping, Judd ordered the driver to wait while he escorted Sukie to the door. He could just as easily have dismissed it and walked home but he wanted no awkward moment on the doorstep while Sukie waited to see if he would kiss her good night. He needn't have worried. She shook hands with him formally as if they were strangers.

'Thank you for a lovely evening, Judd,' she whispered, like a child giving a 'thank you' speech at the end of a party. 'I had a very nice time.'

'Did you, Sukie?' he said, holding on to her hand as he saw her bleak expression. Her lips were trembling and she seemed on the verge of tears. If only – if only he could have offered more. She was a dear girl and deserved better than to be dumped on her doorstep like an unwanted parcel. 'Oh Sukie, Sukie, I—'

'Yes, Judd?' She took a step towards him, screwing up her eyes to stop them flickering, all her hopes in that tentative smile.

'It's late,' he said, scarcely brushing her forehead with his lips. 'You'd better go in. G'night, Sukie. Sleep well.'

She turned away, let herself into the house and closed the door without looking back.

It was Niamh's habit to get up early on a Sunday morning to give the saloon a thorough cleaning throughout. She would throw open the windows to clear the room of smoke and stale air, pile the chairs on the tables, sweep all the floors and then scrub them to remove the smell of stale tobacco and spilt ale; the aftermath of an exuberant Saturday night.

'The better the day, the better the deed, Pa,' she laughed at Tully who frowned at this weekly penance, threatening to employ a cleaner to do it instead.

'No, Pa. Nobody will do it quite so thoroughly as I do,' she said. 'And I like to do it; it's my gift to you. There'll be time enough for me to play ladies when I'm wed – you can take on a charwoman when I'm gone.' She said this last with a wry smile and certain lack of conviction as if the event was still so far in the future, it might never be.

But Tully insisted on dealing with the spittoons himself, rinsing them thoroughly each night before he retired. It wasn't a pleasant task and he didn't care to leave it to his womenfolk.

So by the time Janet dressed herself and arrived downstairs, Niamh was hard at work, tackling the worst of the mess with a millet broom, a scarf around her head and wearing an apron to cover her clothes. Old Sally, well into her seventies and needing less sleep, was also up and about in the kitchen, coughing richly as she clattered the pans in the sink.

'You're up early, Mama,' Niamh greeted her, noting that the smudges beneath her mother's eyes were darker than usual. 'Couldn't you sleep?'

'Sleep?' All Janet's good resolutions to be tactful deserted her as she blurted the reason for her concern. 'Sleep – when all I could think about was that man and the cheek of him, staring at you all night.'

'I don't know who you mean.' Niamh deliberately raised a dust with her sweeping. 'I didn't see anyone.'

'You must have done. That dark-haired man – that boyfriend of Sukie's.'

'He isn't Sukie's boyfriend. He's Albert's new foreman, that's all.' Niamh stopped sweeping for a moment and leaned on the broom. She didn't want to talk about Judd who had been the cause of her own lack of sleep, unsettling her so thoroughly that even now he was invading her thoughts. 'He came in with Albert – oh, months ago now.'

'Aha! So this isn't the first time! You've seen him before?'

'What's "Aha" for?' Niamh frowned, sweeping vigorously again and trying to ignore her mother's taunt. 'He isn't a regular, Mama. It could be another twelve months before he comes back again.'

'I hope so. I didn't take to him – not at all. And I'll have a word with Albert when I see him. What's he thinking of, letting his only daughter keep company with an experienced roué like that.'

Niamh smiled. Janet often used French words to describe anything she thought indelicate. 'Judd isn't a roué, Mama. He's just Albert's foreman.'

'Well, he shouldn't be ogling you, not now you're engaged. It isn't every girl who has a plum like Hollis Maitland fall into her lap. You don't realise just how lucky you are. You have too much luck. Take care that one day the world doesn't blow up in your face.'

'Mama!' Niamh stopped her work to stare at her. 'What a horrible thing to say.'

'No, it's not. Not if it shakes you out of your apathy. You take too much for granted, my girl. And Holly most of all.' Gritting her teeth, Niamh stirred up even more of a dust but her mother wasn't done. 'Look at you now, sweeping and scouring like a Cinderella. It's Sally who should be doing the housework, not you.'

'Sally's old, Mama. She does what she can but she's much too frail to do heavy work.'

'Then maybe it's time she left us to make room for someone who can.'

A strangled cry from the kitchen made them both pause, staring at each other. Niamh narrowed her eyes and glared at her mother, shaking her head. 'If she heard you . . .'

'Nonsense – how could she? You know she's deaf as a post!'

Another gasping cry brought them both running to discover Sally leaning over the sink, wet hands clasped to her chest, her face ashen and her lips turning blue as she struggled to breathe.

'Sally! Sally, my darling, what is it?' Niamh put her arms around the old lady who seemed suddenly to have shrunk into a bag of bones, trembling and fragile as a bird.

'She's having a heart attack, I think.' Janet spoke sharply, regretting her earlier harshness. 'Run for the doctor, Niamh, I'll get her to bed.'

'No. *You* go for the doctor. I'll put her to bed.' Niamh felt the old lady relax as she said this. Janet wouldn't mean to be unkind or rough but she resented the place Sally held in her daughter's heart – a daily reminder of her own shortcomings as a mother. Happy as she had been to surrender her screaming, demanding infant to Sally's care, she was jealous of the rapport that existed between them now her daughter was grown.

*

39

The doctor arrived, unshaven and dishevelled at this early hour, confirming their fears. Sally had suffered a heart attack.

'She shouldn't be working at all, a woman of her age.' He spoke in a clipped, upper-class English manner, accusing them. 'High time you turned the old horse out to grass.'

'Oh doctor, no!' Sally protested weakly.

'You'll do as you're told, my girl.' He patted her hand not unkindly. 'If you get over this – and I'm not at all sure you will – you'll need to take better care of yourself. You can't go on as before.'

'Sally will have whatever she needs, doctor.' Niamh covered Sal's hand with her own as she fixed her mother with a look, daring her to say otherwise.

'Send for my niece – my niece, Gladys.' Sally ground out the words, speaking with difficulty. 'Widowed just now. Lives up Castlemaine. Send for Gladys O'Shea.'

Chapter Four

Arrivin miday Cob & Co from Bendigo. Lov Gladys.

On a piece of well-thumbed, crumpled paper, this was the
message that Sally received from her niece. Niamh smiled at
the painstaking, badly formed letters, imagining the simple
countrywoman who must have written them; a plump, comfortable widow, a younger version of Sally perhaps, hair
moulting from an untidy bun, a nose like a small potato and a
warm, motherly disposition.

Gladys O'Shea turned out to be none of these things. She
was a tanned gypsy with a hawk's beak of a nose and fierce,
predatory eyes that swept the room, assessing them. A woman
whose springy, dark hair stuck out from beneath a wide-
brimmed straw hat and who clasped to her bosom a home-
made cotton bag which seemed ready to burst at the seams,
bulging with everything she possessed. Niamh smothered a
laugh, thinking her father must have collected the wrong
woman from the coach. This lissom, sloe-eyed creature
couldn't possibly be related to Sally.

'Did – did you have a pleasant journey?' she managed to
greet the woman as she readjusted her ideas.

'All right, I suppose.' Gladys had a deep, rather surly voice
with traces of a Welsh accent. Her smile was wide but her eyes
were never still as she glanced around the room, taking in her
surroundings. 'You must be Niamh, then? Aunt Sal used to
drive us mad, talkin' of you. Never bothered with any of us.
With her it was always Niamh!'

Niamh smiled in return, trying not to stare, thinking Gladys
looked too young to be a widow. Her face was unlined, the

41

only evidence of her grief a fine network of crow's feet and dark hollows around the eyes. But she had a piercing stare which Niamh found disconcerting; as if those small, boot-button eyes could see right through flesh and bone to the soul beneath. Gladys seemed like a gypsy indeed.

Later she found out the woman's exotic looks came not from the Romany but from her father, a Sicilian, who had met and married Sally's sister at the gold fields.

'Proper mongrel I am,' Gladys said with her gravelly laugh. 'And I married an Irishman jus' to mix things up even more!' She sighed. 'But we never had no nippers, my John Michael an' me. Such a lovely man an' good with the horses, you know. I couldn't believe it when they told me he'd taken a tumble an' broken his neck. Poor old John Michael – on his birthday, too. Jus' forty, he was.' She spoke of her husband without emotion, having come to terms with her loss.

Her hair was a mass of greasy ringlets, unruly and uninhibited as her laughter. Janet did her best to turn her into a conventional servant but without success. A mob cap and an apron made no difference to the woman's untidy appearance. She just clapped the hat to the back of her head, allowing most of her hair to escape, framing her face; a face that might have been beautiful but for that disfiguring beak of a nose. A nose which confirmed all the woman's unbridled passions or so Janet whispered, grumbling to her husband as soon as they had a moment alone.

'Look at her. Dark as Satan and wicked as a witch, I'll be bound. You should've sent her packing. Straight back to Castlemaine on the next coach.'

Tully winced at her, looking pained. 'Now, Janet – how could I do that?'

'I'm warning you – no good will come of it. A Welsh witch, that's what she is. It's not so long ago she'd have burned at the stake. She'll bring men – they'll come sniffing round after her, wasting her time, you'll see. She's far too good-looking to want to do any work.'

In that at least, Janet was wrong. Gladys was more than worthy of her hire, taking over the lion's share of the cleaning and cooking and nursing her invalid aunt. But while Tully was grateful and willing to overlook the woman's eccentricities, Janet kept finding fault.

'A sensualist,' she pronounced, watching Gladys's hips sway as she carried a pile of linen upstairs. 'And I never trust a woman who paints her lips.'

'Oh Mama, she doesn't,' Niamh protested. 'Her lips are naturally red.'

'Then she bites them to make them that way.' Janet was determined to have the last word.

Upstairs, Sally beamed at her niece. 'Look at me. Out of bed already an' gettin' stronger each day.' Gladys had no breath to reply, too busy heaving her aunt from the bed and supporting her weight until she could put her slippered feet to the floor. 'I'll be me old self again in no time. Then you can leave us an' go back home.' It was taking all her effort to stand on limbs that trembled with weakness; she didn't see the tightening of her niece's lips.

Three weeks after the onset of her illness, the old woman wanted to go downstairs to visit the privy although it took twice as long as using a pan or a commode by the bed.

'I have to get up,' she grumbled. 'Or I'll get weak as water, lyin' in bed.'

'No need to push yourself, Auntie. You had a nasty turn. Maybe you're not so strong as you'd like to think.'

Sal blew a rich raspberry in reply. 'The old ticker's as good as it used to be. Haven't felt breathless in days. I'll be fit as a flea come Christmas an' back on my feet.'

'Better wait and see what the doctor says first.'

'That doctor! I'd be six feet under by now if I listened to him!' Sal had reached the bottom of the stairs and was managing a slow shuffle down the corridor to the back door, leaning on her niece's arm. 'Don't think I don't appreciate you, Gladys, I do. Good of you to drop everythin' an' come at such short notice. But I'm tired of bein' an invalid. Time I got back to me work an' let you go home.'

Gladys raised her eyes to heaven, having been over it all before. 'I've told you, Auntie, I don't have no home now John Michael's gone. His family don't want me no more.'

'Why not?'

'Let's say we didn't see eye to eye.' Gladys tossed her head. 'An' I like it here in the city. I like lookin' after you. So there's no hurry for you to get back on your feet. No one expects it of you, least of all Tully.'

'Mr McDiarmit to you.'

'Oh, Mr McDiarmit, then.' Gladys repeated it with a mischievous twitch of her lips. 'A lovely man, isn't he, Auntie? Reminds me of my John Michael, being Irish and all.'

'Well, he's not your John Michael and don't you forget it!' Sally snapped. She didn't like the turn the conversation was taking and her heart was beginning to flutter alarmingly.

But Gladys wasn't listening. 'Shameful it is, how she treats him – that miserable wife of his.'

'Now that's enough. I don't want to hear no more. You mind your busines, my girl, an' keep out o' their affairs.'

'But he's pleased with me, Auntie, he told me so. Says I can stay here as long as I like. Long as you need me.'

'Which won't be for long,' Sal gasped, feeling as if her life had been taken over and she was no longer in control of it. Breathless and with her heart fluttering, she was grateful to reach the privy. Gladys made sure she was safely seated, gave her plenty of paper and stood waiting outside the door.

Even in winter, the skinny native trees were in bloom with clusters of small, feathery, yellow flowers which gave off a spicy, rather cloying perfume, tickling her nose and making her want to sneeze. Slender grey and yellow wattle birds hung upside down in the branches, sucking the nectar, stopping only to dispute territory with others of their kind, filling the air with their raucous, abrasive cries. Fortunately, the scent of the wattle was strong enough to mask the smells of the city's drainage system. The yard, though it was small, had room enough for a line of washing to hang between the trees; a tiny oasis of green in a busy city. The yard was well shielded from the wind and the sun was surprisingly warm.

When Sally emerged from the privy, she was white-faced and almost fainting with strain. Gladys caught her about the waist to support her, realising that she would have to gather her forces before she could go back upstairs.

'Why not sit out here for a while, Auntie? It's a lovely afternoon for the time of year.'

'So it is, if you don't mind the stink of the cesspool next door. Let go of me, girl. I can stand on my own two feet.' Cantankerous as only a sick person can be, the old woman pushed Gladys's hands away. 'Always fussin' – it's you makes me weak. You keeps me from gettin' well.'

Gladys ignored the criticism. 'The sun will do you good. If we wrap you up warm, you can sit out here for an hour or so. Niamh can read to you while the missus goes to the shops. Mr McDiarmit and I can look after the bar.'

'Got it all worked out, haven't you?'

'Dunno what you mean, Auntie.' Gladys opened eyes too wide to be innocent. 'I'm only thinkin' of you.'

Much as Judd regretted it, there was no way to turn back the clock and return to the easy, platonic relationship he and Sukie had enjoyed before. Outwardly nothing had changed but the barriers, if invisible, were all too real. There was a restraint in her manner towards him, an uncertainty in her smile and he didn't know what to say to put matters right. Careful never to touch him even by accident, she no longer asked him to stay to supper unless she was prompted by Albert.

He couldn't have said she was sulking, she was pleasant enough but she kept her remarks to a minimum speaking only when necessary. If he came to supper, she dished up the meal in silence, leaving Albert to do all the talking. Sensitive to her feelings Judd left as soon as the meal was over and courtesy would allow.

Life at the Bradleys wasn't much better. In the absence of Carl, Daisy sighed about the house, crying over her cooking and salting their food with her tears. At last Matthew, losing patience with this 'female mewling' as he called it, announced he was going back on the road.

'No, Matthew!' Daisy wailed, wringing her hands. 'Your feet are too soft now – you haven't walked with a dray for nigh on two years. The doctor won't like it. An' what will Jake an' Tom say? They can manage without you now.'

But Matthew was stubborn, his mind already made up. 'I never said I was leavin' the game for good.'

So, with Matthew away from home and Daisy moping, Judd spent more and more of his free time at the Silver Star where

Niamh, exasperated yet perversely flattered by his attention, had no choice but to make him welcome.

Judd knew he was being selfish but he didn't care. He laid siege to Niamh, ignoring the diamond which she brandished before his eyes like a talisman, in the hope of warning him off. Her indifference served only to fuel his obsession; she was both a challenge and an enigma, one of the few women capable of resisting his charm. It made him all the more determined to break down the barriers, to get her to like him at least.

She listened attentively when he talked of his childhood in Devon, a childhood so different from her own. He spoke with affection of his mother, shunned by her family for bearing a child to a Spanish fisherman who left her to go back home.

'She was the dearest, sweetest woman alive, if she did have a weakness for unreliable foreigners,' he said, smiling as he remembered her. 'Bad girls don't have babies – isn't that what they say? But there was only my Uncle Jem would stand up for her, and even he let her down in the end.'

'How? How did he let her down?' Hands clasped, Niamh leaned on her elbows to listen, intrigued by the tale.

'My uncle was a seaman, like almost every able-bodied man in Devon. You know how they are. Gone for years and you think you'll never see them again until they reappear. The last time he wrote, he said he'd struck it lucky at the gold fields and his ship was on its way home. He promised to buy my mother the cottage she lived in. He gave her purpose – a hope for the future. Goddamn him. I wish he'd kept his mouth shut and promised her nothing, then she wouldn't have been so disappointed.' Niamh listened, waiting for him to go on. 'That was the last time we ever heard from him. He never showed up. My mother tried to make ends meet by taking in washing and sewing but it wasn't enough. The landlord's patience came to an end and we were to be thrown out on the street. So, against her better judgement, she married a Frenchman instead. A great brute of a man who used to beat her. He made our lives hell for three long years before he took himself off back to France. But she never said one word against Uncle Jem and never blamed him. I did. Raising my mother's hopes only to let her down!'

'Maybe he couldn't help it. The seas are dangerous – even more so in those days, so my father says.'

'How would he know?'

'He was a seaman himself once, a long time ago, on the circle route. His ship was wrecked and he was lucky to survive. She glanced at Tully, busy on the other side of the room. 'It was a bad time for him. He finds it difficult to talk about those days even now.'

Judd was suddenly all attention. 'When was he at sea?'

'Oh, I don't know,' Niamh shrugged. 'In the early days of the Gold Rush. Long before I was born.'

'But my uncle was here at that time.' Judd followed the direction of her gaze. 'Maybe I'll have a word with him.'

'Judd, please don't or I shall be sorry I told you.' Niamh laid a restraining hand on his arm. 'He gets so upset and it's hardly likely he knew of your uncle at all. There were so many seamen in and out in those days.'

Judd looked at her hand on his arm, wishing she knew how her touch affected him. But she was right. He had questioned dozens of seamen and never found anyone who had heard of Jem Burden or the *Sally Lee*.

'All right then, I won't,' he said, leaning forward until he was close enough to kiss her as he looked into her eyes. 'As always, Miss McDiarmit, your every wish is my command.' Uncomfortably aware that it looked as if they were flirting, Niamh took a step backwards, pulling her hand away. Seeing it, Judd smiled, raising his hands shoulder-high in a gesture of surrender. 'Whatever you say, lady. Whatever you say.'

Hollis paused in the doorway, having arrived in time to see the little tableau and draw his own conclusions. It didn't improve his mood. The business meeting with Horace Ironsides had concluded early, Ironsides making it plain that he thought the younger Maitland no more than an upstart born with a silver spoon in his mouth. His own opinion of Ironsides was no better. An old fool who boasted of being self-made, while everyone knew his wealth had come because he was lucky enough to be in the right place at the right time.

With an empty evening stretching before him, Hollis decided to smoothe the ruffled feathers of his vanity by paying a visit to Niamh. He'd been looking forward to telling her about Ironsides and receiving her sympathy and understanding. But now he was here, he didn't like what he saw. *His* Niamh, eyes sparkling, two spots of colour high in her cheeks and clearly engaged in a flirtation, her hand on the arm of the rangy, dark-haired man who lounged at the bar. And so engrossed that she didn't even look up to see him come in. The surge of emotion he felt left him breathless, jealousy ripping at his vitals with sharp claws.

Slowly, watching them, he took off his gloves and hung his hat on the stand before weaving his way through the tables to speak to Tully who was occupied at the other end of the bar. At the piano, the couple engaged to provide tonight's musical entertainment were performing a duet from Gilbert and Sullivan's latest offering, the comic opera style allowing the woman's voice to swoop painfully towards some of the higher notes and making him wince.

'Oh, I know,' Tully nodded, greeting Hollis with a wry smile. 'I'll speak to them tomorrow – she'll have to go.' He pulled a beer and gave it to Hollis who accepted it without thanks, his mind still running on Niamh.

'Who *is* that?' He nodded towards the pair. 'The big man talking to Niamh at the bar?'

Tully adjusted his glasses, squinting at them. 'Ah, nobody much to be sure. Bit of a regular these days. The boys have been teasin' Niamh about him, sayin' she's won herself a heart.'

'And has she?'

Tully polished a glass, looking ill-at-ease. 'Ah now, Holly, it's nothin' to get all riled up about. It don't mean anythin' or I wouldn't have said.'

'But who is he?'

'Judd Burden. Works for Albert Smith at the foundry.'

'Oh, does he. I think I'll drop over and have a word. Can't leave her at the mercy of a fellow like that, monopolising her time.' And he set down his empty glass and squared his shoulders before moving over to join them. He felt somewhat mollified when Niamh smiled, seeming genuinely pleased to see him.

'Holly! I wasn't expecting you. What a nice surprise.' She kissed him briefly as he joined her behind the bar.

48

He took her into the circle of his arms and dropped a kiss on the top of her head. The message he sent to the stranger was silent but very clear. *Keep away from this woman. She's mine!* He expected the other man to take the hint and move off but instead he introduced himself as he reached across the bar, offering Hollis his hand.

'Judah Burden,' he said. 'But most of my friends call me Judd.'

Hollis hesitated, looking at that big hand before he accepted it, hoping his fingers weren't to be crushed against his rings. But the contact when it came was surprisingly gentle.

'Maitland.' He offered only his surname in return with a smile too bland to be sincere. 'And you're from the old Dart by the sound of those rounded country tones. Been in Melbourne long?'

Judd pulled an imaginary forelock, deliberately emphasising his accent in the hope of getting Hollis to unbend and relax. 'Me? Nigh on a twelve-month, gaffer!'

'And what do you think of our fair city? Do we bear comparison with the capitals of Europe or do you find us hopelessly out of touch and behind the times?'

Judd gave up the pretence of being a yokel. 'Streets ahead in some ways. Business is healthy and vigorous, or so it seems from our order books at the foundry. We've enough work on hand to see us through Christmas and beyond.'

'Is that so? Old Albert must think quite a lot of you then, for you to know how his business stands.'

'Oh, stop it, Holly,' Niamh said, jabbing him in the ribs. She had seen him in action before and knew he was trying to provoke an argument. 'Judd doesn't have to explain himself to you. He isn't on trial here.'

'It's all right, Niamh, I'll answer him.' Judd's smile assured her he had little need of her protection. 'I am Albert's foreman. By sharing our skills we can have the best of both worlds, old and new. We hope to provide unique designs for our customers, inspired by the ferns of the Dandenongs and the fauna of the Australian bush.'

'Fascinating, I'm sure,' Hollis murmured, realising too late that in underestimating Judd, he had made a mistake. He was still festering about it later when Niamh walked him to the

49

street to get a cab. Cheated of an argument with Judd, he quarrelled with Niamh instead.

'I don't like the man. Too sure of himself for a common tradesman. And much too taken with you.'

'Oh, Holly! Don't tell me you're jealous?' She tried to tease him out of it. 'You know I have to be pleasant and listen to all of our customers. It's my job.'

'I know. But do you have to make yourself so ...' He paused, searching for the right word. 'So accessible?'

'There's always the width of the bar between us, Holly. Remember that.'

'Niamh, it's almost twelve months since we got engaged. I want to marry you. It's time.'

'But Holly, there's so much to think about – to arrange. And with Sally so ill – I can't just go off and leave my parents in the lurch.'

'They have Gladys, don't they?'

'Yes, but—'

'You worry too much about other people.' He drew her close and she responded at once, closing her eyes and taking comfort from the familiarity of his embrace. 'Think of yourself for once. Think of us.'

'I do, Holly,' she breathed. 'Only ...'

'I want us to be married by Christmas – no later.'

'Christmas?' She opened her eyes to stare at him. 'But that's no time at all. Christmas is only weeks away.'

'I know. I wanted to marry you at Christmas last year and you put it off.'

'I don't think Pa can afford a wedding just yet—'

'No. But my parents can. Mother brightened no end when I suggested it – a party and a ball at The Oaks. I said she'd come around and she has. We'll have the biggest wedding party this town's ever seen.'

He stopped her gasp of surprise with another kiss, giving rise to wolf whistles and good-natured teasing from some young men passing by. She was first to break away.

'Go home, Holly,' she said, pushing him towards the cabs standing in line in the middle of the street, the horses swaying on their feet, half-asleep as they waited for a fare. 'We'll talk about it later. This isn't the time.'

'It's never the right time with you,' he said, full lips almost pouting in disappointment. 'But I do love you, Niamh. Always remember that.'

'Love you, too,' she said. It was the expected reply but she meant it. 'And try not to be jealous, there's really no need.'

She smiled and waved as he climbed into a cab and saluted her as the driver shouted to his horse, whipping it into a brisk canter as it took off up Bourke Street, busy even at this late hour. But her smile faded as she turned back to the Silver Star. Of course she loved him. He was her first love and she expected him to be her last. It was only lately that the doubts had come creeping in. And he had done little to dispel them tonight. He said he loved her and he did – as much as he could love anyone. But already he was thinking more of the social occasion and the business advantages rather than marriage itself and what it would mean. Was this the right sort of love? And was it fair to expect so much of it? Would it last through the next twenty years and prove strong enough to prevent her from falling in love with anyone else? Inevitably, such thoughts led to Judd. If she loved Holly, then why did she watch the door every night waiting for Judd to come in, looking forward to the way he teased her, making her laugh?

There's danger here, Niamh McDiarmit, she warned herself. You know very well that Judd is a practised charmer. Let him into your heart by the back door and he'll wreak havoc in your life. What price then your safe, orderly future with Hollis? The future everyone keeps telling you you're so lucky to have?

Chapter Five

Later, in bed, Niamh was unable to sleep. Her thoughts were running around inside her head like rats, refusing to be stilled. She punched her pillows, flung off her covers and retrieved them again. Her face was flushed, her body hot and damp with perspiration, making her very much aware of it.

Hollis was ready to be married and, as he said, it was time. She had put it off long enough. But, after seeing Hollis and Judd together she was beset by fresh doubts. Holly represented all that was known and secure, while Judd brought an element of excitement and danger into her life – something she had never missed until now. She had always thought herself cool and unemotional like her mother, capable of fondness rather than a heart-stopping, passionate love. Even now she wasn't sure she believed in it but, like it or not, Judd was *there*, digging up the foundations of her security and daring her to be more than an accessory to Hollis. He could raise her heartbeat simply by smiling at her as he came through the door.

Small wonder that Holly was jealous – any man would be, given the circumstances. And she had only herself to blame. She had done nothing to discourage the man, allowing herself to be drawn into a flirtation so subtle, so addictive she didn't want it to come to an end.

Unlike the others who came to the bar straight from work, bringing with them the dust and sweat of their labours, Judd always went home first, to wash himself and change his clothes. But a hint of the foundries always remained; a whiff of burning metal which blended with his natural male musk to create an invisible aura which clung to his hair and clothes.

Reminded of it, Niamh groaned and punched her pillows again, willing herself to get some sleep.

Finally, she sat up and poured herself a glass of water from the carafe which stood on the little gypsy table beside her bed. She drank deeply and pressed her aching head to the glass to cool it, wondering who to ask for advice. No joy from her mother, she could be certain of that. Janet would say, *Marry Hollis, count your blessings and make sure you keep what you already have.* As a rule, Niamh took her problems to Tully but she couldn't embarrass him by asking for his advice on matters of intimacy and sex. Who then – Gladys? She shied away from that idea, repelled by the thought of revealing her innermost secrets to the woman, whose sly smiles made her shiver. Ellie was too close to Hollis. That left only Sukie. She, while no more experienced than Niamh, could be relied on to offer sound common sense

Having made up her mind to see Sukie, Niamh slept at last, only to be haunted by wild dreams of Hollis and Judd, dressed in glittering old-fashioned costumes and fighting a duel, swords spinning as they pursued each other across the tables of the Silver Star. They slashed at each other, drawing blood, and each time they did so she screamed although she knew she was making no sound. Nobody stopped the fight and nobody won. She awoke with a bad headache, no better rested than if she had stayed up all night.

Janet complained when she said she was going to Richmond to see Sukie.

'Oh Niamh, does it have to be today? I've already told Gladys she can have the morning off.'

But Niamh was determined. 'Gladys can have the whole day off tomorrow,' she said. 'I have to see Sukie today.'

'Niamh!' Sukie greeted her with a kiss. 'What a lovely surprise. But is anything wrong? It's not like you to turn up in the middle of a working day.'

'I wanted to see you, that's all,' Niamh said, glancing past her into the cramped office of the foundry, hoping Albert wouldn't be there. She was in no mood for his teasing, however well-meant. 'Not too busy, are you? I was hoping you'd have time for a chat.'

'I'm always busy – but what are friends for?' Sukie grinned. 'Don't worry, the coast is clear. Pa's gone to the wharf to see if his pig iron's come in while Judd and the others are down at the furnaces – got a big order to go to Bendigo in a hurry.'

'Uhuh,' Niamh nodded, not much interested in the day-to-day business of the foundry.

Because of her poor eyesight, Sukie had to peer into Niamh's face in order to see her clearly. 'Good heavens,' she said. 'You look awful. Is everything all right?'

'I didn't sleep very well, that's all.'

'Oh – not your mother again?'

'No, no more than usual,' Niamh said, growing impatient with Sukie's innocent questions. 'I came to see you because I need your advice.'

The other girl pulled a face. 'That sounds very ominous. Sure I'm the best person to ask?'

'You're the *only* person I can ask.'

'Sit down here, then.' Sukie indicated the visitor's chair with its crumpled cushion. 'I'll dig out some oatmeal cookies and make us a fresh pot of tea.'

'Do you still make those oatmeal cookies? I used to love them when you brought them to school.'

'Sometimes I think the foundry runs on them. Most of the men don't bring any lunch.'

Moments later they were drinking tea and munching their way through a plate of the crisp, nut-covered biscuits. It occurred to Niamh that in their sensible, everyday clothes, she and Sukie looked more like a pair of governesses than the daughters of successful businessmen.

'Now then,' Sukie said, brushing some crumbs from her lap. 'Tell me what's up and how I can help.'

Niamh looked at Sukie for a moment, set down her tea-cup and burst into tears. Sukie found a clean handkerchief and offered it, waiting for her friend to recover enough to speak.

'Sorry about that.' Niamh blew her nose vigorously. 'Caught myself unawares. Holly wants us to be married and soon. And I will, oh I will, only . . .'

'Only what? Niamh, what's wrong? Isn't this what you've

54

always planned? You asked me to be your bridesmaid, remember? Oh . . .' She nodded, after thinking for a moment. 'So it's *his* mother, this time?'

'No, it's nobody's mother. Aunt Lil came around eventually and she's been sweetness itself of late. I should be the happiest girl in the world but I'm not – that's what makes it so awful. Oh Sukie, I think I'm falling in love with somebody else.'

'Ohoh. Now that *is* serious.' Sukie sat up straight, suddenly all attention. 'Who?'

'Can't you guess? It's Judd Burden, of course. Your father's foreman.'

'Oh? Oh, and has he – does he—' Sukie bit her lip as Niamh burst into tears all over again.

'No, I don't think he has any idea. And it's all my fault. I should've seen it coming and put a stop to it long ago. I was flattered, I suppose, and I let him get too close.'

'Well,' Sukie whispered, 'I'm staggered. I don't know what to say.'

'You do know he comes to the Silver Star almost every night?'

'No. No, I didn't,' Sukie said slowly as she stood up to stack the teacups with shaking hands, almost choking on her words. 'Niamh, I'm sorry. I'm just not the right person to ask.' She swore mildly as she tipped over one of the cups and spilled the dregs of tea on her father's desk.

Niamh looked at her, understanding at once. 'Oh Sukie, no. Not you, too.'

'Me?' Sukie's eyes were fluttering but she managed a shaky laugh. 'Good lord, no. What makes you think that?'

'It's just – you do seem a bit put out.'

'No. I'm surprised, that's all. Surprised to see a sensible girl like you taken in by such an obvious rogue as Judd – a man who spreads charm about as if it were honey.'

'He – he does?'

'Oh, yes. And I'm telling you, Niamh, you'd be a fool to cancel your wedding plans and ruin your life over him. I've seen him in action before. His smiles are for everyone. Girls wait for him outside the foundry almost every night. One of them was in tears – I felt so sorry for her, poor thing.' Sukie dropped her voice to a confidential whisper. 'With my eyesight I couldn't be sure, but she looked to be in the family way. She was *very* upset.'

'Oh. Oh, I see.' Niamh hid the shock of this revelation by noisily blowing her nose. 'I was a fool, then, to have taken him seriously. Thank you, Sukie. Thank you so much. What a good thing we had this talk before I did anything rash.' Impulsively, Niamh rose and hugged her friend, only vaguely aware that Sukie was too tense to respond.

The door burst open at that moment to admit Judd himself, naked to the waist apart from a sweat-stained navy singlet and bringing with him the heat and smell of the furnaces. He was dirty, unshaven and wild-eyed with anxiety, his hair a dusty black halo around his face. Niamh and Sukie exchanged glances, wondering how much he'd heard but he had something more serious on his mind.

'Sukie, quick – the first-aid box. Tim's had a of bit an accident. A nasty burn.'

'Oh dear!' Sukie opened a cupboard and squinted inside, wasting time as she searched for the box. 'Pa always keeps it in here. He's the one who takes care of first aid.'

'Sukie, let me look.' Niamh had recovered enough to take charge. 'I know a bit about first aid.'

'Better not waste any time, then.' Judd hustled her towards the yard where the men had stopped work and were standing in a semi-circle around the lad, uneasy and embarrassed by his pain. At fifteen, Tim was the youngest and least experienced of Albert's workers. Pale and shocked by the pain of his injury, he had sunk to the ground, knees bent, leaning against the fence and nursing his right hand in his lap. The men fell back to let Niamh approach but Tim whimpered, holding up his good hand, warding her off.

'No, no. Just let me alone, miss. Gimme a moment and I'll be right.'

'Tim, you're injured.' Judd crouched beside him. 'This lady knows about first aid. Let her take a look.'

'No-o.' He screwed up his face, protecting his arm. 'It hurts too much.'

Niamh also sank to the ground beside him, careless of the mud and the scraps of metal attaching themselves to her skirts.

She spoke gently, reassuring him. 'Tim, I won't hurt you, I promise. Just let me take a look.'

'Wouldn't have happened if we had proper safety measures – a proper place for the iron to cool off,' someone said. 'We should come out on strike over this!'

'Strike? What good would that do, yer silly old bugger?' Another man growled.

'Silly old bugger, yerself!'

'Shut up the pair of you,' Judd snapped. They did so, although they continued to glare at each other.

Judd peered over Niamh's shoulder, anxious to see the extent of the boy's injury. It was a bad burn on the soft under-side of his forearm, scorching several layers of skin and leaving a painful open wound. 'Shouldn't you wash it?' he murmured. 'My mother used to put honey on burns.'

Niamh shook her head and, with care, began to bandage it loosely, wincing in sympathy, when Tim whimpered again. 'Nearly done,' she said. 'Now, has anyone a scarf or a big handkerchief perhaps to make him a sling?'

Willing hands offered several and she picked one that looked clean, securing the boy's arm so that it was supported against his chest.

'Are you able to stand?' she said as Judd reached out to support the boy with an arm round his waist. 'Come to the office and Sukie shall make you a cup of tea. Then you should go home and rest to get over the shock.'

'I can't.' The boy's face twisted in misery. 'How can I earn any money if I don't work?'

'But the injury happened at work. I'm sure Mr Smith will pay you – something at least until you're well enough to come back.'

Hearing this, somebody gave a snort of derision – the same man who had been talking of safety measures before. 'Yeah? The day I see Albert Smith put his hand in his pocket for anythin' other than pig iron, I'll go hee.'

Sukie had tea ready and waiting by the time they brought Tim up to the office. After drinking it, his colour returned a little and Niamh offered to walk him home.

'No,' he protested. 'I'm all right, Miss. I can work one-handed, for sure.'

'And have another accident? No.' Judd was firm. 'You're

going home, Tim. And don't you worry about Mr Smith, I'll square it with him.'

'Will you, indeed?' Albert spoke up behind them. 'What the hell's going on? I leave the place for more 'n five minutes and everyone crowds into the office, drinkin' tea.'

'There's been an accident, Pa,' Sukie told him. 'Tim's burned himself badly and Niamh's offered to see him home.'

'And I'm going with them,' Judd said firmly, giving Albert no opportunity to object. 'The Bendigo order's complete. Only needs to cool off and it can be loaded on to the dray.'

While Albert stamped off to the furnaces to get the men working again, Niamh and Judd set off with Tim towards home. Home was just a few streets away but he went unwillingly, protesting all the way.

'You tell the old man I'll be back tomorrow,' he warned Judd. 'Don't you let him give my job to anyone else.'

'Tim, he can't. You're apprenticed to us. Take as much time as you need—'

'And let a doctor take a look at that arm,' Niamh put in. 'You might need some laudanum or something to ease the pain. Albert will pay.'

'Fly to the moon more like,' the boy said, voicing the opinion of the other men at the foundry.

With Tim safely delivered into the care of his mother, Niamh expected Judd to leave and return to the foundry. She was surprised when he boarded the horse-drawn bus which would take her back to town.

'You do realise that this is the first time we've been out on our own?' He grinned. 'I should thank poor old Tim for providing me with the chance.'

'We're not out together at all,' she snapped. 'And I don't need an escort – I'm quite capable of going home on my own. Aren't you needed back at the foundry?'

'Albert can cope for once,' he said, ignoring the rebuff. 'He can't say he doesn't owe me the time. It's a rare thing for me to see you away from the Silver Star.'

'You shouldn't be seeing me at all. I *am* engaged, you know. I expect to be married quite soon.'

'All right. You don't have to be so defensive.'

'Who's being defensive?'

58

'You are. You're shouting at me.'

'Fares, please!' the driver interrupted, tapping the glass box half-full of coins. Judd paid up for both of them before Niamh had time to open her purse.

'And I can't let you pay for me, Judd. It won't do at all. I want you to stop chasing me, stop teasing me and – and I want you to stay away from the Silver Star!'

'That's a lot of wants,' he said, pretending to consider them, head on one side. 'I don't think I can do all that. Not unless I have something from you in return.'

'What can you possibly want from me in return?'

His smile was all devilry. 'Give me a minute. I'm sure I'll be able to think of something.'

'You're enjoying this, aren't you? Laughing at me up your sleeve.'

'Bourke and Elizabeth!' the driver yelled, making Niamh spring to her feet, ready to get off. Judd stood up with her.

'The next stop will be mine. Don't get off and don't follow me – I'll have enough explaining to do as it is.'

'Until tonight, then,' Judd grinned, raising his cap, his dirty, unshaven face giving him a demonic look. 'Go on then, Niamh. Get off. You don't want to to miss your stop.'

'Look lively, Miss,' the driver grumbled as she hovered on the step, anxious to have the last word. 'Got a timetable to keep.'

As Niamh went about her business that afternoon she rehearsed her speech, determined to take up the argument where they left off. She almost wavered in her resolve when she saw him come pushing through the swing doors, grinning as usual, until she remembered Sukie's words. *He spreads charm as thick as if it were honey – his smiles are for everyone.*

'I mean it, Judd. I mean what I said.' She folded her arms. 'I don't want you to come here any more.'

'Oh dear,' he said, pulling a face and imitating her grim expression. 'What happened to, *Good evening, Judd* or even *Hello*? What have I done to turn you against me? I'm clean – I don't come straight from work like the great unwashed.' He jerked his head at the group of men in dirty boots at the other end of the bar. 'I don't drink too much or throw chairs. I don't swear.'

59

'It's not that at all, as you very well know. You're just here every night, upsetting me, crowding me—'

'Upsetting you? Crowding you – how? How can I crowd you from this side of the bar?'

'Judd, please. Do you have to make this so difficult for me?'

'But I like coming here. I like your father – like the atmosphere of this place. I even like that ghastly woman who sings. But most of all I like talking to *you*. That's what you're here for, isn't it? To entertain the customers, talk to them?'

'But not to conduct a flirtation when I'm engaged to somebody else. Please, Judd. You can talk to other girls in different bars. There must be other places you'd like to drink. Just do me a favour and don't come in here any more.'

He regarded her for a moment, unsmiling. 'Whose feelings are you afraid of – mine, or is it your own? Do you really want me to leave you in peace to marry your dull-as-ditchwater lawyer? To become a boring, orderly housewife like all the other women here?'

'Holly's *not* dull. You don't know him at all! You have no idea what he's like.'

'Oh yes, I do. All business, that's what he is. Anything else has to take second place in his life. Do you know what you're letting yourself in for? A round of dinner parties with self-important men who can advance him in business, followed by endless tea parties for you with their wives. Oh Niamh, you're a practical person who needs to be useful and active. Look how you rose to the challenge of that crisis today. Sukie was in a panic—'

'Only because she can't see.'

'And I wasn't much better. I turn green at the sight of blood.'

She smiled. 'Do you, Judd?'

'Yes. Just because I'm strong, doesn't mean I'm invincible. But you, you bound up his wound and looked after him as if you'd been doing it all your life.'

'It wasn't so bad as it looked. Anyone could have done it.'

'I don't think so. Don't sell yourself short, Niamh. And do yourself a favour – don't marry that man. You'll live to regret it, if you do. You'll be making a big mistake.'

'What gives you the right to point out my mistakes? Why

60

should I listen to you? I'm sure you're not offering to take his place and marry me instead.' Much as she expected, Judd blinked, rendered speechless at the thought. 'Oh, don't panic, I didn't mean it,' she said wearily. 'Just calling your bluff.'

'Right, then,' he said, eyes glittering with suppressed anger. 'It shall be as you wish. I shall banish myself from the Silver Star. But before I do, I'll have something from you in return.'

She folded her arms. 'Not till I know what it is.'

'All right. You know Harry Campion's in town?'

'Not *the* Harry Campion, the showman?' she said, intrigued in spite of herself. 'The man who flies around in a hot-air balloon?'

'The very same. Well, he's building a big house in Camberwell and we're commissioned to do the verandahs and some of the ironwork inside. He's offered to take me up for a joyride.'

'Oh!' Niamh breathed. 'Oh Judd, you lucky—'

'So I took a chance,' he interrupted, pausing to pick an imaginary hair off his sleeve, 'and asked him if I could bring a lady friend with me. Maybe *you*.'

'Me?' She almost squealed her delight. 'But I've always wanted to ride in a hot-air balloon. What did he say?'

'He thought about it a bit and said yes. It would be a novelty to take up a girl.'

'So when do we go?'

'Sunday morning – early. I'll meet you outside the back door of the Silver Star. Say, half an hour before dawn.'

Her shoulders slumped in disappointment. 'But I can't, not possibly. It'll still be dark at that hour – the middle of the night.'

'Come on, Niamh. I've gone out on a limb for you. Do you want to be in it or not?'

'Of course I do. But I—'

'No buts. I'll have you back before breakfast, we'll part as friends and you need never see me again. Now can I say fairer than that?'

He made it sound so simple, so easy, that Niamh, thrilled by the prospect of fulfilling a long-held ambition, didn't realise how harebrained the scheme would sound to anyone else.

She broke the news to Holly and her parents over lunch the following day as they were seated around the big pine table in the kitchen. Janet glared at her daughter and pressed her hand to her heart while Hollis choked on a mouthful of biscuits and cheese.

'You're going to do *what*?' he spluttered, coughing into his napkin. Janet poured him a glass of water and patted him on the back, shaking her head at Niamh. She wasn't to be deterred.

'I said I'm going for a ride in a hot-air balloon. It leaves from the Cricket Ground early on Sunday morning. You can come too, if you like.' She knew this was rash – the invitation had not been extended to Hollis. 'I'm sure they won't mind. It's only for half an hour.'

'No, thanks,' he said when he could speak. 'I'd rather keep my feet on the ground. Ballooning is for circus performers, not people like us. Certainly not for you as my future wife. We have certain standards to uphold.'

Dull! Dull! Judd's words returned to mock her, chiming in her head. 'Oh Holly, how can you be so stuffy?'

'You're not to do this, Niamh. I don't want you to go.'

Janet glared at her daughter, supporting him. 'Quite right, Hollis. Quite right, too.'

Niamh looked around the table to see two shocked faces staring back at her. She appealed to her father who had so far said nothing. He was eating quickly and economically, anxious to finish his lunch and return to the bar. 'Papa, tell them they're being ridiculous, please!'

He pushed his plate away and pressed his napkin to his lips before he spoke. 'I'm sorry, Niamh, but this time I have to side with Holly.'

'Thank you, sir.' Hollis smiled his relief and glanced at Niamh, waiting for her to accept the decision as unanimous.

'But Papa, why? You know I've wanted to do this for years – ever since you took me to the Cremorne Gardens to see a balloonist when I was a little girl. It was my birthday. You must remember?'

He smiled, wagging a finger at her. 'No, no, sweetheart, you won't catch me with sentiment. Not this time. Ballooning is a dangerous pastime, unsuitable for a girl. I'm surprised at Burden for suggesting it. I know a little about balloons. Sometimes the gas is too heavy and the thing won't lift except to give

62

the passengers a bumpy ride along the ground. Or the fabric of the balloon can give way and tear. You could be injured, even killed. And as for these so-called aeronauts, I've seen them too often before. Drunken show-offs, most of them.'

'Not Harry Campion. He's a gentleman. Judd told me, he's building a big house at Camberwell and—'

'Niamh, I don't care if he's building the Taj Mahal. You're not going.'

'Judd wouldn't put me at risk, Papa. What can possibly go wrong? We'll be in full view of spectators the whole of the time.'

'And there's another thing.' Tully leaned on his elbows, regarding her. 'What do we know of this Burden, really? Nothing, except that he works for Albert Smith.'

'Of course you know him, Papa. He's in here every night.'

'And that's *all* we know about him, darlin'. For me that's just not enough. To be honest, I've never liked the man. I don't trust him.'

'Oh? Why wait until now to say so? You've always made him so welcome before.'

'I have to, darlin', I'm running a public house. Unless he gets blind drunk and starts causing trouble, I have to serve him. That don't mean I have to like him – and I like him the less for making trouble between you and Holly.'

'He hasn't.'

'No – then why are we arguing? I don't believe in playing the heavy father, Niamh, I never have. But I don't think you should see Judd Burden away from the Silver Star. Thank him kindly and give an excuse. You'll think of something, I'm sure. Say you're needed here and you're much too busy to go.'

Niamh bent her head and looked at her plate, letting them think she conceded defeat. Tully sprang to his feet, summoned by the shouts of his neglected patrons in the bar.

'C'mon, Tully. Let's be havin' yer! Me stomach thinks me throat's cut!'

'Are ye there, missus? A man could be dyin' o' thirst out here!'

Propped on her pillows, Sally was sitting out in a basket chair while Gladys was re-making her bed. 'Look at me, girl, when

I'm talking to you.' She was tired of staring at the stubborn curve of her niece's back.

'What is it now, Auntie?' Gladys snapped. 'If I have to stop every time you open your mouth, I'll never get done.'

'Just don't make me sorry I sent for you, that's all. I don't like it, what you're plannin' for him.'

'Dunno what you mean, Auntie,' Gladys sniffed, tossing her head.

'Oh yes, you do. I'm not so green as I may be cabbage-lookin'. I might be weak and feeble in body but not in mind. Think I haven't seen you, sashayin' about the place, shakin' your tits at the man and drivin' him wild?'

As Gladys came and stood over her, Sal's heart gave a painful thump. She looked up at her, threatened by the malice she saw in those glittering, boot-button eyes.

'For someone who's tucked up in bed all day, Auntie, I think you see far too much.'

'I shan't be abed for ever. I'll be on me feet an' at work again afore long.'

Gladys smiled, cruel and smug. 'I wouldn't count on it, Auntie. I think you'll be there quite a while. You could be chained to that bed till you rot. And when you're dead and buried, I'll still be here.'

'You're cruel, girl. Heartless and cruel,' Sal whispered, looking down at her gnarled, work-worn hands, and gripped the blankets firmly to stop them from trembling. 'No wonder John Michael's family don't want you back.'

Gladys finished making the bed then turned to help the old lady get in. Blinded by tears, Sal pushed away the helping hands, trying to stand alone.

'Don't be silly, Auntie. Let me help or you'll fall.'

Reluctantly, Sally allowed her niece to put her to bed, falling back against the pillows with closed eyes. 'I could say somethin' – tell Mrs Janet . . .' she began.

Gladys gave a snort of laughter. 'An' cut off your nose to spite your face? She'd have us out on the streets in a moment. Which one of us d'ye think would fare better then?'

Tears of weakness and frustration leaked from Sally's eyes and soaked into her pillows.

'I want him, Auntie. And if I can get him, I will.'

'Stop it!' The old woman cringed away. 'I don't want to hear it.'

'Besides, I've nothing to feel guilty about. I'm not the one who's married, he is.'

Sally shook her head. 'The voice of a guilty conscience if ever I heard one. It's up to the woman to resist a man's carnal passions and keep things nice.'

'But what about *my* carnal passions?' Gladys pressed her lips to Sally's temple. She did it seductively, as if she were kissing a lover, making Sally shrink from her in disgust. 'Trust me, Auntie. You wait an' see. We'll be livin' high on the hog afore long, you an' me. I'll be the next Mrs Tully McDiarmit or me name's not Gladys O'Shea.'

Chapter Six

Harley Maitland frowned as the door of his office opened and his son came breezing in without knocking. Full of suppressed excitement and confidence, Hollis unrolled some architectural drawings across his desk, covering the files his father was studying and disturbing another pile of legal case-notes awaiting attention, neatly folded and bound with red ribbons.

'Pa, can you spare me a moment to take a look at this?'

'Oh Holly, not now.' Harley put his hand to his side in the hope of quieting the unpleasant feeling of tightness in his chest. 'Can't you see I'm up to my eyes in it? I have work to do here.'

'I promise, it won't take a moment. Just do me the courtesy of glancing over these plans—'

'I don't need to.' Harley looked up into his son's face, sorry he had to be the one to dampen his enthusiasm. 'Because I've seen it all before. I told you – I don't want my name, or the name of Maitland and Maitland associated with the dubious business of suburban railway shares or the subdivision of land.'

'Dubious? How can you say my plans are dubious when you won't even look at them? You know nothing about it!'

'Yes, I do. You're trying to get on the bandwagon with Horace Ironsides and I have to say I don't like it. At best his scheme is short-sighted and at worst it's downright dishonest. I want no part of it.'

'Then you'll be the one to lose out, Pa. Not me.'

'Fine,' Harley said easily. 'At least I can sleep at night with a clear conscience.' Briefly, he glanced at the plans, shaking his

66

head. 'These are back blocks, Holly, to be sold at inflated prices – and under false pretences as well. The land isn't even cleared; it's not much better than virgin bush. There'll be no proper services out there for years.'

'All we need is time. Victoria is expanding faster than we can keep up with it. Prices can only go higher. I don't see how we can lose.'

'There speaks the optimist – the promoter of every get-rich-quick scheme I ever heard.'

'It's a solid business proposition even if we are expecting to get rich quick.' Impatiently, Holly made a fist of one hand and punched it into the palm of the other, pacing the room. 'Why do you always suspect my motives? Why do you always take me for a fool?'

'It's not *your* motives I suspect but those of Ironsides and his cronies. Playing hard to get while they're working so hard to convince you at the same time. You're nobody's fool, my boy, just inexperienced and a little naïve.'

'You're the one who's naïve, Pa, for letting these opportunities pass you by. D'you know how much Horace Ironsides made from that land at the beach? It was positively indecent.'

'It was. I couldn't have put it better myself.' Harley's tone was dry. 'I don't blame Ironsides for trying to get ahead and making the most of his chances. A man with no education, pulling himself up by his boot-straps. But as an established, respectable law firm we don't need to resort to such questionable business tactics.'

'Oh? So what would you have me do, Pa? Stick my well-bred, educated nose in the air and pretend it's not happening, while everyone else cashes in all around us?'

'Yes, I do. We should keep our integrity. That way we'll still be in business when the bubble has burst.'

'It's not like you to be so shortsighted, Pa.'

Harley smiled; the pain in his chest wouldn't let him laugh. 'No no, son. I'm too old and wily a campaigner to be caught with that one. You won't goad me into it. Speculate with your own money, if you like. You'll probably be more careful with it than mine.'

'Pa!'

'You're of age now and about to be married. You'll be

67

responsible for your own family soon. I can't block you indefinitely if you're determined to be a part of this. But don't expect me to go guarantor for you or invest any money of my own. And remember, if anything goes awry, I will say *I told you so*.'

'Nothing will go awry. And when I've doubled my money twice over, I'll be the one who's saying *I told you so*.'

'I hope so, son.' Harley's smile was thin. 'Believe me, I do.'

On Saturday night Niamh couldn't have slept if she'd wanted to; she was plagued by a mixture of nerves, excitement and also a guilty conscience. She knew she was defying the wishes of her parents and Hollis, but she was determined to keep faith with Judd. He had called in earlier to remind her of her promise and that he would be waiting for her in the lane outside the back door of the Silver Star. Harry Campion had told him the balloon must be launched at sunrise to take advantage of the favourable winds.

Customers lingered as usual on Saturday evening and it was almost two before the McDiarmits could retire to bed. With only an hour to spare before leaving, Niamh didn't dare try to sleep. To refresh herself, she washed and put on a red flannel petticoat under her skirts, buttoned a warm riding jacket over a light silk blouse and sat up in the chair beside her bed to wait until it was time to leave. Gentle snores told her the rest of the household was asleep and when the clock in the bar chimed the hour of three, she wrapped a mohair shawl about her shoulders, rejecting a warm beret in favour of her newest hat. Designed to perch on the coil of hair at the back of her head, it was a frivolous confection of silk ribbons and artificial flowers, the colour of autumn leaves. The salesgirl said it enhanced the rich deep bronze of her eyes. Shamelessly feminine, it went a long way towards softening the severity of her clothes.

Not even Gladys was awake to challenge her when she crept through the house and let herself quietly out of the back door, locking it behind her. With luck she would be home again before anyone realised she had gone and, if she were late, she could always say she had been to church.

As promised, Judd was waiting with a cab to take them to

Richmond. She greeted him with a brief smile, feeling both furtive and traitorous and the cab driver's greeting did nothing to set her at ease; he looked her over with a knowing grin, touching his hat with his whip. It was obvious that he thought himself party to an assignation and Judd did nothing to make him think otherwise, kissing her hand and smiling at her under his eyelashes as he handed her up.

At the Cricket Ground, she was surprised to see a blaze of lanterns and torches making it light as day. The flight was to be a very public event. Judd had mentioned spectators, but she had not anticipated anything like this. A huge crowd had gathered and a brass band was in full swing, in spite of the early hour. Harry Campion was nothing if not a showman and many tickets had been sold with the promise of music and entertainment, along with the spectacle of the flight. Deliberately, he had chosen Sunday morning as the time most people would be free, ignoring the censure of church and civic authorities. The show would be over and the money pocketed, long before the protests came in.

Keeping a firm grip on Niamh, whose steps were faltering now she realised she was to be in the forefront of so much publicity, Judd fought his way to the barriers and waved to Harry Campion who signalled to his men to let them come through.

'Good, you're on time,' he said as Judd made the introductions. 'Conditions are perfect for a smooth flight. Please be patient, just for a moment. We're almost ready for take-off.'

'Judd.' Niamh plucked at his sleeve, whispering urgently. 'Judd, I'm sorry but I really don't think I—'

'No,' he said firmly, reading her mind. 'This is no time for second thoughts.'

Niamh looked up at the balloon, straining at the ropes and pegs which secured it to the ground. Close to it, she saw it was much larger than she'd expected. The fabric was a brilliant orange, painted with curls and highlights to resemble red hair around the features of a white-faced clown. The mouth was open, laughing, showing a huge tongue behind a row of white, even teeth. In the air it would look like a disembodied head. Niamh fancied it was laughing at her right now, rocking with secret mirth. Campion was a man in his early forties, wearing a

69

seaman's cap over thinning hair and a pair of metal-rimmed spectacles perched on the end of his nose. Contrary to her father's predictions, he was sober and she thought he looked much more of a scientist than a showman.

A box was found for her to use as a stepping block, and willing hands reached out to help her into the basket. The breeze gave her a battle with her skirts, causing a ripple of amusement to pass through the crowd. Larrikins whooped and whistled, hoping for a sight of frilly underskirts and feminine ankles. The crowd took up the whistling and stamping, impatient with the delay.

Harry nodded to his assistants, warning them to keep a firm hold on the ropes as he turned up the burners to warm the air inside the balloon to make it rise.

Out of the corner of her eye, Niamh could see a commotion on the edge of the crowd as a party of a dozen men worked their way to the front and broke through the barriers, urged on by their leader, a thin scarecrow of a man dressed in mouldering black and wearing a battered, tall-crowned hat.

'Halt! Halt this blasphemy! If the good Lord intended us to fly like his angels, he would have given us wings! Sacrilege! The heavens must not be invaded. Not on the Lord's own day!'

Niamh glanced at her companions, beginning to be scared. Clear of the barriers now, the men were racing towards them across the field, their leader hobbling behind them, shouting encouragement in ringing, biblical tones.

'Go to it, lads! Seize them! Burst the balloon. Foil the plans of these followers of Beelzebub!'

Harry's assistants murmured curses. Unable to move or defend themselves as they stood there, holding the ropes, they were most vulnerable to attack.

'Look lively, Harry!' One of them pleaded. 'We're sittin' ducks here.'

Harry shrugged. There was nothing he could do until the air in the balloon was hot enough to allow it to rise. At last he raised his hand, giving the signal for them to release it. But not before the first of the intruders reached them, clinging to the side of the basket and clawing at the fabric.

Judd reacted by landing him a sharp punch on the jaw and

70

Niamh winced, certain she heard it break. The man let go at once with a cry and dropped back out of sight.

Free of its restraints, the balloon lurched into the air just as the others reached the spot it had occupied only moments before. Thwarted, they clutched and stabbed at the empty air, yelling and shaking their fists at the balloon which was now rising, moving swiftly and steadily away.

Judd found a handkerchief and wrapped it about the knuckles of his right hand which was skinned and beginning to bleed.

Those few moments had been filled with such drama that Niamh had quite forgotten to be nervous about the ascent.

Now she caught her breath, feeling a wave of dizziness as she looked over the side, seeing the earth drop away. The sensation was strange and the silence complete, except for the occasional roar from the burners. She steadied herself and looked again, seeing the oval of the Cricket Ground and the stands reducing in size to look like toys, the people, like ants, closing in on the troublemakers. Dawn broke, the sun appearing through the clouds to give them a golden sunrise and on this clear, summery morning, they could see for miles. Her fears were forgotten as she gave herself up to the pleasure of identifying familiar landmarks and seeing Melbourne from this unusual vantage point in the sky.

There was the city spread out beneath her with its strange mixture of old and new; trees growing on the steeply sloping banks of the Yarra and the mansions behind them; she thought she recognised The Oaks which led to a further pang of conscience. There was the university, set in its formal gardens, the bank buildings of the city with their sombre Corinthian columns, the wide main streets with the back-streets and alleys connecting them, quieter than usual as it was Sunday. She was unable to pick out the roof of the Silver Star although she identified the Post Office and other landmarks in Bourke Street. She felt guilty all over again for deceiving her parents and Holly – for deliberately flying in the face of her father's wishes. Then she reminded herself of the peace of mind that would follow. It would be worth it. She was keeping her part of the bargain and, if Judd were a man of his word, he'd be obliged to keep his.

71

She looked down at the Yarra, ponderous as a huge snake the colour of churned mud, moving sluggishly on its way to the sea. There were the tanneries and foundries that crowded the banks of the river and the suburbs of Richmond and Hawthorn grown up on either side; squares of cultivated garden and shady trees which shrank again as they rose still higher, making Niamh grateful for her warm clothes.

Harry adjusted the burners to remain at the right height for cruising, allowing the balloon to leave the city and travel south, following the coastline but taking care not to drift out over the sea.

Niamh looked down at the various shades of ochre that formed the sands and the white caps on the bay which contrasted with the dull green of forest on the distant hills. 'Why, it's beautiful,' she whispered. 'It's only when you see it from up here that you realise just how vast this land really is – how little we have managed to tame.'

'And would you want to tame it, Niamh?' Judd asked softly, taking pleasure in her wonder and enjoyment and looking at her with new respect. In the face of danger she had remained calm and unruffled when most women would have panicked.

'Tame it? Oh no.' She answered his question at last, reluctantly tearing her gaze away from the scenery to smile at him. 'Australia is wild and rugged because that's what it's meant to be. It isn't for taming, Judd. This is an old, old continent, maybe the oldest in the world, and our pathetic attempts to civilise it have made no impression at all. Look at those ships.' She pointed downwards at the collection of vessels anchored in Hobson's Bay. 'Brigs and three-masted clippers, capable of crossing the world, yet from here they look no bigger than a child's toys on a pond. No wonder those fanatics wanted to stop us – it's too magical, too good. Oh yes, I can believe in a God who is jealous of His skies.'

Harry cleared his throat, reminding them of his presence. 'Sorry folks,' he said. 'Discovered a bit of a hitch. No need to panic but I think there's a tear in the envelope and we'll have to land before it gets worse. Those idiots must have done us some damage after all. I had hoped to return us to the Cricket Ground or a bit of parkland nearer the city. As it is, we'll have to set down here.'

'Oh no!' This was the first time Niamh had shown any sign of dismay.

'Don't you worry, love,' Harry said. 'I'll aim for that bit of open ground – the bluff near the beach. We might land with a bit of a bump but we'll be quite safe.'

'It's all right, Mr Campion, I'm not scared,' Niamh said. 'Nor do I doubt your skills. But I'll have some explaining to do if I'm not home for lunch.'

'Where *is* Niamh, then?' Janet fixed Gladys with a stern look. 'Didn't you see her go out?'

'No.' Gladys twitched a shoulder, giving her attention to the pot of lamb stew on the stove. 'She was long gone before I was up and about.'

'And look at me when I'm talking to you!' Janet snapped. 'You must have some idea.'

'Church? It's Sunday mornin', after all.'

'But the early morning services will be over by now.'

'Well, I don't know!' The woman's patience gave out. 'I'm not her keeper, am I?'

'St Paul's – that's where she'll be. I'll walk up and meet her,' Janet said, half to herself. She fetched her hat from the stand in the hall, slapped it on her head and pinned it without looking in the mirror. 'Keep stirring that stew, Gladys, and keep it from burning until we get back.'

Tully straightened himself and sighed as he stood up from checking the casks and bottles in the cramped little storeroom behind the bar. 'How many times must I tell you, Gladys? you're wasting your time. I said no and I meant it.' His voice rasped, showing he was under a strain. 'So be a good girl now and let me alone.'

'I don't believe you,' she said in her mocking sing-song voice. 'Relax ... give yourself a treat.' Coming up behind him, she slid her arms around his waist and pressed herself against him, tall enough to breathe on the back of his neck and whisper into his ear. He closed his eyes and groaned, almost tempted by the smell of warm female body and fresh soap. 'Come on,' she gave him a little shake. 'You want it as much as I do – I can tell.'

'*No!*' He threw her off with such force that she fell against a rack of bottles and bruised her arm. She winced, rubbing it and he almost relented as she looked at him, eyes wide with reproach. 'Go on, Gladys. Let me get on with my work. Leave it now and we can forget it – pretend nothing happened.'

'Nothing has.' She sniffed. Without asking him, she picked out a bottle of his best double malt, broke the seal and pulled the cork with her teeth, before offering it. 'Come on. Take a little something to oil the wheels.'

He took the bottle from her and snapped his fingers for her to give him the cork. He forced it into the bottle and put it back on the shelf. 'I don't drink. One thing you learn if you want to stay in this business and keep your sanity, is not to soak up the profits.'

'Please, Tully. This is the best chance we'll ever get. No one will know.'

'*I'll* know.' He gave her a slap on the bottom, aware that she wouldn't feel it through the thickness of her skirts. 'Whatever you think – whatever you hoped – forget it. I'm a married man. And if there's anything I've ever said, ever done to encourage you, then I'm sorry.'

'But the way you look at me sometimes . . . The way you—'

'Men are always looking at women, Gladys. They don't mean nothing by it.'

'But—'

'Give yourself time, girl,' he said, not unkindly. 'You've not been a widow for long. You'll meet a man one day – a good man who'll appreciate that you waited. Then you'll be glad you left me an' my marriage alone.'

'You haven't a real marriage. Not with *her*.'

'Yes, I do. However things seem to you, Janet is still Niamh's mother and my wife; my business partner too. That's never going to change.'

'Why not?' Gladys shrugged. 'Businesses are sold every day and the profits divided.'

'Not this one – not the Silver Star! I've put too much into it. Too much of my life. Ye see, I'm a creature of habit, Gladys. I like things as they are.'

'Have it all, then.' Her voice was low and persuasive and she held him with the intensity of her gaze. 'Your business, your

74

wife, and me, too.' She took his hand and pressed it into her breast. Her corset was of the sort that pushed up her breasts so that they were crushed against the low-cut neckline of her gown. Only a couple of layers of muslin separated the breast from his fingertips which instinctively closed on her nipple. She tensed, holding him with her eyes, waiting to see if he'd push her away. He didn't. Instead, he kissed her thoroughly, filling her mouth with his tongue and grazing her chin with his stubble as he forced her back against the rough brick wall of the storeroom. She gave a muffled cry, somewhere between pain and pleasure, certain she had him now. Just as suddenly, he let her go and stood breathing heavily and watching her as she stared back at him, wiping her bruised lips with the back of her hand.

'All right, you,' he said, speaking softly but with no tenderness. 'Now you know I can be tempted the same as any man. Maybe we'll come to it in the end, you and I. But I'll decide when and where and the guilt will be mine.'

'We'd be takin' nothing from her that *she* wants.'

'Her name's Janet. And she is still me wife.'

'But – but I love you!' she tried as a last resort. Choked with self-pity, it was easy for her to let tears stand in her eyes.

'Bollocks!' He laughed, being deliberately coarse. 'Your tears don't cut any ice with me. Go on with ye, ye baggage. The stew will be on the way to burnin' by now. Get back to your work in the kitchen and let me be.'

Niamh closed her eyes and braced herself for the moment of impact; the ground seemed to be rushing towards them so fast. But Harry was too skilled an aeronaut to give them a rough landing. Instead of the bone-shuddering crash she expected, there was only a slight jarring of the teeth as the basket tilted and settled itself on the ground.

After congratulating Niamh on her courage and assuring themselves she was unhurt, Judd and Harry left her to admire the surroundings while they retrieved the balloon which was in danger of suffering further damage in the scrub. Harry showed Judd how he wanted it folded, rolling and squeezing the last of the air from the envelope until it was small enough to pack into the basket.

Niamh saw they had landed on an exposed headland covered in coarse, tufted grass. Behind them were some sand dunes and a few stunted trees; in front of them the gentle curve of a sandy beach. In the middle distance she could see a pier, stretching out into the sea. Several boats were tied up and people were promenading, enjoying the sea breezes. Just now, every face was turned towards them. It was unusual to see a balloon in flight at all, let alone coming to land so unexpectedly, narrowly missing the disaster of being blown out to sea.

A small crowd had gathered around them on the headland and Campion was quick to enlist their help, bribing two boys to fetch a carrier to take himself and his basket to the train.

'Well, Judd,' Harry said, clasping his friend's hand and shaking it in farewell. 'Sorry the show didn't work out according to plan.'

'Never mind, Harry. That's half the fun of ballooning, isn't it?' Judd grinned at Niamh and pointedly cast an eye at the clear blue sky, free of rainclouds for once which could have spoiled an otherwise perfect day. 'What do you say, Niamh, to an afternoon at the seaside? Lunch first, followed by a leisurely stroll along the beach.'

She shook her head. 'Tempting as it sounds, I think I should go with Harry. I'm in trouble enough as it is.'

'All the more reason to stay.' Judd was at his most persuasive. 'If you're slightly late, people are irritated at first and then they get cross. Later yet and they start to worry. But if you're really late, they're so relieved when you do turn up that they forget to be angry at all.'

'I can't put my family through all that.'

'You worry too much. Enjoy yourself. Let's have a day out.'

'Oh Judd, I really can't.'

'Better make up yer mind, Miss.' The carrier rolled the match he was chewing to the other side of his mouth. 'Sunday services today. Miss this one an' there isn't another till after six.'

'Niamh, please stay.' Judd was exerting every ounce of his charm to keep her. 'I'm famished and you must be, too. It's all this fresh air.' He took a deep breath, relishing the clean, salty smell of the breeze coming off the sea.

'No, really,' Niamh protested until her stomach growled

76

treacherously whereupon she relaxed. 'Oh, all right. I haven't been to the seaside in years. Sal never liked the sands and Mama used to tell me off for tucking up my skirts and showing my knees.'

'I promise not to look at your knees.'

'But I'll be too hot in these winter clothes.'

'Then take off the heavier things and give them to Harry.' He had an answer for everything. 'I'll get them back to you later.'

Judd's fun-loving, carefree attitude was infectious and Niamh laughed for joy as she ran to take cover behind some bushes to take off her red flannel underskirt. Harry groaned at the delay, shaking his head as he looked at his pocket watch. She rolled the skirt into a ball and tucked it inside her winter jacket before giving the parcel to Harry. The shawl she kept in case the weather turned cool later on.

Harry grinned and saluted them as the carrier waved his whip ineffectually and swore at his unwilling horse. The animal responded without warning, plunging forward and almost spilling Harry and the basket from the cart. Finding its rhythm, the bad-tempered pony took off at a spanking trot, the cart bouncing behind it across the uneven turf, Harry clinging to his basket for dear life.

'I should have gone with them,' Niamh muttered, watching the cart disappear down the road.

'Why?' Judd took her hand and tucked it in his arm. 'It's boring to do the expected all of the time. Everyone ought to kick over the traces once in a while.'

She gave him a sharp look, not encouraged by his words.

'You'll feel better when you've had something to eat,' he said, deftly changing the subject and pointing ahead. 'That looks to be the main street over there.'

Conversation lapsed as Niamh had to break into a trot to keep up with his long stride as they walked down the single thoroughfare which was the hub of civilisation in the newly developing seaside town. As it was Sunday, only tea shops and kiosks were open for trade.

As they walked, Niamh saw the bold, speculative glances Judd was receiving from other women out on the street. Sukie's words came at once to mind: *His smiles are for*

77

everyone. They weren't a couple and she had no business to be promenading with him on a Sunday afternoon, behaving as if they were. Yet he was an enviable escort for anyone, a muscular figure in a leather jacket and matching waistcoat over a newly laundered calico shirt. She wished she weren't so aware of him in those tight-fitting breeches and the knee-high boots which emphasised the strength of his calves. He wore a red spotted bandana at his neck which gave him a jaunty, piratical air. And while most men would feel uncomfortable without a hat, he preferred to go bareheaded, his thick dark hair swept straight back and falling almost to his shoulders. It gave him the look of a glamorous titan, dangerous and attractive. Small wonder the local girls stared after him, eyes bright with envy.

And as always there was that whiff of burning metal clinging to his hair and clothes; that heady hint of the furnaces which seemed to be as much a part of him as his smile.

He steered her towards a café on the beachfront with freshly painted windows and clean curtains. Inside it was busy, if a little cramped, with only one waitress serving the tables. But they received a warm welcome and were seated at once by the window where they could look out on the beach and the sea. The tablecloth was red gingham and Niamh fingered it, pleased to discover it crisp and freshly laundered, the cutlery in front of them also clean.

On the waitress's recommendation they ordered the catch of the day, flounder served whole – a large flatfish almost too big to fit on the dinner plate, accompanied by another piled high with fresh bread and butter. Judd also ordered a pot of strong English Breakfast tea. Good, plain food which was just what they needed. Niamh gave it her undivided attention, eating quickly and greedily, too hungry to make conversation.

'That's what I like to see,' Judd said as she sat back with a gentle sigh, pushing her plate away. 'A woman who isn't afraid to eat.'

'Oh, I'm sorry,' Niamh mumbled, eyeing the debris of bones and skin. 'I didn't mean to be rude.'

'You weren't,' he grinned. 'I told you, I like to see a woman enjoying her food.'

He ordered a second pot of tea and they took their time over it, finishing the remains of the bread and butter with

78

some home-made strawberry jam. They laughed at the antics of children playing on the beach and around the bathing huts which lined the shore, and admired the courage of one or two brave souls who had elected to swim so early in summer, ignoring the chill breeze.

Later, they strolled along the promenade arm-in-arm, attracted by the sound of a band playing in the shade of a nearby rotunda.

'Oh, this is so good,' she said, turning her face to the sun and taking a deep breath of fresh sea air. 'A stolen afternoon. And all the more to be savoured because I shouldn't be here.'

The band was playing *Little Brown Jug* to the rhythm of a polka. Half a dozen couples, encouraged by the catchy tune, were already dancing on the grass. Judd spread his arms, inviting her to join them.

The polka finished almost as soon as they started and the band launched immediately into the familiar strains of *I'll Take You Home Again, Kathleen*. This wasn't at all like the energetic, rather childish gallop of the polka and Niamh was very conscious of Judd's hand on her waist, drawing her close as he whirled her into the dance. For a man of his size he was light on his feet and she could follow his steps with ease. Before long she sensed his mood had changed and looked up to see him studying her intently.

'What is it?' To break the tension she said the first thing that came into her head. 'Is there a smut on my nose?'

'No,' he said softly. 'I was just thinking how easily, how naturally we dance together – as if we belong. And I was thinking how it might have been and how it could still be if . . .' He broke off with a mild curse. 'But you won't hear me, will you? There isn't a damned thing I can do.'

'Please, Judd.' She stopped dancing and put her fingers to his lips to silence him. 'Today is perfect. Let's leave it just as it is.' Gently, she disengaged herself and took off, running awkwardly in the direction of the beach, leaving him standing among the other dancers on the grass. She ploughed her way through the dunes and didn't stop until she reached the water's edge where she paused, holding a stitch in her side and gasping for breath. His nearness, the intensity of his gaze, her own

79

tension was all too much. She sensed rather than heard him catch up with her.

'I'm sorry,' she said, without looking at him. 'It's not your fault, Judd, it's mine. For encouraging you and letting you think I was something other than what I am. I knew I should have taken the train with Harry. I should have gone home.'

'Niamh, stop it.' He reached out as if to take her shoulders and thought better of it, letting his arms fall to his sides. 'So much guilt isn't good for anyone. We've done nothing wrong.'

'Not because we weren't thinking about it. I was, anyway.' Suddenly, she faced him. 'You knew this was going to happen, didn't you? You knew the balloon had no chance of returning to the Cricket Ground.'

'I should hope not – with those fanatics waiting to catch us on our return. Ballooning is unpredictable at the best of times. You know that.'

'Do I? How do I know you didn't arrange all this in advance, you and Harry?'

'What?' He squinted at her, genuinely nonplussed.

'To set us down here – at the beach.'

'Oh, Niamh.' He stared at her for a moment, lips twitching. 'I've heard of girlish vanity but you take the cake. If I wanted to abduct you, I wouldn't need to hire a balloon. I could have carried you off in the cab.'

Feeling silly for thinking the worst of him, she gave him a sheepish smile. He laughed until she laughed with him, releasing the tension. He sat down, pulled off his boots and rolled up his breeches, showing strong calves covered with soft brown hair.

'Come on,' he said. 'Take off those boots and stockings and get some sand under your toes. And while you're at it, you can take off that prissy little Sunday bonnet as well.'

'Oh – don't you like my hat?'

'No.'

She knew he didn't mean it and, caught up in his mood of exhilaration, she took off her boots and stockings and then the hat, winding the elastic around one of the buttons on her boots to stop it from blowing away. Then she walked to the water's edge and let the sea ripple in over her feet, surprised to find it warmer than it looked. She enjoyed the gentle tug of the waves as she dug her toes into the soft, waterlogged sand and squealed like a child when Judd saw a larger wave threatening the hem of her petticoat and grabbed her by the hand to pull her clear of it. Recklessly, she hitched her skirts even higher before venturing into the water again, allowing the waves to lap around her ankles this time. Laughing, she dodged the larger ripples that chased her ashore and this time the sea won, soaking her skirts. Some time later, laughing and exhausted, they sat down to rest.

Looking back, she was surprised to see how far they had walked. Paddling and dodging in and out of the sea, they had walked around the headland and into the next cove. The family parties and bathing huts were no longer in view. They were alone on a small, deserted beach, surrounded by dunes.

'Our boots!' She leaped to her feet. 'And my hat. We left them miles away up the beach. Someone could—'

Smiling he held up his boots and her own, caught in the elastic of her hat. He had carried them all the way in his other hand. 'So we don't need to retrace our steps.'

'But we've come so far. I had no idea—'

He shook his head, whispering her name. 'Oh, Niamh. I brought you here to relax and take some time away from your workaday life. I have to work in a place where iron is forged; a place of searing heat and earsplitting noise. The sound of the sea, the smell of seaweed on the beach is refreshing to me. Now we'll sit on the sands, watch the sun go down and give thanks for the beauty of it all.'

'Indeed an' we won't.' She reverted almost to her father's brogue. 'I've lost count of the time. Come on, Judd – we have to go. What if we miss the last train?'

He wasn't listening, absorbed in a world of his own. Collapsing on the sands, he lay flat on his back and turned his face to the sun, composing himself for sleep.

'Judd!' She stood looking down at him, giving him a cautious jab in the ribs with her toe. 'Don't just lie there like a log. Get up.'

Lazily and without opening his eyes, he reached up and caught her by the wrist, pulling her down until she was lying in his lap. He held her there while he kissed her not forcefully but thoroughly, taking his time about it, refusing to let her move until she gave in, responding to his touch. She sat up, ready to argue, only when they had to come up for air.

'You lied to me.' She stabbed a finger at his chest, making him wince. 'You told me this wasn't planned.'

'It wasn't.' He opened eyes too wide to be innocent. 'I didn't know you were going to kiss *me*.'

'What cheek! You were the one kissing me.'

Avoiding her gaze, he started pulling the pins from her hair and shaking it free. 'You must get awful headaches, torturing it like this.'

'No!' She tried to stop him but it was hopeless, her hair was already down and blowing free. She clutched at it, trying to capture the strands at the nape of her neck. 'And don't lose those pins in the sand or I'll never get it back in a coil.'

He wasn't listening. 'Look at it – like spun gold in the sun. Now you look like a mermaid, some creature of myth come out of the sea to torment me,' he whispered, pulling her down beside him and stopping her protests with yet another extended kiss. This time she gave herself up to the pleasure, threading her fingers into his hair and opening her mouth to his kisses, accepting his tongue and delighting in her own power to enthrall. She meant to show him it was she who was in control here. So intent was she to 'punish' him that she didn't pause to consider her own reactions; how close she would come to losing control of her own emotions. For now she gave herself up to sheer physical pleasure, her mind spinning away into fantasy as her fingers greedily clutched his hair and she revelled in the delicious roughness of his stubble rasping her chin, his strong heart thundering close to her own. And that wonderful smell of scorched metal and musk, so peculiarly his own.

Nor did she make any move to stop him when she felt the practised touch of his fingertips at her breast, seeking and finding the hard button of her nipple, swelling against the soft silk of her blouse and the thin camisole beneath.

She sighed under these caresses, her pleasure heightened by the cries of the seagulls flying high overhead and the rhythmic soughing and slapping of the waves on the shore. Lulled into a sense of security by these sounds and the ministrations of his lips and tongue, she lay with her eyes closed, too lost to

82

sensual pleasure to call a halt, and ready to give herself up to what must inevitably follow. She shuddered in ecstasy, no longer aware of herself as Niamh at all but as a creature of sense and taste, licking the salt from his skin as he licked hers and raising a livid bruise on his throat with her own teeth and tongue until he broke free and sought her lips again with his own.

He stopped her mouth with more kisses as he unfastened the buttons of her blouse and left a trail of small kisses from her lips to her throat and, naturally, from there to her breast, rasping the softness of her flesh with his chin.

'Oh yes, yes please,' she murmured as he took the turgid nipple into his mouth, shuddering as she felt him expose the other, coaxing it to life under his rough yet sensitive fingertips. Hollis's hands and lips never thrilled her – not like this. *Hollis!* The thought of him brought her back to earth with a shock. It was like receiving a bucket of cold water full in the face. She opened her eyes and looked down to see Judd looking back at her, watching her reactions as he suckled, pleasuring her body with tongue and teeth. He hadn't progressed so far as to raise her skirts but he was nudging her legs apart with his knee and she knew, if she didn't resist, that their lovemaking would progress to its natural conclusion.

Ignoring the pleasurable pain in her breast and the ache in the lower part of her body, now clamouring to be fulfilled, she took a deep breath, sat up and gently pushed him away, wondering how she could have forgotten herself so far. Her cheeks burned as she realised anyone could have walked through the dunes and seen them. Shamed, she turned her back on him while she put her clothing to rights, fastening the buttons of her blouse.

Sensitive to her change of mood, he sat up and placed his hands on her shoulders, talking to her quietly.

'Niamh, don't do this. Don't turn your back on me – not now you know how it can be between us. How I feel.'

'How you feel doesn't come into it, Judd. I've already made my promises and I must keep them. You're a luxury I can't afford. This isn't safe.'

'Safe?' Frustration made him lash out at her. 'And is that all you want or expect from life? To be safe? Oh, you'll be safe enough with that milk-and-water lawyer of yours. Or is it his money that makes you feel so secure?'

'That's not fair.'

'And you? Are you being fair to me?' He came back at her. 'Professional virgin. Cheat.'

'No. You are the cheat, Judd. Your smiles are for everyone – Sukie told me.'

'And you believed her?'

'Why not? She sees you every day of her life and must know you so much better than I do.'

'Sukie! She sees the world through a haze . . .'

'Don't attack Sukie. It's cruel.'

'Why not, when it's clear she's doing her best to make trouble between us. Are you sure she has your best interests at heart?'

'Of course. She's my best friend.'

'I love you, Niamh.'

'Do you?' She shook her head. 'You love me. That's too easy to say. Three magic words like an incantantion to bring me tumbling into your lap. My father warned me. He said I shouldn't see you away from the Silver Star.'

'Niamh, listen to me.' He brushed her hair aside to drop a kiss on the back of her neck and making her shiver. 'Please – before it's too late. Hollis Maitland will give you half a life, half a love. I know men like that, I've seen them before. They burn with their own ambition until there's nothing left for anyone else.'

'He isn't like that.'

'Are you sure?'

'Of course. We've loved each other since we were children.'

'Exactly. Everyone wants to cling to that first love – long after the time has come to let it go. Oh Niamh, can't you see? We were made for each other, you and I. I love you more than I expected to love any woman, more than life itself. Maitland would be just as happy with anyone.'

'You don't know that!'

'What do you think I want from you? A shoddy, hole-in-the-corner affair? No. I want you to own up to your feelings and make some changes before it's too late.'

84

'It's too late already. Today is a mistake, a lapse, nothing more. I won't let it happen again.'

'And what if I give you no peace? Refuse to take no for an answer? What if I won't stay away from the Silver Star?'

'Then I'll get somebody else to serve you. Holly is my future. He is what's real to me and you're not. You're just a crazy moment of magic.'

He turned her in his arms, making her look at him. 'So you felt it, too. You felt the magic as I did. Oh Niamh, don't do this. Don't turn your back on us now.'

'I've promised to marry Hollis and that's what I'll have to do.'

'Then answer me this: if you're so desperately in love with Hollis, how come you're here with me?' He seized her left hand, holding it up to the light. 'And where's the Maitland badge of ownership – your diamond – today?'

She pulled her hand free, realising he'd picked on the one thing which was a bone of contention between herself and Hollis. 'I was afraid of losing it.'

'No. You don't love him enough. If you did, you couldn't bear to let it out of your sight. You'd wear it on a ribbon right next to your heart.'

She hung her head, not knowing how to answer him.

'You are a passionate woman, Niamh. Own up to it. We are like two halves that can't make a whole unless we're together.'

'One man for one woman? One true love in the whole of the world? I don't believe it,' she said, shaking her head.

'And I don't believe you'll choose that tame, bloodless lawyer over me.'

'He's not tame. He could be a lion in the couch for all you know.'

'He could be, but I'll lay pennies to pounds he's not. You respond to me like a creature starved of affection.'

'Starved? No. Your kisses would rouse any woman unless she were made of stone. But I do know the difference between true love and a moment of lust.'

'Oh, I lust after you all right. But I do love you, Niamh.'

'Only to be perverse. Because you can't have me.' She was slapping the sand from her feet, wiping the last of it on her petticoats before she put on her stockings. He was looking at her feet in a way that both alarmed and excited her. Quickly, she pulled on her stockings and wriggled her feet into her boots, finding it a struggle to fasten them without a button hook.

Having retrieved most of her hairpins, she held them in her mouth while she twisted her hair into its customary knot. Then she put on her hat, feeling it into the right place and tying the ribbons firmly beneath her chin. Lastly, she wrapped her shawl around her shoulders to hide her breasts which still tingled and peaked, betraying her. A mermaid no more, she was herself again, her mother's daughter, the cool unapproachable miss.

'Hurry up,' she said. 'We don't want to miss that train. I told you before – my promises are made and I mean to keep them. Too many people will be hurt if I don't.'

'It doesn't matter that *I'm* hurt?'

'You, Judd?' She gave a short laugh. 'You're one of life's survivors. You'll soon find a new girl to replace me – another unattainable love.'

'Is that what you think of me?' He took hold of her upper arm, squeezing it until she cried out. 'A poor fool who hangs around bars, sighing over women he can't have?'

'Judd, let me go. You're hurting my arm.'

'Be thankful I don't break it!' he grated, almost pulling her off her feet as he kissed her, briefly and savagely before letting her go. Her lips felt bruised from his kiss and she winced, touching them with her fingertips as he strode away through the dunes and disappeared, lost in the thorny bushes lining the road. It was only then that she remembered she had come out without any money. She could be stranded if he were to desert her, leaving her to find the station and take the train on her own. But when she ran through the dunes and the scrub to find him, he was still there, waiting for her at the side of the road. Unsmiling and silent, he offered his arm.

Chapter Seven

'Spurned you, didn't he?' Sal was sitting up in bed, propped on her pillows, ready to rub salt in Gladys's wounds when she saw her sullen expression and red-rimmed eyes.

'How d'you know?' Gladys frowned, still smarting from the pain of rejection. 'You wouldn't hear anything, not up here.'

'Your face tells me all I need to know. Learn to hide your feelings, girl. You're like an open book.'

'Only to those who can read,' Gladys snapped.

'All set to make the most of it, weren't you? The Missus all of a flap because Niamh's out gallivantin', and me stuck up here helpless in bed. There's you with the rest of Sunday mornin' stretchin' in front of you, an' Tully alone in the stores. Couldn't help yourself, could you? Threw yourself at his head – but he sent you packin', didn't he?'

'You stupid, malicious old bitch, what do you know?'

'Plenty!' Sally cackled, a little of her old vigour returning. 'Think I was always like this, do you? Old and crabbed, with a skin like a crocodile's? No, time was when I was young and juicy, like you. Not near as stupid, neither. Or how d'ye think I've kept meself going, all of these years?'

Gladys shrugged, tugging the bedclothes viciously into place, pinning the old lady to the bed.

'Oh yes,' Sally nodded. 'An' over the years I've made it me business to keep an eye on them two. So I don't want you comin' here, upsettin' the applecart. Why can't you be content to leave things as they are?'

'Because I'm not goin' to end my days as a maid of all work like you. I want more out o' life.'

'You're paid well enough.' Sally brooded. 'Thought you'd be grateful to get away from your penny-pinchin' in-laws.'

'Grateful?' Gladys spat the words, making the old woman flinch. 'Grateful to work for that sour-faced Janet, forever at me, finding fault all the time? I'm here for your sake, Auntie, not mine.'

'That's a lie. You came because you saw your chance to get back to the city. An' now you *are* here, you go chasin' another woman's husband – who won't even look at you.'

'Give him time.'

'Time? The only time you're wasting is your own. I'm telling you – you'll get nowhere, not with him.'

'Oh yes, I will.' Gladys spoke softly but her eyes were gleaming and the tone of her voice made Sal shiver. 'I always get what I want when I set my heart on it – no matter how long it takes.'

Niamh was gone, leaving Judd outside in the street, staring at the back door of the Silver Star. He had lost her and there was no one to blame but himself. He had bungled it, spoiled his chances by rushing her and showing his feelings too soon. He had gambled everything on this one day – gambled and lost . . . Now, if he were to keep his promise, he must stay away from the Silver Star or run the risk that Niamh would ignore him, leaving him to be served by Ted Farrelly, the old halfwit Tully employed as a potman and who sometimes helped out behind the bar.

This feeling of desolation was new; he wasn't used to failing with women. Once again he went over all that had passed between them, trying to see exactly where he'd gone wrong. Why must his charm fail him now? Now, the one time it mattered so much. He'd had his chance and he'd lost it. She would never leave herself vulnerable to him again.

Had she struggled against his advances, repelled by them, it would have been easier to bear. But she had fallen into his arms so naturally, as if it was where she belonged, returning his kisses with an ardour that matched his own. He had been so close; she had so nearly been his. But time wasn't on his side, granting him just one day to get her to change her mind. He had not done so. If anything, she was more determined

88

than ever to keep her engagement to Hollis Maitland – the man who had everything.

His fingers curled as he imagined them closing on Hollis' slender, boyish throat and squeezing until those pale green eyes lost their scornful expression, glazing over in death. He shook his head to dispel the vision, ashamed of harbouring such murderous thoughts. No woman was worth swinging for, not even Niamh.

During the train journey from Brighton she had been polite but distant and, instead of sitting beside him, she had chosen the window seat opposite. And when other people wanted to occupy the remaining seats in the carriage, she had smiled and invited them in, relieved that they wouldn't be travelling alone. In minutes, the carriage had filled with red-faced, exhausted people, smelling of salt water and perspiration. Fathers smoked, mothers yawned, sunburned children whimpered and a baby howled, making everyone miserable until it was pacified and persuaded to sleep.

Judd leaned his elbows on his knees, attempting to speak to Niamh, whispering so as not to disturb the child.

'This isn't the end, Niamh? We're still friends?'

She gave him a tight little smile, no more than a twitch of the lips without showing her teeth. 'You promised, Judd. You gave me your word. I've kept my side of the bargain – now you must keep yours.'

Her manner frustrated him. She was slipping away behind her barriers and he didn't know how to reach her.

'Niamh, please . . .'

'No.' She too leaned forward to whisper. 'I know what you hoped – what you wanted – but it isn't to be. I'm engaged to Hollis and I'm going to marry him.'

Raising his voice, Judd threw caution to the winds. 'But you don't love him!'

'I do. I do!'

'Oh? And would you love him as much if he wasn't so filthy rich?'

'If you please, sir, not so loud,' the baby's mother cautioned him. A fat, freckled woman, her cheeks were glowing from too many hours in the sun. 'I've only just got him off. We're all goin' to suffer if 'n he wakes.'

Niamh stared out of the window at nothing and Judd slumped back in his seat. They travelled in silence until the train driver gave a shrill blast on the whistle, warning them that the train was arriving at the terminus.

Forgetting their weariness, people stood up to gather their clothes and luggage, waking the baby who howled in earnest this time. It was amazing how much noise could come out of such a small body. Niamh left the station at a trot, ignoring Judd's suggestion of taking a cab. She would give him no further opportunity to talk in private.

Outside the back door of the Silver Star she paused and looked up at him, meaning to shake hands before going in. He clasped her hand in such a firm grip that she almost winced.

'Whatever you think of me, Niamh, I do have your best interests at heart.'

'Please, Judd, no more speeches. I must go in.'

'Give me one more moment.' It was useless to plead and he knew it but he couldn't help it. 'It's now or never.'

'It must be never, then. You agreed.' He was exerting emotional pressure and she wouldn't look him in the eye. 'Goodbye, Judd. If only things had been different . . . ' She left the sentence unfinished. 'But I wish you luck in life and all the happiness in the world.'

It sounded so final, he couldn't bear it. 'Niamh, please. Please don't do this!' But she was there one moment and gone the next, leaving him staring at the door which had firmly shut in his face.

Inside, Niamh took a deep breath to gather her forces as she leaned against the other side of the door. Judd was a master of charm and persuasion and she'd be a fool indeed to let him chip away at her armour any more. But now she faced a more pressing problem. How to account for her absence, the many hours that she'd been away?

Her mother stood up as soon as she walked in. Outwardly, she seemed calm but Niamh knew the signs; inwardly she would be seething with suppressed anger. Her father was seated at the kitchen table, rubbing his temples as if he had a headache. Peaceful by nature, he hated domestic discord, almost as much as his wife seemed to thrive on it. Gladys was there, too, her face alive with mischief, looking forward to witnessing a family drama.

Unexpectedly, Hollis was also seated at the table, white to the lips and with a strained expression. Everyone glanced at Tully, waiting for him to speak. Uneasy with the role of inquisitor, he cleared his throat before he stood up.

'An' would ye mind tellin' us, darlin,' just where you've been till this hour? You've been gone all day with no word. Ye must've known we'd be worried sick.'

'Oh Papa, I'm sorry. So sorry.' She threw herself into his arms and hugged him, full of remorse when she saw how exhausted, how defeated he seemed. Her mother, more angry than anxious, with her arms folded tightly across her chest, was physically holding her temper in check. 'Mama – oh, I didn't mean to worry you, or to be out so late. There was an accident—'

'An accident!' Tully stood her away from him at once to look at her. 'You're not hurt?'

'No, no. It wasn't that sort of accident.' Exasperated she turned to Janet. 'And Mama, do stop glowering as if I've committed the crime of the century. I've done nothing to be ashamed of.'

'You're not ashamed?' Janet could hardly speak through clenched teeth. 'Not ashamed of deliberately flouting your father's wishes? It was you at the Cricket Ground, wasn't it? Making a peepshow of yourself and getting caught in a riot? That *bold and daring young lady* was my daughter – behaving like a cheap circus performer – riding about alone with two men in a hot-air balloon.'

'Yes.' She saw no point in denying it. 'But you make it sound awful – it wasn't like that. And now, if you don't mind, I'd like to speak to Hollis. Alone.'

'And that's it, is it? We're to be offered no explanation?' Janet would have said more but her husband grasped her by the elbow, steering her towards the door.

'You too, Gladys,' he ordered. 'It's the young people's business, not ours. Let them deal with it on their own.'

Reluctantly, Gladys did as she was told while Janet broke free to whisper a last word to Niamh.

'Apologise! And say no more than you must.'

Hollis said nothing until all the doors were closed and he was certain they were alone.

'All right then, Niamh, I'm listening, but your story had better be good.'

While she gathered her thoughts, she unpinned her hat and stared at her reflection in the mirror of the hall-stand. Her cheeks were unusually flushed – she had caught the sun.

'Good to see you, Holly,' she said at last. 'I wasn't expecting you today.'

'That much is obvious,' he said, having no intention of sparing her. 'Niamh, what's come over you? If you had to do something that stupid, did you have to do it in front of half the population of Melbourne?'

'Holly, I'm sorry. I thought it would be just a joy-ride, that we'd be up and down in a matter of minutes. I didn't realise the event would draw such a crowd – what a public spectacle it would be.'

'You do realise you've made us a laughing stock? Everyone seems to think it's a huge joke – everyone except your parents and me. First and foremost Campion is a showman. A balloon can never go up without attracting a crowd. I told you I didn't want you to go—'

'Oh Holly, what's the use of rehashing it now? It's over and done with. For once, just once in my life I wanted to do something reckless, yes, even dangerous without weighing the pros and cons or thinking it through.'

'And having a final fling with the handsome Burden, before resigning yourself to marriage with me?'

His perception shamed her, making her look away. 'It wasn't like that. Not at all.'

'How was it, then? Did he play the gentleman, or use this opportunity to take advantage of you? More to the point, did you let him?'

Niamh took a deep breath, resisting the urge to slap him. 'Nothing happened.'

'No? But not because you didn't want it?'

She did slap him then and he returned it with interest. In the silence that followed the moment of violence, they stared at each other, shocked at their childishness.

92

'Oh Niamh, forgive me.' His voice broke with emotion as he held out his arms to her. 'I was angry and jealous but you didn't deserve that.'

'I'm sorry, too,' she said as they stepped into the familiar circle of each other's arms, both choked with unshed tears.

'It's just – just the thought of that man,' his voice cracked again, 'and how he looks at you. Niamh, you won t leave me, will you? I can't bear it if I lose you.'

'You're not going to lose me. I've told Judd not to come here any more. I won't have to see him again.'

He drew away from her for a moment to look into her eyes, making sure she meant it. Then he gathered her into his arms and dropped a kiss on her head, feeling an involuntary tremor pass through her body as she settled against his shoulder.

'Holly,' she said softly, 'I'd like to be married as soon as possible, if you still want me.'

'You are sure, Niamh?'

She nodded, holding back tears. Gently and as if he could hardly believe his luck, he took her face in his hands and looked at her intently, tracing the angry mark he had left on her cheek with his thumb. 'I do want to marry you, Holly,' she said, meeting his gaze without flinching. 'Just as soon as it can be arranged.'

'Niamh! For goodness sake stop shaking or I'll never be able to fasten this veil.' Elinor tossed the froth of fine, hand-made lace in the air, catching it as it floated down again, fragile as gossamer.

Dressed in her bridal finery, she was almost ready to face the day. Ready except for the veil which Elinor insisted she would fasten herself.

'Agnes would crush it onto your head and make you look like a cow in a wreath of roses,' she laughed, as soon as the maid was out of earshot. Looking at their combined reflection, Niamh didn't think much of Ellie's efforts either, although she was too tactful to say so.

Falling in with the Maitlands' arrangements, including their suggestion that the bridal party should leave from The Oaks instead of the cramped quarters behind the Silver Star, Niamh had been caught up in plans which had taken off like a whirlwind, outside her control. Even Aunt Lilias – she who had been so bitterly opposed to her son's marriage – was now doing all she could to ensure their happiness.

Niamh was seated before the mirrors of an ornate dressing-table in the suite of rooms she was to share with Hollis when she became his wife. Most of his clothes were already hanging in the wardrobes of the other dressing-room alongside her own. The bedroom itself was spacious, with huge windows commanding a view of the park and the curve of the river beyond. On the first floor of the mansion, it was directly opposite the rooms occupied by the elder Maitlands.

She felt strange and quite unlike herself in these sumptuous clothes. Since that Sunday evening, only a month ago, everything had fallen into place with astonishing speed. They would be married a few days before Christmas, waiving the overseas trip which was the usual honeymoon for wealthy Australians, in favour of remaining for the Christmas festivities at The Oaks. Niamh suspected this was an excuse on Hollis's part. He wouldn't want to leave his business ventures at such a crucial stage in order to take an extended voyage abroad.

She fingered the bridal gown of lace panels and striped silks which had been designed to follow the contours of her slim body, watching her reflection as Elinor pinched the sleeves to make them sit up – sleeves which were wide at the shoulders and tapered to fit snugly, fastened with dozens of tiny buttons at each wrist. Only the hem was a riot of pleats, ribbons and lace, the train secured with a massive bow at the ankles. In this age of extravagance where high fashion decreed that as many flounces, loops, buttons and bows as possible should be crowded onto one gown, Niamh had insisted on clean lines, a style as simple as the dressmaker would allow. Madame Céleste was a Parisian, chosen by Ellie. Relatively new to Melbourne, Céleste was anxious to capitalise on what she saw as a golden opportunity to show off her expertise. She wanted to create a showpiece whilst Niamh insisted on something restrained. Many a battle had followed until they had reached a compromise which wasn't entirely satisfactory to either.

Niamh plucked at the frill on her collar and fingered the set of perfectly matched pink pearls at her throat – Hollis's wedding gift.

Her second bridesmaid, Sukie, was with them as well, sitting on the bed, feet dangling as she nursed Niamh's bouquet, enjoying the smell of the flowers, content to hide herself behind the confection of white roses and carnations, twisted into a posy and nestling against a background of starched lace and asparagus ferns.

'Will you look at these poor flowers,' she started to say. 'They're soon going to wilt in this heat.'

'They will if you keep clutching them in your hot, sticky hands,' Elinor smiled. 'And if you keep sniffing them, they won't have any perfume left.'

'Oh, I'm sorry – I didn't think.' Not realising Ellie was teasing, Sukie left them lying in her lap. Lost and out of place in the midst of so much grandeur, she was beginning to wish Niamh had allowed her to come as an ordinary guest and not a bridesmaid, particularly as Elinor, also a bridesmaid, was so assured. Elinor's luxuriant fair hair was parted, drawn back and now dangled over her ears in obedient ringlets while Sukie's must be submitted to curling tongs to produce something similar. The hairstyle emphasised rather than concealed her disability and, in addition, the apricot lace of the dress was more suited to the Maitland girl who was as curvaceous as Sukie was slim. Elinor looked magnificent, having chosen the style to enhance her well-covered creamy shoulders and plump breasts.

Niamh stared at her image in the mirror, not quite believing that this elegant, well-groomed bride was herself. Of the three of them, Ellie was most at ease, looking forward to the party after the wedding and the night of dancing that lay ahead.

'Oh Niamh, look at you,' she teased. 'That's a face for a funeral, not a wedding. You look more like a tragedy queen than a bride. And do try to stop shaking. There's no need to be nervous. It's Holly you're going to marry, remember? Not some ghastly old lecher, smacking his lips and looking forward to legalised rape.' Niamh glanced at her, looking still more alarmed. 'You don't have to look so scared. Only sex, isn't it? Been around since Adam and Eve – the most natural thing in the world.'

Natural to Ellie, Niamh thought, recalling how she had shocked them by diving in the river with no clothes on when

95

she was scarcely into her teens. Ellie, whose mother was a semi-invalid who suffered from headaches, neglecting her only daughter and allowing her to run wild. Ellie, who was at ease with her developing body, happy to divest herself of bodice, camisole and bloomers for the joy of swimming nude.

'Cheer up, Niamh. Losing your virginity is no such momentous event. This time tomorrow you'll be wondering what all the fuss was about.'

Niamh responded with a twitch of her lips that wasn't really a smile. How could she explain her feelings to Ellie when she couldn't explain them to herself? Her misgivings were much more than pre-wedding nerves; she was wondering if she ought to marry at all while such doubts remained in her heart. She gave a half-smile, wondering if it was Ellie's abundant cheerfulness that made her feel so dispirited. Where was the joy and the radiance – the elation a bride was supposed to feel?

'It's time,' Ellie said, drawing the veil over Niamh's face, helping her negotiate the train as they made her way to the stairs.

In the hall, her parents were waiting for her, Janet looking smart and severe in dark green as she took in her surroundings, somewhat daunted by the grandeur of The Oaks which had been scrubbed, polished and decorated with enough flowers to fill two shops. No expense had been spared on the entrance to the mansion which was designed to impress; the walls panelled with dark wood imitating an earlier age, the bronze statues and crystal chandeliers a testimony to Lilias's taste for the Italianate and her husband's success.

Niamh paused on the landing before descending the second flight of stairs, looking down at her father who was smiling up at her. She smiled back, grateful that he was still Pa in spite of a brand-new suit of clothes. His eyes twinkled and his face lit up with pride as she descended the last few steps and took hold of his arm.

Outside she was surprised to be greeted by a round of applause from the Maitland servants, gathered around the front steps to catch a glimpse of the bride. The sun was blinding, the sky cloudless and the spicy smell of hot eucalypt promised that it might be sweltering by mid-afternoon. Several carriages were drawn up outside to carry the wedding party to church as well as the coach and matched pairs of white horses to carry the bride and her father. The horses stood, shaking their heads as if trying to dislodge the white ostrich plumes decorating their harness.

Ellie helped Niamh to negotiate the steps with her train while Sukie clung to her own posy as well as the bride's flowers.

'Give the bouquet to Niamh, Sukie.' Ellie was teasing again. 'You'll have your chance to catch it later if you're so anxious to be wed.'

Niamh bit her lip as she watched her bridesmaids climb into the next carriage along with her mother, wishing Ellie would be a little kinder to Sukie. Elinor was thoughtless rather than mean, but Sukie wasn't used to her particular brand of teasing and would be hurt. Both Niamh's friends were dear to her and she was at a loss to understand why they didn't like each other but the friction between them was clear.

Inside the carriage, Tully looked at his daughter more closely, dismayed to see her so pale.

'Sure you're all right, princess?' he whispered, receiving a tight smile as she nodded behind the veil. 'I wouldn't like to think you'd been rushed into this or coerced. It's not too late to have second thoughts. Better before the event than after – an' to hell with the fuss.' He patted her hand. 'I'd support you, whatever you decide. The scandal doesn't matter to me.'

'It's all right, Pa.' Niamh smiled, knowing he wouldn't have dared to say as much in her mother's hearing. 'It's only nerves.'

He squeezed her hand, not entirely reassured.

For Niamh, the brief church service passed as a blur. The church was filled with people she didn't know – Maitland friends and acquaintances. At the back of the church she recognised one or two regulars from the Silver Star. She looked to see if Judd were among them, relieved and perversely disappointed when he wasn't.

'Good on yer, Niamh!' a man shouted, seeing her looking in their direction.

'Ye look lovely, lass. Good enough to eat!'

She gave them a wide smile, acknowledging their good-natured shouts of encouragement which caused some of those

97

from the Maitland ranks to turn towards them and frown. In less than no time the brief service was over and she was signing the register with her husband, writing *Niamh McDiarmit* for the last time. Niamh Maitland now. How odd that sounded. Not like herself at all. Mrs Hollis Maitland, who now wore a wide band of gold as well as the diamond, weighing down the third finger of her left hand.

Back at The Oaks she felt better. Divested of the veil, a family heirloom, whisked away to be stored in camphor until it was required for the next Maitland bride, she began to relax. She wasn't hungry but she took a deep draught of champagne before joining Holly to commence the dancing, allowing him to steer her around the polished ballroom floor.

'I can hardly believe it,' he told her. 'Married at last. This is one of the happiest days of my life.' She looked up at him, wanting to tell him the same but somehow the words stuck in her throat and wouldn't be said. So she kept smiling, instead. After a few rounds of the floor, she caught sight of her Aunt Maggi, who smiled and beckoned them, anxious to exchange a few words.

'Congratulations, Holly,' she said, kissing him briefly. 'Now be a good man and chase us up a glass o' champagne. I want a quiet word with the bride.' Having dismissed him, she turned her attention to Niamh. 'Lord love us but you look wonderful. It's no time at all since you were a skinny waif from the city an' I was teachin' you how to ride.'

Remembering those old battles, Niamh smiled. 'How are the boys?'

'Don't ask,' Maggi winced. 'Growin' in wickedness almost by the hour. At least I haven't been called to the school this term to hear the catechism of their sins!' She held up a pair of fingers crossed in case she was speaking too soon. 'But I'm not here to talk of the boys but of you. Are you happy, me dear?' She answered the question herself without waiting for Niamh's reply. 'Well of course you are! Lil's boy and my brother's girl – like a fairytale comin' true.'

'You're looking wonderful too, Maggi.' Niamh had never been able to bring herself to call this vital, puckish creature 'Aunt' although Holly insisted on doing so, making her laugh. Tonight Maggi looked more youthful than ever, wearing a

98

dramatic, low-cut gown of feathers and flounces which exactly matched the bright red flame of her hair. Red hair still so vibrant, without even a hint of grey, Niamh was certain it had to be dyed. Maggi, who was also known as 'Mary Gold, the Southern Songbird', almost a legend of the music halls in her own time. Although she didn't concern herself with her appearance when she was home with her horses, when she came to the city she took care of her looks and would never appear in public less than perfectly groomed. Tonight she looked well. Vital and full of fun, she was drawing almost as many admiring glances as the bride, particularly as she was without escort, attending the party alone.

'Where's Uncle Cal?' Niamh missed him at once. 'Why isn't he here?'

'Yes, he'll be sorry to miss your day.' Maggi's expression clouded. 'But we can't both leave the property – not at this time of year. We've had no rain for weeks and now it looks as if we're heading into a summer of drought. The dams are as low as they've ever been and already he's been feeding the sheep by hand.'

'You won't lose them? You will be all right?'

'Yes, of course,' Maggi smiled. 'Don't you worry about us. Cal sends you his special love and good wishes and promises faithfully to see you when next he's in town. Better still, why don't you come up and see him? Pay a visit to us instead?' At that moment Hollis arrived with her champagne. 'Oh, thank you, Holly,' she took a deep draught. 'You're a life-saver. Even the Southern Songbird can't be expected to chirp on a dry throat.' Later she knew she would be persuaded to sing. 'You're looking peaked and overworked, my lad. I was just saying to Niamh – why not take a holiday? Come up and spend some time with us in the country. Get some fresh air in your lungs.'

'Oh, I don't know, Auntie Mags.' Holly used her old family nickname. 'Got a lot on at the moment. Can't afford to be away from the office. Have my finger in too many pies.'

'Well, don't waste all of your young years chasin' money.' Maggi was no longer smiling. 'S'only dirty old bits of paper when all's said and done. And later, when you look down the years, it'll be the love and the laughter ye remember, not how much money ye made.'

'Precious little to laugh about when you don't have any, Aunt.' Holly's smile was becoming fixed. 'With respect, in matters of business and money, you don't know what you're talking about.'

'Oh yes, I do.' Far from being offended, Maggi grinned. 'Time was when I thought as you do – that money was all you needed to get along in the world. Time was when I had a fortune in stolen cash stitched into my skirts.'

Niamh was intrigued. 'Maggi, you didn't? I never heard that story before! Whose money was it? And who stole it?'

'Never you mind.' Maggi's laugh was deep and rich. 'You should be dancing the night away with your groom, not rakin' over the past with old folks like me.'

'Oh Maggi, you'll never be old folks.' Niamh blew her aunt a kiss as Hollis led her back to the dance. At the same time Maggi herself took to the floor, accepting a dance from a young man who had been hovering, waiting for her to be alone before he screwed up the courage to ask.

Later Niamh danced with her father who took the opportunity to quiz her again. 'Better now?' He waited anxiously until she nodded. 'It really was only nerves?'

Ellie intruded, saving Niamh from lengthy explanations, catching them as they danced by. 'Niamh,' she said. 'Let me dance with your handsome father while you have a word with Sally. The old duck's almost beside herself because she hasn't seen you all night.'

'Oh no!' Full of remorse for neglecting the old lady, Niamh left them standing in the middle of the dance-floor and hurried towards the row of comfortable chairs lining the wall, where Janet and most of the older women were seated, watching the dance. Anxious to catch the attention of the bride, they leaned forward in turn, clutching at Niamh's hands as she passed. She nodded and smiled, receiving good wishes and compliments as she weaved her way towards Sally.

'That's odd,' Tully said, looking at Elinor from under raised brows. 'Old Sally seemed perfectly happy with her nose in a glass of champagne when I left her not five minutes ago.'

'Oh I know,' Ellie laughed, 'but I wanted to dance with you. Is it a well-kept secret then? I never knew Niamh had such a handsome father!'

100

Tully gave a snort of laughter, flattered although he knew she was only teasing, and whisked Ellie into a lively polka, holding her easily in his arms, energetic as a man her own age. Her body was pliant and fitted neatly into his arms as if she were meant to be there. He breathed her perfume appreciatively; it was something foreign and disturbing, nothing like Janet's simple cologne. A scent that reminded him of warm nights in tropical places, awakening urges which had lain dormant for so many years; a perfume not entirely suitable for a young girl. *She is half your age, you fool*, he scolded himself. *She's Hollis's cousin and your daughter's friend!* But forgot all of that as he looked into a pair of eyes which stared back at him, alive with interest and, he supposed, innocence, clear and blue as the sea in summer.

He felt a quick stab of desire – desire, rather than the moment's lust Gladys had stirred in him and which had been easy to ignore. He had a lovely girl in his arms and she liked him, so he gave himself up to the pleasure of dancing, laughing so loudly that the row of dowagers, including his wife, turned towards them and frowned. He didn't care; he would suffer the censure later. For now he was catching up on all those lost years of his youth. Dancing and laughing with Ellie, he was having the time of his life.

Chapter Eight

'You'll suffer for this tomorrow morning,' Gladys scolded, as she helped Sally upstairs and into bed. The old lady had come home flushed from the celebrations and rather the worse for drink. Seeing her, Gladys felt impatient and resentful, very much the poor relation, left behind to take care of the Silver Star while everyone else had been out enjoying themselves.

'Don't care!' Sal was truculent. ''S'only once in a lifetime. You should ha' seen her, Gladys. I was that proud of our girl – she made a lovely bride.'

'Most people do.' Gladys's resentment boiled over. 'It's a poor sort of girl who can't brush up to look good on her wedding day.'

'An' what's got into you?' Sal peered at her niece, who was stripping her of her finery none too gently, hurrying her into her nightclothes.

'I'm tired, that's what,' Gladys burst out. 'I've had to look after this place all day and keep that stupid Farrelly on the move. I feel like a Cinderella who didn't get to go to the ball.'

'Well, somebody had to stay at home. I didn't think you cared to see Niamh wed?'

'I'm sorry I missed the party, that's all. It wouldn't have hurt them to close the damned place for once, on their own daughter's wedding day.'

'Ooh, an' you missed a treat.' Sally didn't mind rubbing it in. 'I've never seen such silks an' satins. You wouldn't get a finer turn-out at a Governor's Ball. Should ha' seen Mr Tully – danced his legs off all night wi' one o' the Maitland cousins.'

'Oh, he was probably just being kind.' Gladys wasn't about

to show how much this news disturbed her. 'A poor thing, was she? One of the old maids?'

'Not she. Right taken with her, he was, an' she as plump an' pretty a morsel of female flesh as ever I seen.'

Gladys listened, feeling a burning sensation on the back of her neck, a sure sign that her temper was building. 'Don't be silly, Auntie.' As she was speaking she pulled the old lady's ribbons too tight at the throat. 'How could the girl be pretty, if she was fat?'

'Loose it – loose,' Sally gasped, red in the face, eyes bulging. Gladys gave a snort of impatience and tugged the ribbons free. Sally had to take some deep breaths before she could speak. 'You tryin' to strangle me, girl? If that's how you feel, I wish you'd gone to the party – not me.'

'An' how could I do that? Now tell me about the girl.'

'Who – Niamh?' Sally was being deliberately slow.

'No, you old fool! The girl who was dancing with Tully.'

'I'm not saying no more about it – not if it makes you so mad. He was just bein' social – dancin' an' all.'

'You told me they was dancing all night?'

Sally blinked at her. 'Did I?'

'You know you did!' Gladys snarled, making Sal shrink back against the pillows. 'How d'you know he was so taken with her? Did Janet say anything?'

'Not her. Too busy keepin' her end up wi' that Mrs Maitland an' her friends. Should've heard 'em. Proper bawdy lot wi' their talk an' them supposed to be ladies. Mrs Janet didn't like it – didn't hold with it at all.'

'Never mind about bloody Janet.' Gladys stood over Sally in an agony of impatience, twisting a pillow in her hands. 'I want to know about Tully an' that girl.'

'There's nothin' to know. They danced a lot an' they laughed, her smilin' up at him with her dimples.'

'Dimples?'

'I – I only meant to say she looked young,' Sal stammered, unnerved by her niece's suppressed fury. 'No more'n a child, to my way o' thinkin'. An' after the dance he took her into the supper room an' fetched her an ice.'

'Then what? Did you see them walk in the garden? Go outside?'

'How should I know?' Sal was beginning to whine. 'I wasn't watching them all night. I didn't see. What's it to you, anyway?'

'Did you see him make love to her? Kiss her?' Gladys whispered, leaning close and making her aunt's heart swoop and flutter ominously.

'Are you mad, girl? How should I know? But this much I *do* know.' By now Sally was upset enough to hurt her niece in return. 'If he's goin' to kick over the traces an' break his marriage vows, he'll be a damned sight better off with *her* than with a scrawny, dried-up widderwoman like you!'

This last taunt was too much for Gladys. Sally realised it when the last thing she saw was the pillow descending on her face, like a white cloud shutting out the light and stifling her efforts to scream. The scream lasted only a moment, cut off by the more urgent need to get air.

For a woman so old and sick, she struggled quite hard before her heart stopped beating and she was still. Gladys removed the pillow and looked at what she had done, the eyes glazed and the mouth open in its last gasp.

'Oh God!' she heard herself saying, a sob in her voice. 'Oh Aunt Sal, I didn't mean it. Please, oh please, don't be dead.' But she knew, before she felt for the old woman's pulse, there was no life left in her.

'Heart failure,' the doctor pronounced, standing away from the prostrate form of Sally on the bed. The tiny attic room seemed airless with the four of them crowded in there; Tully, Janet, Gladys and the doctor himself, looking pensive and stroking his chin.

'A sad thing to happen,' Tully said soberly, 'and on Niamh's wedding day, too. The excitement must have been too much for her.'

'Hmm.' The doctor's frown deepened. 'Anything amiss at the wedding feast? Was she breathless – distressed?'

'No, Doctor,' Janet assured him. 'Full of herself and better than we've seen her for many a day. Ate a good meal too and drank more than her share of champagne. Why, is there something wrong?'

'Don't know,' he said. 'Just a feeling I have. This isn't a typical death from heart failure, you see.'

'What do you mean – a typical death?' Gladys broke in, unusually shrill. 'Every case is different, surely?'

'Ye-es,' he said slowly. 'Certainly, there's no doubt of the cause – the old lady's system gave out. But see how the body seems strained and twisted in death? The hands are clutching the bedclothes in spasm.'

'Well, she was in pain, wasn't she? Threshin' about a bit at the end,' Gladys said quickly. 'I had to hold her down to keep her in bed.'

'Ah well, maybe that's it,' the doctor shrugged. 'I'll sign the death certificate, no doubt of that. I'm not quite happy about it, that's all.'

'No one's happy about it, Doctor,' Janet said sourly. 'A fine thing to happen on Niamh's wedding day.' She folded her arms and glared at the body as if the old woman had done it on purpose to spite her.

'Oh, and Niamh's not to be told. Not yet,' Tully put in. 'She loved Sally like a m— like a grandmother. I don't want her happiness spoiled, not today.'

'If not today, then tomorrow,' Janet insisted. 'The burial can't wait, not in this hot weather. And Niamh would never forgive us if we let it take place without her.'

The doctor covered Sally's face with the sheet and they crept from the room as if she were only sleeping and they were afraid of waking her.

'Well, Gladys,' Tully spoke up as soon as the doctor had left. 'Looks like you've got yourself a permanent job.'

'You should have waited and talked it over with me,' Janet carped at her husband as soon as Gladys was out of earshot, humming quietly as she clattered the pans in the kitchen. 'This is my business just as much as yours. I think we should employ a married couple this time – a couple with no nonsense about them, who would live in.'

'Live in where? You can't expect a man and his wife to occupy that poky attic.'

'I don't know – I haven't thought about it.'

'A married couple will cost twice the wages, as well. Be fair, Janet. We can't throw Gladys out on the streets because we

don't need her to look after Sal any more. She's reliable and a
good worker, too. Better the devil ye know . . .'

'A devil, indeed. You hit the nail right on the head. The way
she stares at everyone with those hard little eyes . . . I've never
liked her.' She paused to give him a sharp look. 'And I'm sure I
don't need to tell you why.'

'Ah come on, Janet, the woman knows where she stands –
I've made it plain often enough. I've asked her to stay an' I'm
not goin' back on my word. Look on the bright side. Now she
has more free time, she might find herself a fella an' leave of
her own accord.'

'I doubt that *very* much,' Janet said with a wry smile.

Hollis lay back and sighed in the darkness, his arm flung
across his face, shielding his eyes. It wasn't the sight of Niamh
he wanted to shut out but those other images, the ones he had
suppressed for so long, thinking them left behind in the past
and forgotten. Now they had come back to taunt him, rearing
up between himself and his bride.

'I'm sorry, Niamh. So very sorry.'

'Holly, don't be unhappy about it – I'm not,' she lied,
turning towards him and leaning up on one elbow so as to
look into his face, ready to provide the excuses he needed.
'It's so hot. There isn't a breath of air in the place and we're
both exhausted. Tomorrow I promise it'll be all right.
Tomorrow . . .'

'Tomorrow?' He took his arm away from his face to look at
her. 'Why should tomorrow be any different after a week of
failure? A week of not getting it right?'

'Holly, married love must be learned just like anything else.
It needs patience and practice. We're both novices – we can't
expect to cast off our inhibitions and turn ourselves into
experts at lovemaking overnight.' She wanted to bury her face
in the pillow and weep with disappointment but her instincts
told her to stay calm and reasonable, suppressing the frustration she really felt. It was an effort, also, not to make comparisons between her husband and Judd. She had to work hard to
banish the vision of that dark, brooding face which kept rising
in her mind's eye, tormenting her. He might have been in the
bed between them, saying: *See now, Niamh! See what you've*

106

done! Mocking her for her loyalty, laughing at Holly's ineptitude.

Also, unreasonably, she blamed Hollis for being so true to her. Most men would have taken the trouble to gain some experience. They wouldn't leave a bride roused and frustrated, her marriage unconsummated. This would never have happened if she'd been married to Judd.

She took a deep breath and closed her eyes, feeling like a traitor as she lay there remembering the warmth of his kisses, the sureness of his hands on her skin. If he were here now, he'd know exactly what to do; how to draw the best response from her. Unlike Hollis who had come to bed shaking with nerves and who wound his hands in her hair, kissing her roughly in the hope of breaking down his own inhibitions, forcing his body to do as he willed.

She had been a wife for a week and was still a virgin as yet. One or two attempts had come close but he had never succeeded in penetrating her fully. There had been no blood and, in spite of her tension, no pain, and the pattern of their lovemaking was becoming depressingly familiar. They would kiss and for a few moments she could believe that their troubles were over, until he lost the erection at the very moment her body was ready to join with his own.

The first time, on their wedding night, she put it down to mutual inexperience and nerves. But after a week of failure they were both so tense and apprehensive, she knew the situation could only get worse.

'Perhaps it's my fault.' She tried taking the blame on herself. 'I'm so stunned, so upset about Sally.' That at least was true. Strange to think that her first official appearance as Mrs Hollis Maitland should have been at Sally's funeral. Strange to arrive at the church in the Maitland carriage instead of walking through the streets with her parents and Gladys. The Maitland wealth and her new position set her apart from her family and it saddened her, knowing they must feel it as she did. The differences were brought home again when Hollis offered to pay for the old lady's tombstone. Tully was about to refuse until Janet stayed him with a hand on his arm.

'Thank you, Hollis. That's very generous of you,' she said, accepting before her husband could say otherwise. Was this then to be the pattern of their married life? Her mother forever thanking Hollis for favours, taking whatever she could get?

'But Sally was old, my love.' Hollis spoke, breaking in on her thoughts and bringing her back to the present. 'Old people die. It happens all the time.'

'Yes, but so suddenly after the wedding. Poor Sally – she was having so much fun.'

'Best way to go,' Hollis said, determined to be cheerful. 'Laugh, drink too much champagne and die in your sleep. I hope I can go as painlessly when my time comes.'

'But it wasn't so painless was it? And Sal didn't die in her sleep. She—'

'Forget it now, Niamh. Don't be morbid.' He was becoming bored with the subject of Sally. 'The old woman's at peace now wherever she is – and she wouldn't want you to grieve.'

'I know. But I do grieve and maybe that's one of the reasons why I'm unable to please you as I should.'

'Never think that, Niamh. You're beautiful.' He kissed her deeply, hoping to reassure her. 'And I do want things to be right between us. I love you so much.'

'Perhaps we should wait a while, Holly. Stop demanding so much of ourselves – try again when we're more relaxed.'

'No. We'll try again now.' He dragged her nightgown from her shoulders and pressed his lips to her throat, making her wince as he marked it with his teeth. She lay and suffered it without complaint as he lowered his mouth to her breasts and bit into their soft flesh as well. But his body felt hot and feverish against her own and she no longer desired him; for herself at least the moment was past. Sensing her withdrawal, he turned on her, whispering viciously.

'You have to help me! How can I make love to you when you lie there, unresponsive as a log? You don't care, do you? You wouldn't care if we never made love.'

'Of course I do. I married you because I love you and I want us to have children.'

'And the wealth and security marriage to a Maitland can provide?'

'That's not fair! I've never considered your father's wealth and you know it.'

He turned away, ashamed of the unkind words, born of his

own anger and frustration. Cautiously, Niamh laid a hand on his shoulder. 'Holly, could you talk to someone? A doctor maybe?'

'No!' He whipped round to glare at her. 'What can a doctor do for me?'

'Perhaps I should talk to Ellie.'

'Are you out of your mind? She'd be sniggering about us to her friends.' Niamh paused, biting her lip, thinking he might be right. 'I'd rather not take the risk. Honestly, Niamh, all we need is a little time. It'll be all right.' And he gave her a tight smile and a quick buss on the lips. 'Least said, soonest mended, eh? Let nature take its course.'

'But it's not natural, Holly. And it *isn't* all right.'

'Leave it now, love.' He was becoming drowsy, murmuring almost to himself. 'Lot on my mind, these days. Tired out. Under a strain. Tomorrow, you'll see. Tomorrow it'll be all right.' He rolled away from her, turning his back and moments later his even breathing told her he was asleep.

But Niamh lay wide awake, hearing the hours marked by the tinkling chimes of Lilias's various French clocks throughout the house. Sleep was impossible, frustration leaving her mind active and her nerves stretched to breaking point. Had they been in their own bed in their own home, she could have shaken him awake and ranted at him, making him face the fact that he needed medical help. Maybe she did, too. Maybe it *was* her fault. Maybe she wasn't made like other women and had some deformity which made it impossible for them to achieve proper congress.

But to cause a scene here at The Oaks – in her mother-in-law's home, and in the middle of the night . . . Unthinkable! In her mind's eye she could see Lilias now, lying awake across the hall, ears cocked for the slightest sound of marital discord.

During those long, lonely hours she had plenty of time to consider that in taking the safe option, doing the right thing and keeping her promise to marry Hollis, she had been forced to turn her back on Judd. Judd, for whom she might once have sacrificed everything. Until Sukie pointed out his shortcomings, warning her off. No doubt she'd had a lucky escape. That chapter of her life was closed and must remain so. Judd was nothing but an irresponsible adventurer, happy to flirt with her because she was safely promised to someone else; a dangerously attractive man who might have ruined her life. She had been right to stand by her principles and marry Hollis, the familiar suitor whose body she knew. Except that she didn't 'know' him in the Biblical sense, not yet.

Confused and unable to sleep, she tried to look down the long years ahead, the days filled with empty pleasures – the dinner parties and picnics, the morning and afternoon teas. How long would it be before she started to get pitying looks from other women because of her inability to conceive? Everyone would say it was her fault. Outside the four walls of this room, Hollis was never going to admit that the blame lay with him.

Sukie pressed her fingers to her temples, trying to ignore the headache because she was busy, working on her father's accounts. The office was small, and the sun had been shining on the tin roof all day, making the room airless and hot. This, in spite of the fact that she had the doors open front and back in the hope of creating a breeze. Summer made people lethargic, particularly about paying their bills, and there seemed to be more outstanding accounts than usual. She squinted at the list and sighed, occasionally wiping her brow with a handkerchief already limp from being screwed up in her hand. Absorbed in her work, she was unaware of Judd until she glanced up, seeing the vague figure of someone standing in the doorway.

'Who is it?' she said, peering at him until she could focus and recognise him, whereupon she sat back and smiled. 'So it's you, Judd. Why didn't you say something?'

'Because I needed your full attention. Sukie, I have to talk to you. It's important.'

'I'm listening,' she said, turning back to the books. 'Fire away. But don't be too long – I haven't got all day.'

'Sukie, put that away for a moment and listen to me.'

She sighed. 'Not now, Judd. These accounts are long overdue and if I don't send reminders when I think of them, they'll mount up.'

'So? Let them mount up, for once.'

'I can't.' She raised her head then to peer at him again. 'How shall I pay your wages if *we* don't get paid?'

110

'I don't care. I don't care about bills, wages or any other damned thing.' She raised her eyebrows, warning him not to swear. 'And to hell with your Sunday-School morals as well. I want you to marry me, '

'No!' she answered crisply and without hesitation.

He stared at her as if he couldn't believe his own ears. 'You're saying no, just like that? That's not very flattering, is it? You could have thought about it for a moment before turning me down.'

'And your proposal isn't very flattering to *me*,' she said, mildly and without malice, 'when we all know it was Niamh you loved. Niamh you wanted to wed.'

'But *you* love *me*.'

'What if I do? I still have my pride, Judd. I don't care to be such an obvious second choice.'

'You're not. You wouldn't be.'

She pushed the papers away and massaged the bridge of her nose with her fingers, willing the headache to go away.

'Don't lie to me, Judd. I deserve better than that. You should learn not to make your feelings so plain. I see more than most people think, if not with my eyes. I sensed your eagerness – how you couldn't wait to torture yourself and hear all about the wedding. And I thought you'd weep when I told you about her dress.'

'Me? In tears over a girl's wedding dress?'

'Yes, you. Do most men want to know what flowers a bride carried? How she looked on her day? No.' Sukie paused, taking a deep breath. 'But you wanted all of it, didn't you? Everything she said and did. And I? I'm ashamed to say I took pleasure in telling you – turning the knife in each little wound. How tender the bridegroom – how he kissed the tips of her fingers and how she gazed up at him through her veil, her face radiant with love for him, eyes brimming with tears. And you? Didn't you wonder how I could see so much with these poor eyes? To be truthful, I didn't see the half of it, Judd. Only how you suffered when I told you what you most dreaded to hear. Not very noble of me, was it?'

'Oh, Sukie. How could I have been so—'

'Blind?' She gave a small, bitter laugh. 'I love Niamh but I could have hated her then, as if it were all her fault. I hated her for having so much when I had so little. For winning the heart of the man I wanted as well as Holly's.'

'Oh, Sukie.'

'So now you know all about it. Now you can stop feeling sorry for me and start hating instead. Goodness knows I deserve it. A jealous, embittered woman – crippled in mind as well as in body. Oh, and there's more.'

'Sukie, don't. I don't need to hear it. The offer still stands.'

'Then you're a fool.' She almost laughed, shaking her head. 'And I won't make you a bigger one by accepting you. Thank you, Judd, but no thanks. I have problems enough without hitching myself to a man who loves somebody else.'

'And if I told you it was a moment of madness – a crazy infatuation that's already over?'

'Then I'd say you were lying – to yourself as much as to me.'

'It's finished, I tell you. Over and done.'

'More unlikely than ever.'

'Marry me, Sukie, and I'll make you a good husband. I'll never give you cause to reproach me and we'll never speak of Niamh again.'

'Of course we will. She's my friend and I'll see her. In any case, I'm not marrying you on the rebound.'

'What I feel for you is quite different,' he whispered, taking her little workworn hand in his own. He turned it over and kissed the palm until she shivered with delight. 'Marry me, Sukie. Marry me and you won't regret it, I promise. I'll devote the rest of my life to making you happy.'

Contrary to the expectations of his workforce, Albert Smith didn't enthuse about his daughter's forthcoming marriage. He wriggled in his rickety captain's chair which had suddenly become as uncomfortable as Judd's news.

'Well,' he said after a long sigh. 'So that's the way the wind blows. I wish you'd said something to me first. Susannah may be of age,' he was being unusually formal, making Judd realise with a jolt of surprise that he had never known Sukie's full name, 'but she won't marry if I withhold my consent.'

'Why should you do that?' Judd couldn't understand the old man's reticence. 'Don't you want her to be wed?'

'It's not something I've ever thought about,' Albert said, frowning. 'Weren't you sweet on the McDiarmit girl?'

'Mrs Maitland now.'

'Exactly.' Albert filled his clay pipe and began to smoke furiously – a sign of his discomfiture. It was unusual for him to smoke before the close of a business day. 'And what about Sukie, then? What does she say?'

'She refused me at first – said she didn't care to be second choice.'

'Sensible girl.'

'I'm happy to say I persuaded her otherwise.'

Albert sat back and puffed at his pipe, filling the small area of his office with the foul-smelling fumes while he absorbed the news.

'Look here, lad,' he said at last. 'I don't want you to take this the wrong way, but you don't need to marry my lass to get your foot in the door. I was going to offer you a partnership, anyway.'

'I'm marrying Sukie for herself, not to "get my foot in the door" as you put it. That's not very flattering to either of us, is it? I thought you loved her.'

'So I do. And I'll break the nose of anyone who says otherwise. What are you getting at?'

Judd spread his hands. 'You love her. So why is it so amazing that I love her, too?'

Albert shrugged. 'Point taken. Where will you live?'

'Ah, Sukie was going to speak to you about that. If you're agreeable, we'll start married life with you. That way you're not losing a housekeeper while I gain a wife.'

'Got it all worked out, haven't you?'

'Not really. I'm ready to marry and Sukie is, too. We shall deal well together.'

'Hmm. I can't say I don't have my doubts, but if it's what our Sukie wants, I must give you my blessing and consent.'

'Thank you, sir!'

'Hold on a minute, there's more. If the business is to succeed in the long term, to keep you an' Sukie and any family you might have, the foundry will need to expand. Been thinkin' of it meself for some time. And we'll need to put on a decent

113

show for the International Exhibition at the end of the year. New patterns, new lines. Can't let those fellows from Sydney have it all their own way, showin' us up on our own turf. Marry my Sukie if you must, but if you want a partnership in the business, you'll have to put up some capital of your own. That's what I had in mind.'

'You need me to put up some funds?'

'Why not? You've been with me twelve months and more, and live cheaply enough at our Daisy's. You must have some money put by.'

Judd thought of Daisy and the money he had 'loaned' her towards Carl's defence and which she was unlikely to return. Matthew had refused point blank to contribute to his son's legal fees, saying the boy deserved all that was coming to him and it was no use throwing good money after bad. Unfortunately for Judd, he was right. The expensive lawyers Daisy hired had been able to get him a reduced sentence but Carl was to serve on the road gangs for two years – a sentence which would have been more severe if he'd been caught with a gun. His companions were all bearing arms.

So Judd looked at Albert and found it impossible to tell him where all his money had gone.

'I'm sorry, sir. I must have been living too well. I don't have much put by for the future as yet.'

'A pity. Because if you can't, I'll need to look for a partner elsewhere.' Albert narrowed his eyes at his prospective son-in-law as a new thought came to mind. 'Either way, your position as foreman is secure, but I can't offer a partnership just because you're marrying Sukie. And if that's what you were hoping, then . . .'

'Nothing was further from my mind.' It was Judd's turn to be exasperated. 'You're the one who raised the subject of partnership, Albert – not me.'

'All right, lad. No need to fly off the handle.' Albert laughed, looking sheepish. 'It's just a bit sudden, that's all. My little lame duck is precious to me – she's all I have. I have to be convinced you won't hurt her.'

'Can anyone be sure of a passage through life without grief or without getting hurt?' Judd spread his hands in query. 'We all have to take our marriage partners on trust. But you can depend on it, sir. I'll give your daughter no cause to shed any tears over me.'

'Beware of making too many promises, son. You'll find chickens can have a nasty habit of coming home to roost.'

'About that partnership, sir.' Already Judd's mind was at work on the problem. 'There might yet be a way. What figure do you have in mind?'

'Ah no, no. I'll not have you borrowing money, Judd. I've always lived free and clear. I want no assessors or bailiffs leaping around, laying claim to my home or my business.'

'No, indeed. I was thinking of an inheritance which could be due to me. I've been a little tardy in following it up.' Judd muttered, half to himself, 'If I can find out what became of my Uncle Jem . . .'

'An inheritance? But that's splendid news!' Albert's expression cleared. 'Is it mebbe a thousand pounds?'

'You need that much?' Judd stared at him.

'Let's say five hundred for starters. And another five hundred from the profits, later on.'

Judd shook hands on the deal. But even as he did so, his heart sank. He had shaken hands on a promise he wasn't at all sure he could keep. He had no way of knowing if he had an inheritance to claim, let alone how much it might be.

Chapter Nine

Over the evening meal, Judd broke the news of his forthcoming marriage to the Bradleys. Unable to ignore the protests of his feet, Matthew was back home, albeit reluctantly, leaving his business in the care of his sons. Daisy, having visited Carl once or twice in prison, had decided things weren't so bad after all and cheered up enough to start cooking again. She greeted Judd's news with small cries of delight, practically smothering him with kisses until Matthew grew impatient and growled.

'Lay off him, woman, will yer. He'll get kisses enough when he's wed.'

'Oh, but I do so love a wedding.' Daisy wiped tears of sentiment from her cheeks with a corner of her apron. 'Who'd have thought it? Judd gettin' married to our Sukie. Poor little Sukie we never thought would—'

'Woman!' Cabbage Tree frowned, warning her not to let her tongue run away with her.

'I'll bet Albert's pleased,' she concluded with another sniffle.

'Not entirely,' Judd confided. 'He's made it quite plain that he doesn't expect a penniless son-in-law.'

'Oh?' Daisy's smile became a little tremulous as she remembered the money she had borrowed for Carl's defence and had not yet returned.

'So I have more than just sentimental reasons to find out what happened to my Uncle Jem Burden now.'

'What? What name did you say?' Matthew stared at him.

'Jem Burden. He was a seaman—'

'But I used to know a Jem Burden back in the old days. Why

116

didn't you ask me about this before?'

'But I did!'

'No, you didn't. You talked a bit about your uncle and told us he was a seaman. But you never said his name was Burden, same as your own.'

Judd rolled his eyes heavenwards, trying not to lose patience with the old man for his earlier inattention. 'Well, spit it out, Cabbage Tree. What do you know?'

'Not much at all.' Matthew leaned forward on his elbows, considering. 'But I'll tell you who does – Tully McDiarmit at the Silver Star. Thick as thieves they was in the old days, three of 'em – your Uncle Jem and some other bloke, Hobley from Cornwall. He went to sea with them, too. Buggered if I can remember the name of the ship . . .'

'But I told you that as well.' Judd couldn't hide his exasperation. 'It was the *Sally Lee*.'

'That's it – the *Sally Lee*. Well, I'll be—' Matthew thought for a moment. 'But you won't get much change out o' Tully. Don't like to talk o' them days. Ship was wrecked an' he was the only survivor – the rest of them were eaten by sharks. Him an' his dog, they was the only ones who came back to tell the tale. Someone left him holdin' a bag o' gold nuggets that gave him enough to buy into the Silver Star.'

'You don't say,' Judd whispered, suddenly thoughtful, reminded of Niamh's protective attitude towards her father and the gleam of anxiety in Tully's eyes when they were first introduced. How neatly the pieces of the puzzle were falling into place. Perhaps this was the reason for the Irishman's reticence and unfriendly attitude which he'd put down to a father's natural suspicion of a man who had no business to be admiring his daughter. 'Well, thank you, Cabbage Tree. You've helped me a lot more than you know.'

The bullocky shrugged, pleased with himself. 'Dunno why you never asked me about it before.'

Elinor plucked a small sugared plum from the centre of the display on the supper table and sucked on it, relishing the crisp sugar on the outside and the sticky sweetness at the centre of the fruit. If she didn't control her greed, it was likely to carry her into stout middle age, but that day was far in the future as

117

yet. With the assistance of whalebone and laces, she presented a perfect hourglass figure, her bosom surging towards the frothy neckline of her gown.

She snatched another plum when no one was looking and spread her fan to conceal her chewing as she smiled with her eyes, casting among the well-known faces at Aunt Lil's supper party, looking for someone – anyone – who might be of interest. Somebody new. No. Only the same boring assortment of lawyers, influential politicians and merchant bankers who attended Aunt Lil's parties accompanied by well-groomed wives and their oh-so-suitable sons. No challenge at all. No one to bring a sparkle to her eyes, making her heart step up its beat – not as Niamh's father had done . . . A pleasant surprise and an experience Elinor would have liked to repeat although she couldn't see how. She wondered how she could run into him 'accidentally' without paying a visit to the Silver Star; something of which she knew her mother wouldn't approve.

Celia Maitland was a professional invalid, a woman of delicate constitution who spent her days draped on a couch, leaving her daughter to do as she pleased. Prizing her freedom, Elinor kept it by allowing herself to be courted by some of the 'suitable' young men and taking care not to infringe the boundaries of good taste. Celia might be neglectful but even she would be roused from her apathy if her daughter were to encourage a man like Tully McDiarmit, who wasn't only unsuitable but married, as well.

Yet the Irishman continued to fascinate Ellie, smiling into her eyes as he danced through her thoughts. The attraction had been mutual. She had seen the admiration in his eyes and there had been nothing avuncular in the way he held her as they danced. She remembered the firmness of his hand at her waist, the whimsical sadness of his smile and the wings of silver at his temples which distinguished the sandy redness of his hair. He was a musician, too; another point in his favour. He played tinkling American tunes on the Maitlands' grand piano, shocking the older women and setting the younger ones' feet a'tapping. Oh yes, she remembered far too much about Tully McDiarmit, and the only way to exorcise those feelings was to see him again – if only to prove he wasn't special at all but just an ordinary man.

118

Once more she looked round the room. The mixture as before – the usual Christmas party at The Oaks. A pile of expensive coloured bon bons decorated the table and wreaths of myrtle surrounded the candles instead of traditional holly. And there was Aunt Lilias, showing off as usual, boasting of her newly refurbished assembly rooms, fishing for compliments and daring her guests to offer less than whole-hearted praise.

She turned from Lilias to look at Hollis and Niamh, standing in line to greet their guests. They were thanking someone for a belated wedding present, and Holly put his arm across Niamh's shoulders and gave her a squeeze, as he dropped a kiss on her head. They really are lovebirds, she thought, with a momentary pang of envy. They made a handsome couple all right, especially as Niamh had given in to the social pressures and allowed herself to be better dressed. The young bride was transformed in a gown of cherry-red silk, her hair looped into an elegant chignon with a decoration of matching silk flowers on the crown of her head. It was a pity Hollis was letting the side down, looking pale and strained. Ellie reminded herself to have a quiet word with Niamh. A honeymoon was all very well, but Hollis was looking shattered and worn out.

She had no chance to catch Niamh alone until after supper, when Hollis left her to perform a duty dance with one of his mother's friends.

'Be careful, Niamh.' Ellie was speaking behind her fan so that no one else should overhear. 'Go on like this and you'll have a baby to mark every year. You can't expect to keep jumping on Hollis's bones and have nothing come of it.'

Niamh blushed scarlet, not knowing what to say. She was mortified that Ellie should speak so frankly, particularly as the opposite was the truth.

'Oh Ellie, be quiet. Sometimes I wish you were a little less forthright.'

'Nothing to be ashamed of. You're a respectable married woman with a licence to prove it – which is more than some people can say around here.'

Niamh stared at Elinor, unsure whether to confide in her or not and deciding it was time to share her problems with her friend. She was badly in need of a sympathetic ear. 'Ellie, can I tell you a secret? But first you must promise not to breathe a word of it to anyone else.'

Elinor's eyes twinkled. 'A secret? How intriguing!'

'But not now. I feel as if everyone's looking at us.'

'Oh Niamh, I'm sure they're not.'

'Meet me outside on the terrace in half an hour.'

'Let's go now while Hollis is stuck with old Mrs K. She loves dancing and she'll keep him on his feet for ages. And when she's had enough, she'll expect him to find her a seat and bring her an ice. If anyone asks after us, we'll say we felt faint and needed a breath of fresh air.'

The terrace wasn't a good choice; it was impossible to be private. Some of the older men had gathered there to smoke in the hope of finding it cooler than inside. Immediately, Niamh was beset with heavy-handed compliments from elderly gentleman trying to be gallant.

'Where's that young husband of yours? Neglecting his bride already? Should know better than to leave such a tender morsel to us.'

'Don't be silly, Uncle Henry.' Skilfully Elinor steered Niamh through their ranks. 'Aunt Maud's looking for you and she's in a bad mood.'

'Oh Christ!' The old man threw his cigar on the ground and stamped on it, casting anxious glances in the direction of the assembly room, anticipating a roar of disapproval from his spouse.

'Ellie, how could you?' Niamh giggled. 'He was enjoying that cigar.'

'And he'll be enjoying a permanent sleep underground if he won't give them up,' Ellie said, ever-practical. 'The conservatory then. It's too hot and humid for most people – we shan't be disturbed in there.'

She was right. Apart from a pair of tropical love-birds softly cooing to each other in a cage, an assortment of palms and ferns around a fountain designed to look like a waterfall, the water trickling over a pile of moss-covered stones, the conservatory was deserted. But now she had Elinor's full attention, Niamh was suddenly shy.

'What's all this, then?' Ellie prompted her. 'Don't tell me the worst has happened and you're pregnant already?'

120

She was astonished when Niamh raised her hands to her face and burst into tears. She could hardly speak through her sobs.

'That's just it. I'll never be having a baby, never! And everyone's going to say that it's my fault!'

'Oh Niamh, that's nonsense. Give yourself time. You've only been married a matter of weeks. It's too early to know if you can't bear a child.'

'But Ellie, that's what I'm trying to tell you. How am I going to have a child if he can't – if we don't— ?'

'Oh, no.' Elinor sank down on a marble seat, nowhere near as shocked as Niamh expected her to be. 'The idiot. And I did tell him. I told him to go to Lucky's Place and get some experience first.'

'You told Hollis to go to a—'

'Why not? Don't look so horrified, Niamh. Men use those places all the time. My father's been going to Lucky's for years and Mother turns Nelson's eye. Your father probably goes there too, for all I know.'

'I'm sure he doesn't.'

'Are you now?' Ellie looked pensive, tapping her teeth with her fan. 'But that doesn't solve your little problem, does it? What are you saying, then – that in all this time, ever since you've been married, Holly hasn't . . . ?'

Niamh nodded miserably, ready to burst into tears again. Ellie gave a rich chuckle which developed into a full-throated laugh, making Niamh glare at her.

'Holly *said* this would happen! He told me you'd laugh!'

'Oh God, I'm not laughing at you, love. But is it any wonder, really? Who'd think of making love in this awful museum of a house? Aunt Lil, awake in the next room, listening for every creak of the bed . . . The answer's quite simple, my girl. Tell Holly you want a home of your own. Why not ask Uncle Harley about the house in Brighton?'

'You think that's it – that Holly is too inhibited to make love in his mother's house? That if we can only get some privacy, we'll be all right?'

'Of course.' Ellie smiled. She liked solving problems and was confident she had given the right advice.

'Oh, thank you Ellie, thank you.' Niamh was almost

121

gabbling with relief. 'Such a load off my mind – I can't thank you enough. Holly said I wasn't to tell anyone and least of all you, but I'm so very glad that I did.'

'Think nothing of it, sweetie,' Elinor grinned, plucking some grapes from the vine and eating them quickly, talking with her mouth full. 'Consult the oracle any time.'

Pink from one of the hot flushes that bedevilled her lately, Lilias stared at her son and daughter-in-law. 'But why must you move so far away from the city? That house was to be a holiday home – a family retreat – or else rented as an investment. I had no idea you were thinking of occupying it yourselves. And I'm deeply wounded that you want to leave us so soon, when I've taken so much trouble to make you comfortable here.'

Harley Maitland raised his eyes heavenwards and gently coughed into his fist. 'Really, Hollis. You might have waited till after dinner to break this news to your mother. You must have realised it would upset her.'

'Upset?' Lilias fanned herself with a scented handkerchief. 'That would be putting it mildly. I'm devastated by their ingratitude.' She rounded on Niamh, making her start. 'It's the bedroom, isn't it? I should have known you wouldn't appreciate chestnut and peach.'

Niamh blinked. Having so much else to worry about, she had scarcely registered the colour scheme of their room. 'No, not at all. The room is perfect – Mm – Mother Maitland.' She stumbled over the words, attemping to break the life-long habit of calling her 'Aunt Lil'.

'And for goodness sake stop calling me Mother Maitland! It sounds like Old Mother Hubbard and makes me feel about a hundred. Just call me Aunt Lil as you always do.'

'All right, Aunt Lil.' Feeling reprimanded and wretched, Niamh stared at her hands in her lap.

'Come on, Holly, is this Niamh's idea or yours?' Lilias tapped the table with an immaculate fingernail. 'I smell a conspiracy here and I mean to get to the bottom of it.'

'More coffee first,' Harley said, holding out his cup so that his wife had to stop glaring at Niamh to serve him. Sighing, she did so, handling the elegant coffee service with practised

122

grace. Harley cleared his throat before going on. 'In principle, Hollis, I agree. It's reasonable that you and Niamh should want to start married life in a home of your own—'

'Harley!' Lilias broke in again.

'Let me finish, Lil.' He raised his hand to silence her, still watching his son. 'It's just the timing that's out of step. I do mean to finish the house but my finances may be stretched if I have to put up the whole of the money right now.'

'You see?' Hollis sounded aggrieved. 'You wouldn't *be* stretched if only you'd only take advantage of some of these land deals. There's a whole new parcel of land about to be put on offer at Box Hill, but if we want a stake in it, we'll have to move fast – before it gets snapped up by somebody else.'

'Later, Holly. Bad manners to talk business at the dinner-table in front of the ladies. In any case, there's no point in rehashing it. You already know how I feel. I'll put up the money in stages and finish the house in Brighton. But for dubious speculation in land you can count me out.'

Hollis sighed irritably. 'It's not dubious speculation but a golden opportunity, Father. In six months' time you could build not one house in Brighton but two – one for us and one to sell at a profit.' He brightened, struck by another idea. 'If you don't want the firm's name involved, I could do it alone. You're the trustee of Granpa Maitland's inheritance. I could have it now when I need it, instead of waiting until I'm thirty.'

'Out of the question, Holly. Your grandfather was no fool when he took that precaution in making his will. He didn't want you to have access to that money until you have the wisdom and business acumen of a man of mature years.'

Holly made an impatient sound in his throat. 'I have business acumen now – why must I wait another eight years?' He turned to his wife. 'How about your father, Niamh? The Irish are known to be gamblers. He'll have an eye for a bargain, eh?'

'Oh, I'm not sure.' Niamh chewed her lips, knowing Tully had little cash to spare. He managed to keep a good face on it but money was always tight at the Silver Star.

It was Harley who came to her rescue. 'Forget about land, Holly, and forget Granpa's legacy until nearer the time.' He held up his hand for silence as Holly drew breath to argue. 'Remember, it's not my decision, it's Granpa's. The lawyers

123

won't let you touch a penny of it before time. Wait and see. Stand on the sidelines this time. And if the tide of expansion doesn't turn, there'll be just as many opportunities later on.'

'Old man's talk.' Holly hunched himself and put on a quavering voice. 'Wait an' see! Wait an' see . . .'

'Enough! I won't be mocked at my own dinner-table.'

'Sorry, Pa.' Holly had the grace to look shamefaced.

'So you should be. The house in Brighton is feasible – we own the land and the foundations are already laid. We can build in stages and pay as we go.'

'But Pa!'

'And that's my last word on it.'

'I can't believe this, Harley.' Lilias sniffed delicately, wiping the corners of her eyes with a small lace handkerchief. 'You're encouraging them to leave. I'd rather you made the investments as Hollis wants you to, in land and in shares—'

'Don't be ridiculous, Lil,' Harley snapped. 'You have no idea what you're talking about.'

'Anyone would think you wanted them to go.'

'Don't be silly, woman!' They all stared; it was unusual for Harley to speak so sharply to his wife. He lowered his voice when he saw he had their attention. 'But nor do I want them crouched here, waiting for us to die. Waiting for us to leave them a home of their own.'

'Harley! That's a horrible thing to say.'

'Not if it's true. Two generations rarely live in harmony for long and this place runs like clockwork already; it doesn't require two mistresses. How is Niamh to spend her time, then? Playing second fiddle to you?'

'No. She can do what she's supposed to do. Hurry up and give us some grandchildren while I look after the house.'

'She isn't a brood mare,' Harley laughed. 'And she's far too intelligent to sit around with nothing to do.'

'She doesn't have to. She can come with me to The Briarley Children's Hospital and join the Committee of Friends.'

'Oh, thank you, Aunt Lil, I'd love to!' Niamh showed signs of animation for the first time. 'I'm sure I could make myself useful there.'

'Matron doesn't need us to be useful, Niamh. Just to come up with ideas to raise funds.' Lilias's smooth white brow creased in a frown. Having made the offer on impulse, she was regretting it already.

'The hospital's all very well but the girl still needs to be mistress of her own home.' Harley returned to the previous topic of conversation. 'She'll want to arrange her own dinner parties – entertain her own friends.'

'Well, I'm sure *I'm* not stopping her.' Lilias's frown deepened and she wriggled her shoulders impatiently, beginning to sulk.

Harley laughed. 'Yes, you are. Look at you now – prickly as a cactus at the very thought. A young housewife has to learn from experience and her own mistakes. The last thing she needs is you hanging your nose over everything, criticising every move she makes.'

'I wouldn't! You make me sound like an ogre, Harley.'

'No, you're not,' he said mildly. 'Just a mother-in-law.'

But he was twinkling as he said it and fortunately Lilias could see the humour of the remark. The exchange broke up in laughter. But Niamh remained less than satisfied. Although they were to have a home of their own, the building would take some time and the problems with Hollis were getting worse. Outwardly, they presented a picture of perfect accord, a married couple in post-honeymoon bliss but the reality was that they lived like her parents – as brother and sister, rather than husband and wife.

In response to Niamh's pleading, Lilias agreed to take her to The Briarley Hospital the very next day. Set in manicured grounds, the building was large, imposing and even frightening, Niamh thought, to sick children, particularly those who lived in cramped conditions at home. They would be daunted by rooms with high ceilings which echoed with the booming voices of doctors, the clink of surgical instruments against porcelain and the muffled whimpers of other children in pain.

Matron greeted Lilias politely but with a mild reproach.

'Delighted to see you, Mrs Maitland – delighted – so grateful for your interest and support. But it's a little difficult on a Friday and in the midst of the specialists' visits and ward rounds ... Sir Robert Ainslie is waiting for me to join him right now.'

'Then don't let us detain you, Matron,' Lilias said easily. 'There's only myself and my daughter-in-law today. She's going to join us on the Ladies' Committee.' The Matron and Niamh exchanged nods, sizing each other up as they acknowledged the introduction. 'We'll show ourselves around.'

'Oh, that won't do at all.' Matron looked faintly shocked at the suggestion. 'My deputy, Sister Kearney, will act as your escort.' She picked up a small silver hand-bell and rang it briskly, causing a door to open at once like a jack-in-a-box to admit a woman in a crackling, highly-starched uniform, her grey hair concealed beneath a triangular nurse's cap.

Niamh disliked her on sight. Sister Kearney had a pinched expression and small grey eyes, the colour of wintry skies. There appeared to be nothing motherly about her at all and Niamh suppressed a shudder at the thought of leaving a sick child in her care. Lilias greeted the nurse with a smile, having no such misgivings.

'Mrs Maitland.' Surprisingly, the woman's voice was low and quite pleasing. 'I'm afraid we can't give you more than a quick glance at the facilities and a walk round the wards today.'

'Matron already said.' Lilias cut short the woman's explanation. 'Sir Robert is here and we shouldn't have come on such a busy day.'

'If only you'd come on a Tuesday as you always do . . .' Assuming they would keep up with her, Sister Kearney set off ahead of them at a brisk trot, forcing the Maitland ladies to increase their pace to keep up with her. They passed through a gloomy hall which she described as Out Patients where a row of anxious, wide-eyed mothers waited doing their best to comfort squalling babies or whimpering, feverish children. They looked as if they had been waiting for some time.

Lilias and Niamh were allowed to stand in the doorway and look in on the rooms where surgical procedures usually took place, dark and empty today. Having always taken an interest in medical matters, Niamh would have liked to take a closer look but Sister Kearney hurried them on.

But it was when they reached the main ward that the plight of sick children really tugged at her heartstrings. They were lying in neat rows, tucked in their beds, turning frightened eyes towards the doors and retreating beneath the covers, fearing the approach of trolleys laiden with – to their way of thinking at least – instruments of unspeakable torture. One little boy, aged about four, was sitting high on his pillow, hugging his knees as he rocked himself, shaken by uncontrollable sobs. Tears poured unchecked down his cheeks and it was obvious he had been crying for some time. Sister Kearney stood at the foot of his bed and glared at him.

'Stop that, Paulie – stop it at once. You're not in pain today and there's nothing wrong with you now.'

'Except that he's frightened.' Niamh defended the little boy, perching on the side of his bed to comfort him.

'Don't want any more nurse. I want my mummy!' He roared, increasing the volume of his cries so that the children nearest started crying as well.

'There now! See what you've done?' Sister Kearney turned the force of her glare on Niamh. 'It'll take hours to pacify them now!'

'Do they have infection that can be passed on to somebody else?' Niamh asked softly.

'A bit late, isn't it, to ask about that?' Sister Kearney watched the little boy take hold of Niamh's hand, clinging to it as if he would never let go. 'As it happens, no. These are dental and surgical cases, well on their way to recovery.'

'Then why don't you let their mothers come in and sit with them?' Niamh said.

'And upset hospital routines?' A dark turkey red was spreading to Sister Kearney's face from her throat, contrasting dramatically with the starched white of her uniform. 'Visitors may come in once a week, on Sunday afternoons.'

'But why? Aren't the children wretched enough as it is? They must feel as if they're in prison, being punished for something they haven't done.'

'Niamh!' Lilias thought it was time to intervene. 'This is your first visit here and I don't think you ought to—'

'Make waves?' Niamh completed the sentence for her. 'Changes are never made without treading on somebody's corns, Aunt Lil. Why shouldn't the mothers come in? Each one could see to the needs of her own child.'

'I take it you yourself have some qualifications, Mrs Maitland?' Sister Kearney's tone was cool.

'Why, no. No, I—'

'Perhaps you are a mother yourself?'

'Not yet. I've only been married a short while.'

'Then don't you think you should wait until you have some experience before trying to effect such radical changes here? You have no idea how devious a child can be in seeking attention. Sick children cannot be indulged or we shall end up with total lack of organisation here.'

'Oh?' Niamh didn't like Sister Kearney and was warming to the task of getting the better of her. 'Then who is the hospital for? The children who come here because they're sick, or the nurses and doctors who run the place?'

'Niamh!' This came from Lilias as a shocked gasp.

'For your information, Mrs Maitland,' Sister Kearney was clasping her hands in order to hold her temper in check, 'The Briarley is a charity hospital. We nurses receive the minimum in the way of a salary—'

'How's that?' Niamh seized her opportunity. 'Because you can't obtain a position elsewhere which would pay you more?'

Sister Kearney ignored the jibe but her eyes widened, showing it had struck home. 'Our doctors and surgeons are good enough to donate their services and their time—'

'Oh? In return for what?'

'You're not implying, I hope, that these children could be the subject of medical experimentation?'

'You said it, Sister, not I.' All the same, Niamh saw it was time to tread warily. 'I meant only to suggest that you could use a lot more heart and a little less science.'

'Niamh!' Lilias hissed again, plucking at her daughter-in-law's sleeve and sneakily pinching her arm. 'We must leave. I have an appointment at four and I don't want to be late.'

As a matter of course Sister Kearney offered them tea which Lilias refused, whereupon the woman escorted them to the front door, making sure the carriage was rolling before she went back inside. Lilias said nothing, leaving Niamh to her thoughts until they turned from the main thoroughfare and into the meandering drive leading up to The Oaks.

'We're going home.' Niamh stated the obvious. 'I thought you said you had an appointment, Aunt Lil?'

'I lied.' Lilias turned on her. 'Really, Niamh. If ever I wished

128

for the ground to open and swallow me, it was today. Medical experiments! How could you!'

'I didn't say it – she did.'

'Only because of your insinuations. Never have I been so embarrassed, so mortified in my life. I don't know when I can face going back there again. *You* certainly can't.'

'Oh yes, I can. I shall present myself on the doorstep on Monday morning. And I'll have the mothers allowed to sit with their children in less than a week.'

'Oh, will you, indeed?'

'Yes, Aunt. Or my name isn't Niamh Maitland.'

Chapter Ten

It was mid-February and Judd had been married a month before he could prepare himself sufficiently for the awkward task of making enquiries about his uncle at the Silver Star. It was more than two months since he last set foot in the place and, at first glance, little had changed except there was a new barman, dapper in a crisp white shirt and red waistcoat, dispensing drinks behind the bar.

While Judd's common sense told him Niamh wouldn't be there, his heart refused to believe it and set up a painful rhythm of anticipation. He expected her to walk in from the kitchen at any moment, lighting up his world with her smile. *It won't happen, you fool!* he told himself harshly. Niamh was safely married to Hollis Maitland and to make her doubly inaccessible, he was married himself to Sukie. Susannah Burden now – Mrs Judd Burden, his wife.

He had gone to her like a wounded animal, conscious only of his own pain and marrying her to ease it. He was both astonished and gratified to discover how well she succeeded. He had always known her to have a warm and generous nature but their wedding night had been a revelation. At first she had been shy and reticent, trembling under his advances and reluctant to let him see her without her clothes. But after wooing her with soft words and gentle caresses, his patience was rewarded. He had married a woman willing to match his passion with her own and whose body was more lithe and comely than suggested by her shapeless nightgowns and sensible, everyday clothes. Her skin was clear and translucent, free of blemishes, her breasts high and perfectly formed, traced with a network of fine blue veins and crowned with neat, rose-pink nipples which responded immediately to his touch.

'But Sukie, you're beautiful,' he had whispered, humbled by his good fortune which he didn't feel he deserved. And, so long as she kept her eyes closed, it was true.

Married a month now and healthily addicted to his love-making, she welcomed him nightly, willingly spreading her legs; long, slender legs which she tangled about his own. Although she had come to him virgin, she accommodated him with a joy beyond his expectations. She was one of those rare women, a natural wanton, born to give pleasure to her man. And because she loved him, she trusted him enough to experiment and grow in experience, fulfilling all of his sexual fantasies with a lack of inhibition that took his breath away.

So it was for her sake that he now screwed up his courage to question Tully McDiarmit about Uncle Jem. He had sense enough to know he must tread carefully. There was little to go on, apart from Matthew's hints and the scenario he had built from his own suspicions. He had no proof that Tully had made off with his uncle's gold and, truthfully, little enthusiasm for the task of challenging Niamh's father and accusing him of such perfidy but he needed to know. If not for his own sake, for the wife who was becoming more dear to him each day and the father-in-law who had recognised his talents and given him the opportunity to make the most of them.

He had been standing at the bar with a beer in his hand for less than five minutes when Tully came from the kitchen and saw him, greeting him less than cordially.

'Evening, Judd. What are *you* doing here?'

'Having a drink.' Judd raised his glass and smiled, meaning to start off by being civil.

'Well, if you're here to see Niamh, she's gone. Married now, in case you've not heard.'

'I heard. I got married as well.'

'So you did.' Tully managed to put a wealth of scorn into his next words. 'To the boss's daughter, wasn't it?'

'The very same.' Judd smiled, taking the remark at face value and raising his glass. 'To my Sukie, God bless her.'

Tully leaned forward, speaking softly, but there was no mistaking the menace behind his words. 'This is a public house

131

and I can't make you leave. But there are other places to drink. Other bars. Don't make a habit of coming in here.'

'Oh, don't worry, I won't. I came here to get some answers to one or two questions, that's all.'

'What sort of questions?' Tully's eyes narrowed with suspicion which made him look more like a fox than ever.

'I'd like you to cast your mind back some twenty years ago. When you were at sea . . .'

'Twenty years is a long time.'

'And I want to know what became of my uncle, Jem Burden. He sailed with you once on a ship called the *Sally Lee*.'

Tully's reaction was spectacular; he flushed a brick red which contrasted badly with the paler red of his hair. 'I told you – it was a long time ago.'

'Not so long that it doesn't embarrass you to remember. You know what I'm talking about. You know what happened to Jem and to the bag of gold nuggets which should have come to my mother and me.'

Tully rested his hands flat on the counter and took a deep breath, considering a lie. Deciding against it, he let go a long sigh.

'How much do you know?'

'Very little. Only what Matthew Bradley can remember.'

'I see. Better come through to the office where we can be private. Johnnie –' he clicked his fingers to catch the attention of his barman ' – you're in charge till I'm back.'

Inside, Janet was seated at the desk in the small parlour which had once been her father's office, the walls still decorated with the yellowing souvenirs of those who had visited or performed at the Silver Star. When she saw who was with her husband, she rose to her feet.

'What's *he* doing here?'

'Never mind.' Tully waved her queries away. 'Will you give us a few moments in private, my love, and see that we aren't disturbed? We have to talk.'

'What about?' she said, making no move to leave.

Tully was quiet but insistent. 'If you please, Janet.'

She would have said more but decided against it, knowing better than to argue with her husband in this mood. He closed the door behind her and opened it immediately to make sure she had gone. Satisfied they wouldn't be overheard, he opened a drawer and took out a bottle of best bourbon, broke the seal and poured a generous measure into a pair of cut-crystal glasses before handing one to Judd.

'I don't usually—'

'No, son, nor do I.' Tully knocked back half of it and immediately refilled his glass. 'But I'm going to need strong drink to tell you this tale and you're going to need strong drink to hear it. So sit down and make yourself comfortable. We could be a while.'

'Before you begin, d'you want me to show you some proof – some legal document that I am related to Jem?'

'No need for that, son.' Tully shook his head. 'I saw the likeness the very first day you came in with Albert. You're like him for all that you're dark and he was fair.'

'Was?'

'Oh yes, he's dead. Has been for some time. I'm sorry – maybe you were fond of him?'

'No. To be honest, I can hardly remember my uncle at all. Just a loud voice and a laugh that used to frighten me when I was small.'

'That's Jem all right; always larger than life. At first I thought you were his son.'

'You thought that and you never said anything?' Judd frowned, watching Tully shake his head. 'Why not?'

'Sleeping dogs,' Tully whispered, staring at nothing. 'All right. Where d'ye want me to begin?'

Judd shrugged, waiting for him to go on.

'The gold fields? Or when I joined the crew of the *Sally Lee*? Me sister was dead set against it but Jem told me to cut the apron strings – used to say there was no better place for a lad to grow up than at sea. Oh, we patched it up later, me sister and me, and we're friends of a sort, but I don't think she ever forgave me for leavin' – for choosin' Jem and the sea. Herself and Janet have never got on – that doesn't help . . .'

'So you left Melbourne with my uncle aboard the *Sally Lee*?' Judd didn't want him to be sidetracked into reminiscences about his sister.

'The voyage was doomed from the start. The captain was old and he got sick and died. The mate took over as master of

133

the ship. A bully, riding on a stolen ticket. A man who knew nothing about ships and even less about navigation. Jem tried to stir up the old hands but they hadn't the heart for mutiny – too starved and exhausted after heaving the ship through the gales as we rounded Cape Horn. The *Sally* was old too, ye know, only on this run because all the good ships, the new ships, were needed to go to the Crimea. I didn't know *that* at the time. God, I was green!'

'Yes, but if everyone had joined forces against the mate, surely you could have—'

'No,' Tully said shortly. 'You don't know what it was like. Bad food, the fear of a floggin' and sheer exhaustion made cowards of us all. And if we weren't ground down enough already, when we got through to the tropics the ship was becalmed. We lay roasting for days like so much meat on a slab. We could see the sun even with our eyes closed. And our lips, still cracked from the salt and frosts of the South, were now blistered and burned. Some of the men couldn't stand it and threw themselves into the sea. Then the storm came. I shall never forget it, the ship groanin' in her death throes and the wind wailin' through the masts like a thousand banshees. Jem was a good seaman – he knew we were in for the worst and the ship was about to break up. I don't remember it – got knocked on the head while we was gettin' into the boat.'

'So you and my uncle – you both survived?'

'Yes. But that was only the start of the troubles between us, your uncle and me.' Judd remained silent, almost holding his breath, aware that they were reaching the crux of the matter. Tully sighed and passed a hand over his eyes, remembering. 'He blamed me for Hobley's death.'

'Hobley?'

'His lifelong friend. Came out from England with him on the same ship. They'd been sailing together for years – even went to the gold fields and shared a mine. Hobley never had much to say but we used to think of him as Jem's shadow. He jumped into the water to rescue Pieface – my dog. The dog swam up to the boat and I managed to pull him aboard but Hobley was taken by sharks – dragged under the water and eaten alive. It must have affected your uncle's mind. He was never the same.'

'Go on,' Judd prompted as Tully sat there, reliving the horror, shaking his head.

'We had no water, no food an' we didn't dare sleep for fear of the boat fillin' up with water. I couldn't have slept if I'd wanted to, with your uncle ravin' at me all night and half the next day. Said I'd cost him his dearest friend, and for what? The life of a mangy dog! He sharpened his knife and said we should cut the dog's throat – we could survive by drinking his blood. I tried to stop him. We struggled over the knife, I caught him off-balance and he went over the side.'

'So you pushed him?'

'No, I don't think so. The sun and the heat drove him mad. He'd have murdered me just as easily as the dog.'

'And then you left him to drown?'

'I had no choice. The boat drifted on and he was too weak to swim or to float. He was there one moment and gone the next. Vanished under the waves.'

A silence fell between them as Judd absorbed this news, considering it.

'I suppose you blame me for what happened. And you'd be right.' All the weariness of his guilt was in Tully's voice. 'Don't think I haven't been blamin' meself ever since. I came back looking for happiness and it turned to ashes in less than a year. I thought fate was punishin' me, that I didn't *deserve* to be happy because of what happened to Jem.'

'And the gold?'

'Ah yes, the gold. I was wonderin' how long you'd take to get round to that. Jem used to talk of helpin' his sister, but that's all we thought it was – talk. I didn't know where he kept the gold nuggets till I took a look at his boots. If he'd been wearin' them at the time, they'd have gone to the bottom with him and been lost. They were a pair of sturdy seaman's boots with hollow heels where he kept the gold. I didn't expect to live long enough to enjoy it meself, but a ship picked us up that same day – me and old Pieface, the dog. I put on Jem's boots and never said nothin' about the gold.'

'So where is it now?'

'Gone, of course. Long gone.' Tully blinked behind his glasses, finding it hard to focus, red-faced and owlish with drink. 'Spent to buy me a share in all this.' He spread his arms as if to embrace the shabby room. 'My cross and my penance. The Silver Star.'

Judd could stand the man's smile no longer. He stood up and seized Tully by the lapels of his jerkin, hauling him out of his chair as if he weighed nothing at all. 'You bastard! That gold was for my mother. She waited for it, depended on it and you stole it without a thought.'

'Oh, I thought about it, all right. But how could I find Jem's successors? I didn't know where you lived.'

'You didn't even try.'

'Well, that's true. But I—'

'You have no excuse. If my mother had received the gold as my uncle intended, she wouldn't have married the Frenchman. She wouldn't have suffered as she did.'

'And you wouldn't have learned the man's trade.' Tully was already aware of Judd's skills and how he came by them. 'There's good to be found in everything if you look for it, son. You can't unravel a lifetime of *what-ifs*, Judd.'

'You make me sick. And don't try to justify yourself because you can't. You're no better than a common thief.'

'Show me the man who isn't, one way or another. Think I have it easy, do you? Trade places with me for a week and you'll see. Live with a cold-hearted woman who thinks you've blighted her life. Lose the one precious thing in your life – your child – to an arrogant fool.'

Mention of Niamh made Judd realise he had his hands at her father's throat. He let go of Tully at once, allowing him to fall back into his chair.

'Don't think I haven't gone over it a thousand times, wishin' it could have been different,' Tully said, covering his face to hide a mouth which was working and eyes filling with tears. 'If you knew how often I wished Jem had lived and I'd been the one to drown.'

Suddenly, there seemed to be no more to say; certainly not now, not tonight. Judd opened the door and left, unsure whether to feel loathing or pity for the man who was sitting beside the half-empty bottle of whisky, his face in his hands.

'So what happened about the inheritance?' Sukie whispered.

Not wanting to talk about it in front of Albert, she had waited until they were in bed.

'Quite simply, there isn't one.' Judd shrugged. There was no point in denying it.

'But what are you going to tell Pa? You said—'

'I know what I said.' His face twisted with remorse. 'Don't you worry, Sukie, I'll find a way. I'll get the money for the partnership somehow. I won't let him down.'

'He doesn't want you to borrow.'

'I know that already! Stop nagging me, woman.' It was the closest they had ever come to a quarrel and Sukie put her fingers to his lips to silence him, tears standing in her eyes. 'He told me of the shipwreck and – Ah God, Sukie, how could I press the man? He was beside himself.'

'And you think Pa's not beside himself, too? He's relying on you and you gave him your word. On the strength of your promise he's committed himself to take over the bigger premises up the road.'

'Then he shouldn't have done! He should have waited until I had the money in hand.'

'A bit late to think of that now.' In her anxiety Sukie's eyes were rolling, out of control, making her less than attractive. 'Niamh's father's not wealthy but neither are we. And he's had the use of your uncle's money – *your* money – free and clear without interest for twenty years. Isn't it only reasonable to expect him to give it back?'

'But Sukie, he doesn't have it. All his capital is tied up in the Silver Star!'

'And all we have is tied up in the foundry. You should have pressed him, Judd. It's not as if he's old and feeble, deserving of pity – he's years younger than Pa. Threaten to sue him. Let *him* go to the moneylenders, not you. Let *him* borrow the money to pay you back.'

'He's Niamh's father, Sukie, or have you forgotten?'

'No, I haven't. It's always Niamh with you, isn't it? Niamh! Niamh! Much as I love her, I'm beginning to hate the very sound of her name.' She had raised her voice and Judd winced, miming that she should keep it down. 'No, I won't be quiet – I don't care any more. Niamh always comes first with you, doesn't she? Her father must be considered before mine!'

'Sukie! Sukie, it's not like that. Not at all.'

'Isn't it?' She burst into tears and turned away from him, curling into a foetal position and stifling her pain by weeping harshly into the pillow.

'Sukie – ah, don't.' Judd tried to make her face him.

'Leave me alone!' she said, racked with sobs.

'No. We've been so happy till now. I won't let the sun go down on this, our first quarrel. You're right. You and Albert are my family now – you must come first. I'll go back and ask him again.'

'Tomorrow?'

'No, not tomorrow.' Judd's heart lurched painfully at the thought of going back to see Tully at all. 'But soon.' He kissed Sukie's shoulder still hunched away from him, feeling it warm through her nightgown. He pushed her hair away from her hot, tear-washed face to look at her. Weeping, she looked like a little girl. Very gently he kissed the lips pursed against him until he felt her sigh, beginning to respond to him, when he kissed her all over her face, drinking her tears. He tugged off his own nightshirt and threw it away, pulling her against him so that she should feel his erection against her small flat belly. The tension between them excited him and he wanted her badly now; he wanted to bury himself in her willing moistness, feeling her arch against him as he plunged, making her moan in ecstasy, too. He could scarcely wait while she sat up and took off her nightgown, pinching her nipples as soon as they were revealed. She twisted and lay on top of him, kissing him passionately as she teased him, rubbing her breasts against his chest. Still kissing him, she slid from his lips to his throat, continuing down until she encountered the hot silk of his erection, taking it into her mouth. He groaned for a while, letting her work him with tongue and lips but just as suddenly he moved her, lifting her head away.

'No, Sukie,' he whispered. 'I want to come inside you – I want you with me this time.'

Eyes closed and smiling, she let him lift her on to him until she straddled him, groaning his pleasure as her body closed around him, fitting so perfectly to his own. He stroked her breasts and then her belly so that she could feel him inside and

138

at last her hips and buttocks, moving her in time with him until she took up the rhythm on her own. Never had he had such a responsive lover, who catered so instinctively to his needs. Keeping her eyes closed, she let her head fall back. 'Ummm,' she sighed, close to orgasm and then, 'Aahhh!' as they climaxed together, moaning without inhibition, uncaring that Albert might hear them through the thin wooden partitions of the house.

Later, still not ready for sleep, she roused him again. Judd groaned but he responded all the same.

'Susannah Burden, you are a natural harlot,' he teased her when she was done.

'Am I?' She tensed, looking down at him, lying between her legs, peering at him, trying to read his expression. 'But only for you, Judd – and only because I love you. I love you so much.'

'I'd have you no other way, my love,' he said, coming up to loom over her, kissing her breasts and smacking his lips. 'You are quite delicious.'

He rose further then to kiss her closed eyelids before pulling her down into his arms again, her hair spread across the pillow and his chest. Finally, exhausted, he slept. But Sukie lay awake, listening to his heart beating strongly against her cheek. She was his wife, yes. But did he mean it when he said he loved her? Or was she no more to him than a private harlot, kept to receive his thwarted passion? A convenient means of relief? Impossible to ask.

Her mind veered around to the problem of his inheritance and whether he would find the courage to be forceful with Tully or not. Therein lay the answer to her problem. That's how she could have proof of how he felt; how she could find out once and for all where his affections lay. His actions would show her much more than his words. If he was prepared to put pressure on Tully, even to the extent of employing legal means to recover his money, it would mean that she and her father came first, that they were more important to him than Niamh. But if Judd were to delay, making excuses . . . Sukie squeezed her eyes shut, not wanting to pursue that thought to its logical conclusion. Too late she realised that in devising such a contest, the rules known only to herself, she was placing her fragile happiness at risk. Wouldn't it have been better not to know?

139

The following morning, Albert waited until Judd rose from the breakfast table and went outside to the privy before leaning forward to speak to Sukie. While the house wasn't small and included a parlour and a dining room at the front, these rooms remained closed and were seldom used. Like most busy people they took their meals in the kitchen; a large, rambling family room which was the focus of the house. It was here that they spent their time when they weren't at the foundry.

'By the regular creaking of that bed . . .' Albert smiled at his daughter, speaking frankly. Having taken the place of mother as well as father to Sukie there was less of a barrier between them than between most men and their girls '. . . you've a mind to make me a grandfather before too long.'

Sukie was feeling a little queasy today but she put it down to a hasty breakfast on top of a late night. She peered at Albert, trying to gauge his expression, but there was no hint of reproof. All the same, she blushed. It was one thing to suspect he could hear their lovemaking but quite another to know it.

'I'm sorry, Pa, I didn't realise . . .'

'Be sorry for nothing, my dear.' Awkwardly, he covered his daughter's hand with his own. 'I'm pleased to see you so happy – in love with your man. But such – er – vigorous activity means you'll be increasing before too long. We'll have to make plans.'

'What sort of plans?'

'Oh, I have one or two ideas up my sleeve.' He smiled, looking secretive. 'You wait and see.'

The morning at the foundry turned out to be busier than usual with several new orders as well as visits from some of the older customers, ordering repairs and additions. Judd was supervising some fine work, needed for an internal staircase and, with Albert off on some mysterious errand in town, Sukie gave no more thought to her father's words until he returned to the foundry at lunch-time, flushed with triumph and the effects of drinking whisky before noon.

'Young Holly Maitland is a genius,' he said. 'More forward-looking and go-ahead than his father. Made me take quite a different view of the future. Now I see it in a whole new light.'

'What have you done, Pa?' Sukie shivered, suddenly feeling the chill of foreboding although the morning was far from cold. In a rare moment of disloyalty Niamh had told her that Hollis exasperated his father with grandiose schemes and also that he was a fluent salesman, clever at convincing others to part with money to invest in his plans.

'I've broken the habit of a lifetime, that's what I've done. Overturned all me own rules. Man at the bank was delighted, too – I was welcomed with open arms. He says a firm as long-established as ours is an excellent risk.'

'A risk against what?'

'The money, of course. The money we'll need to buy land and some shares in the railways. Speculate to accumulate – that's what young Maitland said.'

'But Pa, you've always stood so firm on it. *Neither a borrower nor a lender be.* That's what you've always said.'

'I know what I said.' He waved her objections away. 'But we must move with the times, lass, like everyone else. We can double our money by the time of the Exhibition in October. You'll see. Smith's foundry will be the talk of the town. We'll put up a showin' to knock their eyes out.'

Sukie knew Albert had to be drunk as he was talking in clichés. 'Pa, just tell me plainly. What have you done?'

'Oh, stop lookin' so po-faced and disapprovin', my girl. We'll double the money and pay back the loan ourselves or else pay it back earlier when Judd comes through with his inheritance. Either way, we can't lose.'

'But have you discussed this with Judd? Does he know you're putting the business at risk? Dear heaven, Pa. I thought we needed Judd's money to move into larger premises, not this.'

'But we'll do it in half the time if I can double our investment. Why, on the profits alone . . .'

'What makes you so sure there'll be any profits, Pa?' Sukie could hear herself getting shrill with anxiety.

'Because Maitland said—' Albert paused in mid-sentence and frowned. 'Look here, I don't have to explain meself to you, me own child. Pay attention to women's things, Sukie, and don't go pokin' your nose into matters you don't understand.'

'But I *do* understand, and only too well. You've committed us to one of Hollis Maitland's harebrained schemes. How

141

could you, Pa? What if the loan is recalled and you can't pay it back? What if Judd doesn't get any money at all?'

'What if? What if?' Albert was drunk enough to mock her. 'Of course Judd will get the money. He gave me his word.'

Sukie's eyes rolled out of control, Albert thought. He couldn't know she was merely raising them heavenwards.

So now she had more than her husband's loyalties to concern her; there was her father's foolhardy investment as well. As the days passed into weeks and the weeks into months and Judd made no further move to reclaim his inheritance, her confidence was shattered and her heart seemed to shrivel and harden as her respect for her husband died.

However she tried to tell herself the 'contest' was foolish, now the thought had taken root she couldn't set it aside. Judd's affections rested on whether he would speak to Tully again or not. She could have put herself out of her misery any time by asking him outright, but to force the issue now would be cheating; she would be breaking her own rules. No, Judd must make the choice of his own free will and without any prompting from herself. But as the weeks passed and a damp autumn gave way to a winter sharp with frost, Judd had still made no move.

And, on top of these other concerns, she thought she was pregnant as well. A few months ago she was so close to her husband, she'd have told him of her suspicions at once. Now, as relations were strained between them, she chose not to mention that her monthly courses had been absent for several months. And he didn't think to ask. She examined her stomach each night when she undressed, surprised to discover it flat as ever. If anything, she looked thinner than before. Marriage had fined her down and, since those first few weeks, she had never been sick. She found it hard to believe there was a baby growing inside her at all. Yet her nipples itched and she pushed Judd's hands away whenever he tried to touch them. She didn't want him to make love to her at all.

Things came to a head between them when she turned her back on him, refusing him the comfort of her body for the second time in a week.

'But why?' he whispered, curling around her and hugging

her close so that she felt his arousal against her back. 'Is it the time of your courses? Do you have a pain?'

'No, it's not that,' Sukie snapped, choked by unshed tears, convincing herself his tenderness was a sham and he wanted her only for the relief of his masculine needs. 'I just don't feel like it, that's all. I need a rest. My body is sore from letting you use me night after night.'

'Use you, Sukie?' He withdrew a little, shocked by the brusque cruelty of the remark. 'I've never taken you for granted. You've always enjoyed our lovemaking. Taken as much pleasure in it as I do.'

'If that's what you thought you were wrong,' she said, wondering how she could lie so easily, destroying in a sentence all the happiness they had brought to each other before. 'I do it to oblige you and because it's my wifely duty. But I'll be more careful in future – much less of the natural harlot.'

'Oh my darling, you're not still festering over that. A few careless words which I meant as a compliment.'

'A compliment, is it? To call me a whore?'

'No no, never that.'

'Well, you won't have to criticise me for being wanton again. I can be straitlaced as any middle-aged matron you ever saw.' She wriggled away from him and lay there, tense, clinging to the outside edge of the bed.

'Ah, Sukie, I knew it, knew there was something.'

'I don't want to talk about it. Not now and maybe not ever. G'night.' And she squeezed her eyes shut, causing two hot tears to spill over and run down her cheeks. Perversely, she half-hoped he would pull her into his arms, laughing her out of her foolishness and kissing away her tears. But he didn't. Instead he sighed and moved away to lie on his back alone in the middle of the bed. She knew if she turned to look at him he would be lying there with his eyes open, staring at the ceiling. But she stayed where she was, tense and listening, until he flung himself away to the other side of the bed, robbing her of most of the bedclothes as he composed himself for sleep.

Chapter Eleven

Niamh had passed the summer, autumn and now most of the winter months in an agony of impatience, waiting for the house in Brighton to be completed. Convinced that everything wrong with her marriage would be put right as soon as she and her husband could commence life together alone, it never occurred to her to question Ellie's advice. Fortunately, while she waited, she had something to do. She spent most of her time at The Briarley Hospital, ignoring the protests of her mother-in-law and her Committee of Friends who distanced themselves from the day-to-day work of the hospital, preferring to limit their activities to the provision of bed linen and raising funds. Niamh took up the cudgels on behalf of the sick children and their mothers who had been too daunted by authority and too nervous to complain. But with Niamh as their champion, they found the courage to assert themselves and demanded to visit their children each day. Niamh pestered the Matron, arguing that if the children were happy they would recover more quickly and vacate the beds to make room for more. It was due to her efforts entirely that these changes were made.

She walked the wards, giving time to those who had no visitors because their mothers had to work or mind other children at home. She read to the children who were well enough to enjoy it or sat quietly holding the hands of those who were not. Only Sister Kearney belittled her efforts.

'Look at her,' she sniffed, pointing her out to the Matron as they passed. 'She takes too much on herself entirely. She thinks she's Florence Nightingale here.'

The Matron responded to the remark with the slightest of smiles, having no wish to cross swords with anyone who carried the name of Maitland. If the young woman cared to amuse herself by lightening the load of her nurses, who was she to complain?

Niamh visited The Briarley almost daily, refusing to listen to Holly who said she was wearing herself to a shadow, becoming a hospital drudge. Not that he had any time for her, anyway, as he was busy himself. Harley was ill, succumbing to a bronchitis which only narrowly missed turning into pneumonia, this, on top of a heart condition which was gradually getting worse. His recovery was slow and he hated the restraints his illness imposed. Most of all he chafed at not knowing what was going on at the office. And with good reason, Niamh thought.

Hollis, while having no money to invest in the new land himself, was making good use of his father's name and reputation by encouraging others to do so and taking a commission for his services. So far everything had gone smoothly and according to plan, but she knew it needed only one client to lose a substantial amount of money for a scandal to break over their heads. In addition, while Harley was unwell and the business needed Hollis's undivided attention, no one troubled to supervise the building of the new house. She tackled him about it after breakfast one morning, catching him on his way out.

'I can't worry about it now, Niamh,' he frowned. 'There's too much to do at the office while Pa's away. But there's nothing to stop you going down there. You can give old Wakefield a kick in the pants and jolly him along. As I understand it, the house is at lock-up stage. The roof is in place and the glass is in, so the shell is already there. The choice of decorations will be up to you, anyway.'

'Oh Holly, you know they won't take any notice of me. Tradesman have an in-built dislike of taking orders from women; it was the same when anything had to be done at the Silver Star.'

'The building of a house, my love,' Holly kissed the air vaguely in her direction, 'can hardly be compared with a lick of paint at the Silver Star. Well, if you can't cope with it, the

145

builders will have to get on as best they may. Just don't come whining to me if you don't like it at the end of the day. Make up your own mind. Got to go.'

So she opted to drive down to Brighton and tackle the tradesmen on her own. She had all her arguments ready. If they were truculent, she would remind them that she was a Maitland, if only by marriage, and the firm of Maitland and Maitland were paying their bills. She was rehearsing her speeches when Elinor called to see if she wanted to go into town.

'No, Ellie, I can't. Not today. But why don't you drive down to Brighton with me?'

'Brighton at this time of year? In weather like this? Brrh, no thanks!' Elinor snuggled into her warm cloak with its fur-lined hood. 'Drive all that way to visit an empty house with no fires, no servants and no food?'

'The sun's shining and I'm taking the pony and trap. Come on, Ellie, we'll take the coast road. It's a lovely day to be out.'

'And bitterly cold in the wind. In any case, I can't. I have an appointment in town.' Niamh looked at her sideways, certain she hadn't. 'If you're so desperate for company, why don't you ask Aunt Lil?'

'Thanks, but no thanks. You know what she's like. She'll take over entirely and I'll end up with everything decked out in chestnut and peach.'

Elinor laughed but she wasn't to be persuaded. So Niamh changed into the warm, serviceable dress she used to wear in the bar of the Silver Star and put on several petticoats underneath, including her old red flannel, to keep out the cold. She pinned a shawl across her body in the style of an Irish peasant and set out, the only indication of her status as a Maitland being a stylish, burgundy-coloured hat in the new 'flowerpot' design. Hats were her only extravagance – although her husband never questioned her use of his money. In her view, an old dress could always be made to do another turn with the help of a stylish hat.

Only Harley seemed concerned that she would travel alone. She found him seated by the fire in the library when she looked in to say goodbye. Lilias was sitting opposite him, picking away at some fine needlework in a frame.

'But my dear,' he said, 'Brighton's a long way. And darkness falls early now that the evenings are drawing in. Who knows who or what else might be on the road.'

'No bushrangers now, Uncle Harley. Captain Moonlight was hanged in January. Even Ned Kelly's been captured and most of his gang have been killed.'

'Bushrangers are like mushrooms, my dear – knock a few down and more will spring up overnight. Why not take Johnson, the new groom. He could drive you.'

Niamh had no intention of going to Brighton with Johnson who leered unpleasantly and smelled of rum, stale sweat and the stables.

'No thank you, Uncle Harley. I'd much rather drive myself – I'll do it in half the time.'

'Just make sure you leave in plenty of time to get back before nightfall,' he called after her as she blew him a kiss. He shifted in his chair, shaking his head. 'It's disgraceful, Lil. Holly should be going with her. Fancy letting the poor girl drive down to Brighton alone.'

'Send him after her, if you're so concerned. He'll come in for lunch in an hour or so,' Lilias shrugged. Most of her old resentment towards Niamh had returned. For a while she had hoped her daughter-in-law would be quiet and biddable, but the girl had a stubborn mind and a will of her own.

Warmly wrapped, with a rug around her knees and the pony jogging briskly in front of her, Niamh was enjoying her drive. She took the main road out to St Kilda, very much a resort these days with hotels and houses crowded together along the beach-front, competing for views of the Bay. From St Kilda she followed the meandering coast road to the seaside resort of Brighton, named in honour of its English counterpart. She had no way of knowing how it compared with the Brighton which had grown up in Regency days on the other side of the world, but she had a shrewd idea that it wasn't much like it at all. In winter even the scrub seemed to bend, hunching itself against the wind, and it had lost the jaunty, holiday atmosphere which characterised it in summer. The sea looked grey and choppy, having lost the smooth cobalt blue she remembered before. She hadn't been near the sea since the day she had been there with Judd. The day which had proved to be

147

such a turning point; a lifetime ago. Now she was married to Hollis and Judd to Sukie.

She turned away from the beach road, steering the pony towards the wide street at the back of the township which was the site of their new home. Instead of buying a beach-front property which would have been both expensive and small, the Maitlands had chosen a larger piece of land set back from the sea. Her heart lifted as she caught sight of the house, so far known to her only through plans and sketches. She was thrilled to see how near to completion it was. So this was to be her domain, her new home.

Outside she saw a man she had met only once before and recognised him as Wakefield, Hollis's builder. As she drove up, he was in the process of locking the front door and he didn't look pleased to see her.

'Well then,' he said, glancing at his pocket-watch. 'If you'd let me know you was coming, madam, instead of driving down here on impulse . . .'

'Leaving already, Mr Wakefield?' Niamh was equally crisp, matching his mood. 'It's scarcely five minutes after noon.'

'I know what time it is, madam.' He spoke with exaggerated patience. 'I keeps me own hours. I been waitin' all mornin' for the man from Smiths to come an' measure the verandah an' the staircase inside. Can't rely on sub-contractors, these days – always got some excuse for lettin' you down. Ah well, no more I can do here today as he's not arrived.'

Niamh wasn't listening. Instead she was looking at the wide verandah which ran down the length of one side of the house. 'Won't that make the back of the house rather dark? We'll need shade in summer, I know, but it'll be cool at this time of year, and I don't want to lose all the light.'

'That's the way it was shown on the plans an' the way Mr Maitland wanted it. If you want it taken away again, it'll cost you extra on top of—'

Niamh sighed. 'Oh, all right then, let it stay. Give me the key to one of the doors and I'll let myself in and out.'

With obvious reluctance, he fished in his pocket and found one, hesitating before he handed it over. 'You'll make sure you lock up proper before you go?'

148

'This is my home, Mr Wakefield – *my* home. I'm not likely to leave it open to vandals.'

Still muttering to himself and shrugging, the builder climbed aboard his cart. He clicked his tongue at his old horse and saluted Niamh with insincere politeness before driving off down the unmade, uneven road.

Niamh watered her horse and secured it and walked all around the house to get the feel of it before going inside. Externally, she could find no fault, not even with the verandah, on second thoughts. She let herself in through the back door, her boots echoing as she walked on the flagstones of the kitchen and then bare boards. As she expected, the house was complete apart from the internal fittings and it had that poised, expectant feeling as if waiting for someone to occupy it and its life as a home to begin. Not a showpiece like The Oaks with its ballroom, reception rooms and well-appointed guest bedrooms, all the same it would make a comfortable family home. The fireplaces and marble mantelpieces were in, the back stairs completed with simple turned wooden rails and on the landing above the front staircase a leadlight panel already inserted, depicting a stag at bay. The staircase had been started but lacked the curved banisters and the wrought iron on which they would rest. *Wrought iron!* As the thought occurred to her, she stopped dead in her tracks. She had been so exasperated with Mr Wakefield that she had paid little attention to what he said. But there were few craftsmen in Melbourne who worked wrought iron.

A loud banging at the back door made her start, wondering whether to answer it or not. If it was someone to see Wakefield, it wasn't likely that she would be able to help. The knocking came again, more insistently this time. Whoever it was had seen the pony and trap and knew there had to be someone within.

She went to the door and opened it, flinging it wide. The man on the doorstep said nothing, waiting for her to speak. She leaned against the doorpost, realising she wasn't surprised to see him at all.

'Judd!' she whispered, raising her eyes to look up at him, having forgotten how tall he was and how broad. 'Judd, what are you doing here?'

*

149

Sukie looked at the note on the desk and then beneath it for the plans of the house. They weren't there. The note was from Horace Wakefield, Builder, and when she first saw it, she had registered only the requirement from the foundry. *Quotation to be given for six wrought-iron panels for the outside verandah plus an ornate wrought-iron support for the main staircase within.* Only now did she see the small note added at the bottom of the page. *To be subcontracted on behalf of Mr Harley Maitland, c/o The Oaks.* The Maitlands! This work was for Niamh's new home.

She ran outside towards the furnaces, looking for Albert. Because of her poor eyesight she rarely left the office, afraid of tripping over old moulds and odd pieces of iron. She had done so many times in the past, painfully bruising her shins.

'Pa! Pa!' she called, peering at the faces which appeared to her from a distance only as blurs. 'Has Judd left already to price that house job in Brighton?'

'Get inside, girl, do you want to break your neck?' Albert was suddenly at her side, steering her back to the office and past a pile of recently discarded moulds. 'What can be so blasted urgent it brings you out here?'

'A new job for a hotel in town. They need a price now – today.'

'Then I'll get Tom to go.'

'No, they need someone with more experience. If Judd hasn't left already, Tom could go down to Brighton while he goes to town.'

'Too late, I'm afraid.' Albert shrugged. 'Judd left here nigh on an hour ago.'

'Oh,' Sukie said, leaning against the door. A few months ago he wouldn't have gone down the street without telling her where he was going and kissing her goodbye. Of course, she comforted herself, she was behaving like a fool. Judd would be dealing with Wakefield, the builder. Niamh was most unlikely to be there. And if she were? They would deal together formally with the builder; the mistress of the house instructing her tradesmen. And that would be all.

'Dammit, Father, I sent Niamh to Brighton because I can't go myself. I haven't the time.'

150

'Then you should have made the time. It's unkind in you, Holly, to send her on such an errand, expecting her to deal with builders and tradesmen, unescorted and alone.'

'Niamh isn't as delicately bred as you think, Pa. You haven't seen her as I have, sharpening her tongue on the drunks at the Silver Star.'

'She's a lady, nevertheless, and should have her husband's support.'

'All right, all right. I'll go, if you insist. But I'll have my lunch first.'

'Why not take a picnic and have it with Niamh? I don't think she thought of refreshments before she left.'

'Plenty of cafés in Brighton.'

'And most of them closed for the winter. Don't be such a boor, Holly.'

But it was Lilias who insisted that he should sit down to the hot meal, so he didn't mount his father's old horse and set off for Brighton until well after two.

When Niamh opened the door and found Judd on the doorstep, she stared at him for what seemed like an age but was probably only half a minute. And he looked just as dumbfounded to find her there.

'Niamh, it's you,' he said, stating the obvious. 'What are you doing here?'

'This is my home – this is where we shall live.'

'This far out of town?'

Niamh shrugged and Judd consulted the piece of paper and plans he had in his hands.

'I've an appointment,' he said at last. 'Supposed to see some fellow called Wakefield about a set of panels for the verandah and a bit of fancy work in wrought iron to decorate the front stairs.'

'Wakefield's gone. He waited as long as he could but you're late.'

'I know. His directions were a bit sketchy and it took me all morning to find the place. Oh well,' his smile was cautious as he half-turned, ready to go, 'tell him I'll catch up with him some other time.'

'Judd, don't go!' The words were out before she could stop them. 'How are you?'

151

'Well enough,' he said without smiling. He looked at her properly then, deciding that marriage didn't agree with her. She was thinner than he remembered and there was a wary look in her eye. Somewhere along the line she seemed to have lost some of her joy in life, and with it her bloom. 'Well as I deserve to be, anyway. And you?'

She nodded. 'Are you happy then, Judd – you and Sukie?'

'Why don't you ask her,' he said softly. 'I thought you were friends.'

'Because I'm asking *you*,' she said, hugging her shawl more closely around her, suddenly chilled.

'Are you here on your own, Niamh?'

Her first instinct was to lie and say, 'No', and she paused for a moment until she decided against it. 'Yes, as it happens, I am. So I can't ask you to come in.'

He glanced back up the driveway and grinned. It was a shadow of his old mischief but she thought it made him look older now, rather tired. 'Who's to see me, here at the back door?' He leaned in the doorway, beginning to relax. 'Are the fireplaces in?'

'Yes, but the chimneys have never been used. They'll probably smoke.'

'Only one way to find out.'

'No, Judd. You're not stopping and you're not going to build a fire. I don't think you ought to come in.'

'Make up your mind. A moment ago you were asking me not to go. You're chilled already – I'm not letting you drive back to Melbourne like that. You'll catch your death.'

'I really should be on my way. I'm all done here.'

'And I'm not. Listen, Niamh, we're both married – if we meet in public, we can't exchange two words apart from the normal courtesies. This could be our last chance to talk to each other in private.'

'I shouldn't be talking to you at all.'

'I'm going for twigs and some wood to make up the kitchen fire. If I do, will you give me your word you won't lock me out?'

She looked at him for a long moment before saying yes.

The fire was a blessing. He laid it in the kitchen stove so that they could close the door on it if it smoked. It didn't. Instead it gave off the warm, medicinal smell of gum nuts and eucalypt as the kindling crackled and caught. Soon he added logs and the fire blazed, cheering them and warming the empty room.

Niamh sat on the floor in front of it, hugging her skirts around her knees. She had taken off her hat and left it on the windowsill. Judd's peaked working-man's cap lay beside it. He sat on the floor next to her, as relaxed as she remained tense and watchful, his long legs stretched out in front of him, ankles crossed, leaning back on his elbows.

'So you still have that dress,' he said at last. 'You used to wear it at the Silver Star. I thought you'd have—'

'What – given it to the servants? Thrown it away? What do you think, Judd, that I spend my time all dressed up, playing ladies?'

'I suppose so. Yes, I did.'

'Then maybe you don't know me quite so well as you think. I'm not completely idle, as it happens. I do voluntary work at The Briarley Hospital.'

'For sick children?'

'That's it. Oh, they won't let me do anything menial – my mother-in-law sees to that. She's on the Ladies' Committee and that's what she thought I should do – go to their boring meetings as well. But I wanted to do something practical – something more.'

'And your husband allows it? He doesn't mind that you prefer to do something positive for the children rather than hob-nob with the ladies of the Committee?'

'I don't think he gives it much thought. He's so busy just now, he doesn't care what I do, or how I spend my days.'

'Oh.'

'And don't say *Oh!* like that.'

'Like what?'

'I don't know – hinting at something more. And what about you? Have you been back to the Silver Star?'

'You told me not to, remember?'

'Only while I was there. I didn't mean you to stay away after I'd gone.'

'I did go, once.' He stared into the flames, reminded of Tully, crying into his whisky like a broken man. 'But somehow it wasn't the same without you.'

153

'If – if only things had been different, Judd. If only I'd met you before . . .'

'If only! Don't you dare say that, not to me! You knew how I felt but you married him anyway. It wasn't too late – you had plenty of time to change your mind.'

'No.' She spoke softly, also staring into the flames and realising that somehow they'd drifted onto dangerous ground.

'I loved you, Niamh. God help me, I still do.'

'I don't think you should say that, Judd.'

'Why not?' He was leaning towards her now, his brows meeting, dark eyes flashing in temper. 'Why shouldn't I say it? I was a fool to be so gentle with you. If I'd forced myself on you – made you admit that you love me – we wouldn't be in the position we are today.'

'Say what you like – it's too late.'

'No.' He placed one hand on the back of her neck, the other to cup her chin, covering her mouth with his own. His kiss wasn't rough but insistent and all around her was that particular smell of his, the sharp odour of metal and furnaces mingled with masculine strength and good health. She opened her mouth to receive his kisses which were becoming hungry now, responding with all the pent-up frustration of a woman whose married life didn't satisfy her most secret urges and needs.

'Oh, Niamh!' Her name burst from him like a sob. 'Give yourself to me, just this one time. I promise it's all I'll ever ask of you and I'll make it last for the rest of my life. I'll never ask to see you again.'

'I remember,' her voice was no more than a whisper, 'you promised me something like that before.'

Having no answer for that, he kissed her again. He too was the victim of pent-up feelings. Had Sukie remained the responsive lover of the early days of their marriage, this situation might not have developed; this encounter might never have taken place. But he didn't think of those days. Instead he thought of his Sukie today – sullen and sulky, punishing him for that thoughtless slip of the tongue, denying him the comfort of her body. He pulled Niamh's shawl away and kissed her again, feeling her breasts, loving the rounded softness of them beneath her gown. He started unfastening buttons until she stopped him, covering his hand with her own.

154

'Judd, wait a moment. Think about this. What we're doing is wrong.'

'Think? I don't want to think. Not about anything but ourselves. Please, Niamh, just give me this moment. Don't stop me again. God knows I won't be depriving your husband of much. One afternoon. One memory to last me a lifetime.'

He went on unfastening the buttons and tore her undergarments aside, baring a breast. She closed her eyes, letting him feast on her, stroking his hair and holding him close. Nor did she stop him when he reached under her skirts, unfastened his own garments and without any more foreplay thrust himself into her. She gasped, surprised by that first thrust which was unexpectedly painful and then cried out as his body made room for itself inside her, finding its rhythm. But she held on, squeezing her eyes shut and clinging to him until he shuddered, reaching his climax and gaining relief. She continued to hold him until his heartbeat steadied and when she opened her eyes it was to find him staring at her unsmiling and with an intensity of expression she couldn't fathom. Gently, he withdrew from her and pulled her skirts aside to examine her petticoats, finding them stained not just with semen but bright red blood.

'Oh Niamh, your maidenhead.' He scarcely breathed the words. 'Why didn't you say?'

'Would you have taken my word for it, if I had?' she said unsteadily, sitting up to fasten her buttons and pull down her crumpled skirts.

He let go a long sigh. 'You do know you can leave a husband for this? You can get an annulment.'

'Can I?' she said with a wry smile. 'I think I'd run into one or two problems if I tried to plead virginity now.'

'I didn't know.'

'Would you have acted any differently if you did? What's a slice of a cut cake – isn't that what they say? Would you have believed me if I'd told you the cake was still whole?'

Judd looked away for a moment, unable to meet her gaze. They had just performed the most intimate act between a man and a woman, yet he was embarrassed to question her further. All the same, he felt bound to try. 'But don't you . . . Doesn't he . . .?'

155

'We used to try. But now he's so frightened of failure he won't even do that.'

'Poor Niamh.' He kissed her gently, sorrowing for her. That a woman of her warmth and potential passion, should be denied married love. 'Let me love you once more. I want to show you the best of it, what it can really be like.'

'I think not,' she murmured. 'Haven't we done enough betraying for one day? Not just to Hollis but to Susannah as well.' She used the full names of their partners on purpose, reminding him of their commitments elsewhere.

'Sukie?' A smile flickered across his face and left. 'We were happy together once – happier than I ever deserved or expected to be – but something's changed between us of late. She keeps watching me as if she's waiting for me to say something, some magic word to put everything right and I can't because I don't know what it is. That's why I've been dragging my feet about taking up that partnership with Albert.' Once more he averted his eyes, remembering that in order to take up the partnership, he would have to put pressure on Tully.

'But Judd, I'm sure you're mistaken in Sukie. She loves you so much, and she's the most loyal of friends.' Suddenly her voice was unsteady. 'Much more loyal than I've been to her. She'll be a loyal and loving wife to you, too.'

'Well, something's wrong. I don't know what it is and Sukie won't say. God, what a mess. I love *you* – Sukie loves *me*. And you, Niamh – who is it you love?'

'Does it matter?' She kissed him to silence the queries, lips trembling against his own. The touch of her lips ignited his passion and he began kissing her, fiercely, hungrily, refusing to part with her. She sighed, giving herself up to the pleasure of being with him. If she was to be damned for adultery, she was damned already. One time or two – what difference did it make?

He unfastened the bodice of her gown and stripped her to the waist, enjoying the fullness of her breasts. They weren't high and pert like Sukie's but heavier, like rich fruit, her skin darker too, the nipples large and brown. Raising her skirts he lifted her into his lap and on to his member, feeling her tense as she waited for it to be painful as before, moving only gently until she relaxed. At last she smiled into his eyes, catching his

156

rhythm and grinding herself against him, at the same time placing his hands on her breasts, encouraging him to touch her. He smiled into her eyes, seeing the dawning of comprehension as they grew sleepy with passion and she discovered the pleasure to be gained from making love with someone who cared for her and who loved in return. With Niamh he had the eye-contact that had been missing from his relationship with Sukie.

'Oh! Oh Judd, that's just – so wonderful – so good!' She gasped, reaching orgasm for the first time and collapsing against him, filling his mouth with her kisses and smothering him with her hair.

Later, much later, she remembered the time.

'I have to go,' she said, dressing herself in haste, her body still shaking from the violence of their lovemaking. 'They'll be worried sick. I promised to be back before nightfall and I haven't a light on the cart.'

'Let me ride with you, then. I'm on Albert's old horse.'

'No! We mustn't be seen together. I have to go first.'

He parted with her reluctantly, handing her up into the cart. She leaned down, placing a hand on his cheek, unable to resist a last, lingering kiss. 'Goodbye, my love,' she said tenderly. 'Be of good heart and try to make Sukie happy.'

He didn't mount up and follow until the pony and trap had gained the main road and she was lost to sight.

Hollis took his time on the road to Brighton, hoping that by dawdling he would run into Niamh on her way back. This didn't happen and by the time he turned into their drive, which resembled a quagmire due to the coming and going of builders' drays, it was late and he was in a bad mood.

At midday it had been bright and sunny, but now there was no warmth in the winter sun which was well on its way to setting. The light was fading fast.

Silently cursing both Niamh and his father for bringing him out on this fool's errand, he was about to ride up to the front door and announce his arrival when he saw Niamh coming around the side of the house. She was accompanied by a man whom he took to be one of Wakefield's labourers. Aware that if he should be drawn into the negotiations at this late stage, it

157

would take even longer to get away, he reined in under a stand of wattle, preferring to see without being seen. And, in common with most people who spy on others, he saw and heard a lot more than he bargained for, including that last, lingering kiss. A kiss that, in his opinion, could only have been exchanged between long-term lovers.

But even in the midst of his emotional shock and jealousy, his lawyer's mind was at work, sifting the evidence. An assignation? Unlikely. She had no time to arrange it. Wasn't it he himself who had told her to visit the half-completed house? So, who . . .

Even if he hadn't remained half-hidden, he doubted if Niamh would have seen him. She clattered past, half-blinded by tears, her hair falling down and flying behind her like a flag as she whipped the pony into a canter as soon as she reached the main road. He thought of confronting her lover but he decided against it when he saw the breadth of the man's shoulders and his grim expression as he rode past on Albert's clumsy, ponderous horse.

Holly's heart lurched unpleasantly as he recognised the rider as Judd Burden, the man who had paid Niamh so much attention at the Silver Star. His mind whirled in shock as he assimilated this news, scarcely able to believe the evidence of his own eyes. What hurt the most was the thought that Judd might be succeeding with Niamh where he himself had failed. How often did they meet, then? Writhing together, legs entwined, flesh against flesh . . . *No!* He wouldn't think about that. Such thoughts always roused those bad memories; the memories he had suppressed and buried for so many years.

Boys. Boys surrounding him in a circle of cruel faces, laughing at him for his bookishness, for being a cosseted only child. Jeering at him, mocking the womanish fullness of his lips and his babyish fair hair. Then later, in the darkness of the dormitory, there were hands reaching out for him; hands that reeked of food and tobacco clamped over his mouth to stifle his cries, hot breath steaming in his ear. Boys larger and stronger than he was threatened to hurt him if he told; as if they weren't hurting him enough already. Hollis didn't tell. He didn't have to. His work suffered and his parents took him away from that school. At the day school he kept himself to himself. His marks improved, his parents were pleased and no more was said.

But he had been scared of big men ever since; men like Judd Burden, physically larger and stronger than he was. He had disliked the blacksmith on sight and had double the reason to hate him now.

He calmed himself as he rode home, setting his mind to work on the best way to make his enemy pay. He'd be in no hurry: a good revenge needed proper planning and ought to cost Burden a good deal more than a bloodied nose.

Rejecting the coast road chosen by his wife and her lover, he turned sharply inland and rode home another way. He wanted to be there before his wife, ready to greet her, to see how practised a liar she was. He looked forward to hearing her explanation for being so late.

Chapter Twelve

Supper was on the table by the time Judd stabled the horse and came into the kitchen, shivering and rubbing his hands against the cold. Sukie had cooked one of his favourite meals, a rich stew made from a sheep's head with a sauce of brains, served with boiled potatoes and carrots. His stomach growled in response as he smelled it, reminding him that he'd eaten nothing since breakfast.

'Where did you get to?' Sukie snapped. 'It can't take all day to talk to a builder about a staircase. We were about to send out a search-party.'

Judd kissed her absently and smiled, thinking it best to say nothing.

'Don't nag the man, daughter,' Albert said mildly. 'Can't you see he's half-starved with the cold? You're beginning to sound like a shrew.'

By way of an answer Sukie slammed the casserole in front of them on the kitchen table and flung down the spoon beside it. 'Help yourselves,' she said. 'I'm not hungry any more. I'm going to bed.'

'Ah, now now,' Albert began. But she had already left the room.

Judd knew it would serve his case much better if he followed Sukie to bed and made peace with her at once, but the food was too tempting. With a guilty smile at Albert, he ladled it out for both of them and set to, wolfing his share.

'Steady on, lad. Anyone would think you hadn't eaten for a month. Must be the sea air,' Albert grinned, saying nothing more until both of their plates had been refilled and cleared.

'How did you find the job, then? Bit o' profit in it, is there?'

'Maybe. The verandah's straightforward enough and I measured the stairs,' he lied. 'Have to go back, though. Wakefield wasn't there.'

Albert raised his eyes to heaven, sympathising, until he was struck by another thought. 'What took you so long then if the builder wasn't there?'

'Horse cast a shoe on the way home,' Judd lied easily. 'Had to walk him to the forge to get him fixed up before I could ride him again.'

'Ah,' Albert nodded, accepting the explanation.

Judd stood up, having finished his meal. 'Night, Albert. I'd better go up and make peace with Sukie.'

'Sure you won't have a bit o' Dutch courage? A glass of ale before you go?'

'Better not,' Judd smiled.

'Good luck.'

Upstairs, Sukie was lying curled up on her side of the bed, the clothes pulled up to her ears. Judd undressed quickly and slipped in beside her.

'Sukie.' Tentatively, he reached towards her. 'Sukie, what have I done? I don't know, if you won't tell me. Sukie, talk to me, please.'

She whipped towards him, her face red from weeping, eyes fluttering, out of control. 'I smelled her on you. You stink of it – d'you know that? That special lavender water she wears.'

'Oh, Sukie.'

'One of the things you should know about blindness is that it makes the other senses more acute. Touch, hearing and smell – I can recognise smells much better than most people. Tell me, Judd, did you know where you were going when you set out? Did you know it was Niamh's house? Or did you arrange beforehand to meet her there?'

'Of course not, Sukie. We met quite by chance.'

'You kissed her, then? Did you make love to her, too? Did you sit her up in your lap, in that special way; the way you do it for me?'

'No! How could you possibly think that? No!'

'Liar. I can hear the lies in your voice.'

'All right then, I did. I spent the whole afternoon shagging

161

Niamh until she was sore and she begged me to stop. There! Is that what you wanted? Are you happy now?'

Sukie fell back on the pillows, weeping bitterly.

'Sukie, I kissed her, that's all. The house is still empty; there aren't any beds, not even a chair.' The lies came more easily as he mingled them with the truth. 'What are you thinking of? Niamh's your friend, for God's sake. She isn't a whore.'

'Then why did you kiss her? Did she kiss you back?'

'Yes, if you must know. For old time's sake, to say goodbye – it wasn't much more than a peck. The last thing she said to me was to make you happy. Not doing very well at it, am I?'

'Oh Judd, I am so . . .' Sukie looked shamefaced although she couldn't quite say she was sorry. 'Will you send Tom down to Brighton to finish the job? I'd rather you didn't go there again.'

'Whatever you say, my love. Whatever you like.' He sighed as if he were the injured party.

She peered at him, trying to see his expression before she spoke, changing the subject yet again. 'I was wondering, and so was Pa,' she was almost choking on the words until she managed to get them out, 'when you mean to see Niamh's father about that legacy of yours? Pa went and borrowed money to put into that land and it looks like being more of a long-term investment than we thought.'

'I'll go tomorrow,' he promised. 'And Sukie, stop breaking your heart over Niamh. Nothing happened. Whatever there might have been, it's over between us. It's finished.'

'Oh, Judd!' Sukie flung herself into his arms and kissed him passionately, burying her hands in his hair and exploring his mouth with her tongue. With a moan of pleasure tinged with relief, he kissed her in return, sufficiently tense and wound up emotionally to respond to her advances. Unexpected but opportune. It seemed the more he made love, the more ready he was. He ripped off her nightgown, flung it across the room and lay across her, preparing to take her quickly in the missionary position.

'No, Judd, not like that,' she whispered. 'Do it the way that makes it special for me. Let me sit in your lap.'

He didn't have to fake any eagerness. His wife was a warm and responsive sexual partner and he knew how to please her, gently pinching her nipples and doing everything that she liked in order to coax her to her usual noisy climax.

And as Sukie shivered and gave herself up to erotic pleasure, her hair falling in a curtain across his face, she told herself: *He's mine, he is truly mine. How could he do this with such abandon, if he'd spent the afternoon making love with somebody else?*

Had Sukie's eyesight been better, she would have seen the puffy eyelids and dark circles of debauch beneath her husband's eyes. She would have realised that the mark she took for a smudge of dirt on his throat was a bruising love bite left by another woman's teeth.

Niamh returned home to find Hollis and his mother awaiting her at the stables. Lilias was first to comment on her dishevelled appearance, relief making her scold.

'Niamh! We've been so worried, and when Holly came back a few moments ago, saying he'd missed you on the way . . .'

'Oh?' Niamh's heart lurched on hearing this news. How could Holly possibly miss her on the coastal road? And if he hadn't, how much had he seen? 'I'm afraid I got carried away with my planning and didn't start back until late. I didn't realise it would get dark so early and lost my way.'

'And that's all?' Lilias had a better chance to look at her daughter-in-law as she advanced into the light, leaving the pony and trap to the care of the stable hands. 'You look as if you've been pulled through a hedge backwards. And where is your hat?'

Niamh had a quick mental picture of the hat and where she had left it, sitting on the windowsill beside Judd's cap; a vivid reminder of the way she had spent the afternoon. That and the stickiness on her skirts and between her legs as she walked made her feel as if guilt must be written all over her. She hugged her shawl around her, peasant fashion, preparing to face the inevitable inquisition.

It was Hollis who came to her rescue. Hollis who had so far said nothing, standing back in the shadows and leaving his mother to scold and reproach.

'Save the questions for later, Mother. Can't you see Niamh's tired out? Right now she needs a hot bath and something to eat. You must be starving, my love. You missed out on lunch.'

Niamh gave him a searching glance. It wasn't like Holly to be so solicitous and she looked for some hidden meaning behind his words. But his expression was bland, showing nothing but mild concern.

'Oh, I'm sorry, Niamh, I didn't think.' Lilias hugged her. 'Heavens child, you stink of wood smoke and furnaces. What were you doing out there – lighting bonfires?'

Niamh gave a thin smile, thinking the least said, soonest mended, happy to let herself be ushered indoors, clucked over and washed by Lilias's personal maid and tucked into bed like a child with the promise of milk pudding on a tray.

'But I hate milk pudding,' she protested. 'I'm cold and hungry, that's all. I'm not sick. I'd much rather go downstairs and have cheese and cold meats at the table.'

'I have my instructions, madam.' The maid was equally adamant. 'You're to have somethin' hot, wholesome and easy to digest – the cook made it special. And it's more'n my job's worth to let you downstairs.'

Niamh climbed into bed and sighed, seeing it was useless to object and also, in spite of the warm bath, she was aching in every limb. She really was tired. As soon as she was in bed there was a knock at the door and another maid entered bringing the pudding on a tray complete with starched napiery and a fresh posy of flowers. To refuse it would have been less than gracious and Niamh was famished enough to do justice to the bland, invalid's meal.

Left to herself, she pondered her situation, wondering belatedly if the activities of the afternoon could result in a child. Someone as overtly masculine as Judd was sure to be potent. Passion spent, she wondered how she could have taken such a risk? She had behaved like the heroine of a cheap novel, falling into Judd's arms like a lovesick fool. Lost in the gloom of self-recrimination, she started when the door opened and Hollis came into the room.

'Why, Niamh,' he said softly. 'Did I startle you? Who did you think it would be?'

She shrugged, offering a small smile.

'I thought I'd join you,' he said, heading for his dressing-room. 'Have an early night.'

164

'Don't you want me to tell you about the house?'

'It'll keep,' he said, pulling off his cravat as he went. He called out to her as he undressed, raising his voice. 'What really kept you, Niamh? What did you find to do out there all this time?'

Niamh paused, thinking of saying she'd spent the whole day with Wakefield until she realised she could easily be found out in the lie. 'After Wakefield left, I started planning the garden,' she called back to him. 'Holly, do you think there's room for a small fountain and a parterre?'

'A parterre?' He gave a bark of laughter. 'It's a modest suburban home, Niamh, not a mansion complete with a tower and a widow's walk. Have a rose garden instead.' He came back into the bedroom, his nightshirt flapping about his thin, white shanks. She compared them unfairly with Judd's muscular limbs. Oh lord, is this to be my punishment, she thought. Forever making comparisons between my husband and Judd? The bed creaked as Hollis climbed in beside her. Without asking, he turned down the oil-lamp on the table beside the bed.

'Don't do that, Holly.' She tried to stop him. 'I might want to read.'

'No, not tonight,' he said, making her heart sink, hearing purpose behind his words. She wanted to protest, to say she was tired, that she couldn't face another of those futile attempts which left them both in despair. But before she could speak, he began kissing her with unusual intensity, his eyes open, watching her. She gasped as he clutched at her breasts with sharp fingers that pinched rather than coaxed as did Judd's more experienced hands. The whole of her body objected, rejecting him, still tender from her lover's ministrations earlier in the day.

But Hollis was seething with suppressed rage, angry enough to want to punish his wife rather than pleasure her, and this time when he pressed himself against her, he remained hard, ready to possess her – and it seemed their lovemaking would proceed to its natural conclusion.

Niamh closed her eyes, every nerve screaming, every particle of her body wanting to repel this violation. But to refuse her husband now would be tantamount to admitting her guilt. Squeezing her eyes shut, she guided him to the right place, relieved when he climaxed almost immediately with a small sigh.

So you are safe, said the demon of guilt at her shoulder, his silent laughter filling the room and mocking her. *Safe now even if you give birth to your lover's child.*

Hollis neither praised nor condemned her, nor did he offer any explanation for the sudden release of his inhibitions. Niamh knew better than to ask, allowing him to bury his face in her neck and sleep in her arms like a child. But she herself lay awake in the darkness, plagued by her thoughts. Whatever the outcome, the deception would have to go on, night after night, week after week, perhaps even year after year. Not just for the sake of her husband, immersed in business rather than family matters and who would take her for granted yet again, but for Sukie Burden, the friend she had betrayed.

'I told you before, I don't *have* any money to give you.' Tully's voice swooped an octave higher in his anxiety. Unable to remain seated he stood up to pace the tiny office of the Silver Star, unsettled by Judd who was calmly waiting for an answer, having stated his demands.

'I'm not asking for charity, sir – for something you have to spare. I am claiming what is rightfully mine.'

'But a thousand pounds!' Tully's mind was reeling at the amount. 'You must be insane. Those few chips of gold didn't amount to anywhere near such a sum. How much gold d'ye think a man can carry in the heels of his boots?'

'I don't know. But you've had the use of it, haven't you? The use of my inheritance all these years. I hoped we could reach an agreement and save us both the expense of dragging the matter through the courts.'

'Through the courts? Ridiculous! Who's going to care about an incident that took place twenty years ago and more?'

'Myself, to name but one. I must say I'm surprised. I took you for a man of honour, sir.'

'Honour? Ho yes, when I was a boy I used to indulge meself with such high-flown ideals. Nowadays I think honour's for those who can afford it.'

'All I need is enough to buy into a partnership with Albert – to enjoy the same advantages my uncle's money gave you. Is it so much to ask, when you have all this?' Judd looked around the little room which served as the office of the Silver Star, the walls papered with past glories and fading testimonials.

'*All this*, as you're pleased to call it, is more of a millstone than a money-maker, these days. My wife has been ailing of late and there's staff to be paid . . .'

'Spare me the domestic details, I've problems of my own.' Judd felt under no obligation to be gentle with Niamh's father whose excuses were beginning to irritate him. 'I came to you in good faith, to see if this matter can be settled out of court. If not then I give you fair warning, you may have to deal with my lawyers.'

'Your lawyers? Why, you young—' Tully stared at him in disbelief. He had never taken to Judd Burden and liked him even less now he was here as the voice of Conscience, digging up the past, reminding him of matters he would rather leave undisturbed. He smiled but it was a travesty; the grimace of a man trapped by his nemesis and with his back to the wall. To Judd it resembled the smile of a fox, all sharp teeth and sandy hair. 'Without written evidence you won't find it so easy to make a case. What do you have, after all? The word of your mother when she was dying, her mind wandering in her pain. You'll have to come up with somethin' better than that. I'm a respected citizen of this town and the law is unlikely to find in favour of a newcomer like yourself – the relative of someone already known to have broken the law. A seaman who smuggled gold bullion out of the country instead of surrendering it to the Treasury for the going rate.' He went to the door and opened it. 'So, if you've nothing further to add, you may as well leave. We've wasted enough of each other's time already.'

Judd's temper flared. 'Curse you, Tully McDiarmit! You know damned well I'm in the right. Goddamn you for a bare-arsed Irish tinker and a thief!'

Instead of taking offence, Tully laughed. 'Lord'n it's a long time since anyone cursed me like that,' he said. 'Makes me feel like a spring chicken again!'

Judd slapped his hat on his head and left, squinting into the sunlight and pulling his scarf up to cover his mouth and nose against the bitter wind blowing in from the sea. His inheritance was gone. And Tully was right. Without evidence, he hadn't the smallest hope of getting it back.

But he had promised Albert the money and he needed that partnership to establish himself. There had to be some other way of obtaining it. Almost without realising it, he found himself mounting the wide stone steps which led to the impressive, brass-handled oak doors of his bank.

The manager received him in an office which smelled of old leather and ink. A plump, self-important little man with oiled hair, his high, winged collar forced him to keep his nose in the air. But he greeted Judd cordially enough, nodding as the young man explained his circumstances and the purpose for which he would need such a sizeable loan.

'I see no problem with this, Mr Burden,' he said. 'No problem at all. The only stumbling block could be one of collateral. As I understand it you're not a property-owner yourself, and you live in your father-in-law's house?'

'That's right, but—'

'As I say, I see no immediate problems. You're young, healthy and look more than capable of working to pay off the debt. But you do understand that in the bank's interests, enquiries will have to be made? A formality only, I assure you, but I won't be able to give you an answer today.'

'But soon?'

'Patience, Mr Burden.' The man sat back and smiled benignly, steepling his hands. 'Taking a loan is rather like embarking on matrimony. Neither ought to be conducted in haste.'

With that, Judd had to be content. He left, choking down his resentment at the man's patronising attitude but having exacted the promise that he would have his answer within the week.

Two weeks later Albert was sitting uncomfortably amid the indoor palms and aspidistras which decorated the offices of Maitland & Maitland. In the absence of Harley, he was once more facing Hollis across his father's desk.

'I see nothin' for it, me boy. Looks like I'll have to pull out of the scheme a bit earlier than I thought. I must ask you to find me a buyer for that lump of land.'

'So soon?' Holly lolled back in his seat, pinching his lips and frowning. 'That's a pity, Albert, because I'm not sure I can help. I thought you understood this was going to be a long-term investment?'

'Not entirely. I said I hoped it would be, but I might need to get my hands on the money earlier if – if other plans didn't work out.'

'Oh dear.' Hollis opened his eyes, looking innocent, secretly pleased to see Albert discomfited. Not because he had anything against him personally but if the old man were to experience a financial setback, it would have the added bonus of causing difficulties for Judd. 'I wish you'd made that clearer to me at the time.'

'I did.'

'Not as I recall.' Hollis was firm but he made sure his expression reflected only concern. 'And you do realise there are penalty clauses – to protect the other investors, you understand? You'll retrieve only half your investment, if you insist on taking it now.'

'*Half?*' Albert choked, horrified. 'I had to borrow the money to make this investment in the first place. You made it sound so easy, so cut and dried. And now you're saying I shall lose half.'

'So you blame me, then, for your predicament?'

'No, I wouldn't say that . . .'

'Why not look at your figures again and see if you can find some other solution. There's a handsome profit to be made if you can leave the money where it is for the next three to five years.'

'I know,' Albert sighed. 'And I'll be the first to admit I got carried away with the thought of the profits. I thought I'd be able to make a quick killing and get out.'

'Then I'm sorry to disillusion you.' Hollis's smile was thin. 'The money's already been put to work building railways and services to the new estates. You must see how it is. If all the investors were like you, demanding the return of their money before the due date – why, it would be like a run on the bank.'

'I do see. But in my case there's no choice. It's August already and we're gearing up for the International Exhibition. It's my daughter's husband – I blame him more than anyone else.' Albert was too upset and irritated to be fair. 'I wouldn't have done all this but for his boastin' of some legacy he thought he had comin' his way.'

'Ah.' Holly paused, waiting until he was sure he had Albert's attention before going on. 'I think I can throw some light upon that. As a rule, I'd never breach client confidence but this is all in the family, so to speak. He gave Albert a sly wink. 'Niamh's father had a word about it only the other day. Your son-in-law has some mad idea that McDiarmit ran off with his inheritance. He was quite abusive, threatening even.'

'Threatening? That doesn't sound like our Judd.'

'Good old Albert. Loyal to the last, eh?' Hollis enjoyed watching Albert squirm, as he painted the worst possible portrait of Judd's behaviour. 'Oh, there was some mix-up over a few scrapings of gold – probably not worth more than twenty pounds or so on the open market today. All hearsay – nothing on paper. I told my father-in-law to go home and forget it. Burden's clutching at straws.'

'All the same, I can see why Judd's put out. He had such high hopes, promisin' me the money for the partnership, then findin' he hasn't a legacy, after all. I just hope he won't try to borrow the money elsewhere.'

'Keep an ear to the ground, shall I?' Hollis spoke softly, taking care not to sound too eager. 'Let you know if I hear he's applying for any substantial loans?'

'Good lord, no! He's my Sukie's husband – I don't want you spyin' on him!' Finally irritated beyond endurance, Albert stood up, ready to leave. 'It's all right – I can show meself out. And as for the other matter, let me give it some thought. Mebbe I'll see a way to get round it without takin' the money out.'

'You do that, Albert,' Hollis called after his retreating back. 'And I'd look for another man to take up the partnership, if I were you.'

Also in August, Niamh and Hollis moved into the house at Brighton, bringing their tensions with them, in spite of Elinor's rosy predictions that their troubles would be over as soon as they were established in their own home.

Niamh was aware of a little man, fast becoming her shadow,

who seemed to appear as if by magic whenever she went to town. He followed her to the hospital and waited until she was ready to go home. She didn't speak to Hollis about it, believing the man to be a bodyguard, employed to protect her on the long journeys to and from home.

Really she didn't give him much thought, far more concerned with securing reliable help for their new home. Good household servants weren't easy to come by at any time, let alone in the seaside suburb of Brighton, away from the amenities of the city. Girls were more attracted to working in factories which gave them set hours and extra time to call their own. Niamh engaged only one, a plump Irishwoman named Brigid McGinty; a woman well past her middle years and who suffered from bad legs. Niamh got used to her standard excuse: 'Oh, I'd love to help you, madam, if it weren't for me poor auld legs . . .'

In compensation, Brigid was an excellent cook, bringing to the new household a wealth of recipes handed down from her mother who used to cater for one of the best families in Ireland – or so she never tired of saying. In spite of Holly's insistence that it was demeaning for his wife to do her own housework, Niamh preferred to attack the house while he was away, relishing the task of caring for her own home. He tackled her about it again one morning over the breakfast-table.

'You're looking tired, Niamh – peaked,' he said. 'And you do far too much. Don't you think it's time you gave up that work at The Briarley? Surely they don't expect you to travel from here to the outskirts of Melbourne two or three times a week?'

'But I like to do it, Holly,' she insisted. 'And it's no hardship, really. I want to honour my commitment as long as I can. We've formed a Sub-committee of Friends of the Hospital now and as the mothers gain confidence and can do more for themselves, I shall be able to do less. The nurses depend on us now, to take over the nurturing and motherly duties they don't have time for.'

'Sister Kearney doesn't like it. Mother said—'

'Too bad. Sister Kearney's had everything her own way long enough.'

171

'Really, Niamh, sometimes you take too much on yourself. No one expected you to be so – so aggressive about this. Mother feels you're doing it just to spite her, and to make her own ladies feel guilty and inadequate for not doing more.'

'That's nonsense. We're not doing this for personal glory but for the sake of the children. They need more than just money, Holly. They need practical help.'

'And I need you here.' His voice rose as he grew more petulant. 'This is nothing but a thwarted maternal instinct. You'll soon get over it when we have a child of our own.'

Niamh ran her hand over her stomach which remained stubbornly flat. She wasn't sure whether to be relieved or disappointed when her courses arrived on time, informing her nothing momentous had taken place on that autumn afternoon. No child had been planted in her womb by either her husband or Judd. Holly was right about one thing, though – she was longing for motherhood; a longing which only intensified when she heard Sukie was expecting a baby, making her feel her own deficiency still more.

Having proved himself as a husband, Hollis approached her maybe once or twice a week. But since that first time when he had taken her after her visit to Brighton, his interest in sex had waned. She had hoped to compensate for her guilt by throwing herself wholeheartedly into a relationship with her husband, but this wasn't to be. His lovemaking soon fell into a boring, established routine and he was shocked when Niamh tried to steer him towards more innovative sex, coaching him by saying what pleased her.

In the wake of Judd who had gone to the trouble of showing her how to achieve the pinnacle of her own sexual desires, her husband was a tame and colourless lover, sadly lacking in expertise.

'And don't sulk over the stupid hospital,' Holly said, misinterpreting her thoughtful expression. 'Go there all day, every day, if you want to. Wear yourself out, then. I should care.'

Janet had been ill for weeks. She could take little food and was becoming thin, her complexion sallow. At first Tully thought it must be because she was pining for Niamh, but when she rose

172

from the kitchen table for the third time that week, leaving her half-eaten supper to rush outside, he set down his knife and fork, unable to continue eating his own meal. He stared at Gladys who stared back as they listened to the pitiful sounds of Janet voiding the contents of her stomach within yards of the back door. Gladys was first to look away. She shrugged and carried on eating, unwilling to waste her sympathy on a woman she didn't like.

'I seen it before,' she said, almost relishing the words as she aired her small amount of medical knowledge. 'Could be a growth inside her – a malignant tumour. Well, she's askin' for it, isn't she? Sour as a green apple, full o' bile.'

'Her nature has nothing to do with it, Gladys, unless it's the pain that makes her bad-tempered. Illness can strike the most sunny-natured of people.'

'If you say so,' Gladys smiled.

'Janet's never suffered a day's illness in her life – not until now.'

'Ah, but she's gettin' on a bit, isn't she?' Gladys never lost an opportunity to remind him that Janet was older. 'The closer they get to fifty the worse it becomes.'

'What does?'

Gladys leaned forward, dropping her voice confidentially. 'The change of life,' she nodded. 'Takes people different ways. Can be the death o' some women.'

Tully sighed. While he and Janet had spent more years living separately than as man and wife, he was a creature of habit and found it hard to imagine his life without her. 'Maybe I ought to get her to see a doctor.'

'Whatever for? If it's a tumour, it's too late already – nothin' no doctor can do. An' if it isn't . . .' She shrugged again. 'Well, it's just a natural part of agein',' far as a woman's concerned.'

But Tully decided to speak to the doctor, anyway, unwilling to dismiss his wife's illness so casually.

Brighton was still a distant suburb for most people and Niamh didn't have many visitors at The Hollies – named not because the gardens were full of holly trees but as a humorous pun on Hollis's name. The only friend who came regularly was Elinor and on this particular morning she was in the garden, admiring Niamh's fountain which had just been installed as the centrepiece of the parterre. It was a sculpture in bronze representing a larger-than-life-sized heron, standing beside a small waterfall. Niamh loved it and was pleased she had held out for her parterre.

'You are clever, Niamh,' Ellie said, considering the little waterfall, cascading over the stones. 'I'd never have thought of it – and a heron as well, so lifelike I'm almost waiting for it to take to the air. It must have been made by an artist. Where did you get it?'

'It came from Smith's,' Niamh said, unwilling to attribute the heron entirely to Judd. She remembered the day it arrived and the young man called Tom who delivered it, along with the wrought iron for the stairs.

'Best piece o' work I seen in my life,' he said, scratching his head. 'An' I said so at the time – told Judd he oughta come an' see it installed for himself. Says he's too busy with the other items for the big exhibition. Won't take no payment, neither – says you can count it in wi' the cost o' the work on the stairs.' This last remark was punctuated with a sniff. Tom made it clear that he thought the Maitlands more than capable of paying for everything twice over and saw no reason to give them something for nothing.

Niamh was overcome and didn't know what to say. She knew the heron had been made with particular care and Judd intended it as a present, a parting gift.

'Made by Sukie's husband, probably.' Ellie appraised the metal figure, head on one side. 'The dark and brooding Burden – a little bit like that bird. Oh, I know Sukie's besotted but he's far too intense for my taste. I like my men a bit older, too – more mature.' She glanced at Niamh with a flash of mischief. 'Particularly if they have sandy, red hair. How is your wickedly attractive father, by the way?'

'Fine. I wish I could say the same for my mother, though. She s not at all well, these days.'

But Elinor had little interest in Janet, preferring to talk about Tully instead. 'Does he come here often, my reynard? My fox with the beautiful red and white mane?'

'Don't be daft, Ellie,' Niamh giggled. 'And don't go entertaining romantic notions about my Pa. He's charming to

174

everyone, it's his livelihood, his stock in trade. He has more blarney than any Irishman I've ever known.'

'Oh, you're just saying that to put me off. I loved dancing with him and I'm sure he liked *me*. Why don't I remember meeting him when we were small?'

'Because you didn't. He was always so busy at work – at the Silver Star. Uncle Harley always sent the coach for me, if you remember. I used to pretend I was a great queen or a princess, sitting up on the cushions all by myself. It was the most wonderful treat.'

But Elinor's mind was still running on Tully. 'Such a lovely man. If he were mine I'd be in a lather of jealousy day and night. All that controlled sexuality . . .'

Sexuality was the last thing Niamh wanted to discuss, particularly in relation to her father. 'You're wrong about Pa, you know. He talks a good tale but he's no ladies' man if that's what you think. And I love him far too much to let him fall into your grasping little claws.'

'Spoilsport, Niamh! Always so serious, so—'

'I mean it, Ellie. It isn't a joke. My Pa has enough on his plate without trouble from you. Find some other man to pick on – someone who can take it. He can't.'

'All right, all right,' Ellie said with bad grace. 'You don't have to labour the point.'

Chapter Thirteen

Judd was at his wits' end, having received yet another refusal from a bank, but he didn't discuss it with Sukie until they were alone and in bed.

'I can't understand it,' he said. 'I've been to every reputable institution in town but the answer's always the same. They didn't even bother to give me an explanation this time. And I used to think I belonged. I thought I was beginning to count for something in this town.'

'You are! You know you are.'

'A month ago I'd have said so, too. But this blank wall is getting me down. It's as if someone's working against me, pulling strings behind the scenes.'

'Now you *are* imagining things.'

'Am I?'

'Yes. Pa's reputation is unblemished. And as my husband and a prospective partner in his business, so's yours.'

'Oh Sukie.' Judd kissed her gently. 'I wish – but I'm afraid that isn't the case at all.'

'Then let me speak to Pa in the morning – get him to put in a good word for you.'

'No, Sukie. He made it clear from the outset, he didn't want me to borrow. If I take out a loan, it must be without any guarantees from him. I have to do it alone.'

'But he's changed his ideas since you spoke to him last. Even borrowed money himself to invest in—'

'And regretted it ever since. Paying it off leaves him short, especially as I haven't been able to come through with the money as promised. No, Sukie. This is a matter of my

176

self-esteem – my pride, if you like. I have to do this for myself.'

But in spite of his pleas and impassioned promises, the doors of the finance houses continued to close in his face.

In an attempt to compensate Albert for the lack of funds he threw himself into the task of preparing a special display for the International Exhibition. He made bird and animal figures in cast iron, life-sized emus and kangaroos, possums and wombats emerging from logs. If he had no money to bring to the partnership, at least he could offer the best of his craft. But, in spite of his efforts, Albert was somehow distant and withdrawn. Sukie spoke to him about his attitude one morning when they were alone in the office and Judd supervising the work in the yard.

'It's not like you to be so unappreciative, Pa. Judd has done all this extra work on top of the regular business of the day and not a murmur of thanks from you. What's come over you these days? I thought you were friends.'

Albert looked up at his daughter, blooming in her fourth month of pregnancy, glowing with health now the baby had begun to show. She still insisted on coming to work in the office and he was grateful, although he knew somebody else would have to be trained to take over, and soon.

'I don't know, Sukie. But sometimes I wonder if Judd has been quite honest with us about his past. No house of finance will entertain him – oh yes, I know all about that,' he said in answer to Sukie's frown. 'How not? When he's applied to every reputable institution in town and one or two others besides.'

'You know why, Pa. They've already told him. He has no background, no references other than ourselves and he doesn't own his own home.'

Albert sighed, realising for the first time how much his daughter must share her husband's dilemma. 'That's their excuse but I can't help thinking there must be more to it.'

'What?' Sukie thrust her face forward, blinking rapidly as she tried to read his expression. 'What?'

'Now don't get yourself in a state, girl. It's not good for the child.'

'Tell me, then. Just tell me what you heard.'

'Bit o' loose talk – nothin' for you to worry about.' Albert wriggled in his seat, wishing he'd kept his mouth shut as Sukie

177

stood over him, eyes fluttering out of control. 'Sit down then and I'll tell you,' he said as Sukie sank back in her chair. 'Came out on the *Castle Belmont* – right? Seems he travelled with some woman for most of the voyage – very chummy – moved into her cabin from steerage. But as soon as the *Belmont* came into port, he left her standin' beside her luggage on the wharf.'

'Oh Pa, it must be a lie. How could you let yourself be influenced by such malicious gossip!' Sukie's heart sank as she heard this, remembering the lies she herself had invented to tell Niamh. Lies which tipped the balance, encouraging her friend to go ahead and marry Hollis rather than cause a scandal by throwing him over for Judd. Now she had the feeling that fate was mocking her, showing her there was some truth in the lies she'd invented. All the same, she defended him.

'And you took all this at face value – the word of gossips and scandalmongers? Giving my husband no chance to explain himself?'

'Well, it isn't my place to ask.'

'Whose is it, then – mine?'

'No. No!'

'But you let it prey on your mind enough to hold it against him. These are just rumours, Pa,' she said stoutly, tossing her head. 'Nothing but rumours put about by people jealous of Judd's talent – of his craft. We won't speak of this again because I'm going to put it from my mind. And I strongly suggest you do the same.' She found she was breathing deeply and shaking after making this speech. 'And now, I think I'll go home. I don't feel very well.'

'Oh, Sukie!'

But she was already at the door. And she wasn't lying, she *did* feel sick. And although she charged her father to set aside the rumours, she found it impossible to do so herself. Time and again her doubts returned to torment her, quiet, insidious, like whispers inside her head, reminding her she was only a second choice, a substitute wife. It tarnished her happiness and took away her joy. Worse, she couldn't afford the luxury of thrashing it out with Judd. He slept badly himself, having his own dragons to fight.

She put up with these nagging doubts for a fortnight before

she made up her mind to see Niamh. Niamh was the only other person who knew her husband so well. She wasn't sure whether she would have courage enough to own up to the lies she had told before, or whether Niamh would understand and forgive her if she did. She was ashamed of both the lies and the suspicions she had once entertained. Her husband spent every waking moment at the foundry and had neither the time nor the energy to conduct an affair. She decided not to cloud the issue by mentioning the matter of Judd's inheritance and the connection with Tully.

She set off early from Richmond, taking a train to the end of the line at Brighton Beach. There she hired a cab to take her the last mile or so to The Hollies. When she arrived, Niamh insisted on paying the fare while Sukie peered around, getting her bearings, making sense of the blurred shapes which later she identified as plants and trees.

'But Niamh, it's lovely,' she said, sniffing the spring growth and the heady scent of the wattle newly in bloom. 'Only an hour out of town yet we might be in the depths of the country. And the air is making me dizzy, it's so pure.'

'Welcome to The Hollies!' Niamh embraced her friend and led her towards the house, tucking her hand in her arm. 'Oh Sukie, it's so good to see you increasing and blooming like a rose. Motherhood suits you. But take care you don't do too much. I see dark circles beneath your eyes.'

'Only because I haven't been sleeping so well.' Sukie took a deep breath, thinking it was too early to plunge into the real reason behind her visit. 'So much excitement with the Exhibition only a week away . . .'

'Why yes. I'm surprised Albert can spare you.'

'I didn't ask him,' Sukie said, unsmiling. 'I just told him I was going out for the day.'

Niamh's smile also faded as she waited to hear more. She sensed there was trouble and it saddened her. It wasn't like Sukie to be at odds with her father.

'Oh Niamh, you do have your fountain, after all!' Hearing the sound of running water, Sukie turned towards the little circular garden where she could just make out the shape of the rocks surmounted by a large bird. 'You always said you were going to have a fountain and a parterre.'

179

'Let's go inside now. We can look at the garden later on.' Niamh shivered in the chill of the damp spring morning, dragging Sukie away. 'I came out without a shawl. First, I want to show you all over the house and then we'll have tea and muffins by the fire.'

Sukie smiled, allowing herself to be steered towards the back door.

'Now then, Sukie, what's bothering you?' Niamh said later when they had completed the tour of the house and were comfortably seated, drinking tea in Niamh's little parlour before an open fire. 'I'd like to think you came to see me in my new house but I have a feeling there's something more.'

'Is it so obvious?' Sukie sat back and sighed. 'I feel like a traitor coming to ask you at all. You won't know any more than I do.'

'Try me.'

'It's – well, it's about Judd.'

Niamh's cup clattered in her saucer as her hand shook. *The idiot! The crass, self-indulgent fool! He's gone and told her!* This was her first thought, the words screaming in her mind. Then she dismissed them as foolish. Would Sukie be sitting there smiling and asking her for advice, if that were so? She forced herself to remain calm as she poured two second cups of tea and waited to hear more. The atmosphere in the room was heavy with expectancy as Sukie gathered her thoughts, sipping her tea.

'Lovely,' she said. 'You always did make a good cup of tea, Niamh.'

'I didn't make it, Brigid did,' Niamh snapped, anxiety making her sharp. 'Now, what's all this about Judd?'

Sukie chose her words carefully. 'I'm not sure. Niamh, remember – before you were married – when Judd used to spend so much time at the Silver Star?'

'Yes?' Niamh held her breath.

'Did he ever talk to you of his past?'

'His past?' echoed Niamh, not quite sighing with relief. 'He told me about his mother, that's all.'

'Because . . .' Sukie hesitated and then the words came out in a rush. 'No one will lend him any money and Pa seems to think there's a sinister reason behind it. And I – I feel like a traitor, talking about my husband behind his back.'

180

'Sukie, we're friends.'

'So, I just wondered,' Sukie said lamely, 'if he ever let anything drop – about his past?'

'I'm sure you know more than I do,' Niamh said slowly, thinking. 'You're the one who told me about the girls waiting for him outside the foundry – remember?'

'That was a lie,' Sukie confessed, eyes fluttering.

Niamh said nothing for a moment, absorbing this news. When she spoke, she sounded tired. 'Oh Sukie, why?'

'Can't you guess?' Sukie asked, not without difficulty. 'I'm sorry, Niamh. But you seemed to have everything while I had nothing – and all I ever wanted was Judd. And you have to admit I was right. Here you are with this beautiful house and a husband who loves you . . .'

'And no child,' Niamh said, hardly able to speak as she stared at Sukie's expanding waistline. For a split second, she was so angry, she wanted to scream and kick Sukie in the abdomen, making her lose the child. But she took a deep breath, closed her eyes, and the moment passed. 'Sukie, I don't know why you want to tell me all this just now. It can't do either of us any good.'

'I'm so sorry, Niamh.'

Niamh looked at her, irritated by her friend's anxiously fluttering eyes and thinking of shocking her with a confession of her own. She decided against it. Whatever Sukie had done in the past, it wouldn't help anyone if she were to destroy the girl's happiness now.

'Forget it, Sukie,' she said at last. 'We can't put back the clock and change it all now. Look forward to the future and don't go digging up the past. You're Judd's wife now and remember you're the one who's bearing his child. You have so much more than they have already – the women he loved before.' Even to her own ears, the words sounded trite and less than sincere. The truth was that she hated the thought of any other woman bearing Judd's child.

'Sometimes, I feel as if there's a cloud of misfortune waiting to overtake us all. I feel so afraid.'

'It's nerves, Sukie. Just nerves.' Niamh put down her tea and took her friend's hands in her own, finding them chilled in spite of the warmth of the room.

181

'But most of all, I'm afraid the baby will be born half-blind. Oh, Niamh, what shall I do if the baby is born with eyes like mine?'

'Sukie, you mustn't think about that.'

'But I want my baby whole and perfect in every way.'

'I'm sure that's what we all hope for, Sukie.'

Later, Niamh drove her friend to the station in her own trap, embraced her and promised to see her again before long. Sukie left, cheered and in far better spirits than when she came. Her shadows were left with Niamh. Smiling and waving her handkerchief at the departing train, Niamh knew it would always be so but the burden of guilt was hard to bear. She was used to it now – that painful lurch of the heart when somebody spoke of Judd, reminding her. Having tasted his lovemaking she longed to lie in his arms again, to feel the touch of his lips on her body and breathe that dizzying smell of burnt metal, so peculiarly his own. She didn't care that he was a faithless husband or that the rumours were probably true. He'd given her a taste of fulfilment and like a flower, drooping and parched for the want of water, she could only wait, longing for more.

Sukie awoke to a typical October morning. The chill of winter had gone, giving way to the indeterminate weather of spring, the sun warming the air but hiding behind low clouds which left the skies grey and overcast. She was up at first light, shaking her husband awake.

The Burdens and Albert had dined late the night before, the menfolk returning weary but satisfied, having put the finishing touches to the exhibit representing Smith's Foundry and leaving it in place overnight.

'One thing they're not goin' to see,' Albert had wagged his head, speaking with his mouth full, exhausted enough to be irritable, 'an' that's Albert Smith paradin' alongside his workers behind an Eight-Hour Banner.'

'Oh, Pa!' Sukie sat back from her own meal, heaving a sigh. 'We've been over all this before.' It had taken all her powers of persuasion to prevent him from pulling out of the exhibition, when he heard the unionists meant to form a procession behind the flag and march to the Exhibition Buildings, making use of the occasion to promote their cause. 'For most people the eight-hour day is already a fact of life. It will come to us too, eventually, whether you kick against it or not.'

'That's as may be. But I don't have to give it my stamp of approval by joining the march. Isn't it enough that I've given the men the day off?'

Sukie laughed. 'You've given them nothing, Pa. It's been declared a Public Holiday – you had no choice.'

'More's the pity. In my father's day it was the employers who set the hours an' the men who were obliged to keep 'em, take it or leave it. An' if I can put in a ten-hour day at my age, why shouldn't they?'

Sukie shook her head, exasperated. 'Because it's *your* business, Pa. You can't expect the men to feel the same dedication as you do. Get down off your high horse for once and join us. All trades will be represented – shipwrights, bootmakers, printers, masons ... everybody you know. There'll be brass bands and as many as twenty-six Fire Brigades.'

'And monkeys on sticks, I'll be bound! I should be deafened, girl. Thanks, but no thanks. I'd rather get inside the buildings early an' be one of the first to welcome the Governor when he arrives.'

'Suit yourself, Pa. But I'm going to march. I shall be joining the others behind the flag.'

'Oh no, you won't.' Judd had watched the exchange in silence but now he stretched a hand across the table to cover her own. 'You're expecting a child, Sukie. What if you feel faint in the midst of the crowd?'

'Listen to him, daughter. He's talking sense.'

'But Pa, it's the procession of the century and you're saying I can't be there!'

'We are united in this.' Albert raised his eyebrows at Judd who nodded assent. 'I'd rather see you miss a bit of the rah! rah! than take any risks.'

Sukie continued to grumble but was persuaded to go into the city early and wait inside the exhibition with Albert, leaving her husband to march with their men. Fortunately, wearing wide skirts and a generous cloak, she looked merely bonny and plump. A month or two more and she would be too obviously pregnant to appear in public at all.

While Albert was occupied with their exhibit before the

arrival of the official party and the crowds, she took the opportunity to look around in comfort, admiring the brightly-coloured murals which decorated the high ceilings of the new Exhibition Buildings and domes to let in the light.

It was a truly international gathering of merchandise. Cotton from Manchester, tin-plate from Birmingham and iron-work from Germany. The work was competent and impressive but, loyally, Sukie felt it lacked Judd's artistic flair. Against a background of French technique, he had developed a style uniquely his own. She passed on through the halls, looking at the latest gadgetry from America, the slab of Illawarra coal sent all the way from New South Wales, the portrait of Henry Parkes and then the other local exhibits, including a huge pyramid of Swallow and Ariell's biscuits alongside phials of Joseph Bosisto's famous eucalyptus oil. She had almost completed her circuit of the exhibits when the doors were flung open and trumpets blared announcing the arrival of the Marquis of Normanby, Governor of Victoria. The National Anthem was sung and three deafening cheers were raised for the absent Queen and Prince of Wales. Following this, a choir sang an Exhibition Cantata, the words of a local poet being set to the music of Sullivan. Then came the speeches during which most people shuffled, longing for them to come to an end.

As Sukie returned to their simulated forest with its life-sized emus, kangaroos and wombats – the Australian fauna Judd had created in iron – she realised they seemed oddly familiar and she was struck by a sense of déjà vu. Yes! A bird created in bronze rather than iron and which she had only glimpsed in passing with her failing, unreliable vision. How could that be when Judd had drawn what he wanted and carved them in wood before going to the forge to create them in iron? All of a sudden it came to her where she had seen it – a large waterbird, a heron or a crane, standing by a fountain in the middle of a small parterre.

She felt the blood drain from her face and she pressed a hand to her chest, suddenly giddy.

'Steady on, lass.' Her father caught her before she swooned, steering her to a chair. 'This is what I was afraid of. Sit here now an' recover yourself – I'll get you a glass of water.'

184

While her father was gone, she remembered everything. She knew exactly what was on the Maitlands' account, having prepared it herself. In her mind's eye she could still see it, set down in her own painstaking hand:

Eight panels of cast iron installed and fitted to the 'Renaissance' design.
Two matching sets of wrought iron for the stairs – 'Old English Brambles and Ivy'.

No mention of a bird cast in iron or bronze. Was she making too much of this? If she questioned him, Judd would shrug and say it was a housewarming present from all of them. But Sukie knew exactly what that bird represented. It was an expensive gift from her husband to the woman he truly loved.

Involved in establishing a home and keeping pace with her work at The Briarley Hospital, it was November before Niamh found time to visit her parents at the Silver Star.

The weather that day had been warm and balmy with little breeze, heralding the summer to come. She had warned Hollis not to expect her home early as she wanted to look in on her parents before heading back to Brighton. Intuitively, she had an idea that something was wrong.

Although she didn't set out to spy on Gladys, some instinct made her pause in the doorway to watch her before going in. The woman was standing behind the bar looking tidy and confident, much more the hostess than the kitchen maid these days, making the most of the opportunity to establish herself while Janet was sick. But what shocked Niamh the most was that Glady was wearing her mother's clothes.

'There's lovely you look,' the Welshwoman greeted her, sharp eyes measuring the cost of Niamh's own wardrobe. 'And every inch the lady, these days. Get you in here, Tully McDiarmit!' she yelled in the direction of the kitchen. 'There's a stranger come to visit us. Wanna see who it is?'

Niamh's heart sank as soon as she saw her father. He looked older than she'd ever seen him, his expression pinched with anxiety.

'Keep your voice down, woman,' he snapped at Gladys. 'My wife is trying to sleep.' But his face lit up at once when he saw

185

who it was. Niamh ran into his arms to embrace him, hugging him close. He swept her off her feet, swinging her round like the old days and making her laugh.

'God'n you weigh nothin' at all, girl,' he said, setting her down again. 'Lookin' tired, too. Lost a bit of your bloom. Sure you're not doin' too much?'

'I could say the same of you, Pa.' She touched the new lines of strain she saw at his mouth. He looked rumpled and dishevelled, his clothes in need of a wash; no longer the well-groomed host in the tailored waistcoat and crisp white shirt that her mother provided. She must be sick indeed to allow him to go about looking so shabby. 'How is she, then? How's Mama?'

'Ah, not so well.' His smile faded. 'Not well at all. This week she's taken to her bed an' the cramps in her stomach are worse. Says the pain never stops now and she can't hold down solid food.'

'What does the doctor say?'

'Not a lot.' He paused, wondering how much to tell her. 'Ah, ye may as well know, Niamh – it's hopeless. Only a question of time. But Gladys has been marvellous – taken over everything here.'

'Including my mother's clothes,' Niamh said softly, causing Tully to give her a sharp look. Out of the corner of her eye she could see Gladys, straining her ears to hear what was said. 'Let's go into the kitchen – we can be private there.'

'Dunno what I'd do without Gladys – she's been a tower of strength,' Tully said, anxious to avert his daughter's criticism. Niamh made a strong pot of tea and set it between them while she collected the cups.

'You should've told me, Pa. Sent for me before.'

'You've enough to do, girl, with a brand-new home and your work at the hospital. An' what could you do that's not being done already?'

'She's my mother, isn't she? I ought to be here.'

'But darlin', there's really no need. Gladys takes care of everything.'

'Gladys! I'm sick of hearing what a saint she is. Didn't do much for poor Sally, did she?'

'Sally was old, darlin', it was her time.'

'Maybe.' Niamh folded her arms. 'And when did you give her permission to wear Mama's clothes?'

'Does she?' Tully blinked at her, looking bemused.

'There seems a lot going on that you don't know, Pa.'

'Now look here, girl. You don't come near us for weeks an' now you *are* here, all you can do is find fault.'

'Right. I'll come back home for a while and help you.'

'You don't have to do that.'

'But I want to, Pa. If my mother's sick, I should be the one to care for her.'

'Leavin' your husband to forage for himself?'

'Not for long.'

'I wouldn't hear of it, darlin'. You're a married woman an' you can't go upsettin' your husband, not for us. We'll manage. Gladys says—'

'Gladys has you wound round her little finger. She can't wait for my mother to die, so that she can step into her shoes right away.'

'I can handle that one.'

'Exactly – that's what I'm afraid of.'

'Good lord, Niamh, what sort of a fool d'ye take me for? D'ye think I'd be carryin' on with Gladys, with your mother lyin' in agony over our heads?'

'No, of course not.' Niamh blushed because she had been thinking just that. 'But Mama's never liked Gladys and I don't think she should be nursed by a woman she hates.'

'It shall be as you wish.' Tully nodded slowly. 'It goes without sayin' I'll be delighted to have you home again – a load off my mind.'

'That's settled then. I'll send Brigid to her sister until after Christmas and close up the house.'

'What about Holly?'

'Don't lose any sleep over *him*. He spends as much time at his mother's house as at home, these days.'

'Does he now?' Tully gave his daughter a long look which she ignored, pushing her teacup away and standing up.

'I'll go up and see Mama now.'

Outside Janet's door she hesitated, half-afraid she would find her lying in a dirty, unmade bed. Her fears were unfounded. Inside, although the room smelled of strong

187

disinfectant which had been used to cover the smell of vomit and other bodily functions, her mother's bed was clean and recently made. Janet lay there flat on her back, her eyes closed and her arms at her sides. She looked like an old woman, her hair almost white, her skin jaundiced and slack, halfway to being a corpse already. Even as Niamh watched, she gasped and her face contorted with pain as she curled into a foetal position, trying to fight it. When the spasm left her, Niamh approached the bed, and reached out to take her mother's hand which felt abnormally hot.

'It's all right, Mama,' she whispered. 'It's Niamh. I'm here to take care of you now.'

'Don't let her – give me any more!' Janet gasped, clinging to Niamh's hands. 'She's killing me – killing me with that filthy brew.'

'You must have your medicine,' Niamh said, brushing a damp strand of hair away from her mother's face. 'It will ease the pain.'

But Janet showed no sign of recognising her daughter. She just groaned and turned her face to the wall.

Niamh sent her husband home to his mother and moved back to the Silver Star. But it was to no avail. Less than a week after she did so, Janet died.

Chapter Fourteen

Sukie looked up from her work and frowned at the sound of voices engaged in conversation and footsteps approaching the office. Heavily pregnant now, she was finding it hard to concentrate on the accounts and she didn't want any interruptions today. Albert had been showing someone around the foundry and was now bringing his visitor to the office, expecting her to make tea. The day was unusually warm, taking everyone by surprise so early in summer and Sukie felt heavy and lethargic, in no mood to deal with new people today.

The light from outside was momentarily blocked as Albert ushered a shambling overweight figure before him into the room. The man was unsuitably clothed for the weather, dressed in thick, dark-coloured European clothes. He, too, was feeling the heat, sweating profusely and mopping his face with a large red silk handkerchief. Caught unawares by the pungency of the man's body odours, Sukie's eyes watered and she coughed; the smell of garlic seemed to be coming not just from his breath but his very pores.

'Sukie – oh, Sukie love,' Albert said, 'I'd like you to meet Mr – M'sieur Jean-Louis' (he pronounced it John Lewis) 'de Vesinet.'

'Oh?' Sukie said, on guard at once, recognising that syrupy, ingratiating note in her father's voice.

'Mrs Burden – my daughter,' Albert completed the introductions. 'Takes care of the books and the office.'

'Madame!' de Vesinet bent over her hand and Sukie flinched, hoping he wouldn't kiss it. 'But surely a place of business, a foundry, is no place for so lovely a lady, particularly

189

one who is *enceinte*.' His heavily accented English was good but to Sukie it sounded like the hiss of a snake. 'You should be at home, madame, preparing for the birth of your child.'

'I am perfectly well, m'sieur.' She knew she was being less than gracious. 'And I'll make myself useful here just as long as I can.'

'But in future, there will be no need . . .' The man gave a typical Gallic shrug.

'That's right, Sukie love.' Albert was smiling, not at all like himself. 'You can relax – put your feet up, when Jean-Louis takes over the office.'

'And why should he do that?'

'Your father and I have just signed a deed of partnership, madame.' The Frenchman was clearly irritated at having to explain himself to a woman.

'A partnership? Papa, have you gone mad?' Sukie heard her voice rising in hysteria, unable to prevent it. So it had come to this; this was the reason for those huddled conferences at the Exhibition Buildings and her father's secretive behaviour.

'No. Come to my senses, more like.' Albert rocked on his heels, truculent in the face of her criticism. 'If you can't beat 'em, join 'em, isn't that what they say?' He was talking in clichés as he always did when he was nervous. 'Two birds with one stone, eh? Taking on a new partner and disposing of competition at the same time.'

'But you offered the partnership to Judd!'

'And he couldn't take it up, could he? Dammit, girl, I waited longer than I'd have waited for any other man, and now it's too late. I must do what's best for the firm.'

'And to hell with everyone else – including me.'

'No, no. It's you I'm thinkin' of, Sukie love.'

'Oh, is it? Papa, how could you do this to us?'

'Joining forces with Jean-Louis will make the business secure.'

'Madame, listen to me.' The Frenchman added his voice to the argument, forcing Sukie to hear what he had to say. 'Your papa has made the position clear. Your 'usband, he is the craftsman, yes? Not so much a man of business . . .'

'You don't know anything about it!'

190

Jean-Louis gave yet another Gallic shrug. 'Better to let him continue with the practical work of the foundry, leaving matters of money to your papa and me.'

'If he wants to continue working for you, at all.' Sukie was close to tears and, as always when she was anxious, her eyelids fluttered, the eyes rolling beneath them, out of control. 'We might even set up in opposition to you ourselves.'

'Now, now, Sukie, I know you're upset but let's not do anythin' hasty, love.' Albert made a placating gesture with his hands. 'When you calm down you'll see I've acted for the best – for all of us. Sukie, stop!' He almost stumbled as she pushed past him rudely, grabbing her straw hat from its peg behind the door. 'Wh-where are you going now? Why don't we all sit down and have a nice cup of—'

'Tea?' she said through gritted teeth. 'If you want tea, Pa, you can make it yourself. I'm going home.'

'Women!' Albert smiled weakly, motioning the Frenchman to sit down. The man did so, mopping his face again, looking bemused. It was outside his experience to see a girl defying her father so blatantly. 'Don't you worry about our Sukie. Give her an hour or so to get used to the idea an' she'll come around.'

Gladys was peeved. A week had passed since Janet's funeral and Niamh stayed on to work at the Silver Star, showing no inclination to go back home. She had hoped to have Tully to herself at this time, while he would be at his most vulnerable, newly bereaved. So she did her best to conceal her delight when Tully captured his daughter in the kitchen and suggested it was time for her to go home.

'I don't want you to think I'm ungrateful, darlin', but you're a married woman. You have a duty to your husband, a life of your own.'

'Are you throwing me out, Pa?' Niamh grinned.

'No no, darlin', perish the thought.' Tully was mortified that she should mistake his intentions. 'But Gladys an' me can do all right on our own now.'

'Is it your intention to marry Gladys, Pa?'

Even Gladys paused in the midst of her washing-up, shocked at the bluntness of the question.

191

Tully looked from Niamh to Gladys and back again, frowning. 'Good heavens, no! With your mother scarce cold in her grave? What are you thinking of, girl?'

'Fine. That's just what I thought. So I'd better stay.'

'I don't understand.'

Niamh folded her arms, shaking her head. 'For a middle-aged man, Pa, you're surprisingly innocent. If you live here alone with Gladys, people will talk. Then you'll be forced to make a decision; to marry her or to send her away.'

Gladys gasped.

'Oh, I see.' Tully frowned, scratching his chin. 'I never thought.'

'I know. So it's lucky I'm here to do the thinking for you.' Niamh giggled, including Gladys in her smile. 'I'll have to stay until you make up your mind.'

Gladys poured hot water into the sink and rattled the pots in the suds. Niamh knew it was to hide the sound of her grinding teeth.

Niamh was wiping the bar the following day when she looked up, surprised to see Ellie standing in the doorway, removing her gloves and taking stock of the room. Hovering behind her was an escort, shuffling from one foot to another and looking uncomfortable, unable to understand why Elinor Maitland wished to patronise such a second-rate bar.

'Ellie!' Niamh leaned over the bar to kiss her friend on both cheeks. 'What are you doing here?'

'I wanted to see you,' Ellie said. 'And to find out when, if ever, you're coming home.'

'Did Holly send you?' Niamh was suddenly thoughtful.

'No. I thought of coming to see you all by myself.' She glanced around, faintly amused yet at the same time enchanted by the old-fashioned mirrors, the potted ferns, the solid brass spittoons which had been polished until they gleamed like gold, the sawdust on the floor and the general quaintness of her surroundings. 'Cosy,' she pronounced at last, nodding her approval. 'Why didn't I come here before?'

'How's Holly?' Niamh felt a pang of guilt for her neglected husband. 'Has he been asking for me?'

'Not that you'd notice,' Ellie said. 'Too busy trying to keep in with that slippery Horace Ironsides. You haven't seen him then?'

'Not since Mama's funeral,' Niamh said with a significant glance at Elinor's escort. She didn't want to discuss such a private matter as the state of her marriage before an unsympathetic audience.

'You can go now, Peter.' Elinor waved a hand, dismissing him. 'Thank you for bringing me. I'll be all right now.'

'Oh Elinor, I hardly think . . .' he began.

'That's your trouble, sweetie,' Elinor kissed the air in his direction. 'I don't think you know how to.'

'I was about to say I don't think it proper to leave you here all alone.'

'Well, I'm not alone, am I?' she said, beginning to lose patience. 'There's a room full of people. On your way now, Pete, there's a good boy.'

'But Elinor . . .'

'If you think this is a den of iniquity, it's not. You do know who this lady is, don't you?' She nodded towards Niamh.

'I – um –' the young man looked at Niamh and then at the ceiling, like a schoolboy caught without the answer to a difficult question.

'She's Niamh Maitland,' Ellie answered for him. 'Hollis's wife.'

'Oh.' His expression cleared immediately. 'Oh, that's all right then. Well, if you're sure . . . The chaps did say something about a fisticuffs at the Haymarket.'

'Then go and enjoy your fisticuffs, Peter dear. I'll see you next week.'

Peter smiled, raised his hat and left almost at a run, happy to be dismissed. Elinor shook her head, watching him go.

'That's the last we'll see of *him*,' she grinned at Niamh. 'He'd much rather be out with his chaps than with me. But his mother is friendly with mine, and they have fond hopes – you know how it is.'

'And are the fond hopes likely to . . .?' Niamh raised her eyebrows, waiting for Ellie to answer.

'Good God, no!' Ellie gave her familiar throaty laugh. 'What sort of a fool d'you take me for? When I marry, I want a husband. Not a grown-up child.' She stopped smiling and

193

changed the subject. 'How are you, Niamh? Sorry to hear about your mother.'

'Oh, I'm all right,' Niamh said listlessly. 'It's Papa I'm worried about. That's why I'm staying on.'

'Ah. Not because you're leaving Hollis, then?'

'No! Why – is that what everyone thinks?'

Ellie shrugged. 'It's nearly Christmas, after all. And you showing no sign of coming home. I thought I'd better visit and see how the land lies.'

In whispered tones, Niamh gave Elinor a quick sketch of the situation at the Silver Star; her misgivings about Gladys and her fears that the woman wanted to take advantage of Tully in his bereaved state. From time to time she broke off to serve a few of the regulars, some of whom were staring at Ellie with frank admiration. At last she came to the end of her tale, concluding with a sigh, 'Poor Papa. He might have taken it better if he and Mama had been close. She didn't even leave him her share of the business – she willed it to me. I've tried to give it back to him but he won't take it. I think he feels guilty now for not loving her more.'

Elinor nodded her understanding and then she walked across to the piano which had remained silent and neglected since Janet fell ill. Slowly, she removed its dark red shawl, raised the lid and gave an experimental riff off the keys. It sounded in need of attention, slightly out of tune. 'You poor thing,' she said, seating herself on the stool and cracking her fingers, preparing to play. 'Your voice is about as rusty as mine.'

'Oh Ellie, no,' Niamh protested. 'We haven't had sing-songs here since . . . I really don't think—'

Ellie smiled and shook her head to reassure her as she started to play. Avoiding the rousing popular songs which most people expected from a pianist in a bar, she chose the light, classical music she played in the drawing room. It was like a blessing, a fitting requiem for Janet, soothing and enchanting her listeners as her fingers flew over the keys as easily as water cascades over a gentle fall. One by one, people stopped talking, engrossed in music familiar enough to bring tears of sentiment to their eyes. Niamh too was affected and Tully also came up from the storeroom to see who was coaxing such beautiful sounds from his old piano.

194

His expression softened at once when he recognised Ellie and he came up behind her on tiptoe, not wanting to break her concentration.

She sensed him there immediately and broke off in the midst of a concerto, turning to look up at him. 'I'm sorry,' she said. 'I didn't mean . . .'

'It's all right. I like it. Go on,' he whispered, reassuring her.

'Don't stop now, miss!' another man called out, anxious for her to continue. 'I've paid good money to go to the Town Hall and not heard playin' like yours. Lovely as a concert all on your own, you are.'

Elinor smiled and broke into a tinkling, joyful piece of music that must include all the notes of the piano, fingers flying up and down the scales. She finished with a flourish to shouts of 'More!' and 'Bravo!' as well as a round of applause.

'Oh Elinor,' Tully said, his smile highlighting the crow's feet around his eyes and making her heart ache. 'I can't tell you how lovely it is to have you here. Welcome. Welcome to the Silver Star.' He let her take both his hands in her own and leaned forward, meaning to give her a fatherly peck on the cheek. Having no intention of letting him get away with that, Elinor turned her face at the last moment so that his kiss met her lips instead. He stared at her, overcome by a mixture of emotions, eyes wide with surprise.

Lost in that blinding moment of self-discovery when two people realise, simultaneously, that they might be falling in love, they were conscious only of each other, oblivious to the outside world. Niamh was the only one to see Gladys, who had come from the kitchen attracted by the applause and was now standing in the doorway watching them, eyes glittering like dark coals in her sallow face. She couldn't know how murderous she looked, her mouth closed like a trap, the kitchen knife she had been wielding to cut up vegetables, still clenched in her hand.

Another unexpected visitor appeared on the doorstep the next day. She came with a trunk and several hat boxes, which her cab driver left in a pile just inside the door of the Silver Star.

'Maggi!' Tully recognised the diminutive form of his sister at once in the sensible riding habit she wore for travel. He caught her up in his arms, smiling widely to conceal the tears that were always close to the surface these days, touched that she should come to him in his hour of grief.

'Careful and mind my hat,' she laughed, covering what might have been a moment of painful sentiment with a joke. 'You don't know your own strength, my lad. Never got over that sailor's bear hug, have you?' She peered into her brother's face, assessing him. 'I'm sorry I didn't get here in time for the—. Sorry I didn't get here before.'

'Well, you're here now and that's all that matters. Good of Cal to spare you at Christmas-time.'

'Oh, we've had lots of good Christmases at Lachlan's Holt and we'll see a lot more,' she said comfortably, linking her arm in his. 'Besides, he's not alone. The boys are home with schoolfriends in tow, wreaking havoc. Lilias is come with Harley; she wants him to convalesce and breathe in some fresh country air. Even your husband is there,' she grinned at Niamh, offering her cheek to be kissed. 'Yes, even Hollis has been persuaded that no one wants to discuss business at Christmas-time. You should be with him, Niamh.'

'Oh, Aunt Maggi, I can't,' Niamh murmured, wilting under her aunt's inquisitive gaze. 'How can I leave Pa now?'

'Quite easily,' Maggi said, releasing herself and pulling off her gloves, taking stock of her surroundings. 'I'm here to look after him now so you're free to go.'

'Yes, but—'

'It's all right,' Maggi said softly. 'Lilias told me about the Welsh termagant and I have the measure of her now.'

Within twenty-four hours Niamh found herself packed and despatched on the early-morning train to Wangaratta and Beechworth. The journey was long, passing through the thick forest which covered a large part of Victoria, the train stopping at all of the small towns on the way. Towns which until recently had been terrorised by Ned Kelly and his gang. Too unsettled to read, Niamh looked out on a countryside only partially civilised, reminded that the last time she had travelled by train was with Judd. That thought made her no more easy. In addition, she had plenty of time to consider her husband and what she would say when she saw him again. Their marriage had not begun well but perhaps this Christmas holiday, away from the distractions of the city, would afford them a second chance. Silently, she promised to do what she could to mend their differences and make the marriage work.

Shivering, with a sudden awareness of being watched, she looked up and into a face she knew. The man looked away immediately, hiding behind his newspaper, not wishing to be caught. She recognised him at once as the little man who followed her everywhere, doing his best to be inconspicuous in his plain, grey clothes; the man she now thought of as her bodyguard. So Hollis must care for her, after all. Why else would this little man be instructed to follow her so faithfully, even onto a country train?

She had to change trains at Wangaratta and take the branch line which was much less comfortable. There weren't enough carriages for the amount of passengers and although people accepted the inconvenience cheerfully and a Christmas spirit prevailed, Niamh was squashed into a corner, clutching her bag. She was grateful when the train pulled into Beechworth Station and the passengers dispersed.

She stood beside her bag, getting her bearings, wondering who was to meet her, hoping, perversely, that it wouldn't be Holly. The twins with their teasing or even surly Pat Hegarty, the MacGregors' overseer would be more welcome at this time. Her heart rose when she saw Uncle Callum and, better still, he was alone.

'Maggi got there safely, then?' he said by way of greeting, speaking softly in the gentle Scottish accent he had never lost although he could scarcely remember his native land. 'And she persuaded you to come? One slightly abrasive wife in exchange for a niece, worn out and in need of a holiday.'

'I wasn't persuaded so much as ordered, Uncle Cal. I had no choice.'

'Good to see you, anyway,' he laughed, taking up her bag and steering her towards the buggy which he had parked under the spreading shade of a large gum, allowing the sturdy ponies to crop the grass while they waited. Out of the corner of her eye, Niamh caught sight of her shadow, the man who had followed her on the train from Melbourne and nearly lost her in the crush on the branch line. He was pointing at Callum and making enquiries, probably learning that he was from

197

Lachlan's Holt. Idly, she wondered if he would follow her out to the homestead as well.

Safe and comfortable with her uncle, she didn't reopen the conversation until they were well on their way.

'Oh, Uncle Cal,' she said, looking up at trees taller than she was used to seeing in Melbourne, their silver trunks and sickle-shaped grey-green leaves outlined against a clear blue sky. 'I keep forgetting how lovely it is up here till I see it again.' He smiled, still in love with his home territory and enjoying it all over again through her eyes. He turned the horses towards the track which ran alongside the river and which would eventually lead to his home.

'Although it's drier than it ought to be this early in summer,' he said, nodding towards the grasses already brown and dusty on the side of the road. 'We'll see a few bush-fires later on if the weather keeps so hot.'

Niamh looked at him and saw the lines of care seaming his face; the tanned weatherbeaten face of a man who spends most of his life out of doors. These lines and the fact that there was more grey than gold in his curls gave away the fact that Callum was no longer young. But he was still lean and sinewy, his legs now slightly bowed; the typical figure of a horseman. Not wanting to talk about bush-fires, unfortunately a natural part of the cycle of life in Australia and an ever-present danger during a hot summer, she changed the subject again.

'And how is everybody at home?'

'Maggi you've seen. The boys? Growing so fast we can't feed them enough, sprouting pimples and getting tongue-tied in the presence of pretty girls.'

'No?' Niamh laughed, thinking of her noisy, ebullient cousins whom she hadn't seen since they were small. 'I find that hard to imagine.'

'They have friends staying so we don't see so much of them now. Just as well. Your Aunt Lil's driving me mad, as usual. No sooner here than she starts complaining of our country ways and sighing to get back to her palace. Pity about poor Harley. That heart attack knocked him about a bit – seems to be diminishing right before our eyes.'

'Is he?' Niamh frowned. 'I know he's been ill but nobody said it was that serious.' She felt guilty now. She had been so

198

busy with her own projects and problems, she had given little thought to Hollis's parents. It was easier to dismiss them, believing that because they had money they had no need of her time or care.

'Maybe it isn't so bad,' Callum hastened to reassure her. 'I'm not a doctor – I wouldn't really know.'

'No, you're probably right. Holly's already taken over most of his father s work.'

'Ah yes. Holly . . . I was coming to that.' Callum paused and looked at her. 'Niamh, what's happened between you two? What went wrong?'

'Why?' Niamh was staring at her gloved hands, lying in her lap. 'What's he been saying about us?'

'Nothing, which is far more significant than if he had. Scarcely a word about you.'

'Oh, well. He's been very busy lately, so have I.'

'I think there's more to it than that. You've been living apart?'

Niamh blinked at this bald statement of fact. 'Not really – not intentionally. I went home to look after Mama and afterwards I felt I should stay on.' She thought it would sound lame to mention her fears about Gladys.

'This isn't usual, Niamh. You've been married scarcely twelve months, yet you don't act like a young couple in love.'

'I – oh, it's all my fault, Uncle Cal. I shouldn't have married him!' Suddenly, she was crying; the floodgates were open and she was letting it all come out. Callum provided a handkerchief, letting her weep. Hesitantly, and because there was plenty of time, she told him everything. How she felt about Holly and most of the truth about Judd, except they were lovers. Understanding as her uncle might be, he was still of an older generation and might find it hard to condone such behaviour. So she was ready for the question when it came.

'So that's it, then? That's as far as it went?'

'Of course, ' she answered quickly, hoping he'd interpret the colour that swooped to her cheeks as embarrassment rather than guilt. 'Sukie's my best friend. How could I look her in the face if I—'

'But your feelings were involved? On both sides?'

'Yes. Oh yes. I've been such a fool, Uncle Cal. He was there

199

for me all along and I pushed him away; I thought I should stand by my promise to marry Holly. I couldn't see how much I loved him till it was too late.'

'And now what? You've made a martyr of yourself, and you're wondering why Hollis doesn't appreciate the sacrifice and love you all the more?'

'No, Uncle Cal. It's not as simple as that!'

'Affairs of the heart never are.'

'It's not that I don't love, Holly – I do. But I'm not *in love* with him.'

'As you are with the other. And what about him, this Judd? Is he going to sit back and accept it?'

'He has to, because I won't have Sukie hurt. That's why I'm here to spend Christmas with Hollis. To see if we can patch up our differences, put the past behind us and make a fresh start in the New Year.'

Callum tilted his head to give her a sideways glance, his eyes very blue and glittering under his wide-awake hat. 'New Year resolutions are made to be broken, Niamh,' he said soberly. 'You're asking an awful lot of yourself. But you can count on my support. I'll stand by you, whatever you decide.'

'Thank you. Thank you, Uncle Cal.' Touched by his kindness and ashamed of lying to him, even in part, she started crying again.

Much as I love you, dearest Mags, you're turnin' my household an' my life upside down!' Tully wailed. His sister had been in Melbourne for less than two weeks but already she was making her presence felt. Elinor had beaten a strategic retreat while she waited for Maggi to return to the country and now Gladys was stamping about upstairs, hurling her few possessions into a bag, to the accompaniment of a storm of tears. Her argument with Maggi had been bitter but brief and now she was taking her leave. This, in spite of the fact that it was past eleven at night and she had nowhere to go.

'Well, it's high time somebody told a few home truths around here.' Maggi folded her arms and lifted her chin, ready to do battle.

'You didn't have to call her a hook-nosed Welsh harpy with an itch in her pants.'

'Well, that's what she is. Let her go, Tully. You'll be storin' up nothin' but trouble for yourself if she stays.'

'Gladys knows where she stands.'

'Oh, does she? Then why is she cryin' her eyes out, eh? You're such a great fool when it comes to women, Tully McDiarmit. Your wife scarce cold in her grave an' you've two of them after you already, pussyfootin' around. One of them young enough to be your own child!'

'She's not. Elinor's much older than Niamh.'

'Oh yes – by six months or twelve?'

'Maggi, you must have known how it was with Janet an' me. We spent more years living like brother and sister than man and wife. An' I did stand by her – to the end.'

'Oh, bravo! Give the man a medal.'

'So I think I deserve some happiness now she's gone.'

'But why pick on Elinor? She is a Maitland, you know. They'll be wantin' a better match for her than a broken-down barman like you.'

'Thanks for reminding me. Always the tactful one, aren't you. You're not tellin' me anythin' I don't know. Ellie does, too.'

'Aha, so you've already talked about marriage?'

'Of course we have,' he sighed, running his hands through his hair as he always did when he was anxious or upset. 'I don't mean to seduce the girl.'

'Might be better for all concerned if you did. Get it out of your system – and hers.'

'Maggi!'

'Oh come on, Tully, you don't have to play the prude with me.' She pointed to the ceiling where Gladys could still be heard weeping and banging about upstairs. 'What's all that about then, if you haven't been playin' fast and loose with that one as well?'

'But I haven't!' he said, desperate for his sister to believe him. 'Not that she wouldn't have welcomed me with open arms, if I had.'

'Poor Niamh,' Maggi laughed shortly. 'No wonder she was stuck here standin' guard over you, afraid to go home.'

'Ha!' Tully warmed to the battle, finding a chink in her armour. 'Well, she's not here now, is she? Nor anyone else,

201

thanks to you. How will I manage this place on my own now you've sent all the womenfolk packing? I don't suppose you'll be staying for ever?'

'No, indeed. I've the horses to think about and the Easter sales comin' up. To say nothin' of Cal.'

'Ha! You wait. I'll tell him what you said; you thought of your horses before you thought about him.'

'Trouble-maker!'

'Ha! Takes one to know one.'

'Please stop saying "ha!". You're the one who's on toast here – not me. You should advertise for a nice married couple to come and live in.'

'And what about me? I suppose I might as well give up and join the monastery now. You won't be satisfied till you see me living the life of a monk.'

'Oh Tully, it isn't that.' Suddenly, she changed, becoming gentle. 'You're still grievin' but you don't know it. I just want you to give yourself time to get over it; to get over losing Janet before you go plungin' into a love affair with somebody else.'

Chapter Fifteen

Christmas did not turn out at all as Niamh expected, nor did it bring about the changes and resolutions she hoped for. In common with many who keep themselves busy, she and Hollis discovered these hours of leisure moved slowly and served only to show them how far apart they had drifted.

She knew this the moment Callum drove up to the homestead, bringing the horse to a halt alongside the verandah where her husband was seated, playing chess with one of the twins. Engrossed in the game which he wanted to win, even from his young cousin, he raised a hand in greeting without looking up, unwilling to break his concentration. Whereas Daniel, unable to contain his excitement, sprang up at once, jarring the table and almost spilling the pieces.

'Daniel,' Holly growled. 'Take care!'

But the boy was no longer listening, already leaping down the steps of the verandah, two at a time.

'Merry Christmas, Niamh.' He embraced her at the same time raising his voice to alert those in the house, 'They're here!' before turning back to her. 'And what have you brought us from the city this time?'

Callum frowned at his son's bad manners but Niamh only smiled and hugged him again. 'You know very well, Danny. It's Santa Claus who brings Christmas presents – not me.'

Daniel grinned. Too old to believe in Santa Claus, he was unwilling to let go of the idea. The likelihood of presents increased if he went along with the Christmas myth.

'Taller than ever, too, and leaving me far behind,' Niamh said. 'How's school?'

203

'Hush! School is a dirty word until after Christmas.' This time it was Dermot who spoke, having come up to join them. With him was their friend, Peter, who was spending the Christmas holidays with the MacGregors as his parents were overseas. 'Mrs Hegarty made the puddings last week and we're having a leg of ham, roast pork and two chickens for Christmas Day ...' The boys were growing fast and food was high on their list of priorities.

Niamh fished in her handbag and produced a box of crystallised fruits, receiving more bear hugs from her cousins and whoops of delight which she thought excessive for such a simple gift. Bearing their booty aloft, the young men retreated, leaving her to the adults.

Tired after her journey and then sitting up late after supper to catch up on the local news, Niamh had no chance to speak to Hollis in private until they were retiring to bed.

'I must say I'm surprised to see you at all,' he said, lounging in the doorway as he watched her check the wardrobe and drawers to see where Molly Hegarty, the MacGregors' housekeeper, had stored her clothes. 'I thought you'd find some other excuse not to come.'

'Oh? So my mother's death is an insufficient excuse?' She raised her eyes to the ceiling and took a deep breath to compose herself. 'No. I promised myself I wouldn't do this. I haven't come all this way to quarrel with you, Holly. I came in the hope of patching things up.'

'Our poor marriage, you mean? Only a year old and already covered in more patches than a tinker's raincoat? You do know it was our anniversary last week?'

'Oh lord, so it was. I am sorry, Holly. I forgot.'

'I rest my case.'

'You stop it, too. Stop being so damned superior. Standing there like a smug, self-important spider in a corner, waiting for me to put a foot wrong so you can rush out and trip me up.'

'I don't need to. You trip yourself.'

'Ohh!' Niamh closed her eyes and sighed, falling backwards across the bed. Really, she was exhausted and longing for sleep but she knew that would be impossible with her husband in such a mood.

Lilias had given them Callum's old room; the room he had

204

occupied in his single days before he and Maggi were married. It was spacious and comfortably appointed with plenty of drawers, a wardrobe and a marble wash-stand big enough to hold two jug and basin sets. But although the old-fashioned iron bed was larger than a single, it was still less than full size. No problem for most newlyweds who wanted to sleep in each other's arms, but for Niamh whose relationship was under a strain, the prospect of sleeping in such close quarters with her husband was less than enticing.

After taking a moment to gather her forces, she sat up on the edge of the bed to regard him. 'You should hear yourself, Holly. Sometimes you talk to me as if you were a prosecuting counsel and I was a hostile witness.'

'Not the defendant?' he said softly, leaning forward to thrust his face into her own. She met his gaze without flinching although she was first to look away.

'Oh, I was a fool to come here. I was hoping to take advantage of this holiday – this time together – to start anew.'

'And is that what you want, Niamh?'

'It's what I think we should do. You see, Holly, I know you still care for me. Or why would you employ a bodyguard to protect me – to follow me about?'

'A bodyguard?' He looked mystified for a moment and then gave a short bark of laughter. 'Oh, you mean Simpkin. Blast! Now I'll have to give the little blighter the sack. I told him he wasn't to let you see him.'

'Why not?'

'Because, dear heart,' he said with exaggerated sarcasm, 'if I wanted someone to protect you, I wouldn't employ a five-foot midget like Simpkin. He isn't a bodyguard at all – he's a private detective.'

Niamh stared at him for a few moments while she absorbed this news. 'Are you saying you set someone to spy on me? And you actually have the gall to admit it?'

Hollis shrugged. 'Spy on you? I wouldn't put it quite so strongly as that.'

'Well, I would.' Niamh was so angry her heart had taken up a slow, pounding rhythm, making her breathless. 'But why? What did I ever do to deserve it?' Mingled with her outrage was also a sense of guilt as she recalled that one afternoon she had spent with Judd. Only one. And that had been months ago now. She had been so sure that no one had seen them. There had been nobody but themselves at the empty house. So how could Hollis possibly know?

'I wasted my money,' Hollis was saying. 'You do nothing, go nowhere but the Hospital. In fact, you're so boring and predictable in your habits, I was calling him off. He's given you four stars – a clean bill of health.'

'Well, thank you, Holly. I appreciate your confidence in me.' Wide-awake now, Niamh was far too angry to be tired. She jumped up, grabbed her travelling bag, laid it on the bed and started hunting through the drawers to find the clothes which had just been unpacked.

'What are you doing?' Hollis folded his arms, watching.

'I'm leaving, of course. I should never have come.'

'Don't be a fool, Niamh. It's Christmas, for God's sake. You can't go now. How could we explain it to Callum, or to Mother and Pa?'

'You should have thought of that before you set someone to spy on me.'

'And there isn't a train until Boxing Day. You're here for Christmas, Niamh, whether you like it or not. So calm down and be sensible. Get undressed and get into bed.'

'If you think I'm going to sleep in the same bed with you after—'

'You have no choice. And please keep your voice down. Do you want the whole household to hear you squawking at me?'

'I should care.'

'Oh Niamh, I don't want to fight.' He tugged a lock of hair that had fallen down by her ear, his smile deceptively mild. 'I'm sorry about Simpkin but I was jealous – that's my only excuse.' She averted her face, refusing to look at him. 'And we've been apart for months. Isn't it only natural I should want to be with you tonight?'

'Well, you're going the wrong way about it, if you do.'

'I thought you wanted a child? Your friend Sukie's having one, isn't she?' he whispered, finding her Achilles heel, the one thing which might break down her defences. 'And you spend so much time with those kids at The Briarley . . . I thought you wanted a baby, too?'

206

'Of course I want a baby. You know I do.' She closed her eyes and compressed her lips, wondering if it was entirely by accident that he should bring Sukie into the conversation at this time.

'There's no dressing-room so I'll turn my back while you make yourself ready for bed.' So saying, he turned away, pulled off his cravat and began to unbutton the sleeves of his shirt. She stared at him, trying to fathom his lightning changes of mood but still she made no move to do as he said.

'It's all right,' he said, turning only partially towards her. 'I know you're tired after the journey – I'm not going to bother you tonight. Sleep with the bolster between us, if it makes you feel better, although it'll be damned uncomfortable in that narrow bed.'

Still unconvinced of his good will, she undressed quickly, put on a linen nightgown and climbed into bed. They had no need of blankets as the night was warm. The feather mattress accommodated her in its soft embrace, soothing her weary, travel-worn body and encouraging her to relax. On the borders of sleep she was only vaguely aware of Hollis as he extinguished the lamp and climbed in beside her.

A moment later she was wide awake. He had seized her left arm and was bending it behind her back, forcing her body to arch towards him.

'Holly, what is it? What are you—?'

'Shut up!' he hissed, his breath hot in her ear. He was using his other hand to raise her nightgown and she could feel his erection, hard between her buttocks. She gasped, but she knew that it would be useless to struggle. He had her firmly in his grasp and it would only excite him if she did. She gave a low groan as he forced himself roughly into her from behind. The months of celibacy had left her dry and closed and in the absence of any tenderness, any foreplay, she had never felt less receptive to sex.

'Holly, please don't do this. You're hurting me.' But she knew she was pleading in vain. Determined to humiliate her and at the same time gratify his desires, Hollis wasn't about to stop.

He didn't hear her protests. Mentally, he was back at the boarding school but this time he was the one on top, crushing his victim into the mattress; he was the one in charge. Niamh could only bite her lips and put up with the discomfort, hoping he wouldn't take long. He climaxed just as the clock in the dining room struck the hour of twelve.

'Merry Christmas, Niamh,' he kissed her ear as she cringed away from him. 'Here's hoping I've given you the Christmas present of a child.'

No one would have been more surprised than Niamh, if he had. She curled as far away from him as she could on the edge of the bed and buried her face in the pillow, refusing to give him the satisfaction of hearing her weep.

For the remainder of the Christmas holiday, without making it obvious, she kept out of her husband's way. On Christmas morning, he scarcely looked at her, awkward and ashamed of his behaviour of the night before. He had no gift for her and she didn't feel like presenting him with the silk cravat she had brought for him. To make sure he didn't touch her again, she placed the bolster between them each night but he made no attempt to remove it. Apart from that unfortunate encounter on the night of her arrival, he left her to herself. And, if her relatives thought her unduly morose or subdued, they put it down to the fact that she was still in mourning for Janet.

Callum found her a quiet horse and she rode out with him, sharing his anxiety for his sheep and his concern over the falling water levels in the rivers and dams.

'I don't know,' he was shaking his head after rescuing another animal, too weak to haul itself from the mud after going down to the creek to drink. 'The ewes are failing and we are losing our lambs which is a bad sign so early in summer. We had little rainfall in spring and we're unlikely to get any now. We can't expect much more until March.'

'But you will be all right? This has happened before?'

'Oh yes,' he agreed, looking at the grasses already brown and dried out except on the banks of the river. 'And somehow we survive. But as I grow older, I find it harder to be optimistic. I'm more aware of what can go wrong.'

The four Maitlands stayed until after the New Year, which was ushered in with a lot of forced gaiety and glasses of vintage port. They were joined by the Hegartys who had been with Callum and Maggi for years, Patrick helping with the horses and Molly taking over the post of housekeeper on the death of Sarah Hallam, the elderly cook. Shy in the presence of those they thought to be 'smart city folks', the Hegartys sat on the edge of their seats, contributing little to the conversation. Callum was also quiet, worrying about his stock and missing Maggi's unfailing cheerfulness and support. This was the first time in over twenty years of marriage that they had been apart on New Year's Eve.

On 2 January, Maggi arrived unannounced, saying she couldn't bear to be away from home any longer. Niamh followed her to the stables, which was the first place she visited as soon as she returned.

'You're getting fat, my lad, and in need of some exercise!' she told Orion, her new horse – another grey to replace her beloved Nero who had died the previous year. 'You don't have to worry about your father, Niamh,' she said in answer to her niece's questioning gaze. 'I sent Gladys packing. She's gone.'

'Really?' Niamh made no effort to conceal her relief. 'You're a miracle-worker, Maggi. How did you do it? I thought I'd have to stay there for months, facing her out.'

'Oh, I just told her one or two home truths. Let her know I'd seen through her game. We found a nice married couple to look after your father and he's all right. You and Holly can go on home.'

Home. What would that mean? If Holly had discovered a taste for sexual tyranny, she didn't know how she would cope back at Brighton where they'd be alone apart from Brigid who slept on the other side of the house. Their only other servant was Dayman, a lame ex-jockey employed as a gardener and stable-hand who slept in his own quarters over the stables. Hollis was like a stranger now and she felt as if she didn't know him at all. It would be difficult, if not impossible, to repair the relationship sufficiently to start again. And after his crude invasion of her body on Christmas Eve, she wasn't sure she wanted to try. It would be a long time before she felt comfortable and at ease with him again.

The only person to benefit from Christmas in the country was Harley. The pinched look had left him, his colour had returned and, for the first time in months, he told Lilias he felt like paying a visit to his club.

'Well, don't you go drinking brandy,' she warned, not entirely happy that he should go out alone.

'Brandy at eleven o'clock in the morning! What do you take me for, woman?'

'A fool of a man,' she said promptly 'who doesn't know his own limitations and would rather be sociable with his friends than take proper care of his health.'

Groaning at her prophecies, Harley put on his best top hat and left.

Two hours later he was back, slamming the door before his footman could do it for him and with sufficient force to bring Lilias running from her parlour, complaining about the noise. He held up a hand to stem her complaints while he gave orders to his servant.

'Take my best horse and ride into town with a message for my son. Make sure you catch him before he goes home. Say I have to see him this evening and the matter is urgent – it can't be put off. If he has a prior engagement, he'll have to break it. It is imperative that I see him tonight.'

'Imperative that you see him tonight,' the man repeated, memorising his master's words.

'Why, Harley.' Lilias took her husband's hat and coat, peering anxiously into his face. The sight of him frightened her. He was grey with strain and breathing harshly, all the benefit of his holiday gone. 'What is it? Why must you see Hollis so urgently?'

'Not now, Lil.' He was holding his side as the all-too familiar pain returned. 'It's not the boy's fault entirely I should have realised he's more of a salesman than a lawyer and acted before. I've neglected the business and allowed too much responsibility to fall on young shoulders.' He paused, gasping for breath.

'For goodness sake, Harley, sit down before you fall down. And where are those drops the doctor gave you?'

'Never mind that now, woman!' He waved her concern away. 'I gave the boy too much responsibility and it's gone to his head. And now this business with Ironsides. Never trusted the man, never liked—'

210

'Harley, let me send for the doctor!'

'Not now, I say!'

But Lilias wasn't listening, she was more concerned with his health than his news. 'You shouldn't have gone to the club, it's too soon. And if this is what happens when you do, I'll ask Dr Harris to forbid it.'

'Oh, stop clacking at me, woman, and fetch me a brandy,' Harley said, making her stare at him, round-eyed. 'I must be calm if I'm to deal fairly with our son.'

''If only you'd tell me what all this is about.'

'Later, Lilias. Only fair to speak to him first. Give him a chance to explain.'

Hollis arrived an hour later, hot and dishevelled. Dodging Lilias, who was bound to start fluttering about food and inviting their son to dinner, Harley ushered him into the annexe off the dining room, which he used as a study sometimes. On the darker side of the house, it smelled musty and unused and they shivered simultaneously as they sat down in the comfortless leather chairs. Hollis looked at his pocket-watch.

'Whatever it is, Father, I hope it won't take too long. I've a committee meeting at seven-thirty.'

'Then you'll be late! Your bloody land-grabbers and their meeting can wait,' Harley snapped, getting his son's attention immediately. 'I have plenty to say and you'll hear it. It'll take just as long as it takes.'

Hollis took a deep breath and shrank into the chair, shoulders hunched. His father hadn't spoken to him so severely since he'd been hauled up for a prank at school. He looked with longing at the walnut cigar box on the table but his father didn't take the hint. Finally, he had to ask: 'Can I have one?'

'No, you may not.'

'All right, Pa. Spit it out. What am I supposed to have done?' Anxiety made him flippant. 'Skipped off with the petty cash? Made a pass at Miss Johnson?' As Miss Johnson was well on the way to sixty, he hoped to amuse his father and shake him out of this dark mood. It didn't work.

'I wish it were something so trivial.'

'Miss Johnson wouldn't think it was trivial, Pa.'

'I went to Melbourne today – visited the club.'

'Glad to hear it. Do you good. Time you started getting out and about again.'

'You may not think so when you hear what I have to say. Victor Benham made a point of coming over to speak to me – you do know who I mean? Victor Benham of Grolier's Bank.'

'I do, indeed.' Hollis perked up at once, looking interested. 'Victor Benham, no less. What did he want? What does he have for us, this time?'

'He asked me – and I felt like a fool, Holly, because I didn't know! He asked me what a young man, a talented craftsman by the name of Judah Burden – a craftsman whose work had been singled out for praise at the International Exhibition – he asked me what this man had done that the firm of Maitland & Maitland should take the trouble to blacklist him all over town.'

'Burden, is it? Nothing but trouble all along. You take it from me, Father, he's no good.' Challenged at last, Hollis resorted to bluster. 'A man of dubious morals and an even more dubious background. And he's been threatening Niamh's father – I'll bet you didn't know that.'

'And what if he has? That's not our affair.'

'Niamh is my wife.'

'But it still isn't our business – not unless Tully asks us to act on his behalf. I take it he hasn't done so?'

'Not officially, no.'

'So you took it upon yourself to ruin the prospects and the reputation of this young man? To drag our company, of which I'm still the senior partner don't forget, into some petty vendetta of your own?'

'That's how it looks, Pa. But you don't know the facts.'

'Then kindly explain them so that I do. I have to tell you that Benham has been sufficiently rattled to withdraw his business from us and place it elsewhere.'

'Oh no!'

'Oh, yes. And it was only for old times' sake and our long association that he did me the favour of telling me why. Your spite has cost us the good will of Grolier's Bank.'

But Hollis was no longer listening, already looking for ways to justify himself. 'Burden is a waster. A man who runs away from his problems.'

212

'So? He's not even a client of ours.'

'Too right. I wouldn't have him as one.'

'But where are your *reasons*, Holly? So far you have shown me nothing but schoolboy malice. Worse, you acted on behalf of the firm and now we shall have to make amends.'

'Is that really necessary, Father?' Hollis squirmed uncomfortably in his seat. 'With Victor Benham to take up his cause, Judd Burden won't need help from anyone else.'

Harley looked at him, slowly shaking his head. 'I see I've failed with you, Holly, although I'm at a loss to understand why. I taught you better than that. Go on then, go! Make your schemes with your land-grabbers but don't expect any support from me.'

'That's nothing new. You never have supported me.'

'Just go, Holly. The very sight of you wearies me. And you can go in early tomorrow to vacate my office. As from this moment, I'm in harness again. Tomorrow, I'm back.'

'Is that wise, Father? Didn't the doctor say you needed at least another month of complete rest?'

'Then I'm not going to get it, am I?' He nodded, dismissing him. 'Don't forget to drop in and have a word with your mother on the way out. She'll expect to see you before you go.'

It was only with the greatest forbearance that Tully waited until he had waved his sister away on the train out of Melbourne, before he sacked the couple she had employed for him. If Maggi thought the woman's plump figure and rosy cheeks were the product of country freshness, Tully knew otherwise. Nor was he impressed by the husband's incessant banter. They were a pair of sots who would drink him out of house and home and water the whisky to hide it. At first the woman defied him, refusing to go.

'It was Mrs MacGregor employed us and it'll be Mrs MacGregor who tells us to go.'

'Indeed an' she won't. Me sister isn't in charge here – *I* am. And I'm saying you have to go. I'll pay you for the rest of the week.'

'The rest of the week? The rest of the month more like!' The woman drew a deep breath to summon her husband in stentorian tones. 'Will-yum! Get you in 'ere.'

213

Her husband joined them in the kitchen, hiccoughing and wiping his lips on the back of his hand.

'Tasting the brandy again, William?' Tully's smile was wry. 'Made sure you got the water content just right?'

William's eyes rolled like those of a horse in panic before turning to his wife for support.

'I've seen enough,' Tully said. 'Pack your bags, you two and get out – now.'

'But what about supper tonight?' The woman began to whine. 'The customers . . .'

'They'll understand. I'm sure they'll prefer their liquor full strength and pass on your cooking. That pastry of yours is a recipe for indigestion; it sits on the chest like a lead poultice.'

'Hoo!' The woman began to bawl into her apron as she ran to pack their few things. Distasteful as he found it, Tully watched her do so, making sure they took only what belonged to themselves. Ten minutes later the door slammed behind them and he sighed with relief as he sat at the kitchen table after they'd gone, enjoying the silence broken only by the measured progress of the kitchen clock. He leaned forward on his elbows, resting his chin on his hands. He regretted nothing. It wasn't his intention to be lonely for long.

'But how could you? How could you let this happen to us?' Sukie scolded Judd. Unfairly, she was blaming him for her father's high-handed action in joining forces with the Frenchman behind their backs. Delighted with his new partner, Albert had gone out to take supper with him, leaving his daughter and her husband at home alone.

'Oh Sukie, how could I prevent it?' Judd rubbed eyes gritty with more than just weariness. He had worked hard to provide Smith's Foundry with an exhibit so fine it was still the talking point of the Show and all it had brought him was the loss of the partnership and recriminations from his wife. 'I'm not Albert's keeper, am I? How was I to know?'

'It's your job to know. You're there, aren't you, on the factory floor? And a foreigner of all people – reeking of strange foods and full of outlandish ideas. He'll make trouble with the men, too. He wants to extend their working hours instead of reducing them to bring them in line with other unions.'

214

'I know all about it,' Judd sighed. 'The men are already up in arms, threatening strikes and lockouts.'

'And Pa goes sailing through life blissfully unaware. He's let the Frenchman take over the office, doing me out of my job.'

'That's no bad thing, Sukie. You couldn't have gone on much longer. The baby must be due in a matter of weeks.'

Sukie spread her hands over the swell of her belly. 'Sometimes I feel as if I shall be pregnant for ever and the baby will never come.'

'Oh, but he will.' Judd placed his hand over her own, both hoping to feel the miracle of the baby's movement. If nothing else, the advent of de Vesinet had brought them together to face a common enemy. It was the first moment of closeness they'd shared in weeks. 'There!' He smiled at her as the baby kicked. 'That was a strong one.'

'I know,' Sukie winced. 'He's a boy all right. Sometimes I think he's playing football in there.'

Judd drew her close and would have kissed her lips but she turned away at the last moment, allowing the kiss to fall on her temple instead.

'Sukie, what is it? What's happened between us? We used to be so close. These changes of mood aren't all because of the child.'

'No. No, they're not.' As always when she was tense, her eyelids started to flutter and she pressed her lips together, fighting for control.

'Then please tell me what bothers you, darling. If you won't tell me, how can I put it right?'

'You can't,' she said dully. 'You can alter lots of things but not the way you feel. I saw the thing, Judd. I – know about the heron you sent to Niamh.'

'What of it? That was a very big order we had from the Maitlands. And besides, it wasn't a personal gift to Niamh, I sent it to both of them – as a gesture of appreciation from all of us.'

'I knew it. I knew you'd say that.'

'Then why did you ask?'

'I can't win, can I? You have the right answer for everything. You've probably got an explanation for the woman on the boat.'

215

'What woman? What boat?'

'The *Castle Belmont*, of course.'

'Sukie, that was a long time ago – long before we met. It's not fair to hold that against me now.'

'So the story was right – there *was* someone.'

'Yes. Yes! But it didn't mean anything – neither to her nor to me. We whiled away the journey together, that's all. She was coming to Melbourne to marry somebody else.'

Sukie pursed her lips and frowned, finding his explanations too glib but nevertheless unable to fault them.

'Oh, Sukie.' He cradled her in his arms. 'You're having a baby and all sorts of changes are going on inside you. It's only natural for you to be emotional and entertain doubts over me. But we have more than each other to think about – we're a family now.' Sukie at last slid her arms round his neck and buried her face in his shoulder, weeping hot tears of relief as he whispered comfort to her, rocking her like a child. 'And if there's anything – anything at all that worries you, I want to hear about it. Don't let it fester, keeping it to yourself. Didn't I promise you once that I'd make you happy?' He waited for her to look up and nod. 'Well, that promise still holds. Even if it means we have to break away from de Vesinet and your father and start a new business on our own.'

'How can we do that?' she said, sounding as if she had a cold, her nose red from weeping, 'when we have no money?'

'I don't know yet. But I met a man from Grolier's Bank who seemed sympathetic for once. I'm sure I'll find a way.'

'Oh, and I nearly forgot – there's a letter for you. Pa brought it home from the foundry.' She released herself and rose awkwardly because of her bulk to collect the letter in its envelope of fine vellum which she had placed on the mantelpiece. He turned it over in his hands.

'A business letter – might be important. I wonder who it's from?'

'Open it!' Sukie could scarcely contain her patience. 'Open it and see.'

Judd ripped it open with his finger, destroying the envelope as he did so. He read the letter, frowning. 'It's from the older Maitland, Harley. Wants me to call on him tomorrow morning to hear something to my advantage.'

'Your legacy!'

'I doubt it. My uncle left nothing in writing.'

'But it does mean money, doesn't it? That's what *something to your advantage* usually means?'

'Don't get your hopes up, Sukie.' He kissed her briefly on the nose. 'Wait till tomorrow and see.'

Chapter Sixteen

Judd stood outside the office of Maitland & Maitland, blinking in the sunlight. In the pocket of his jerkin was a bundle of crisp new banknotes, amounting to the sum of a thousand pounds. He had never dreamed of possessing so much money, let alone hold it in his hands. He walked down Collins Street hill on unsteady legs, almost in a state of shock, unable to believe it had come to him so easily.

On his arrival he had been surprised to see Harley Maitland at his offices at all. Obviously ill, he looked more like a man in his seventies rather than someone with a son scarcely out of his teens. Mr Maitland had addressed him kindly but had found it embarrassing, even painful to own up to the mischief that Hollis had done – how he had quietly ruined Judd's reputation with a whisper here, a nod there, using his father's integrity and prestige to stop him getting the finance he so desperately needed.

'So, Mr Burden,' the elder Maitland concluded heavily, 'I can only say how sorry I am. We can't compensate you for the anguish or the time you have lost.'

'Of course you can't! How can you compensate me for a reputation in ruins? A partnership lost?'

'Oh, I don't know.' Harley sat back to regard him, massaging the old pain in his side. 'Public memory isn't so long. A scandal lives only as long as yesterday's newspaper. It might not be as bad as you think.'

Although he knew it was unfair to rage at this good old man who was only trying to set things right, Judd's temper got the better of him. All he could think of was his Sukie, worn out and heavy with pregnancy, slumped in despair at the kitchen table. Anger stirred like a red mist before his eyes as he stood over Harley, ignoring his pallor as he told exactly how much damage Hollis had done.

But now, out on the street, he felt euphoric, experiencing a sense of release from all the restrictions that had confined him before. Here was money enough to give them a new start in life. To buy Sukie a home of her own and even set up their own business for themselves, if they started small. There was no need to go into competition with Smith's Foundry, producing iron lace. They would start up a small foundry to provide custom-built fountains and bronze pieces for the garden. In his mind's eye he could already see the caption in shining gold letters on the signboard – *Burden & Burden* – a name synonymous with quality rather than quantity.

Recklessly, he ran out into the road and hailed a cab, wanting to get home immediately; public transport would take too long. He couldn't wait to share his good news.

On that same morning, Niamh was facing Elinor in the kitchen of the Silver Star. She too had received some astounding news.

'You – you're going to marry my father? But you can't!' The words were out before she could prevent them. 'He's so much older than you are!'

'Yes, I know,' Elinor said quietly, refusing to be irritated by Niamh's lack of tact.

'And he's been widowed but a matter of months. What will your parents say?'

'No more than they have already. I've presented them with a *fait accompli*. I told them I've already moved in with him and, to add weight to the argument, I said I was pregnant, as well.'

'Oh, Ellie, you're not!'

'No, of course not, silly. But I don't want Pa to come whaling into the rescue, packing me off with some ghastly companion to do a Grand Tour of Europe instead.'

'But – but what did they say?' Astonished as she was by Elinor's daring, Niamh was still curious.

'Oh, there was a fearful row. The servants will dine out on it for weeks. But I stuck to my guns and in the end Pa retreated to his club and washed his hands of me. Mother's had a relapse . . .'

'Oh no, she's not really ill this time?'

'Not she!' Ellie laughed. 'One of her friends has recommended a new Swiss doctor – supposed to be an expert on *crises of the nerves* – well, that's what they call it in English but it sounds more impressive in French. He's a beautiful young man with limp brown hair that falls into his soft brown eyes. He sits there, holding her hand for hours, telling her how brave she is. I could have two society weddings for what he's going to cost Pa.'

'Oh, Ellie!' For all that she was exasperated, Niamh had to chuckle.

Hearing, on her return to Melbourne, that Tully had sacked the couple Maggi just hired, she had gone at once to the Silver Star, expecting to find her father living in a state of squalor and bachelor disarray. Nothing could have been further from the truth. Elinor had arrived ahead of her and had already taken charge . . . but an Elinor so changed that Niamh had to look twice to make sure it was the same girl. The bored, sought-after princess of Melbourne society was gone and in her place was an efficient young woman who had discovered a whole new purpose in life, up to her elbows in dough and wearing a crisp, white apron to protect her clothes. Delicious smells emanated from the stove and Ellie showed every sign of becoming a model housekeeper.

'I just love him, Niamh,' she said simply. 'I can't help it. I've loved him ever since we danced at your wedding. And he's so – so good to me – so delighted to have me. Come on, give me a kiss and wish us well.'

'You know I wish you every happiness, both of you.' Niamh managed to suppress her amazement to give the expected kiss. 'Just don't turn into a wicked step-mama, that's all.'

Ellie laughed richly at such an idea and on hearing it, Tully decided it was safe to come in from the storeroom where he had been hiding in mock fear of his daughter's wrath. Sheepishly, and with an arm around Ellie's plump shoulders, he admitted he had been too much of a coward to face her until he saw how she would receive their news.

It *was* a surprise, although Niamh did her best to conceal it.

But the couple radiated happiness, glancing at each other often and communicating without speech as couples in total accord often do. So she gave them her blessing and would not be persuaded to stay. Seeing them so enraptured, in the first flush of new love, served only to remind her of the shortcomings of her own marriage to Hollis. She needed to get away.

Hollis was swearing under his breath as he ran up the steps of the building on his way to his father's office. Horace Ironsides had made yet another unforeseen move; this time to obtain a seat in the State Parliament. From such a position it would be but a short step to becoming a minister and pushing through measures which would be advantageous to himself and his cronies. That might have been all right, had not Ironsides heard that Maitland Senior was about to resume his former position as head of Maitland & Maitland, ousting his son. Ironsides had poked fun at Hollis, teasing him for being so easy to set aside.

Still smarting from the encounter, Hollis paid little attention to Miss Johnson when she called out to him, as he passed her desk, trying to catch him on the way in.

'Raised voices, Mr Holly. I do hope that man didn't upset him. Your father's unusually quiet in there – hasn't even rung for his letters or for me to go in.'

Hollis burst into his father's office, instantly aware that something was very wrong. To give himself time to think, he closed the door carefully behind him, preventing Miss Johnson from following him.

'Oh you fool, Pa.' He whispered the words which came out almost like a sob as, beset by conflicting emotions, he examined his father's lifeless form. 'Why did you have to go and interfere?'

'Here he is!' Sukie said as Judd came through the back door, rising from the table as swiftly as her bulk would allow. 'I told you he'd be back. He's done nothing wrong.'

The troopers were standing just inside the back door, one on each side as if to prevent anyone from going in or out. They glanced at each other, neither relishing the task of arresting a man in front of his heavily pregnant wife.

'Tell them, Judd,' she said. 'Tell them what you've been doing and where you've been.'

221

'But, Sukie, you know very well.' Judd stared at her and then at the troopers, a slight frown on his face. Looking forward to breaking his news, he had scarcely registered the carriage and four waiting in the street outside their house.

'What is it?' he said. 'Trouble at the foundry?'

'No.' Sukie looked at him imploringly. 'Tell them, Judd. Just tell them where you've been.'

'To the office of Maitland & Maitland. I had an appointment with the elder Mr Maitland at eleven.'

'There!' Sukie lifted her chin as if to defy the troopers although her fluttering eyelids betrayed her nervousness. 'He'd deny it, if he had something to hide.'

Until that moment the troopers had been looking embarrassed, uncertain their information had been correct. But unconsciously Judd gave himself away by pressing his hand to the pocket containing the money. The men pounced at once, needing no further evidence of his guilt.

Ignoring Sukie's cries of protest, they snatched the money from Judd and stunned him by slamming him hard against the doorpost before spreading his arms and legs to search him for weapons.

'Just as we were informed.' The senior trooper flung the money down on the table. 'Now, madam! What do you have to say about that?'

Sukie began to tremble, her eyelids fluttering out of control as she clapped both hands to her mouth. The trooper continued to question Judd while the younger man kept him covered with a rifle, ready to shoot.

'So how did you come by such a large sum of money?'

'Mr Maitland gave it to me.'

'Oh, he *gave* it to you, did he?' Sure of his ground now, the trooper was becoming sarcastic. 'Before or after you broke his skull with the poker from his own hearth?'

'*What?*' Judd whispered, the colour draining from his face. 'What did you say?'

'You heard. Oh, well done. You ought to be on stage with George Coppin if you can put on a performance like that.' He gave a slow handclap. 'I've never seen such a good show of surprise.'

'It isn't a show – I *am* surprised.' Judd spoke softly knowing it wouldn't help to aggravate the troopers. 'Mr Maitland was quite all right when I left him. He was pale and certainly not in the best of health but he was alive.'

The troopers didn't believe him. In spite of Sukie's tears and his own protestations of innocence, he was arrested, handcuffed and thrown into Melbourne Gaol to await his trial. His hopes and dreams for the future had lasted exactly one hour.

'I don't believe it! It's a mistake.' Niamh could no longer stay seated across the dinner-table from Hollis. Her heart set up a slow painful rhythm in her chest; it felt heavy as a stone, as if it had swollen to twice its size. Unable to conceal her feelings, she paced the room, wringing her hands, her appetite gone. Hollis, by contrast, was attacking his roast pork and vegetables as if he hadn't eaten all day.

'One thing I'll say for your Brigid,' he mumbled, speaking with his mouth full, 'she might be an old fraud who likes dodging the housework but she certainly knows how to cook.'

Niamh stared at him, wondering how he could sit there, calmly eating his meal and making trivial conversation when a matter of hours ago his father had been brutally murdered. At last he was finished, dabbing his lips with a napkin and sighing with satisfaction. Her fingers curled into fists and she wanted to strike him.

'Be damned to Brigid and her blasted cooking!' The words burst from her, making him stare at her, eyes wide. 'I want to know how it happened – in detail. And if there *has* been a crime, why are you so certain the culprit is Judd?'

'Niamh! Niamh, sit down.' He caught her hand as she passed, stopping her. 'You don't need to harrow yourself with the details, you'll only get upset. Everything's taken care of. The man's in gaol. No need to distress yourself any further.'

'But I have to know!' Niamh grated the words. 'And if you won't tell me, I'll go to the Melbourne Gaol and find out for myself.'

'You will not.' He glared at her. 'My wife – visiting that hell-hole! What would people say?'

'They can say whatever they like – I don't care.'

'Well, I do. And I expressly forbid it.'

223

Hearing the tremor in his voice, her temper left her. It was, after all, Holly's father who had been so callously murdered; gentle Uncle Harley who had never hurt anyone. Uncle Harley whom she, too, had loved. And if Hollis could eat and she couldn't, she ought not to blame him. It didn't mean that he felt the pain any less. Everyone reacted differently towards grief and Hollis could still be in shock, unable to take it in. So she dropped to her knees by his chair and took his hands in her own. Her hands were feverish and a little shaky, making his seem unusually cool.

'Oh Holly, I'm so sorry. I know this is dreadful for you but really, I need to know. Tell me about it this once – and I won't ever ask you again.'

He sighed and leaned forward, holding her two hands between his own and watching her face intently as he spoke.

'It was a shock to all of us when Pa said he wanted to come back to the office. Mother didn't think he was well enough yet and neither did I. Nor did his doctors, come to that, but you know how stubborn he is – or he used to be . . .'

Niamh nodded, waiting for him to go on.

'He – he said he was taking some cash from one of the trust accounts, to make an investment or something – I didn't pay much attention. You know how secretive he could be, and sometimes, when people are getting on . . .'

'Oh no, Holly. Uncle Harley might have been sick but his brain was as sharp as ever.'

'Maybe.' Holly shrugged. 'And maybe not. I had business elsewhere so I didn't get back to the office till after noon. Miss Johnson was first to alert me that something was wrong. She said Burden had called to see Pa at eleven – Lord only knows what about. She was alarmed when she heard raised voices – Burden raging, losing his temper, and Pa's voice grower weaker, attempting to reason with him. Then silence. And shortly after that, Burden left. Miss Johnson thought it odd that Pa didn't call for her but she's not in the habit of disturbing him at his work. So I – I was the next person to go into that room.' Hollis's face worked and he looked like a small boy overcome with emotion, doing his best not to weep.

'Please, Holly. I know how hard it is. But tell me – just tell me what you found.'

224

'I didn't see Pa right away because he wasn't at his desk. He –
he was lying across the hearth with his head caved in. Poor
dear Pa, struck down from behind by a coward. And a stupid
coward, as well. He must have known he'd never get away with
it.'

'But – but why does it have to be Judd? It could have been
somebody else. Someone who slipped by Miss Johnson when
she wasn't looking . . .'

'Except that it wasn't.' Holly smiled although there was no
humour in it, his mouth a thin line. 'They caught him red-
handed with Pa's money still in his pocket. The notes were in
sequence; the money Pa took out of the bank.'

'Ohh!' Niamh's breath expelled in a sigh as she understood
the weight of the evidence against Judd. 'They'll hang him for
this.'

'I sincerely hope so,' Hollis stared at her, hungry for every
nuance of her expression as he licked dry lips. 'I look forward
to seeing justice done.'

With de Vesinet in charge of the office, Sukie's visits to Smith's
Foundry were rare. After a while she hadn't the heart to go
there at all, fearful of the avid, inquisitive glances she received
from both workers and customers alike. She was no longer
Sukie Burden, an unremarkable woman, expecting the birth of
her first child. Overnight she had become an object of interest
and curiosity – a murderer's wife. She couldn't escape her husband's notoriety, even at home. The night following his arrest
had been the worst. She had been unable to prevent herself
from hearing the shouts of the newsboys, distributing the
evening paper on the streets.

'Read all about it! Blood in the fireplace!'

'Murder in Collins Street! Suspect arrested!'

And every evening the newspaper journalists discovered a
new slant to keep public interest alive. Harley Maitland was
too prominent a citizen for his murder to go unremarked.
Some, bolder than others, had come to the house in Richmond
and knocked on the door, in the hope of getting her to talk.

'Mrs Burden! Mrs Burden, what's it like to be bearing a
murderer's child?'

'Was your husband always a violent, bad-tempered man?'

225

'As a blacksmith, he'd be unusually strong. Did he ever raise a hand against you?'

Blinded by tears, Sukie had slammed the door in their faces, shouting at them and warning them not to come back. But they always did. The same reporters or others.

She must have gone over the scene of Judd's arrest a dozen times, trying to convince herself of his innocence. He had looked so astounded when the troopers accused him, and surely a guilty man would have found an excuse for having so much money on his person? But Judd offered none, insisting it had been given to him. Sukie had reminded him of the letter summoning him to the office of Maitland & Maitland, but he had left it behind there.

There was another difficulty, as well. Since the victim was one of their own, it was hard to find a sympathetic lawyer who was willing to defend Judd. One or two of the less scrupulous offered to take the case for the money but mostly they shunned it. No one cared to mar his reputation by taking on such a lost cause. The newspapers had done their worst; everyone believed Judd was guilty and the trial was just a formality. He was as good as hanged.

So she paid less attention than usual when Albert chattered of the new working hours at the foundry. De Vesinet wanted the men to commence at 7 a.m. to get the bulk of the work done early before the heat of midday. This didn't mean he was willing to release them earlier at 3.30 or 4 p.m. He expected the early start on top of a full working day and Albert approved, boasting of the Frenchman's ability and determination to impose his will. Sukie listened in silence.

'Ho yes!' Albert said. 'He won't stand for their union non-sense – and he'll give them some stick if they try. I should've found me a man like him before. Cut out the dead wood – that's what he's done. Sacked most of the old hands and taken on a team of much younger men.'

'But, Pa, that's not fair. Some of those older men have been with us for years.'

'Too bloody long. Beginnin' to think they own the place. Throwin' their weight about and tellin' us what to do.'

Sukie closed her eyes and sighed, too troubled and exhausted on her own behalf to go into battle for the men at

226

the foundry. She concluded at last that her father cared nothing for anyone unless they were of use to him *now*. Long service and past loyalties meant nothing; he had already washed his hands of Judd.

She felt as if she were the only person in the world who believed in his innocence as she lay awake each night staring at the empty space in the bed beside her, willing herself to find a way to save him. Sleep was impossible now, the baby too big and too active to let her rest comfortably. The date of the trial was looming and still she hadn't found a reliable lawyer; someone she could trust to defend him. At last she decided she must to go the gaol to see if Judd himself had any ideas.

Metal clanging on metal was the first sound she heard. Not the positive, cheerful sound she was used to at the foundry, but the rattle of chains and heavy doors being slammed and locked – and afterwards the very final sound of a bolt shooting home.

As she didn't want to edge around the troopers who were blocking the doorway, she waited for them to finish their business and leave. Already stressed by the heat and embarrassed by the disapproving looks she received from other women for being out and about in such an advanced stage of her pregnancy, she didn't want to draw any more attention to herself than need be. Screwing up the last vestiges of her courage, she approached the doorway and peered in. The smell of the place assaulted a stomach already delicate and she forced herself onward when all she wanted to do was run back outside again and void the contents of her stomach right there in the gutter. The place smelled worse than blocked drains in summer; a mixture of dank places that never saw daylight, excrement, unwashed bodies and human fear. A smell that Judd must be loathing as much as she did. Judd, who liked to put on fresh clothes each day and sleep between clean linen sheets each night. Judd who scrubbed himself every evening to rid himself of the sweat and dirt of the foundry – sometimes more than once if the weather was hot.

When her poor eyesight became accustomed to the gloom, she saw the gaoler, lounging in a chair near the door. It took all her courage to approach him as he looked more like a squat toad than a man. It was hard to see where his skin finished and

227

his clothing began; both were the same uniform, dingy grey. At close quarters, he smelled worse than he looked, a mixture of raw onions and ancient cheese. With a shiver of distaste, she realised he was already evaluating the swell of her belly in pregnancy and the rich curve of her breasts. His gaze didn't reach her face.

'I am Susannah Burden.' She spoke sharply to get his attention and calm her own fears. 'And I want to see my husband.'

'Do you now?' the man said, opening his mouth to pick at his teeth with a grimy finger. 'You're the second one to come askin' for Burden today – mus' be a popular boy.'

'Who was it – a reporter?'

'How should I know? Not every day we have a real, live murderer to put on show. Everyone wants to take a peek at 'im – an' I tell them just the same as I'm tellin' you. This is a place of punishment – a gaol – not a bleedin' hotel for people to come an' go as they please.'

'Will you tell me when I can see my husband then?'

'You can't. Not unless –' he took a quick glance around to make sure they weren't overheard '– unless you've brought me something to make it worth my while. If that other woman can afford to pay me, so can you.' He thrust his face into hers, rubbing his thumb against two fingers to indicate what he meant. 'What's it worth to you? A fiver for five minutes, eh? Give us a fiver an' ole Gusto will look the other way.'

'Gusto?'

'Gusto, that's me. I can't let you go in but you can talk to him through the hatch in the door.'

'I haven't any money – I didn't think I'd need it. But please, sir, in the name of pity let me see him, if only for a moment.'

'In the name of pity?' The man laughed shortly. 'That's a good one. Prisoners are here to be punished, not pitied.' He said the words slowly and deliberately, relishing Sukie's horror. 'They sit in darkness and in leg-irons, some chained to the walls of their cells. Prisoners may not speak – not to each other, not even to me. Do yerself a favour missus an' go on home. Forget yer ole man – he's a gonner. He'll get his neck stretched jus' like Ned Kelly.'

Sukie turned away, feeling dizzy. The room was swimming before her eyes as she felt her way to the door. She leaned in the doorway, waiting for the spell to pass and would have fallen if someone hadn't come forward to catch her, supporting her with a strong arm around her back.

'It's all right, Sukie.' It was Niamh who whispered in her ear. 'I have you safe now.'

'Niamh,' Sukie croaked, weak with relief. 'Oh Niamh, what are you doing here?'

'Same as you are. Trying my best to help Judd.'

'But why should you,' Sukie gave a great sob, 'when they say he killed your father-in-law? And when nobody believes he's innocent except me?'

'But I do,' Niamh said, thinking the time for hiding the truth was past. 'Because I love him, too.'

It was one thing to suspect and quite another to have it confirmed. Blindly, Sukie hit out at her, sobbing. 'This is all your fault – your fault, I know it! He wouldn't be in gaol or in trouble at all if it wasn't for you!'

'Sukie, stop it.' Niamh evaded her friend's flailing hands. 'This won't help anyone.'

'And – and Judd?' Sukie could hardly speak and her heart set up a pounding in her chest. 'Does he love you, too?'

'What does it matter now?' Niamh said sharply. 'You're the one who's having his child.' Sukie paused, looking down at her swollen belly as the tears kept rolling down her cheeks. 'Oh God, Sukie. I'm sorry . . .'

'Just leave me alone, damn you. I want to go home.'

'Then let me take you.'

'No, I don't want you to. I'd rather go by myself.'

'Sukie, stop it. I promised him I'd look after you. Don't you want to hear what he said?'

'No, I don't. Not if his words were for you.'

'Sukie, don't – just don't shut me out. This is hard enough without fighting each other as well. There's no room for jealousy or dishonesty now. If Judd's going to stand a chance of proving his innocence, he'll need all the friends he can get.'

Niamh hailed a cab and half-ushered, half-lifted Sukie inside, giving the driver the Smiths' home address.

'Oh Niamh, how are we to bear it? Poor Judd locked up in that dreadful place, with that evil man . . .'

229

'You mustn't let it prey on your mind, my dear. We won't be able to help him if you go on thinking like that.'

'Then how *can* we help him?'

'I'm not sure, but there must be a way. There has to be.'

Left alone for hours, spaced with meals that were hardly worth waiting for and infrequent periods of exercise during which some of his chains were removed to let the circulation return to his tortured limbs, Judd had plenty of time to review his situation and knew it didn't look good.

Someone had set out to entrap him, spinning a web of lies. Harley Maitland had been a respected citizen and greatly loved. Now the whole population of Melbourne was baying for his murderer's blood. It would take a man of inspiration and genius to get him off. He didn't think there could be such a man and, if there were, it was unlikely he'd take the case. In addition, the imposition of silence was getting him down. Naturally gregarious, Judd missed the simple pleasure of conversing with somebody else.

He heard keys in the door of his cell which swung open on creaking hinges allowing Gusto to come in.

'Quite the ladies' man, aren't we?' the gaoler smirked. 'Two of them sniffin' round after you now. You'll have to give me some tips.'

'You could wash yourself more often, for a start.' The words were out before he considered the wisdom of saying them, earning him a punch in the face and a split lip.

'Prisoners are forbidden to speak. D'you want to be flogged?'

'You asked me—'

'Shut it! Dunno know why I bother.' Gusto used another key to release the iron ball from shackles around Judd's ankles, leaving him hobbled. Then he pulled a dirty calico hood onto Judd's head to conceal his identity before leading him out to the exercise yard. The air was cool and Judd sensed it was already late in the afternoon. He was surprised that he should be allowed to exercise now, at a time when most prisoners were safely locked in their cells. The exercise yard wasn't large and the walls were high, shutting out most of the light, but even with the restriction of the hood, he could breathe more

230

easily than inside the gaol where the sour smells made him sick.

Relishing even this temporary respite, he started to move with more speed, half-running, half-hopping as fast as the chains would allow. He felt that while he had life, he had hope and in spite of the poor food and debilitating prison routines, he should keep himself fit if he could.

'Hang on! Wait for me!' These words came from another prisoner, similarly hooded and apparently in pursuit. Judd could hear the man's chains rattling as he hopped along, trying to catch up.

'Shut up, will you?' Judd hissed. 'D'you want to get us both flogged? They don't need an excuse.'

'Shut up yourself an' listen good. We haven't much time. Old Gusto won't leave us for long. D'you know who I am, Judd?'

'Yes, I do.' Judd was surprised to recognise a familiar voice. 'It's Carl, isn't it? Carl Bradley.' He slowed down to a shuffle, allowing the other man to trot beside him as they continued to move around the yard.

'The same. Got yourself into plenty hot water this time, haven't you, Judd?'

'Tell me something I don't know. An' if you're here to gloat, you can piss off right now.'

'Hold on – don't get on your high horse. I'm about to get out o' here. An' seeing the trouble you're in, I thought you might like to go with me.'

'If I try to escape that's as good as an admission of guilt. And I'm innocent!'

'Oh, I know. That's what they all say. Short of a miracle, Judd, the only way you're getting out of here is feet-first in a box.'

'Give me one good reason why you should help me.'

'A smith, aren't you? Useful man to have around. An' one good turn deserves another. Mum said it was you stumped up the money for my lawyers when Dad wouldn't help.'

'Much good it seems to have done you.'

'Save the sermon. You're in no position to preach, Judd.'

'But I'm not a criminal, I tell you.'

'Save it. I don't care either way. Just make your mind up

231

before Gusto comes back. Are you with us or not?'

'I dunno. Wait until after the trial. I could get off.'

'After what you did?' Carl gave a short bark of laughter. 'Got a better chance of flyin' to the moon.'

Chapter Seventeen

Torn between her grief for the father-in-law she had loved and the fears she secretly held for Judd, Niamh found herself growing still more apart from her husband. Since his father's death, Hollis had built an even bigger wall around his emotions and retreated behind it.

Harley Maitland's funeral had taken place at the Collins Street Independent Church where the Maitland family celebrated all its momentous events – the births and the marriages as well as the deaths. It was no more than a stone's throw from the Maitlands' business premises and, today, it seemed to Niamh, glancing briefly at the hundreds of faces turned towards them, as if half Melbourne had turned out in honour of the occasion. Even Lilias's rigid composure had been shaken as she realised how many people had come to pay their last respects to her husband, filling the church and spilling out onto the street as there wasn't enough room inside.

Niamh sat in the front of the church on the end of the Maitland pew, reflecting that the past twelve months had been overshadowed by death. Sally had been first – Sally who had asserted that funerals always came in threes. It was beginning to look that way. Sally herself and then Janet and now they were burying Harley. Surely, that would be enough death to appease the dark gods without Judd having to make it a fourth?

She shivered to dispel the thought and took a sidelong glance at her mother-in-law, white-faced and heavily veiled, supported between Hollis and Callum who had come down from the country to support his sister, leaving Maggi at home this time. Niamh had never been close to her mother-in-law but her heart went out to her now as she admired the older woman's courage. Lilias coped with the loss of her husband in the same way as she dealt with every other problem in life, rising to the challenge and showing herself to be equal to it. Dressed in the most expensive of black lace, she wore a broad-brimmed hat to keep the veil away from her face and prevent people staring at her. Standing straight and tall with her head held high, she appeared to be in control of her emotions, refusing to make a public show of her grief. As Hollis was supporting his mother, Niamh stood with her father and Ellie, who had been married quietly a few weeks before. Very much a couple, they stood close together, hands and fingers linked as Ellie wept unashamedly, unable to hold back her tears. Niamh herself felt too shocked, too numbed to give way to tears.

After the funeral service at the church, followed by the commitment of the body into the ground, a ceremony attended by only the closest relatives, the family returned to The Oaks for the traditional feast and the reading of Harley's will. Niamh paid little attention, allowing her mind to wander at this time. No one expected any surprises and there weren't any. A careful husband, Harley had provided his wife with a home and made sure she would be more than comfortable financially in the event of his death. With certain provisos in legal jargon which largely went over Niamh's head, everything else was going to Hollis. Or so she thought until she heard the lawyer mention her name in the same measured tones, repeating it and pausing to make sure he had her attention.

'To Niamh Maitland, my son's wife, full title and sole ownership of the house in Brighton which was purchased through Maitland & Maitland and known as The Hollies—'

Hollis waited to hear no more. With an impatient sound, something between a snort and a grunt, he drew back his chair and strode off outside to pace up and down the loggia. Niamh went after him as the lawyer looked up from the document to address the room. 'And that, ladies and gentleman, concludes the last will and testament of—' but she heard no more after closing the door quietly behind them. She wanted no one else to follow or intrude.

'Holly, I'm so sorry,' she said, almost running to catch up

with him. 'I didn't know Uncle Harley was going to do that. I'm sorry about the house.'

'It really doesn't matter, Niamh. Not at all.'

'You've made it very clear that it does. But why – why should he . . .?'

'Lord only knows. I told you he was going soft in the head. Some crackpot idea of protecting the place for the future – for his grandchildren, I suppose. Not that we look like having any.'

Niamh ignored the jibe. 'I'll see the lawyer – deed it back to you, if you like.'

'What for? You're still my wife, after all. If only in name.'

'Holly, don't do this. Don't turn your father's will into another bone of contention between us.'

Hollis shrugged. 'Make my apologies to Mother – I can't stand any more condolences from her twittering friends. Got an appointment with Horace Ironsides. I'll have to go out.'

'On the day of your father's funeral?' Niamh stared aghast at her husband, thinking how ill, how haunted he looked, wishing he would let her get close enough to be more of a support to him. He looked as if he hadn't been sleeping, his face lined as if he were ten years older, the skin white as parchment and drawn tightly across his cheekbones. 'Don't go, Holly. Ironsides won't expect you today.'

'What do you care? Get on home to that precious house of yours and let me be. No need to wait supper either. Brigid can leave me some cold collations and I'll eat them when I get in.'

'But what shall I say to your mother, and to your father's friends?'

But Hollis was already striding across the lawn on his way to the stables, his mind on other things.

Inside, Callum was doing his best to persuade Lilias to accompany him to Lachlan's Holt rather than remain in an empty house on her own. While there were guests present, she could put a good face on it, but he knew she would succumb to her grief as soon as she was alone.

'Another spell in the country, Cal?' Lilias was in no mood to be gracious. 'I don't know if I can stand it – not while the weather's so hot.'

235

'You can always come to Brighton, Aunt Lil,' Niamh felt bound to offer. 'You might find it cooler nearer the beach.'

'No, no.' Callum gave Niamh a quick wink. 'Maggi's expecting you and it's all arranged.'

'Oh all right, then.' Lilias accepted with bad grace as Niamh swallowed a sigh of relief.

Hollis didn't have any business with Horace Ironsides; that had been a convenient lie. Unreasonably irritated with Niamh and unable to face any more of his mother's determined fortitude, he needed to be alone. Without really thinking where he was going he went to the wharf where he stood smoking a cigar and watching a ship being unloaded, the wharfies and sailors sweating in the heat of the afternoon, naked to the waist, muscles bunching as they strained, moving cargo which would have broken the backs of lesser men. He was afraid of big men yet he watched them, rather as someone else would watch a snake or a spider, repelled yet fascinated, unable to look away.

He stayed there, watching them, until sunset when they were through with their work and went to the nearest public house. Hollis followed them, bought a beer for himself and continued to watch them, thinking no one would notice. But it wasn't long before they did.

'What's up, mate? What you gawpin' at?'

'Looks like an undertaker's boy toutin' for custom,' another man sneered, seeing him dressed in black. 'Come to the wrong place, if he has. Fit as fleas, we are. An' if we wasn't, we can't afford no fancy funerals down 'ere.'

Hollis didn't rise to the bait or answer them. He frowned slightly, ignoring their jibes.

'Ah, leave 'im alone, Bill,' another man said in a stage whisper. 'He's just a nancy-boy out on the tear – lookin' to pick up a bit o' rough.'

'Whoo, hoo!' The other man gave a howl of laughter. 'Who wants to take him on then, for a roll in the hay? How much d'yer think he'll pay?'

Hollis slammed his empty glass on the counter. If anyone had asked him what he was doing here, he couldn't have said. He wanted to look but certainly not to touch, and had no intention of getting involved. All he wanted now was to get away from them. Their laughter followed him as he made his way to the street where it was already dark.

'What the hell are you doing here?' It wasn't like Niamh to use strong language but she was so dismayed to see Gladys O'Shea back at work at the Silver Star, that she spoke without thinking.

After visiting church with Niamh on Sunday morning and receiving another string of condolences, combined with the heartfelt wishes of his father's friends that Judd Burden should be taken and hanged without the benefit of a trial, Hollis made his excuses and went off on his own, leaving her free to spend the remainder of the day with her father and Ellie. She had been looking forward to spending a happy afternoon with them and it had come as a shock to see Gladys.

'I asked you what you're doing here! I thought Mrs MacGregor sent you packing?'

Gladys responded with a self-satisfied smirk. 'So she did. But Mrs MacGregor isn't here now, is she? An' the new Mrs McDiarmit is. There's lovely she is an' so pretty. A real lady she is – not like some I could mention.' She narrowed her eyes at Niamh. 'And she says I can stay.'

'Only because she's kind-hearted and she doesn't know you. What about my father, then? I thought he'd have more sense than to let you come back.'

'Ah, but you don't know everythin', miss. We've always understood each other, Mr Tully an' me. Was only other people who got in the way.'

'Why you – you smug bitch!'

'Sticks an' stones,' Gladys shrugged.

'Just don't get too comfortable, Gladys, that's all. You've not heard the last of this.'

But Niamh was surprised when Elinor dismissed her catalogue of complaints against Gladys with a laugh.

'She's welcome to try but she'll be a skinny one, indeed, if she can wriggle between us when we're in bed. Oh Niamh, don't be such a worry-face. I know about her – your father told me – how she set her cap at him in the past.'

'Make sure it *is* in the past. Oh Ellie, I'm serious, I don't like this at all; it gives me a very bad feeling. I just know you're going to regret it, if you let her stay.'

'Niamh, it's only a feeling and that's all. I know you've never liked her and I can understand why—'

'But you don't. You don't understand at all. Both Sally and my mother died in her care.'

'Niamh, be fair. The poor woman did her best for them. She isn't to blame.'

'No?'

'No.' Elinor was insistent. 'She came and wished us every happiness – even brought me some flowers. And she looked so wistful, so lost with nowhere to go.'

'It's a month since she left us. She had lodgings. She must have had somewhere to go.'

'And she asked us so humbly, with tears in her eyes. It would have been cruel and heartless to turn her away.'

'Be very careful, Ellie. That woman never does anything without a reason.'

'And neither do I.' Ellie smiled. 'I've always enjoyed cooking and I don't mind helping Tully behind the bar but housework isn't exactly my style.' She wrinkled her nose. 'I'm spoiled – used to having someone else to clean up for me – someone who'll keep the house tidy and hang the washing out on the line.'

Niamh pursed her lips, unconvinced. 'Just make sure *you're* not the one who's hung out to dry.'

Sukie stayed away from the foundry not only because of her condition but because of her continuing aversion to Jean-Louis de Vesinet. When she heard someone knock at the door that Sunday afternoon, she squared her shoulders, preparing for battle, expecting to find more reporters outside on the doorstep. So she was only marginally relieved to see it was the Frenchman instead. She considered ignoring his knock, allowing him to think she had gone out with her father, when he knocked again, more insistently this time.

'My father's not here,' she told him, disinclined to be gracious. 'And won't be back for the rest of the afternoon. He's gone to the M.C.G. to see the cricket.'

'Good afternoon, madame!' De Vesinet wasn't at all put out by this news. He presented her with his hat, giving her no option but to invite him in. She led him through the house to the family room, only slightly ashamed of the muddle. If the man would come visiting without an invitation, he would have to take them as he found them.

'May I offer you tea perhaps and a slice of cake?' she asked, her nostrils assailed by the miasma of garlic which always accompanied him.

'Tea? *Mais non.*' De Vesinet wrinkled his nose. 'Perhaps a *demi-tasse du café?*'

'I'm sorry, I don't speak French,' she snapped.

Ignoring her rudeness, the man sat down at the kitchen table, making himself so at home, she began to feel uneasy. 'I'm afraid I can't ask you to wait, m'sieur. I don't know how long my father will be.'

'I have nothing else to do. And we can become better acquainted, you and I.' He gazed around the room which had changed little since Sukie's grandmother's day. It was a cottage kitchen, very much in the old-fashioned English style. 'Yes, I like it, Suzi. It is very – how you say – cosy.'

'My name is Susannah or Sukie. But you may call me madame.' She was seething at his presumption.

'Suzi in France. The name suits you. Beautiful Suzi – *enceinte . . .*' He leaned forward, allowing his hand to rest on the curve of her belly. 'And in the full flower of your womanhood.'

Astonished, unable to believe he would touch her so boldly, so intimately, Sukie froze. Taking her silence to mean consent, de Vesinet grew bolder still and raised his hand to fondle her breast, accurately discovering the nipple beneath the light muslin of her blouse.

Sukie cried out in disgust, smacking his hand away. 'I'm a married woman, m'sieur, and about to have a child. My husband will – will –' she swallowed, unpleasantly reminded of where he was.

'You must face facts, madame.' De Vesinet retreated a little but his smile was no less unctuous. 'Your husband can't help you now. He is in gaol for murder, soon to be hanged.'

'No!' The word burst from Sukie like a sob. With as much

speed as she could muster in her condition, she managed to put the table and a chair between them.

'While I, Jean-Louis de Vesinet, am here for you now. I am willing to overlook that you are the widow of a murderer—'

'But I'm not a widow. Not yet! He's not even come to trial!'

De Vesinet raised his hands in a typical Gallic shrug. 'A formality. Be practical, madame. It is only a matter of time. I, Jean-Louis de Vesinet, will take care of you and your little *bébé*. I will even raise the child as my own.' He rose and took another step towards her. She picked up the bread-knife which was the only weapon to hand.

'Don't! Just don't come near me again. You wait till my father hears about this.'

'Your father? *Ah, non.* That would be most unwise. Think – my foolish, impetuous little Suzi. Will it help to have your father fall out with me now? I own half the foundry, already.'

'Oh yes,' she said. 'And with me in your pocket you could inherit the whole of it when Pa dies.'

'So? We understand each other, at last.'

'Oh, I understand you all right, you worm. You evil snake in the grass!'

'Insult me as much as you like, madame, if it makes you feel better. I can wait. You'll come round to my way of thinking in the end.'

'Just get out of here. Go! Get out of this house before I run out on the streets crying rape!'

De Vesinet laughed, believing she'd do no such thing but he made his way slowly to the door, collecting his hat from the stand on the way. She followed at a respectable distance, waiting to pounce and bolt the door behind him as soon as he left. He remained in the doorway a moment longer, to tease her, his gaze resting on the opulence of her breasts which she was unable to hide. She folded her arms and wished she were wearing a shawl.

'So modest. I like that. *Au revoir!*' he said, raising his hat as he stepped over the threshold. Sukie slammed the door behind him and bolted it, leaning against it and breathing heavily until her heartbeat slowed and became normal again.

Contrary to de Vesinet's expectations, she told Albert exactly what had happened as soon as he came in. But he didn't sympathise or give her the support she expected.

'Now, now Sukie,' he said, doing his best to calm her. She was becoming more and more agitated when she saw he wasn't taking her complaints at all seriously. 'You're upset, I know, and I can understand – but you have to realise it's because of your condition. That's what makes you so anxious and start imaginin' things.'

'I'm imagining nothing, Pa! The man touched me – he put his hands on my body, on my breast!'

'He's a Frenchman an' they do things different than we do. He would've meant it as a compliment, not to insult you, girl.'

'Pa, you're just guessing. You weren't there.'

'You have to make allowances, Sukie.'

'No, I don't. I don't have to do anything.' She turned on her heel to go to her own room.

'And where are you off to now? What about tea?'

Sukie didn't answer him. Instead she leaned in the doorway of the room which until recently she had occupied with Judd. It had been hers since she was a child and remained the same apart from their new double bed. It held all the bric-à-brac she had accumulated over the years – old toys and favourite ornaments. With difficulty because of her size she bent down and pulled a travelling bag from under the bed, coughing at the dust she disturbed. Trouble and pregnancy had wearied her, making her less than diligent with her housework these days.

'What are you doing?' Albert said, looking over her shoulder. She ignored him. 'Sulk then, if you want to. I should care.' He stamped off to the kitchen and she could hear him pretending to make his own meal, clattering pans and swearing, waiting for her to come and push him aside, taking over as she usually did when she heard him.

This time, she didn't. Carefully, she packed the little clothes she had made for the coming baby and a few of her own. She took the music box which had belonged to her mother and the tattered rag doll she had loved as a child. She put on her best hat and shawl and picked up the bag, finding it heavy enough as it was without taking more. For the last time she peered around the room at the rest of her treasures which must be left behind.

241

She paused in the hallway and listened. Albert was still banging about in the kitchen, confident that she would come to his rescue before he dented her pots and pans. He was singing to himself, determinedly cheerful, when she let herself out of the front door and closed it gently behind her to make no sound.

Niamh came home to find Sukie waiting for her in the parlour, sitting wearing her hat and shawl, a bag by her side.

'I'm sorry, Niamh,' she said, her eyes swimming with tears under fluttering eyelids. 'It was so awful at home and I had nowhere else to go.'

Brigid fussed around her, anxious for Niamh to know she had been doing her best to make Sukie comfortable. 'I made her some hot milk an' cinnamon, God love 'er, an' gave her some of my bread an' butter puddin' left over from lunch.' She dropped her voice to a stage whisper as if Sukie were deaf as well as having diminished vision. 'To be honest I don't think the poor thing's eaten all day an' she'll be needin' the whole of her strength for the comin' ordeal.' She rolled her eyes significantly at Sukie's pregnancy.

'Thank you, Brigid, that'll be all now.' Niamh briskly dismissed her servant, realising Sukie was finding it hard to control her emotions until they were alone. 'I appreciate that you did all you could to make Mrs Burden feel at home.'

'Mrs Burden?' The old Irishwoman gaped. 'You don't mean . . .? God'n she isn't *that* Mrs Burden?'

'That will be all, Brigid!' Niamh glared at her servant, hoping she'd leave before she was any more tactless. There was no point in pretending that Sukie was anyone other than who she was but, as the wife of the notorious Burden, she became instantly fascinating to Brigid.

'Now then. Tell me what's happened?' Niamh said after pouring a small cognac for Sukie and dropping to her knees beside her friend's chair.

'I'm not sure I should drink this. It might not be good for the baby.'

'I'm sure it won't matter this once. You need something to calm you. What happened? Is it Albert?'

'Not entirely.' In between sips of brandy, the tale emerged

and Sukie broke down in tears again as she told how Albert made light of the Frenchman's advances.

'You did right to come here.' Niamh took Sukie's hand which was cold even though the afternoon had been hot. 'Of all the crass, insensitive—'

'It isn't his fault, Niamh.' Sukie felt bound to excuse him. 'You know what Pa's like when he has an enthusiasm for someone; they can do no wrong.'

'He used to feel that way about Judd.'

'I know.' The whole weight of Sukie's dejection lay in those two small words.

'Don't worry, Sukie. Not about anything. You can stay here just as long as you want.'

Hollis spoke up behind them, making them both start. 'No, she cannot.' They had been so engrossed, they didn't hear him come in. He stood glaring at Sukie, arms folded.

She set down her glass on the table beside her and hauled herself to her feet, awkward with her bulk. 'It's all right, Niamh, I'll go,' she whispered. 'I can't be the cause of trouble between you and your husband.'

'Sukie, sit down. You're not going anywhere.' Niamh stood up to face Hollis, preparing for battle. 'Sukie *will* be staying because I want her to. I've invited her.'

'I can't believe it.' Hollis stood hands on hips, regarding them. The drink on his breath could be smelled from ten paces, he was flushed and his eyes were unnaturally bright. 'You, Niamh – giving food and shelter to the wife of my father's murderer!'

'No, Holly, I'm taking care of a friend. It's incidental that she's Judd Burden's wife.'

'And what if it's *incidental* that I find her presence offensive?'

'Then that's your problem, Holly, not mine.' Niamh stood with an arm around Sukie, supporting her. 'This house is, after all, my property. Uncle Harley left it to me.'

'Ah! I wondered how long it would take you to get round to that. Well, I'm not staying – not under the same roof as Mrs Burden. Either she leaves or I do.'

'I'm sure your club will accommodate you until you come to your senses and decide to be reasonable, Holly,' Niamh said sweetly.

'I won't be at my club – I'll sleep in my old bedroom at The Oaks. And it'll be a long time before I return. You'll have to ask me.'

'You'll be alone there. Your mother's away.'

'Fine. That means I'll get some peace for once. And somebody ought to be there to keep an eye on the servants – keep them on their toes.'

Nervously, Sukie began to blink, plucking at Niamh's sleeve. 'Niamh, I do think I should go. I can't have you fighting with Hollis, not over me.'

'Don't worry, Sukie, it's nothing. Only one of a score of things we manage to fight about, these days.'

Hollis ran up the stairs, taking them two at a time. Brigid reappeared from the kitchen and stood looking after him. 'Will I wait supper, madam, if Mr Maitland's changing to go out?'

'No, Brigid. We will eat just as soon as it's ready. And don't bother to save a portion for my husband. If there's anything left over, you can give it to the dog.'

Niamh sent messages to Sister Kearney, excusing herself from her work at The Briarley Hospital while she devoted herself to Sukie. She would scarcely be missed; there were plenty of willing hands to take over the work these days. Were it not for Judd's trial, set for the first week in February, the two women might almost have been happy. Niamh made Sukie walk to the beach every day to keep fit and was exasperated to find out her friend had engaged no medical practitioner to attend her. She couldn't even be sure when the baby was due.

'But you must have *some* idea! And someone should advise you – look after you. You haven't even a midwife?'

'No.' Sukie pursed her lips, growing stubborn. 'I was going to an' then there was all this trouble with Judd. So I've made a pact with myself. I won't have the baby till after the trial.'

'But that's nonsense, Sukie! The trial isn't until next week and you must be a good nine months already. The baby could come right now – any hour, any minute . . .'

'No, it won't.'

Sukie was right. The day of the trial dawned humid and hot;

244

one of those days in the height of summer when the sun beats down from a cloudless cobalt-blue sky and there isn't a breath of air. Niamh tried to persuade Sukie to stay at home while she went to court on her own but to no avail. Armed with a bottle of smelling salts and wet handkerchiefs to cool her wrists, Sukie was determined to be there. Niamh sat beside her, conscious of the hostility all around them, which manifested itself in a throbbing headache and a burning pain on the back of her neck. Not one friendly face was turned towards Sukie and, for once, she was grateful for her friend's poor eyesight. Even so, Sukie was able to sense the animosity that surrounded them and she shrank in her seat. Nobody wished them well.

The outcome of the trial was never in any doubt. Hollis was lucid and convincing in giving his evidence and when the time came for cross-examination, Judd's barrister was obsequious and in awe of the Maitland name. He didn't check Hollis once, allowing him to wander from the point, saying whatever he liked. Hollis was quick to take advantage, pointing to Judd and then at Niamh with Sukie cringing beside her.

'And to add insult to injury,' he spoke in ringing tones, 'my own wife has turned against me. I've had to move out of my own home while she harbours the murderer's wife.'

There was a concerted gasp from the matrons among the spectators and one or two cries of, 'Shame!' causing the judge to call for order in the court.

Sukie clutched Niamh's arm. 'Please,' she whispered. 'We must do something. He's twisting everything to make it look bad.'

But Judd's lawyer seemed as anxious as the prosecutor to reach a conclusion, scarcely taking the trouble to offer any defence. The jury were out for less than ten minutes, unanimously returning a verdict of 'Guilty as charged!'

Sukie stood up and cried, 'No – please! My husband is innocent!' before she became too overcome by emotion and had to sink back in her seat. Judd's legs also gave under him when the verdict was given and he had to be hauled to his feet to hear sentence pronounced.

'You have been found guilty of the most heinous crime. The brutal murder of a man cherished by this community and who never did anyone a bad turn in the whole of his life. I see no reason to postpone sentence in this case.' With ceremony the judge placed the black cap on his bewigged head. 'Have you anything to say for yourself before I do?'

'Only this, milord.' Judd glanced at his lawyer who was already shuffling his papers and glancing at his pocket-watch. 'I am innocent – as my wife says.' A howl of derision greeted this remark. 'Am I to be given no right of appeal? No more time to clear myself?'

'The evidence we have seen is overwhelming – the jury's decision unanimous. Justice will not be served by wasting any more of the court's time. Prepare yourself to receive sentence. On Thursday next, the day after tomorrow, at nine a.m. you will be conducted to a place of execution within the gaol where you will be hanged by the neck until you are dead.'

A sigh of satisfaction went through the spectators. Sukie slumped beside Niamh, having quietly fainted away. Judd strained towards them, trying to see what had happened as two burly policemen closed in on him, one either side.

'Don't worry, Judd. I'll take care of her,' Niamh said, aware that in speaking to him across the court, she had attracted the interest of reporters who now watched her avidly, some even making a quick sketch of her features.

Sukie groaned and stirred beside her as Niamh waved the smelling salts under her nose to revive her, but she didn't fully return to consciousness until after the court had been cleared and Judd had been returned to the cells.

Chapter Eighteen

Relaxed and totally happy, for the moment sated from their love-making, Elinor turned to look at her husband. They were lying in the big four-poster bed she had brought to the marriage. A bed so large and out of proportion to its surroundings, it filled the modest room on its own, leaving no space for clothes presses or even a wash-stand, all of which had to be moved into the bedroom next door. Ellie had taken over Tully's bedroom entirely and made it her own, even to the extent of placing an ornate, gilt-framed mirror on the wall opposite their bed. Tully had been shy about watching himself at first but Ellie worked hard at freeing him from his inhibitions; she was one of those women who liked to watch herself making love.

But this time instead of turning towards her, kissing her softly and whispering, 'Hello again,' which was his usual post-script to passion, Tully was lying back, resting his head on his hands and staring up at the ceiling. Ellie leaned over and kissed him, enjoying the smoothness of his face. Since marrying her, he had made it part of his routine to shave before going to bed. He smiled and put an arm about her, drawing her close. Whirlwind romance and passion had brought them this far and now they were reaching that stage of the relationship where they were ready to learn more of each other; to test the boundaries.

'I'm sorry, Tully,' she said, tracing the line of his chin with her fingers. 'Sorry I wasn't a virgin for you.'

'Do you think I care about that?' He turned to look at her. 'Oh no, Ellie. You're here for me and you're mine – that's all I care about now.'

'But I must tell you – I need you to know. My first time was when I was staying at Lachlan's Holt. It was a friend of my father's who came to buy horses from Maggi.'

'Then Maggi should have taken better care of you.'

'Oh no, my darling, it wasn't her fault. And she's more used to dealing with boys, not deceitful girls. She couldn't have stopped me anyway. I was determined to have him – I've always liked older men. Idiot that I was, I thought he would marry me. It was only when I got home that I found out he was married already and was only amusing himself. I was so angry I went on a rampage for the next twelve months that took me through most of the officers at Victoria Barracks.'

'Ellie.' Gently he placed a finger on her mouth. 'I don't need to hear this: I don't need this confession. No one can live all their lives without doing something they're ashamed of. Everyone does.'

'You, Tully? I can't imagine you doing anything to be ashamed of.'

'Oh yes, I did. I robbed a man once – not deliberately, mind, because I've never liked the thievin'. My father and Maggi picked pockets for years but I couldn't do it. I was always too scared I'd be caught.'

'*Maggi?* Maggi – a thief?' Ellie was stunned. 'I don't believe it.'

'It's another story entirely – I'll tell you some time. I'm saying I didn't put my hand in a man's pocket and rob him literally, but I did make use of some gold nuggets that came my way. I should have returned the money when I had the chance but chose not to. Because of that, tomorrow a man's going to die.'

'Who then? Who's going to die?' Wide awake now and fascinated by the tale, Ellie turned up her oil-lamp with its pretty, rose-coloured shade, in order to stare at him.

'Judd Burden, of course. I went to sea with his Uncle Jem – I was with him when he died. I found the gold nuggets in the heels of the old man's boots.'

'How many?'

'Some. I should have gone back to England and given the gold to Jem's relatives, but I was young and in love with Janet, you see. So, instead of doing the right thing, I came back here.

I'd forgotten the nuggets entirely till Judd Burden came askin' for them – I knew one day that somebody would. So I panicked and used my connections with your family to protect myself and keep young Burden at bay. But now – now I'm thinkin' if only I'd treated him fairly, maybe he wouldn't have been so desperate an' he wouldn't have murdered poor Harley and stolen that money. He wouldn't be facing the gallows tomorrow.'

Ellie sat up to add weight to her words. 'Tully, that's not your fault. You didn't make a murderer of Judd Burden. He chose that course by himself. You're not to make yourself miserable, taking the blame over this. I won't have it.'

'Oh Ellie, Ellie . . .' He took her in his arms and buried his face in her luxuriant hair which smelled of rose petals. 'I do love you. I love you so very much.'

'Love you, too,' she whispered, drawing him close. 'Tully – what would you say if I told you we might be expecting a child?'

'A baby?' He looked at her in wonderment, eyes wide. 'Oh darlin', are you sure?'

'Not entirely, not yet. But I feel that it's so.'

'Then I'd say,' he took her face in his hands, gently kissing her lips, 'I'd say I'm the luckiest man alive.'

'They're going to hang me tomorrow.' Anxiety made Judd speak loudly and with less caution when he met Carl in the exercise period. This time Gusto had let them meet without the calico hoods to disguise them. 'They're boasting of it. I'm to hang from the same gallows they used for Ned Kelly.'

Carl glanced at Gusto who was lurking in the doorway, signalling them to be quiet. 'Keep your voice down.'

'So if we're going, let's go!' Judd urged. 'It must be tonight.'

'Pipe down! D'you want to get us both flogged?'

'Right now that's the least of my worries.'

'Stop wasting time and listen. It's all arranged. I've already got the money for Gusto – had it for two nights.'

''Then why didn't you—?'

'Go alone? Because, like a fool, I was waitin' for you.' Carl held up a hand to stem Judd's further queries. 'Shut up an' listen. Gusto's made sure he's on for the graveyard shift.

There'll be only one guard on duty – himself with a couple of troopers outside.'

'Troopers?'

'We don't have to worry about them. At night the troopers are always half-drunk or fast asleep.'

'Can we trust him?'

'We have to.' Carl laughed shortly. 'It's the only chance we're going to get.'

The early hours of the evening crawled by for Judd. Had there been no possibility of escape, he might have come to terms with the inevitability of his fate. But hope made him restless and realise that he wasn't ready to die. If only he could escape, somehow, somewhere he might make a new life for them – Sukie, himself and their child. And Niamh? He couldn't include her in his plans. Niamh he didn't dare think about – not at all.

Since he was due for execution the following day, he was given a generous plate of roast beef with three vegetables and a jam sponge pudding to follow. He tried to eat but the food cleaved to the roof of his mouth and tasted like sawdust. He was too tense to salivate. And during the night he listened as the various church clocks in the town chimed nine, ten, eleven and then, in spite of everything, some time before midnight, he slept.

He awoke with a start, hearing the bolts of his door being drawn back and a key quietly inserted in the lock to turn it with the minimum of noise before the heavy door swung open, creaking on its hinges. For a moment he thought he must have slept until morning and they were coming to take him to his execution but instead of police and a parson in black robes, he was relieved to see the grinning faces of Gusto and Carl.

With agonising slowness Gusto fumbled for his keys, grunting as he bent over Judd's leg-irons, taking an age to release him; Carl hopping with impatience behind.

'There!' Gusto hissed, grinning. 'Now take my coat an' my hat – you're nearer my build than he is.' He offered the smelly garments to Judd who accepted them with little enthusiasm; he didn't care to wear clothes that reeked of the gaoler's sour body odours. 'That way, if the troopers wake up an', see you, they'll think it's me. The door's on the latch and the rest's up

250

to you. Just the small detail of the money . . .' He leered at Carl, holding out a grimy, calloused hand to receive it.

Carl slapped a tightly-rolled bundle of notes into his palm and Gusto's fingers closed around it.

'And a small bonus as well,' Carl whispered, moving so quickly that Judd didn't realise what he would do until it was too late. Seizing the gaoler by his matted curls, Carl jerked back his head, expertly cutting his throat with a slim knife. Almost in the same movement, as if performing a dance, he retrieved the money and pushed Judd out of the way to avoid being splashed by the blood which came spurting from the open wound in the man's neck. Sinking to the ground like a felled ox, Gusto didn't even have time to look surprised.

'My God!' Judd stood staring at the twitching, now lifeless body as the blood spread, forming a dark pool around it on the stone floor.

'Come on,' Carl said. 'Let's get out of here.'

'Was that really necessary? Did you have to—?'

'Kill him? Yes, I did.' Carl gave a soft, snickering laugh, disturbingly unaffected by what he had done. 'You didn't think he'd really let us get out of here, did you?'

'Why not? He fulfilled his side of the bargain.'

'Sure. Until he had his hands on our money. We wouldn't have gone two paces before he'd have been rousin' the troopers.'

'You don't know that. You're just guessing.'

'Well, that's what he did to somebody only last week. There's advantages to being held in the cell nearest the front door. These idiots think that because you don't see what's going on, you don't hear. Old Gusto's had this coming a long time – don't waste your pity on him.'

'But you murdered him, Carl. And you've made me an accessory to it.'

'So I did. You were going to be hanged tomorrow, remember? Come on!' Once again he gave that high-pitched snickering laugh. Judd knew if he had to hear much more of it, it would get on his nerves. 'Let's make ourselves scarce, eh? Before they get to bring you your hearty breakfast. You can argue the ins an' outs of it later on.'

*

251

'Niamh! Oh Niamh, wake up – I'm scared. There's water come away from me, soaking the bed. I think the baby's coming – and it's not going to wait until morning.'

Niamh groaned and struggled to consciousness, realising the white figure looming at the end of her bed was no ghost but Sukie standing there in her nightgown, white-faced, her eyes rolling in panic.

'Don't worry, Sukie,' she croaked. 'We'll get help.' She got up, steered Sukie back to her own room and sat her in a chair while she fetched clean linen and re-made the bed. Only when she was out of her friend's sight did she allow herself the luxury of panic. Sukie had never found time to visit a doctor or engage a midwife to attend the birth of her child. Silently, Niamh cursed herself for her laxity – she should have insisted upon it. Enjoying rude health herself, she had never seen it as urgent to make the acquaintance of a local physician in case she needed him; to do so would have seemed like tempting providence.

In this household only Brigid made regular use of a doctor and it was to Brigid she turned in her hour of need. The old woman was fast asleep, snoring richly with her nightcap falling over her face. She didn't take kindly to being shaken from her slumbers.

'Brigid! Oh Brigid, please wake up. I need you.'

'Well, madam,' Brigid sighed, finding her usual excuse even when she was half-asleep. 'I'd like to help you, really. An' if I could do it, I would. But once I've got these poor auld legs into bed . . .'

'Brigid, this is an emergency! The baby's coming! Mrs Burden's about to give birth.'

Brigid blinked owlishly. 'I'm not a midwife, madam. I can't possibly—'

'I know that!' Niamh was clenching her teeth, trying not to lose patience with her elderly servant. 'But will you get dressed and rouse Dayman – get him to drive with you to fetch your doctor – Dr O'Hara, isn't it?'

'Indeed it is, madam, but there's no point in goin' now. I'd trust John O'Hara with my life in the hours of daylight, but he'll be drunk as a lord by this time o' night.'

'Niamh!' This came as an agonised scream from Sukie, caught by another wave of pain.

'All right, Sukie, I'm coming!' Niamh called to her before turning her attention once more to Brigid. 'You! Get out of bed and help me, you lazy old bones. Boil some water and bring me some towels. Then go an' get Dayman. We'll decide what to do after that.'

'Oh madam,' Brigid wailed. 'I'd like to help you—'

'And if you could do it, you would!' Viciously, Niamh finished the sentence for her. 'Do it, Brigid, and quickly. Or you'll find yourself out on the streets with no character.' She didn't like to deal so harshly with her servant but this was the only way to get her to help.

Shaking her head and muttering imprecations under her breath, Brigid moved faster than Niamh had ever seen her, doing exactly as she was told. Niamh knew little about childbirth and wished she had paid more attention to the experiences of labour described by the women at The Briarley Hospital. For all Sukie's initial panic, she seemed surprisingly calm and not unduly stressed by her ordeal.

Dayman arrived in due course, a wizened, dark-skinned little man who looked older than his forty or so years. With his bright, intelligent eyes, colourful waistcoats and fluffy mutton-chop whiskers, he looked a bit like a gnome. He stood in the doorway of the bedroom, regarding Sukie, unembarrassed by the sight of a woman in labour, nodding his approval as she took advantage of the contractions to push.

'She'll do all right,' he pronounced. 'No point in gallopin' all over the countryside for the doctor. That baby's goin' to be here before I get to leave.'

'Can you help us, Dayman?' Niamh wanted someone – anyone – to take the responsibility from her shoulders. Having done what she was told to do, Brigid had taken umbrage and disappeared. 'You know something of childbirth?'

'Childbirth? No. But I've delivered a thoroughbred foal or two in my time. Can't be so very different now, can it?'

'Sukie,' Niamh wiped her friend's face for the umpteenth time. 'Will you let him take a look?'

Sukie looked from Niamh to the groom and back again, nodding to indicate she would trust herself to Dayman until proper medical attention could be found.

Dayman examined her, talking softly as if she were a nervous mare, his hands surprisingly gentle.

'Good,' he said, nodding approval and smiling to reassure her. 'Seems as if everything's where it ought to be at this time. A bit more heave-ho, Mrs Burden, an' you'll be holdin' your babe in your arms.'

'Oh, call me Sukie, please,' she gasped when she had breath enough to speak. 'We can't be formal – not at a time like this.'

With surprisingly little more effort the head crowned and the baby was born.

'Mrs Burden – Sukie,' Dayman retrieved the child. 'I'm pleased to tell you you're the mother of a fine boy.'

'Thank you,' she whispered. 'Thank you, Mr Dayman.'

'Noah.'

'That's a good name – a strong name.' Sukie wiped the mucus from the baby's face and kissed him. 'And bein' born in such wretched circumstances my son's goin' to need one. D'you mind if I call him Noah – after you?'

'I'd be honoured, madam, but surely . . .' Dayman shot an anxious glance at Niamh but she nodded, reassuring him. She passed him a pair of scissors she had boiled to cleanse them in the way she'd seen surgical instruments boiled at The Briarley, for him to cut the umbilical cord. Sukie expelled the afterbirth but Niamh could see Dayman watching her anxiously, still vaguely troubled, as if he were expecting something more. But she didn't question him until Sukie had taken a cup of tea and fallen asleep, her infant in a makeshift cradle – a fruit box provided by Brigid – which they stood on a chair by the bed.

'What is it, Dayman?' Niamh said. 'The baby's all right, isn't he?'

'The baby's fine. It's the mother concerns me.'

'But she's sleeping now and in no pain.'

'Bring a doctor to her as soon as you can in the morning.' The little man frowned. 'I'm not saying there should be a lot of blood, but I'd have expected more. There could be a blockage, something left inside. Not for me to meddle – I might do more harm than good – but you should get a medical man to look at her soon as you can.'

'Thank you for everything, Dayman.' Impulsively, Niamh kissed his cheek. 'I couldn't have managed without you.'

'You didn't do so badly yourself, madam, and you keep a cool head which is half the battle. You can assist me in birthin' a foal any time.'

'Why me, Carl? Why did you bother to save me?' Judd saved his questions until they were clear of the city and out on the open road. Instead of being offered a fast horse, as he expected, he and Carl had been met in a lane not far from the gaol by a man driving a cabriolet – a cabriolet no different from the dozens of others which might be seen touting for trade all over the city at any hour of the day or night. 'You could have finished Gusto and got clear in half the time without getting lumbered with me – a man convicted of murder.'

'I owe you, remember? An' my mum said—'

'Come on, Carl, this is nothing to do with Daisy. I *know* you, remember? I've lived in your home.'

'Exactly. So that makes us brothers.'

'No, it doesn't. And you don't give a damn for your own brothers so why should you care about me? You sprang me from gaol because I can be useful. I want to know how.'

'All right. There's no one aboard the boat with the skills of a smith.'

'Boat? What boat? You said we were going to hide in the hills!'

'Which is what they expect us to do. Troopers are probably heading north in pursuit of us right now.'

'Then where *are* we going?'

'Little place near Sorrento down the peninsula. Friend of mine has a schooner waiting. We're on the coast road already – can't you smell the sea?'

'No, Carl! This just isn't possible. My wife is expecting our child – she needs me here!'

'And you had a date with the hangman, remember? Lot of good you'll be to her, chokin' your last at the end of a rope. This is your only chance, Judd. Better take it.'

'All right, all right. But on one condition.'

Carl snickered. 'You're in no position to make deals, Judd.'

'Oh, I think I am. Are we anywhere near Brighton?'

'Bloody hell! How should I know?'

'Ask him then – ask the driver.'

Reluctantly, Carl leaned forward and exchanged a few words with the driver who told him they were within a mile or so of Brighton right now.

'Good. Then tell him I want to stop off at The Hollies to say farewell to my wife.'

'Have you lost your mind?' Carl's voice rose an octave in panic. 'If anyone sees us – and I mean *anyone* – they'll have the troopers down on us in a matter of minutes.'

'I won't come, then. Not without seeing my wife.'

'Fifteen minutes, then. No, make it ten! And if there's trouble of any kind, you're on your own.'

Judd's heart was in his mouth as he peered into the darkness, wondering if he could remember the way to The Hollies. More roads had been completed, more houses built since he was last there. If they missed the way, he knew Carl wouldn't waste time doubling back. Fortunately, there was a full moon and, more by instinct than memory, Judd found the track which led to The Hollies. He jumped from the cab, leaving Carl and the driver parked under the trees just off the main road.

'And if you're not back in ten minutes, we're gone.' Carl repeated his warning.

Judd moved slowly towards the back of the house. Now he was here, he had misgivings of his own. What if Sukie shouldn't be there? And what if Hollis was back? Could he attract Niamh's attention without disturbing anyone else?

A voice behind him made him jump. It was accompanied by a double-barrelled shotgun jammed into the small of his back. 'Raise your hands slowly, big fella, an' no false moves. Up to no good, I'll be bound. Or why would you be disturbin' a household of women at this time of the night?'

'Must be nearly morning by now.' Judd kept cool but he now hoped the owner of the shotgun, whoever he was, wouldn't panic when he found out who he had in his sights. 'And I'm not a burglar, if that's what you're thinking. I'm here to see Sukie Burden – my wife.'

'Mrs Burden? Then you mus' be—'

'Yes. And whatever you've heard, I'm not dangerous. So please don't panic and shoot.'

256

'Wasn't goin' to.' Dayman relaxed and lowered the shotgun. 'How could I shoot Miss Sukie's husband, when it's meself that delivered her child? Congratulations, sir. You are the father of a fine, healthy boy.'

'I am?' Judd blinked, having some trouble absorbing this news. One moment he was being bailed up and threatened at gunpoint – the next, this little man was offering congratulations and shaking him by the hand. 'Then please will you let me see them? There isn't much time.'

Dayman opened the back door and let Judd into the kitchen where Brigid was muttering about her disturbed night and raking out the coals, preparing to light the stove.

Hearing voices below, Niamh came downstairs. It was Dayman she wanted and at first she didn't see somebody else was present as well as Brigid and the groom.

'Dayman – thank goodness you're still up and about. I need you to ride for Dr O'Hara . . .' She paused in mid-sentence as she caught sight of Judd, wondering for a moment if her eyes were deceiving her. So concerned had she been about Sukie and the child that she realised, with a jolt, that she had managed to block the unpleasant business of the hanging from her mind. 'But Judd, this is wonderful – we couldn't have better news! They saw sense at last? You've had a reprieve?'

'Afraid not.' Judd saw no point in deceiving her. 'I broke out of gaol with some friends and I'm in as much trouble as ever. Probably more.'

'Then you were crazy to come. They know Sukie's staying here. This is one of the first places they'll look for you.'

'But I had to see her – and you – before going to sea.'

'To sea?' Niamh was longing to ask about it but out of the corner of her eye she saw Brigid listening, waiting to pick up every word. 'No, don't tell me anything more. Then, if anyone comes here asking questions,' she glanced at Brigid, 'we can truthfully say we don't know.' She turned to her groom. 'You must be exhausted I know, but—'

'No more than you are, ma'am,' he smiled.

'I'd appreciate it if you'd ride out and fetch Dr O'Hara to Sukie.'

'What's the matter?' Judd's voice betrayed his anxiety. 'You said she was safely delivered of the child?'

257

'Seeing you will be the best tonic she can have.' Niamh assured him. 'But she's running a bit of a fever and I'd like a doctor to examine her, that's all.'

'I'm on my way.' Dayman saluted and left.

Niamh wrinkled her nose. 'Judd I don't know where you got that verminous coat and hat but they should be burned. I can't let you go up to Sukie smelling like that.'

'Oh God, I forgot!' He tore off the foul-smelling garments and, finding nowhere to dispose of them indoors, took them outside to the yard. Niamh heard him pumping water to wash himself. Shortly afterwards he returned, dripping but without the stink.

'That's better.' Niamh smiled, offering a towel. 'You can go up and see them now. They're in the room directly opposite the top of the stairs.'

Judd needed no second invitation and bounded for the front stairs, taking them two at a time, leaving Niamh to face Brigid who watched him disappear into the interior of the house through narrowed eyes.

'Aidin' an' abettin' a murderer, madam, that's what it is. We could all be arrested for this.'

'Only if we're found out.'

'I ought to go for the troopers, an' if I could do it I would. But it goes against the grain for any Irishwoman to have truck with the law.'

Niamh smiled thinly, for once grateful for Brigid's laziness and bad legs.

'Never mind, Brigid. If anyone comes asking questions, I'll make sure you're in the clear.'

'Thank you, Madam.' Brigid pursed her lips and wriggled her shoulders like a self-satisfied hen. 'I don't wish to be difficult, to be sure. But a woman in my position has to protect herself.'

'Quite so, Brigid. Now why not go back to bed for a while? You've had a terrible night and I'm sure you could do with some sleep. If Sukie needs anything, I'll see to it myself.'

'D'you know, madam, I think I will.' Brigid visibly brightened. 'Although how a body can sleep in peace with a convicted murderer roamin' about the house . . .'

'Oh, I think you'll manage,' Niamh smiled. But soon as

258

Brigid had gone, she sank into a chair at the kitchen table, rubbing eyes which felt gritty with tiredness.

In a small, mean corner of her soul she resented Judd's eagerness to go up to his wife and baby son. She had sent both her servants away, perhaps without realising it, to allow herself a few moments with him alone. She told herself this was no time for petty resentment. She'd had her chance with him and she'd let it go. It wasn't his fault she wished she could have been the one to present him with his first child. She pressed the heels of her hands to her eyes to hold back the tears of self-pity as she waited for him to return.

Judd paused on the threshold of Sukie's bedroom to calm himself before going in. He didn't want to frighten her by appearing before her like a wild man. The room smelled strongly of female perspiration and other smells, less familiar, of baby and milk. Both mother and child were asleep, Sukie lying on her back with her eyes closed, nothing visible of the child but a small bundle in a fruit box on a chair by the bed.

He stood by the bed and touched Sukie's cheek with the back of one finger. It was hot. Niamh said she had a slight fever but, maybe because he was chilled having sluiced himself with cold water, she felt as if she were burning up. Her eyes snapped open and she peered at him, taking more than a moment to focus and recognise him.

'Oh Judd,' she whispered, clinging to his hand.' You're here and you feel so real to me but – oh Judd, are we dead?'

'No, my love, thanks be to God – and to the Devil too if He goes by the name of Carl Bradley.'

'Carl?' She frowned at the mention of this name, reminding him of something he had forgotten – that she and Carl were related. 'The Devil, indeed. What's he done now?'

'Never mind. I'm sorry, my love – I can't stay more than a moment or they'll go without me.'

'Go where?' Sukie's eyes fluttered as she struggled to sit up, petulant and feverish. 'But you can't – you've only just got here!'

'I know, love. But I shouldn't be here at all. It puts you and Niamh at risk.' He kissed her temple, realising she was delirious and wouldn't be thinking rationally.

259

'Niamh's been so kind to me. So good . . .' Sukie's mind was beginning to wander until Judd interrupted her gently.

'Aren't you going to introduce me to our son?'

'Oh, yes.' Awkwardly, still unused to handling her baby, Sukie picked up the bundle making the infant whimper at being disturbed and open his mouth like a small fish, searching for nourishment. He looked like most babies who've had a difficult passage into the world; a screwed-up red face and the expression of a peevish old man. The dark tuft of hair on his scalp was the only similarity he bore to his father but as Judd looked down into the tiny face, he felt a rush of tenderness and a desire to protect this baby. His first child.

'Oh Sukie, he's beautiful.'

'No, he isn't,' she smiled shyly. 'Only to us.'

'What shall we call him?'

'I've named him already – Noah. I hope you don't mind.'

'Noah Burden. That's a good name – it will suit him. Oh Sukie, I do thank you – thank you so much for this.'

'Then you're pleased?'

'Pleased? I can't tell you what this means to me. When this morning, this very morning, I might have been . . .'

'Ssh! Don't say it. Don't even think about it.'

'Sukie, it's awful, I know – but I have to go.'

'No.' Sukie's face crumpled. 'Oh no, not yet. I can't bear it – I'm not strong enough to let you go.'

'Sukie, you have to be. And I must leave now or I won't have the strength or the will. I'll just stay here with you and the boy till they come here and take me.'

'No!' Sukie looked up at him, anguished. 'I can't let you do that.'

Very gently he kissed her lips. She looked too pale and fragile for passion. 'Sukie, my love. I've never told you this before because I couldn't deceive you. I can say it now because it's true. I do love you – you are as dear to me as my own life.' He kissed her again, feeling the hot salt of her tears on his lips. 'Ah, Sukie. Sukie, don't cry.'

'If you know how I've waited and longed to hear you say that.' Her voice was low with misery. 'And now it's too late. Too late for all of us.'

'No, Sukie, not when we've come this far. As long as we have life there will always be hope. Goodbye, dearest wife and goodbye little Noah – my son.'

'Oh, Judd!' Eyes squeezed shut, she held the baby close with one hand, clinging to him with the other. Gently, he released himself from her grasp. 'Look out for my cousin Carl. He's a fool – a reckless fool.'

Judd didn't think this was the time to tell her Carl was a cold-blooded murderer, too. He left her, holding the baby to her face and sobbing. Crushed and uncomfortable in his mother's grasp, Noah cried lustily, adding his voice to her own.

'I'm afraid I disturbed them,' he said to Niamh downstairs.

'It won't matter.' She swallowed her own tears to smile at him, ready to act out the part of the sympathetic friend. 'She'd never have forgiven me, if I'd let you go without waking her.'

'God, look at the time!' Judd glanced at the kitchen clock, his eyes widening in panic. 'Carl gave me ten minutes and I must've been half an hour.'

'You don't have to worry about anything or anyone here. Dayman's the salt of the earth and Brigid won't say anything – I'll make sure of that. Go now, Judd – and quickly, before Dayman and the doctor come back.'

'Thank you, Niamh, for everything – for taking such care of them.' Judd raised his eyes to the ceiling to indicate his little family upstairs.

'That's all right.' She covered her tension by being crisp. 'Anyone would have done the same.'

'Oh no, they wouldn't,' he said, cupping her cheek in one hand. Without thinking, she raised her own hand to cover it. 'I daren't kiss you,' he whispered. 'I'd never be able to stop.'

'Just go, Judd. Go now.'

He paused in the doorway fighting his emotions, unable to leave without one last look. 'I don't know what's going to come of this, Niamh, really I don't. God help me, I love you both.'

261

Chapter Nineteen

That same night Hollis slept well, better than he had slept for months, in the certainty that by the time he awoke, took his breakfast and arrived at his office soon after nine, the loathsome Burden would be dangling at the end of a rope. The man responsible for his father's demise would be dead. Justice would have been served.

He rose from his bed refreshed and came downstairs early, sending the servants into a panic by demanding his breakfast half an hour before the usual time. Hastily, they provided a meal of sheep's kidneys and scrambled eggs.

Outside, the sun had come up on a perfect summer's day, a light breeze preventing the temperature from becoming too hot. For the first time in weeks Hollis felt at peace with the world, happy enough to whistle as he rode to the office in his father's carriage.

His mood of contentment was short-lived. On reaching the outskirts of the city, he saw newsboys shouting on street corners, waving the latest edition of the *Argus* which was selling as fast as they could take the money.

'Read all about it! Murder in the gaol-house! Convicted criminal escapes!'

Certain this must be Judd, Hollis yelled for his driver to stop and leaped from the carriage to buy a paper and read it for himself. He resisted the temptation to look at it until he reached the sanctuary of his office, ignoring his law clerk and Miss Johnson on the way. The newspaper report was sensational but accurate. Journalists had gone to the gaol to witness the hanging only to be greeted with the news that the prisoner, Burden, along with a fellow desperado by the name of Carl Bradley, had escaped after killing one of the guards. There followed a lurid description and a rough drawing of how the gaoler had met his violent end. Hollis scowled when his law clerk intruded, tapping at the door and then peering around it, wary of his employer's mood.

'You've not forgotten we're due in court at ten, Mr Hollis? Mr Sloane is expecting—'

'You know as much about it as I do, Jim.' Hollis waved him away. '*You* take the brief to Sloane. Oh, and tell Miss Johnson to cancel my appointments for the rest of the day.'

'But—'

'Don't stand there spluttering like a kettle. Just go.'

'Yes, Mr Hollis.' The young man ducked away, eyebrows writhing with anxiety and blushing from ear to ear.

Miss Johnson didn't think much of Hollis's manners either and said so, calling after him as he stormed past her desk on the way out.

'But what shall I say, Mr Holly? These are your father's best clients, his personal friends.' She was almost wringing her hands with anxiety. 'It's so rude to cancel appointments at the last minute. They'll take it as an insult.'

'Be buggered to them, then! I don't care.'

'Mr Holly! In all of the years I've served here, never have I been spoken to in such terms!'

But Hollis was already leaping into the carriage which was to have taken him to court, instructing the driver that they would be going to Brighton instead. Sukie was staying at The Hollies and a pregnant wife would act as a magnet to a desperate man. On his way to the top of the town to fetch reinforcements, his smile was grim. He had a good idea where Judd Burden and his accomplice were to be found.

Weary to the point of collapse, Niamh was too concerned about Sukie to rest. Even as the baby went from strength to strength by the minute, Sukie diminished. Judd gone, and no longed buoyed up by the triumph of giving birth, she seemed to be sinking into despair. Also she had broken out in a feverish sweat, soaking her bed linen which Niamh had already changed several times. Sukie's cheeks burned, her eyes were red-rimmed and sore, and she slept only fitfully, murmuring in her dreams and crying for Judd. Fearing she might sink into a delirium, Niamh sponged her often. She was lucid only when she was fully awake and feeding the child.

'Ooh!' she said, wincing as the baby fastened his mouth to her nipple, not yet accustomed to feeding him. 'He pulls so strongly, it feels as if he's drawing that milk all the way from my toes!'

'You'll get used to it.' Niamh smiled. Girls at the hospital, new to motherhood, said the same thing.

'Niamh?'

'Yes?'

'You *would* tell me, if the baby wasn't all right?'

'Oh Sukie, of course he's all right. Look at him. See how he kicks? How he exercises those lungs? It's amazing that someone so small can make so much noise.'

'No. I'm talking about his eyes.' Sukie looked down at the child who stared back at her, trying to focus as he suckled. 'I have to be sure he doesn't have eyes like mine.'

Niamh didn't know what to say. Would Sukie believe her if she said that all babies' eyes rolled as they squinted, unable to bring the world into focus during these first weeks of life? It was too soon to tell if Noah had inherited his mother's disability or not. A loud hammering at the door saved her from having to answer right away.

'That'll be Dr O'Hara to see you.' She patted Sukie's hand. 'And not before time.'

Remembering she had sent Brigid back to bed, she ran downstairs to open the door herself, then took a pace backwards, shocked when she saw who was there. Hollis stood on the threshold, flanked by a pair of troopers who had dismounted carelessly, leaving their horses to trample and graze on her flowers. To give herself time to think, she forestalled them, focusing her anger on that instead.

'Get those horses out of my flower beds!' she ordered, making the younger of the troopers leap to do her bidding, securing the horses away from the house where they could do no harm. 'You have a key to the front door,' she glared at her husband. 'Why didn't you use it?'

264

'Because we're here on official business.' Hollis greeted her with a thin smile. 'We have reason to believe you may be sheltering dangerous criminals. These men want to search the house.'

'Well, they can't. Sukie's just given birth and she's still very sick – very weak. I'm expecting the doctor any minute – I thought you were him.'

'You do know that her husband escaped from Melbourne Gaol last night after murdering one of the guards?'

'*What?*' The colour drained from Niamh's face. She had no need to feign her surprise.

'Here's the newspaper. You can read the account for yourself while these men search the house.'

'Look wherever you like but I won't have Sukie disturbed,' Niamh said, although her real fear was that Sukie might let slip that Judd had been there.

Hollis exchanged glances with the troopers and they ran for the stairs, thinking that if Judd Burden were anywhere in the house, it would be in his wife's room. Niamh would have followed but Hollis caught her by the arms, holding her back. She struggled in his grasp as they heard Sukie's terrified cry. 'Let me go to her, Holly! Those men shouldn't be up there – it's not decent.'

Moments later, the troopers came down again, looking shamefaced. They said Sukie had screamed, clutching her baby son to her bosom, for some reason convinced they had come to take him away. Refusing to be pacified, she had kept screaming until they left the room.

Good for you, Sukie, Niamh thought. Aloud she said, 'I hope you're satisfied. Harassing a poor woman who's just given birth to a child.'

'Someone was here,' Hollis insisted. 'I just know it. Those are fresh tracks at the top of the drive – signs that a horse and cart, maybe a cabriolet, left the main road.'

'What of it? We're not the only people who live here abouts.'

The troopers were exchanging glances, beginning to think they had been brought on a fool's errand.

'Go on then,' Niamh glared at them. 'Don't just stand there gawping. Make a job of it and search the rest of the house.

And don't forget the stables or the privy. I want you to be quite sure nobody's here.'

Hollis watched her through narrowed eyes, suspecting she knew more than she was telling. While the troopers were gone, she read the account of what happened at the gaol.

'You see? Look at this.' She pointed to a particular paragraph, reading it out. 'It says, *Due to the manner in, which the gaoler was slain, it is believed to be the work of Carl Bradley. Bradley, suspected of murdering a fellow member of his road gang, was in custody pending further investigation. In both cases the victim was killed in this brutal and bloody manner; the throat cut deeply, enough to sever the wind pipe, killing him instantly and preventing him from making a sound. Although the authorities were certain of Bradley's guilt, the close-mouthed attitude of his fellow prisoners, prevented them from gaining sufficient evidence to bring him to trial. Now, provided Bradley and Burden, his accomplice, can be apprehended, prosecuting attorneys have all the evidence they need.* 'You see?' she said, looking up at Holly. 'They say Judd was only an accomplice. He isn't guilty of this latest crime.'

'You'd defend him to the end, wouldn't you? Well, I want them both hunted down. If necessary, I'll do it myself. I won't be satisfied till they're both hanged.'

'You'll have to catch them first.' Niamh glanced at the troopers who were half-heartedly peering into the bushes, having already finished with the yard. 'And that won't be easy with sluggards like those to help you.'

'Don't you sneer at me, you little bitch!' Hollis seized her by the wrist, gripping her so tightly she feared the bones would break. 'I know damned well he was here.'

'Well, he's not here now, is he?' Niamh jerked free and stood rubbing her wrist. 'Better point your bloodhounds in the right direction. The longer you waste time here, the cooler the trail; the more time they'll have to get away to the hills.' She put her hand over her mouth as if to stop the words, as if she'd said more than she intended.

'Away to the hills, eh?' Hollis grinned. 'Thank you for that, Niamh. Thanks very much.'

'Oh Holly, please. I never meant—'

'I know just what you meant, my darling.' Sarcastically, he

blew her a kiss as he ran for the carriage, yelling for the troopers to follow.

Niamh slumped in the doorway, watching them go, hoping her piece of acting had been good enough to throw them off the scent. With luck, it would be some time before they realised she had sent them the wrong way. She thought about Holly, wondering what had happened to change him from the sunny-natured little boy of her early memories. While it was understandable that he wanted revenge for his father's death, he was behaving like a fanatic, hunting Judd like a man possessed.

She stayed in the garden to calm herself, knowing it wouldn't be good for Sukie to see her so agitated. It was only when Hollis and the troopers had been gone for some time that she saw the smelly old coat and hat which Judd had been wearing, discarded beside the pump. The sight of such obvious evidence, left in full view yet ignored by the troopers, struck her as so ridiculous that she started to laugh, weakly at first and then building until she was doubled up with hysterical laughter, unable to stop.

'What is it, madam? What's happened now?'

It was Dayman who spoke, afraid she was on the verge of hysteria. She had been laughing with her eyes closed and she didn't see him return, Dr O'Hara behind him, riding a snorting, overweight pony. O'Hara was as plump as his pony and red in the face from the effort of riding hard.

'No, I'm all right.' She sobered at once when she saw the doctor giving her an odd look. As Dayman dismounted, she gave him a whispered account of her husband's visit with the troopers and how she'd sent them off in the wrong direction. The groom nodded his approval and led both horses away while Niamh ushered the doctor upstairs, waiting with mounting impatience as he examined first the mother and then the child.

He concluded his examination, poured some water into the basin at the wash-stand and rinsed his hands, a thoughtful expression on his face. Before making any pronouncement, he led Niamh away from the bed, so that Sukie should not overhear.

'Your groom made quite a good job of it.' He spoke quietly

so that Niamh had to lean forward to hear what he said. His breath smelled of whisky although he was clear-eyed and sober enough now. 'Good as any midwife. Lucky he was here.'

'I must tell him,' she said. 'His experience so far has been mainly with mares.'

'Good. Let him keep it that way.' The doctor's smile was wry. 'Can't have him setting up in opposition to me.'

'I thought fever was usual after a difficult birth but you are concerned?'

'That I am.' The doctor nodded, his mouth setting in grim lines. 'It's as bad a case of puerperal fever as I've ever seen. Hard to tell which way it'll go. The fever might break and she'll rally tomorrow, or . . .'

'Or what? You're not saying she could die? Not after all we've been through?'

'I'm sorry.' The doctor shrugged. 'But, apart from keeping her cool and comfortable, there's not much more you can do. We must wait and see. If the girl has the courage, the determination to live . . .' He shook his head. 'Otherwise . . .'

'She can't die!' Niamh whispered frantically, staring at Sukie who was once more plagued with delirium, murmuring in her sleep. 'She has to live, for the sake of her son. Her husband's relying on me to look after her.'

'Yes, where is the husband? It might just tip the scales if he could be here to support her.'

'Unfortunately, he can't.'

'Pity. The girl needs to be cheered, to know that she's loved. Might just be enough to hold her; to encourage her to fight the fever and live.'

Niamh rubbed her face which now itched with tiredness, wondering how long it would be before the doctor made the connection and realised Sukie was the wife of the man convicted of murder who had escaped that morning from Melbourne Gaol.

Albert found it hard to believe that his daughter had deserted him for good. Like many men who take the womenfolk around them for granted, he made light of his daughter's troubles. Every day he expected her to 'come to her senses' and return home, to be the dutiful daughter who kept his life running so smoothly. And each day he was disappointed as he returned to an empty house with no supper prepared and no one to welcome him. But his pride stopped him whenever he thought of visiting her at The Hollies or admitting he might have been wrong.

He missed Judd, too. There was no one at home to go over the business of the day and only de Vesinet at the foundry. And every day something happened to remind him that in taking the Frenchman as a business partner, he had made a gross mistake. De Vesinet cared nothing for quality or craftsmanship, only for profits. Insisting that costs must be kept to a minimum, he cut corners and used the cheapest of raw materials. The result of this false economy was reflected in an increasing number of cancelled orders and customer complaints. Morale at the foundry was at an all-time low. Many of the old hands who had been there for years refused to work for the Frenchman and voted with their feet. In these days of boom and prosperity, other foundries were taking their share of the market. Other foundries where men could work for more money and shorter hours. Soon only the inept, the inexperienced and the troublemakers remained.

One morning he came to work to discover an eight hour banner stretched across the front of the building, declaring in bold red letters:

Eight hours labour
Eight hours recreation
Eight hours rest

He brought a ladder at once and climbed up to tear it down, ignoring the jeers of the men who had formed a semi-circle around him.

'It'll come in the end, Albert Smith – fight it or no,' one of the ringleaders taunted him. 'Tear it down all you want, you an' that French slavemaster of yours, but the banner's still there in our minds an' our hearts. Progress is coming and misers like you won't be able to stop it.'

'Could be worse than a banner next time,' another said meaningfully. 'There'll be rioting in the streets before we're done.'

'Are you threatening me?'

The men exchanged glances, wondering how far to go.

'Me? Nah.' The man smirked. 'I'm jus' warning' you, see – passin' on what I hear. Youngsters is fond o' wreckin' – why, you could come in one morning an' find the moulds is all broke. Set the foundry back months.'

Albert tried to ignore them but the warnings preyed on his mind. That night, when everyone else had gone, he loaded a dray with Judd's moulds – the special ones of the native animals and birds – and took them home. There was a shallow storage area under his house intended for putting down wine which he never kept. Not deep enough to call a basement or cellar, it would suit his purpose. The moulds fitted in snugly as if the space had been built for them and he could relax, knowing the precious templates were no longer at risk, at the mercy of belligerent workers.

Tully was becoming concerned about Elinor. In the early days of her pregnancy, she had plenty of energy, blooming with the radiance of a woman fulfilled. He had to beg her to take it easy and make allowances for her condition. But now she was tired all the time, her complexion lifeless, reminding him unpleasantly of Janet during her last days.

'You mustn't worry, so.' She took his hand as they sat at the kitchen table late at night when the bar was closed. Gladys was there, washing the last of the dishes to give them a fresh start in the morning, her vigour serving only to highlight Ellie's listlessness. 'It's only morning sickness, the doctor says.'

'The mornin' sickness, you say?' He brushed back a limp strand of hair from her eyes. 'No, Ellie, I'm worried. I want you to see another doctor – a specialist, maybe.'

'Oh no.' Ellie wrinkled her nose. 'I don't like seeing doctors at all, let alone strangers. And what can they tell me that I don't already know? Drink milk, exercise gently and make sure I get plenty of rest.'

'That's right, love.' Gladys was irritatingly cheerful. 'All doctors are charlatans – a waste of money so they are. You'll be right as rain, soon as you start to show.' She busied herself at the stove, preparing a hot drink which she set before Ellie. 'Malt and hot milk. Drink it all down now – do you good.'

Ellie shivered, pulling a face. 'Oh Gladys, I do hate the taste of hot milk and the sliminess of the skin – ugh!'

'Then drink it down quick before it makes one.'

'Yes, darlin', drink it up.' Tully reinforced Gladys's argument. 'It'll help you to sleep.'

Elinor sipped it, like a child tasting medicine. 'Ugh! Even with all this sugar, it still has an after-taste.'

'Drink it before it goes cold.' Gladys peered into her cup, seeing half the malted milk still sitting there, forming a skin. 'Your baby needs it, even if you don't.'

Elinor swallowed the rest and coughed. 'I'm for bed. I don't know if I feel queasy or faint.'

Tully was too anxious to sleep well, and he didn't sleep at all when his wife had to get up and vomit into the chamber pot. In the morning over the breakfast table, he tried to talk to her again as she picked at her food.

'Please, Ellie. See another doctor, just to set my mind at rest. An' if he says you're all right, I'll believe him. I won't ask you again.'

Elinor exchanged glances with Gladys and they both raised their eyes to heaven. 'No. Dr Bruce has looked after me for as long as I can remember. He'd be mortally offended if I were to go to somebody else.'

Tully didn't like it but he knew how stubborn his Ellie could be when she made up her mind. Bruce was a fashionable doctor who worked from an elegant suite of rooms at the top of Collins Street. A good-looking man with a sprinkling of iron grey in his hair, he was the perfect choice for a girl who enjoyed rude health and visited a doctor only to confirm it. Not so competent, maybe, if he were faced with a genuine medical emergency.

Chapter Twenty

It was evening before Judd and Carl completed their journey and reached the appointed meeting place at the end of the peninsula. Falling into a morose silence after leaving The Hollies, he had answered Carl's queries in monosyllables, preferring to keep his thoughts to himself.

They arrived in time to see the sun setting like a huge orb spreading flame across the horizon. Judd's spirits lifted at the sight of it, giving him hope. If he hadn't been able to escape from the gaol, he wouldn't have been alive to see it. The waters of the Bay were calm enough to resemble a lake and showed all the corridors of the currents. The ship was already there and waiting for them, standing offshore, a threemasted sea-going vessel which dwarfed the smaller fishing craft out on the bay.

Judd let go a sigh of relief when Carl dismissed their driver with a clap on the shoulder and a small bundle of notes. After what happened to Gusto, he wouldn't have been surprised to see the man paid off with a knife in the ribs. Again he wondered if he were storing up yet more trouble for himself by throwing his lot in with Carl, but he had no choice. Alive, there was always a chance that he might prove his innocence and take up his life where he had left it. Dead, he would be of no further use to anyone. For now, it was easier to set aside his principles and live.

Carl stood on the headland, waving his scarf and milling his arms to attract the attention of the ship's crew. As he did so, Judd was beset by the premonition that it would be a long time before he saw the coast of Victoria again.

'You do realise I've no papers – no passport?' he said.

'Papers?' Carl snickered. 'You don't need no papers to sail with Frits Diedrik. Turn it up, Judd. No use gettin' cold feet now.'

Cowardice wasn't his problem but Carl, having no ties and no one to care about him but his mother, would never understand. He saw this voyage differently, looking forward to it as an adventure rather than a journey into exile. So it was with a heavy heart that Judd stepped into the rowing boat sent ashore to collect them. The oarsman was a Pacific Islander who helped them into the boat, grinning as he introduced himself.

'Jimi Fiji,' he said. He was a big man with a voice to match; deep, vibrant and appearing to resonate in his chest.

Judd accepted the man's hand willingly but Carl took it only with reluctance, making a point of wiping it down his breeches afterwards. The Fijian pushed the boat from the shore and jumped in, almost sinking it. It was fortunate that the waters were calm or they would have shipped water with every stroke.

Having seen few black men, Aboriginal or Polynesian, Judd stared at the Fijian, taken aback by the size of the man. By European standards, he himself was tall but this man towered over him by a good six inches. Naked apart from a necklace of boar's teeth and a pair of seaman's trousers cut off below the knees, he was enormous, with arms and legs as sturdy as the trunks of small trees.

Judd looked back over his shoulder at the shore they were leaving and sighed. Carl grinned, quick to divine the reason for Judd's low spirits.

'No good thinkin' about the missus now, Judd. Out of sight out of mind, eh? You'll soon forget the pasty-faced girls at home when we get in amongst the black velvet.' And to illustrate the point, he clicked his fingers and licked his lips suggestively, shaking imaginary breasts, earning himself a sharp look from the Fijian.

'Black velvet?' Judd was unfamiliar with the term.

'Yeah! The hot-blooded women of the South Seas, who have nothing to do all day but pleasure their men.'

'I'm not interested,' Judd snapped, aware of the Fijian's deepening scowl. He looked up at the ship which was looming closer now, intrigued to see that she was heavily armed as a navy vessel, with guns on either side. 'The ship is French?'

'I dunno.' Carl shrugged. 'Captain's a Dutchman.'

'Then why is she flying the French flag?'

'Why? Why?' Carl mocked. 'Don't look a gift horse in the mouth, Judd. It's a lifeline. Just grab it an' be thankful. Stop askin' stupid questions an' findin' fault.'

'You've already made me accessory to murder, Carl. I'd like to know what you're getting me into now.'

'A life of limitless adventure and fun.'

'Oh? Aboard a pirate ship with a Dutch captain, flying a French flag?'

'Better not let Diedrik hear you say that. He'll have you walking the plank.'

As they drew closer, Judd was impressed by the tidy appearance of the ship. Even from a distance he could see it was well-maintained. The ropes were all coiled, the decks spotless and the hull gleamed with a recent coat of white paint, her scrollwork varnished and the brass fittings polished until they shone bright as gold, reflecting the last rays of the setting sun.

On coming aboard, they were greeted by a chunky, potato-faced Englishman, his age impossible to guess. He wore thick seaman's boots with his breeches tucked into them, a pair of braces over a Crimea shirt. Unlike most white men at sea, he was cleanshaven and wore a red knitted cap, possibly to protect a balding head.

'What kept you, Bradley? We nearly sailed without you. Can't afford to miss any more tides. Cap'n prefers to slip past the heads under cover of darkness – no questions asked.' He looked Judd up and down. 'So this is the smith. He looks handy enough. You can thank your stars you didn't show up without him – Diedrik's toey enough as it is.'

'All right, Diggory, put a sock in it.' Carl punched the man on the shoulder as he introduced him to Judd. 'This ugly old *choom* is Diggory Wood, first mate of the good ship – what is it this time?' He raised questioning eyebrows.

'The *Daisy May* – for now, anyway.'

'First mate of the good ship *Daisy May*. The rest of the crew are kanakas.'

'Kanakas?' Judd frowned at another unfamiliar word.

'The islanders. That's their word for man – kanaka.'

274

'You speak their language, then?' Judd was beginning to feel more than literally at sea.

'Nah. But most of 'em can talk pidgin like Jimi Fiji – they can make themselves understood if they want. C'mon, better go an' pay our respects to Cap'n Diedrik.'

Judd looked forward to meeting the captain. Now perhaps he would find out why a blacksmith should be such an important addition to this ship's crew.

But Captain Diedrik preferred to ask questions rather than answer them. His quarters were cramped but comfortable, containing the usual captain's table covered in charts, a pallet alongside and his captain's chair in which he was now seated. The walls were covered in weaponry, old and new, and to Judd's experienced eye, they were all in the peak of condition and ready for use.

Diedrik was a big man with thick blond hair bleached white by the tropical sun. His beard was a reddish-blond and his skin was that startling golden-brown common to fair-haired people who spend too much time in the sun. He was a modern Viking, reminding Judd of the Danes he used to see on the streets of Plymouth when he was a boy. Judd wasn't small but alongside this Dutch captain and his crew of kanakas, he was of less than average height. Diedrik's features looked as if they had been hewn from rock; a prominent nose, high cheekbones and a strong jaw. A large face, typical of a man whose height and size made him almost a giant. He might have been good-looking but for his eyes which were unusually small and mean, grey and cold as the sea in winter. There was no warmth, no friendliness in them – only calculation.

He had a deep voice and spoke English deliberately, with scarcely a trace of accent. 'So, in trouble again Bradley?' he said to Carl. 'This time you are fortunate – you have brought me the smith. Next time, maybe you won't be so lucky. I might leave you to your fate.'

Carl smiled but he knew better than to answer back. For this man he had no smart remarks.

Diedrik lit a cheroot, filling the cabin with wreaths of blue smoke and the smell of strong tobacco which began to irritate Judd's eyes. He was exhausted and hungry, having had nothing to eat all day, and was longing to get back on deck where at least he could breathe fresh air. Diedrik sat back and studied him through a haze of smoke.

'So, blacksmith – what do you know of fitting a ship?'

'I'm no ship's carpenter, if that's what you want.'

'No. I want the ship refitted below – made secure. Can you do this?'

' If you show me what you want and say what it's for.'

Diedrik ignored the question. 'I want strong bolts and hinges attached to the entry to the hold. Inside I want rings and shackles attached to the uprights. Yes?'

Judd thought it best to be positive. He had the strong impression that if he said otherwise, he might be tossed overboard and left to make his own way back to shore. 'Yes, provided you have the necessary raw materials.'

'We do.'

'But to work metal, I'll need the right tools.'

'We have them.'

'And a fire to generate plenty of heat. That may not be safe aboard a sailing ship.'

Diedrik frowned, growing impatient with these qualifications. 'Then you can do it ashore.'

'Why do you need this? If I'm to build you a prison aboard this ship, I want to know what it's for.'

Diedrik ignored the question and stood up, indicating the interview was at an end. 'You must be hungry. Cook will serve dinner as soon as we pass the heads. Let's hope you don't lose it, blacksmith, when we hit the rough waters of the Bass Strait!'

'But aren't you in the least bit curious? Don't you want to see your own grandchild?' Exasperated, Niamh was staring at Albert. At Sukie's insistence she had driven from Brighton to Richmond to give him the news. But Albert was sullen and still aggrieved.

'I'll talk to my Sukie when she's back home where she belongs.'

'Mr Smith – Albert – please try to understand. Sukie's not well. The birth was a difficult one; she needs someone to care for her night and day.'

'So? Whose fault is that? I'm not to blame. If she'd gone to the Lying-In Hospital as we planned . . .'

276

'Well, she didn't!' Niamh was fast losing patience with the old man but for her friend's sake, she tried to reach him once more. 'Please come. It would mean so much to her. My little horse and cart are outside. I can have you there and back inside the hour.' This was a lie but she didn't care. 'Please, Mr Smith. Won't you come?'

'You expect me to leave now, halfway through a workin' day? You don't know what's goin' on here – nor does she. We're in a competitive situation – my partner's out trying to clinch a big order right now. Lord knows what'll happen if we don't get it. The men are bein' lured away with high wages an' shorter hours, tempted to work in other yards. We've never been so short-handed.'

'Oh? And have you bothered to ask yourself why?'

But Albert wasn't listening. 'An' now we're minus the foreman, I have to supervise all the work at the furnaces on my own. I should be there now; the men will be lounging around having a smoke-o if I'm not present to prod them along.' He stood up, ushering Niamh towards the door. 'Tell Sukie I'll come at the weekend. If it doesn't rain.'

Niamh stared at him, biting her lip. 'Sukie did say I wasn't to tell you but really she's gravely ill. If you leave it until the weekend, you could be too late.'

'Go on with you, girl! You're makin' it up just to scare me. Sukie's young and she's healthy. She won't die.'

'She will if she doesn't find someone to champion her besides me.' Niamh pressed home the point. 'Her husband gone who knows where and her father deserting her.'

'Oh no – I didn't desert her, girlie. She left me.'

'Please Albert, won't you sink your pride and be generous? For Sukie, please?'

Albert frowned, hesitating, and Niamh thought she had him until running footsteps on the gravel outside made them both turn towards the door. It burst open, admitting Tim.

'Mr Smith – Mr Smith – you're needed down at the furnaces!' Some of his urgency left him as he recognised Niamh. 'Oh, it's you, miss. Nice to see you again. Take a look,' he rolled back his sleeve to show her, 'thanks to you the arm's healed up real well.'

'That is good, Tim,' she smiled back at him.

'All right, never mind that now!' Albert growled. 'What d'you want, boy?'

'We think the metal's ready to pour but we need to—'

'You *think?* God's bones, don't you *know?*' Albert groaned, heading towards the door. 'You see how it is, Niamh? I can't come now. Here – ' he fished in his pockets until he found a grubby note which he handed over ' – buy her some flowers an' say they're from me. I'll be there Sunday, if I can.'

And with that she had to be content. On the way back she visited a small market on the bank of the river where she bought a huge bunch of tiger lilies and a light, hand-knitted shawl for the baby.

When she got home she was greeted by Brigid, white-faced and shocked, at the door.

'Oh madam, I've had such a time with her. Thanks be to God that you're back. She got up to go to the privy an' started bleedin' again—'

'You let her get up? Oh Brigid, how could you? I told you particularly to take her a pan to use in the bed.'

'Well, I wanted to help the poor girl, madam – an' if I could do it, I would. But there's only so many times these poor auld legs can go up an' downstairs.'

'Oh, all right.' Niamh swallowed her impatience. 'You sent Dayman to fetch the doctor, I hope?'

'No, madam. Nobody told me to.' Brigid was starting to whine. 'An' Dayman's not always at the stables, not at this time o' day. And I dunno where else to look.'

'Then get out and do so now, Brigid! Look everywhere till you find him. Say it's urgent.'

'I'd like to help you, madam –' Brigid began but Niamh wasn't listening, already halfway up the stairs.

Sukie was lying in bed, white with strain but her expression cleared when she saw Niamh.

'I am sorry, Niamh. So stupid to get out of bed. But it's all right now. The bleeding seems to have stopped.'

Niamh flung back the bedclothes, taking' care not to let Sukie see how horrified she was by the sight of so much blood. But Sukie was right. The bleeding had stopped and, for the moment, her fever had abated.

Niamh ran to the linen press to fetch more clean sheets and

soon she had Sukie washed and comfortable, in clean bedding and nightclothes, a pillow beneath her ankles to raise her feet.

'And this time you stay where you are,' she ordered. 'You're not to get up again till Dr O'Hara says.'

'I won't.' Sukie gave a rueful smile. 'Poor Brigid. Don't be too hard on her. I gave her an awful fright.'

'I hope so, the selfish old biddy. She'll be lucky if I don't give her the sack.'

'Don't do that.' Sukie gave a wan smile. 'She's worth keeping, if only for her calf's foot jelly and those wonderful scones. So tell me – did you see Pa?'

'Yes,' Niamh said carefully, wondering how much to tell. 'I did. And he sent you these.' She presented Sukie with the flowers which, in her panic, she had flung down on the washstand.

'Ohh!' Sukie's eyes brightened as she touched the exotic blooms which seemed to glow with an even brighter flame in contrast to her own pallor. 'How lovely. But I suppose he made his excuses? Won't leave his precious foundry for five minutes to come and see me . . .'

'He's promised to come on Sunday.'

'But only if it's not raining.'

'Yes. How did you guess?'

'Because I know my pa. It's his way of saying he won't forgive me till I go back to Richmond and offer the olive branch myself.'

'Sukie, he'll come. He'll want to see his grandchild.'

'I don't think Noah's quite real to him yet.' She reached out to touch the baby who grasped her index finger firmly and sighed in his sleep. 'So, little man – you're all I have left now. All I have left to remind me of Judd.'

And all I have left of him, too, Niamh thought.

'Niamh, if anything happens to me . . .'

'Nothing's going to happen to you. I won't let it.'

'Yes, but if it does, I want you to promise me you'll take care of Noah?'

'Oh Sukie, you don't have to ask – you know I would. But I don't want you to dwell on such gloomy ideas. You should be thinking of getting well.'

279

'Oh, I am,' Sukie said with little conviction. 'But I told you – I know my pa. And when he realises he has a grandchild, he's going to want him, to grow up and train for the business. I don't want that, Niamh. I don't want Noah turned into another slave to the foundry like I was.'

'But Sukie, I always thought you loved it. I thought you liked working there!'

'I used to, until Pa took it all away. He used to say that working for the foundry was working for our future, our security. I believed it, too. But the foundry isn't our future, is it?' Her voice died to a croak; she was breathless. 'Not mine, Judd's nor even his own – any more.'

'That's enough, Sukie. I want you to rest.'

But Sukie clutched her arm. 'No, listen to me. The foundry doesn't belong to us, not since he let the Frenchman get a foot in the door. I don't want Pa to have my baby – I want you to keep him for Judd.'

'But Sukie—'

'I want you to promise me! Promise me, now.'

'All right. But Sukie, you're scaring me. I wish you'd stop talking as if you expect to die.'

'I'm pretty scared myself,' Sukie managed a wan smile, 'but it's no more than I deserve. I've had time to think about it a lot while I've been lying here. Everything – all that's happened – it's my fault.'

'Oh Sukie, I'm sure that's not true.' Niamh sank down on to the bed. 'You mustn't blame yourself.'

'But you don't know the half of it. How wicked and selfish I've been.'

'You, Sukie? But you've been the best of friends to me. You're one of the most generous, unselfish people I know.'

'I let you think so but it wasn't true. I was always jealous of you; jealous because everything came to you so easily. That's why I lied. I lied about—'

'Sukie, it's over now. Water under the bridge.'

'But I stood between you and Judd – I kept you apart. I stopped you from getting together and making a go of it.'

'No, Sukie. I did that all by myself. I was engaged to Holly and I chose to stand by my promise – nobody forced me. And Judd loves you. He told me so.'

'He told me, too, but it isn't the same. He loves me but he's not *in love* with me – there's a world of difference, you know. I knew it was you he wanted – you he loved. And if I hadn't . . .' By now her voice was no more than a hoarse whisper which Niamh had to lean close to hear . . . 'If I hadn't nagged him so about his inheritance . . . '

'Inheritance? What inheritance, Sukie?'

'Ohh! It could have been so different,' Sukie sighed. 'If *your* father had been his father-in-law and not mine.'

'Sukie, you're rambling. I don't know what you mean.'

'Ask – ask your father.' Sukie lay back on the pillows, drifting into an exhausted sleep. 'Poor Judd. If only I hadn't nagged him, he wouldn't have wanted the money so badly, or murdered someone to get it. He wouldn't be in all this trouble or so far away from me now.'

'Sukie!' Niamh was trying to shake her back to consciousness. 'You don't believe that! Judd couldn't murder anyone, no matter how desperate he was.'

'I drove him to it, you see. That's what I have to live with. No one more guilty than me.' And this time Sukie fell into a deep sleep from which Niamh could no longer rouse her. A sleep that was more like a coma, a prelude to death.

Some time later Dr O'Hara arrived and studied her, gravely scratching his chin.

'Well?' Niamh said sharply, as if it were his fault for being unable to do more.

'I'm sorry,' the doctor said, packing his instruments into his bag. 'She's developing a pneumonia and has no reserves of strength left to fight it.'

'But there must be something you can do?'

Slowly he shook his head. 'She's too weak to stand any more procedures. Too weak from the loss of blood.'

The doctor left, having nothing to add and Niamh was distracted by Noah who woke at eleven, demanding to be fed. Sukie continued to sleep through the baby's cries.

Downstairs, Brigid, too shocked by Niamh's expression to grumble, boiled cow's milk and suggested the baby might be hungry enough to suck it through a clean rag. Noah fretted, complaining bitterly about this makeshift arrangement; a damp rag full of cow's milk was a poor substitute for his mother's breast.

Niamh prepared to sit up all night and keep watch over both of them, wondering about this connection between her father and Judd; a connection which Sukie had been too tired and too sick to explain. In the early hours of the morning weariness overcame her at last and she slept. She was woken by the sun streaming in through the window and also the baby, crying angrily for more food. She reached out to touch Sukie only to find her stiff and cold. Oddly, she put Niamh in mind of a pet kitten she'd had as a child and which she'd found dead in its basket. The sense of shock and loss she felt was so much the same. Sukie had died peacefully and in her sleep, but Niamh felt no less guilty for being unaware of it at the time.

'It's no good bringing him to me, Mrs Maitland.' Sister Kearney eyed the baby in Niamh's arms. 'This is a hospital, not an orphanage. We have no means of keeping the child.'

'I don't want you to *keep* him at all, sister. I've come here for your help and advice.' She tried to stay calm but she could hear herself getting shrill. Having left Brigid and Dayman to inform an undertaker and make the arrangements for Sukie, she had wrapped the baby warmly before putting him in his fruit box and driving to The Briarley Hospital. Now she felt hollow and exhausted, having had nothing to eat for hours. Sister Kearney's criticism was the last straw. 'We can't feed the baby on cow's milk. He keeps bringing it up.'

'I should think so, indeed. A child of that tender age can't tolerate cow's milk – some never do. He could be allergic. Here we keep emergency supplies of excess mothers' milk. They send it to us twice daily from the Lying-In Hospital.'

'Oh, good. That's what I hoped.'

'But for *our* emergencies, Mrs Maitland, not yours.' Sister Kearney fixed her with a steely look. 'If you mean to take charge of that child and keep him yourself, you'll need some certainty of supply. You'll require a wetnurse to be with him full-time.'

'A wetnurse – but of course! Why didn't *I* think of that?' Really, Niamh had been too numbed by the loss of Sukie to

282

think clearly about anything. 'Is there someone you can recommend?'

'Matter of fact, I can, though I wouldn't like you to hold me to ransom over the girl's character. One Becky Willis – a feckless sort who makes a career of getting herself in the family way . . .'

'Beggars can't be choosers, Sister. Where can I find her?'

'Now look here, Mrs Maitland. I wouldn't like you to think—'

'Sister Kearney, at this moment, I don't care if she strips the house to the curtains. I need someone to help me raise this child.'

'The girl is amoral. I didn't say she was a thief.'

Following Sister Kearney's half-hearted recommendation, it seemed to Niamh that everything took place with maddening slowness. At least the baby had stopped screaming, sleeping peacefully after drinking deeply from the supplies of mothers' milk at the hospital. Also someone had seen Niamh's exhaustion and had the presence of mind to sustain her with tea and toast at the same time. Even so, it was after midday before she drove up to the dilapidated, weatherboard cottage in Port Melbourne where Becky Willis and her parents were said to live.

From the external appearance of the cottage, Niamh expected it to be a smelly hovel within. But there was no time to change her mind as, in answer to her knock, she heard the heavy-footed tread of a middle-aged woman, yelling as she approached the door.

'If you're collectin' for charity, we already gave. An' if it's the ole man you want, he's down at the wharf, doin' an honest day's work for once in 'is life!' She finished the sentence as she opened the door, stopping dead in her tracks when she saw Niamh standing on the doorstep with Noah in her arms. The woman looked beyond her to see a smart little horse and cart hitched to the rail at the kerb, incongruous in the dilapidated street. 'Ooh, I beg yours, madam. I thought it was one o' them debt-collector fellers after the ole man.'

'No,' Niamh smiled, reassured by the smell of good, plain soap wafting from somewhere inside the house. 'I came to see Becky Willis – if this is her home?'

'Some o' the time, it is.' The woman raised her eyes heaven-wards and raised her voice to give another stentorian bellow over her shoulder. 'Becky! Lady 'ere waitin' to see you! Step inside, madam, do. Ooh, what a lovely little—' Her eyes flickered towards the sleeping baby in his blue shawl. 'He yours?'

'Er – no.' Niamh's smile faded. 'He has no one. That's why Sister Kearney sent me to Becky. His mother is dead. It was only last night.' Thinking of Sukie again, she felt more tears welling into her eyes.

'There, then, poor little lamb. Warrashame.' The woman didn't sound at all sorry as she dropped her voice to a confidential whisper. 'With our Becky it's the other way round – can't never rear 'em. Just as well, maybe – we'd 'ave us a football team by now. Becky!' She raised her voice again. 'What's keepin' yer, gel?'

The girl presented herself at last, having scrubbed her face and combed her errant blonde curls. Her clothes weren't at all stylish but she wore them with an air of gypsy abandonment and was possessed of a knowing and mischievous smile. The same smile, Niamh surmised, which must have brought her a great deal of trouble already. Whether the girl was older than herself, Niamh had yet to find out but she looked to be in her late twenties.

'Let's see,' she grinned, holding her arms out for the baby who woke and stared at her, trying to focus. 'Who's a pretty boy, then?' She looked back at Niamh. 'That's all right, madam. I'll look after him for you. You can leave him with me.'

'Becky!' Her mother broke in. 'Don't be in such an 'urry. You ain't even arst what the lady's willin' to pay.'

'I don't think you quite understand,' Niamh said. 'I can't leave him here – I promised his mother I'd keep him with me. I need someone to come to my home and stay there.'

'Where's home, then?' Becky said, suddenly not as keen.

'Brighton. It's a very nice house – I'm sure you'll be comfortable there.'

'And bored to tears.' Becky handed the baby back although she continued to look at him covertly and with an expression of longing in her eyes. She also folded her arms to hide the damp patches on her dress; the sight and smell of a baby had brought in her milk. 'I don't know, madam. Brighton's a long way from anywhere – sort of out in the sticks. Nothin' there but big houses an' the sea.'

'Best thing in the world for you, gel,' her mother chipped in. 'Time you had a rest from the ships an' them randy sailors.'

'Mum!'

'Well! No good pretendin' you're other than what you are. Piece o' skirt for the visitin' Navy, that's what you are. Don't suppose Sister Kearney had anythin' good to say for yer, do yer?' She raised a quizzical eyebrow at Niamh who remained tactfully silent.

'Allersame, I dunno.' Becky scowled, gnawing a broken fingernail.

'Becky, please come?' Niamh said. 'Noah has no one and he needs you. I promise I'll make it worth your while.'

'Noah? Is that his name?' Becky held out her arms for the child, crooning softly to him as she unfastened her bodice and gave him her breast right there on the doorstep without embarrassment. 'Ooh!' She grinned at Niamh as the baby responded, fastening himself to the nipple as he clutched the ample breast with his tiny hands. 'He knows what he wants, doesn't he? Isn't he the greedy one?'

That single moment of bonding was all it took. From then onwards, the baby and his new nurse became inseparable. So far as Noah was concerned, Niamh's troubles were at an end.

Chapter Twenty-One

It was only as she was driving home with Becky Willis beside her, hugging the baby and chattering non-stop about the more colourful of her conquests, that Niamh began to wonder how this girl and her cantankerous housekeeper might get along. Brigid was straitlaced and conventional enough to style herself Mrs McGinty although she had never been married, yet Irish enough to be leery of those who enforced the law. Most of the time too lazy to go to church, occasionally Brigid was stricken with a religious conscience and dragged her statue of the Virgin from under the bed, dusted it and propitiated it with fresh flowers.

So Niamh held her breath as she watched the two women get acquainted, hoping it wouldn't be a case of mutual and immediate dislike. To her relief they became fast friends. Brigid spoiled the nurse, feeding her on fresh cream and other delicacies on the pretext of nourishing the child while Becky, who had never seen so much good food in the whole of her life, treated Brigid like a long-lost aunt, and she never complained when the old woman had her running up and down stairs all day.

'I'd like to do more for myself, dear – an' if I could do it, I would.' Niamh overheard Brigid's familiar wail. 'But I'm slave to these poor auld legs. Now if you wouldn't mind runnin' on up to me room now an' bringin' me that bottle o' Row's Embrocation . . .'

'Any time, Mrs McGinty – you've only to say.'

'Brigid, me dear, call me Brigid.'

So with Noah settled, cooing and comfortable in Becky's

arms, Niamh could turn her attention to other things, the most urgent of which was Sukie's funeral. Unwilling to pay another visit to Albert at the foundry, she decided to break the news to the Bradleys instead.

It was Daisy who answered the door, taking a moment to recognise and remember her. Her eyes were already bloodshot and reddened from weeping and she was scrubbing her nose on the back of her hand. When she spoke she sounded as if she had a cold. 'Niamh, isn't it? Land sakes but I haven't seen you for years – not since you an' our Sukie was at school. Quite the young lady now, aren't you? Come on in.'

'Thank you,' Niamh said, gathering her thoughts as she followed Daisy down the narrow passage to the kitchen.

'Terrible, ain't it?' Daisy turned a mournful face towards her. 'What an awful shame.'

'Oh. Oh yes, it is.' Niamh let go a sigh of relief. Somehow Daisy had already heard the bad news.

'Sit you down, dear, an I'll make us a nice cuppa.' Daisy sniffed. 'Such a comfort in times like these. With all this trouble I've not had the heart to bake any scones.'

'Don't apologise, Mrs Bradley. I feel just the same. I couldn't eat a thing.'

Daisy frowned and gave her an odd look. 'Matthew's at the foundry right now, lookin' over the wreckage to see if there's anythin' can be saved. For the life of me, I dunno how I'll break the news to our Sukie. Maybe you'd like to help us out there? Although more bad news won't help a woman in her condition, poor soul.'

'What bad news?' Niamh's heart sank as she realised they had been talking at cross purposes. Daisy was speaking of another matter entirely. 'Will you start from the beginning and tell me exactly what's happened?'

'I thought you knew. Isn't that why you're here?'

'I'm sorry – a misunderstanding. There is something more – something I have to tell you. But what's happened to upset you? Was there an accident at the foundry?'

'It weren't no accident, the rotten bastards. Place has been levelled – smashed to the ground. The men had a meetin' – a union meetin' they called it. Turned into a reg'lar riot. An' all

over nothin' – jus' one o' them stupid eight hour banners.'
Daisy sniffed, rubbing her nose which was already red and
sore. 'You know how it is, how men get all riled up over banners an' flags.'

Niamh didn't know but she shrugged, encouraging Daisy to
go on.

'They knew it'd have to come down; it's happened before.
But this time the stupid Frenchie has to go one better an' burn
it. Tossed it into the furnace, didn't he? That's what set them
off. Broke every damned thing they could lay their hands on,
smashed all the moulds an' threw anythin' that'd burn right
back into the furnaces. It made such a blizzy, you could see it
from here. One o' the stacks caught fire an' some o' them
threatened to catch the Frenchie an' roast him, too. It's a pity
they didn't. He took to his heels an' run off at the first sign o'
trouble an' no one's seen hide nor hair of him since. Poor
Albert was tryin' to stop them, to save somethin' out o' the
mess. But by then they was too crazed to listen. You know
what lads are like when they get full o' the joys o' smashin'
things? They shoved Albert out of the way an' he fell. Nobody
seems too sure about what happened after that whether somebody kicked him or if he cracked his head on one o' the broken
moulds. He's in hospital, not expected to live.' Impatiently,
Daisy brushed away another tear. 'Opened his eyes just the
once to ask after Sukie, an' now they can't wake him at all. I
know they had their differences but surely she'll go to him now
and patch things up?'

'Ohh!' Niamh let go a sigh, wishing she didn't have to bring
more bad news to Daisy. 'If only it were possible, Mrs Bradley,
I'm sure she would but—'

'Talk to her, Niamh. She'll listen to you.'

'I can't, Mrs Bradley.' Niamh was too wretched to hold
back the truth any longer. 'Sukie's dead.'

'Oh, no no.' Daisy put her fist to her mouth, her eyes filling
with fresh tears. 'Was it the baby?'

Niamh nodded, her own throat too full of tears to allow her
to speak. She put an arm around Daisy instead.

'Lordy, Lordy, what's to become of us now?' Daisy said in a
quavering voice. 'My poor Matthew – a broken man over Carl
an' the terrible things he's done. Sometimes,' she said between

sobs, 'I wonder what we've done to deserve all this. Where did we go wrong?'

'Mrs Bradley – Daisy – you mustn't blame yourself. Carl isn't a child any more. You can't take his guilt on your shoulders.'

'There are times when I think there's a curse on this family.'

'I'm sure that's not so,' Niamh said crisply. Without asking permission, she poured another cup of strong tea, adding plenty of sugar before handing it to Daisy who blew her nose into her apron loudly before she accepted it.

'Oh yes, there is.' Daisy's eyes glittered. 'A curse that goes by the name of Judd Burden. Nothing's gone right for this family, not since he came.'

'You know that's not true. Judd isn't a murderer, he's a victim of circumstance!'

'Poor little Sukie, bearin' a baby to that great brute. An' what of the poor little mite? Born dead, I s'pose.'

'No. He's a strong healthy little boy who's going from strength to strength since I found him a nurse. She loves him dearly as if he were her own.'

Daisy's reaction was not as Niamh expected. She reared back, her eyes shining with malice. 'You don't mean to keep him, the spawn of that murderin' devil who had us all fooled? If you've any sense you'll let some other woman raise him. Send him as far away as you can.'

'Of course I won't. He's Sukie's child.'

'No good will come of it, you'll see.' Daisy's eyes had grown wide, staring at nothing. 'And when he brings trouble down on your house, you can't say I didn't warn you.'

'But he's only a baby. An innocent child.' Niamh rose to go. She could see Daisy was irrational, overcome by too much grief but she didn't want to stay to hear any more of it. 'Don't worry, Daisy. You can leave Sukie's funeral to me. I'll send for the minister and arrange for the burial. There'll be a place for her in our family plot at The Hollies. It will be my pleasure to tend her grave.'

'Oh Niamh, you mustn't think we're ungrateful.' Daisy looked shamefaced, sensing the criticism behind those quiet words. 'I know you did all you could for our Sukie.'

'I wish I'd been able to do more.'

289

'Let us know the day an' the time an' we'll be there, Matthew an' me. But I meant what I said, girl. You give that baby away.' She shook Niamh's hand to emphasise the point. 'No good will come of harbourin' a murderer's child.'

Niamh left quickly. She could understand why Daisy was bitter but had no wish to argue with her. And when she saw her at Sukie's funeral, Daisy said Albert had never recovered consciousness. He had died in his sleep.

'What's this, then?' Hollis accepted the banker's note from Horace Ironsides, looking at it long enough to see it was made out to himself and for a handsome sum. Ironsides was seated behind his empty, highly polished desk in his office in Collins Street, flanked by his cronies, some of whom were going through the ritual of lighting cigars, creating a smokescreen to hide their embarrassment.

Until then, Hollis had been looking forward to this meeting with Ironsides and the prospect of new ventures. Now, sensing the tension in the room, he wasn't so sure.

'It's your severance pay. We want to thank you for all you've done for us in the past, Hollis, and hope you'll accept this in the spirit in which it is given. As a gesture of appreciation for services rendered.'

'You're cutting me off – blowing me out the door? But why? What have I done?' Even to his own ears his voice sounded shrill, on the edge of panic. 'I've delivered, haven't I? Brought new investors when you needed them?'

Ironsides paused, measuring his words before he replied. 'Oh yes, you performed well enough in the past. No one disputes that. Unfortunately, you seem to have a talent for attracting disaster. We're in a delicate position here. We can't allow any scandal to rub off on ourselves.'

'What exactly do you mean by that?' Hollis leaned forward on his knuckles, to stare the man full in the face. Ironsides stared back at him, unflinching.

'I don't have to answer that. You've been paid and the matter is closed. But if you insist . . .'

'I do.'

'First there's your father's death. You can't deny he died in suspicious circumstances—'

'You can't hold me responsible!'

'Let me finish.' Ironsides raised his eyebrows, irritated by the interruption. 'Hard on the heels of your father's murder, we have that of Albert Smith – also the victim of an unprovoked and vicious attack.'

'But these two matters are unconnected.'

'Are they?' Ironsides rapped out the words. 'But you were closely associated with both men. Albert Smith was your client – you introduced him to us. And it's hardly a secret that his daughter, the wife of a convicted murderer, is a close friend of your – er – estranged wife.'

'I'm not estranged from my wife.'

'No? Then how come you no longer live under the same roof?' Ironsides inclined his head, waiting for Hollis to deny it which he couldn't. 'People like to know they're dealing with someone stable and reliable, particularly in matters relating to finance and law. It's unfortunate, Hollis, but there are just too many queries hanging over your head. We can't afford to be tarred with the same brush. Regrettable as it is, we must sever our connection with the firm of Maitland & Maitland.'

'Oh, you'll regret it all right!' Hollis thumped the table, making some of the older men start and blink behind their spectacles. 'I'll see to that! You're not the only one who knows how to buy and sell land. You wait and see. I'll raise a mortgage myself and set up in opposition.'

'A mortgage, Holly?' Ironsides laughed softly, mocking him. 'From Victor Benham perhaps? At Grolier's Bank?'

Hollis stormed out, bringing the meeting to a close. One of the older men followed him and tucked the banker's draft into his top pocket.

'You left without this, Hollis,' he said. 'Don't be too proud to accept it. You might need it later on.'

'But how could he do this to me? It's not fair, Tom. I've worked my arse off for him and he knows it.'

'Yes, but you know what they say, lad. It's the reformed sinners who make the best saints. Horace would rather draw a veil over his own less than savoury early activities. These days, Ironsides is whiter than white.'

'But I'll get him, Tom. You wait and see.'

'Take my advice and let it alone, lad. You're young enough to recover and start again. You could find you're better off without him. Put it down to experience and get on with your life.'

'I'll get him, if it's the last thing I ever do. I'll get to be bigger than he is before I'm through.'

Already in a bad mood, he exhausted his horse by riding it hard to Brighton to visit The Hollies. If his wife had to be at his side so that he could be seen as a respectable, model citizen, that's where she should be. There would be a reconciliation. He felt very noble and self-sacrificing to be making the first move.

Niamh was in the garden cutting some flowers when she saw him ride up to the stables, giving his horse to Dayman as casually as if he'd been away a matter of hours rather than weeks. She watched him through narrowed eyes, knowing he wouldn't be here unless there was something he wanted. Still angry with him for his treatment of Sukie and for bringing the troopers down on them, she made up her mind that, whatever it was, she wouldn't make it easy.

Hollis looked around with a proprietary air, measuring the changes, his attention caught at last by the sight of the first grave in the family plot; a new grave, covered in fresh flowers, the headstone reflecting the gold of the afternoon sun. Niamh came over and stood beside him as he read the inscription.

'Susannah Burden,' he muttered, continuing to frown at the headstone, not bothering to greet her. 'I know she died here, Niamh, but did you really have to bury Judd Burden's wife and child in our family plot?'

'I buried Sukie here because I loved her and I owed her that much.' Niamh's temper flared. 'She was my best friend.'

'To bury her here is a slap in the face to our family. An insult to my father's memory.'

'If Uncle Harley were alive, he wouldn't see it that way. He had more compassion in the tip of his finger than you have in the whole of your body.'

Hollis shivered. Smarting from the battle he had lost with Ironsides, he was in no state to cross swords with his wife. 'Oh

Niamh, do we have to fight whenever we meet? I came here today in friendship and good faith. Burden has gone now and Sukie is dead. I think it's time I came home.'

'You do, do you? So what's in it for you?' She had no intention of letting him off the hook. 'The last time you came, you treated us like criminals and let troopers go stamping all over the house. The time before that, if I remember correctly, you said I'd have to beg you if I wanted you home. I'm not ready to beg, Hollis.'

'I am. I was angry and upset about Pa but I shouldn't have brought the troopers. I see that now.' He ran his finger around his collar as if it were choking him. It was almost four in the afternoon and the air was still, no breeze to give any relief. He took off his hat and wiped the sweat from his forehead on his sleeve. 'Lord, but it's hot. Won't you offer me some tea and something to eat before I go back to town?'

'I suppose so,' she said with bad grace, ushering him towards the back door. 'You'd better come in.'

The kitchen presented a comfortable domestic scene. A sleepy-eyed Becky sat at the kitchen table with Noah at her breast. In front of her was a half-finished glass of milk laced with cream. In spite of the heat, a red-faced Brigid was stoking the fire to make a fresh batch of scones. She straightened her back and frowned when she saw who it was. Becky, unaware that this was the master of the house, gave Hollis a sultry look through her eyelashes and a full-lipped pout. He coloured and averted his eyes, embarrassed by the sight of the baby suckling at the girl's naked breast. Aware of this, she made much of shifting Noah to feed on the other side, leaving herself for the moment fully exposed.

'Another charity case?' he muttered to his wife. 'What on earth is the use of a servant who comes with a child?'

'Becky's a nurse,' Niamh said, enjoying her husband's discomfiture. 'I employ her to care for Sukie's boy. A lusty infant, as you can see, and very much alive.'

As Holly looked down at the baby, his expression changed to one of distaste. 'Are you telling me that's Judd Burden's child?'

'Oh yes,' she continued to goad him. 'Can't you see the resemblance? He has his father's eyes.'

293

And Hollis could well imagine the baby looked at him with something of Judd's uncompromising gaze. He hadn't the slightest suggestion of Sukie's squint. 'Then you'll send him packing, and the girl with him or I'll—'

'You'll do what, Holly?' Niamh said softly. 'Do you really think I want you back in my life? No. There was a time when I'd have met you halfway; a time when we might have made some sort of life together. Now it's too late.'

'Must we discuss this in front of the servants?' He was aware that Brigid and Becky were listening, fascinated.

'*My* servants, I think, and also my friends.'

'Ah, Niamh . . .'

'No, Hollis. You won't get around me with false promises. Not this time. This baby is all I care about now. Sukie asked me to take care of him and I will.'

'I can't believe this. After all that he's done, you still put that damned blacksmith and his child before me.' Hollis was breathing heavily. 'You might be the owner of this house, Niamh. Not much I can do about that. But a house needs money to be maintained. So long as you keep that brat, you won't get a penny from me. Make sure you enjoy that cream, girl,' he said to Becky, pointing to the half-finished glass of milk on the table. 'From now on you'll be lucky to get so much as a plate of gruel in this house.'

And he smiled at Niamh, thinking she would see the hopelessness of the situation and give in. But she returned his gaze calmly, not in the least put out. 'No doubt you've found me wanting as a husband – and as a friend. But as an enemy, I could surpass even your expectations. Ladies!' He inclined his head in exaggerated politeness to all three of them. 'I leave you to consider your predicament. Good afternoon.'

They remained silent, listening as he urged his weary horse towards the road, swearing at it and whipping it until it stumbled into a trot. As the hoofbeats died away, they breathed a concerted sigh of relief.

Shortly afterwards, Dayman came into the kitchen in search of afternoon tea, shaking his head and grumbling at the way Hollis was treating his horse.

'The poor creature's done in, an' I told him so. I implored him to borrow another an' leave it behind.'

294

'Don't worry, Noah,' Niamh said. 'In that sort of mood, my husband listens to no one.'

'It's not him I'm worried about, it's the horse. A lovely animal it is, well-bred an' deservin' of more respect. A hot day like this an' he'll be lucky if it don't drop dead under him afore he gets halfway home.'

Niamh looked at her three loyal servants, gathered around the kitchen table. 'I'm glad we're together, because there's something I have to say while you're all here.' They exchanged anxious glances, wondering what was to come. 'No one will go hungry here, no matter what my husband says. Nor will you have to wait for your wages. I have a legacy due to me from my mother. So far we haven't needed it but I shall go into town tomorrow and ask for it now.'

The next day the skies opened and it poured with rain. Both Brigid and Becky did their best to persuade Niamh not to go but she waved their anxieties away.

'A little rain never hurt anyone. I shan't melt. And the pony will appreciate the cooler weather.'

But the pony hated the rain, becoming skittish and hard to control. She was wet through and exhausted by the time she reached the Silver Star. Outside the back door, Niamh wrung the worst of the rain from her shawl and her skirts before she went in. Gladys was first to greet her, laughing at her bedraggled state.

'There's awful you look. Not so much of the lady today, are we? More like a drowned rat.'

'Where's my father?' She had nothing to say to Gladys.

'Help yourself.' Gladys shrugged. 'Out there in the bar. Rushed off his feet, he is.'

Tully was in the saloon, looking crumpled and harassed as he serviced the lunch-time crowd with the help of a barman. Ellie was nowhere to be seen. He embraced Niamh briefly when she joined him behind the bar. Assisting him was second nature to her. She did it as a matter of course.

'Good heavens, darlin',' what brings you out on such a day? You'll catch your death.'

'Not me,' she grinned at him, tucking a strand of wet hair away from her face.

'Well, you certainly know when to call at the right time.'

'But where's Ellie?' Niamh said, when they had time to draw breath. 'Why isn't she helping you?'

Tully's smile faded and his mouth turned down in sorrow, his eyes betraying his anxiety. 'Ellie's not well, dear. Not well at all. She lost the baby and at first I thought she was just depressed. Now I think it's much more. She's so tired all the time – too weak to get out of bed.'

'Oh, Pa. Why didn't you send for me before?'

'Poor girl,' he rested his hand briefly on her head. 'I thought you had enough on your plate, what with Sukie an' all of her troubles, an' the baby . . .'

'But you should have done. Ellie may be your wife but she's also my friend. I care about her.'

'I know you do, darlin', an' I'm sure it'll do her the power o' good to see you today. Go up an' take a look at her now the rush has died down.'

Niamh ran up the twisting, rickety stairs to the room shared by her father and Ellie. Alone in that enormous bed in the dimly lit room, Ellie looked smaller and thinner than Niamh remembered. The air in the room was stale and, whether or not it was a trick of the light, the sight of her lying there, her face pinched and jaundiced, reminded Niamh all too vividly of her mother in her last days.

'Oh Ellie, what's happened to you?' she murmured, taking her friend's limp hand.

Ellie opened her eyes and took a moment to focus on Niamh, recognising her with but a ghost of her old smile. 'I – I lost the baby,' she whispered and covered her eyes with her other hand. She gave a great sob, overcome by her tears.

'Oh Ellie, don't.' Niamh squeezed the hand in her own. 'You'll have other babies, I'm sure. There's plenty of time.'

'But I wanted this one, Niamh. It's as if part of me died. And I feel so sick, so weak all the time. I should be over it all by now – back on my feet and helping Tully downstairs—' She broke off as Niamh dashed from the room. 'What is it? Where are you going?' She waited until Niamh returned a few moments later with a bundle of clothes, including a shawl and a hat, then held up her hands, warding her off. 'Oh no, no. Niamh, I can't. I don't feel well enough to get out of bed.'

'Ellie, you must. I'm taking you home with me where I know you'll be safe.'

'I'm safe here, aren't I? With my husband and Gladys?'

'At the very least you can benefit from Brigid's good food and a breath of sea air.'

When they appeared downstairs – Elinor pale and leaning on Niamh, her clothes hanging heavy on her diminished frame, Gladys was quick to object.

'You'll be the death of her, taking her out in weather like this.' She glared at Niamh and tried to take Ellie's arm, urging her back to bed. Ellie hesitated, looking from one to the other, too weak to decide for herself.

Fortunately, for Niamh, Tully came down on her side.

'You go with her, darlin'.' He kissed Ellie tenderly but gently as if she were made of fine porcelain. 'Stay as long as you like and come back to me well.'

'But I don't want to leave you.' Ellie's eyes filled with fresh tears.

'Of course she doesn't!' Gladys was quick to take advantage of that moment of doubt. 'She should be abed, not traipsin' about in the rain.'

'Typical Melbourne weather – the rain has stopped.' Niamh smiled, determinedly cheerful. 'If we go at once, we'll be home before it thinks of starting again.'

Gladys shrugged, admitting defeat, and turned away to pick up the poker and take out her spite on the coals of the kitchen stove. Before leaving, Niamh quickly took her father on one side and explained the original reason for her visit; that Hollis had left her embarrassed without any money. Tully was quick to mend the deficiency, insisting it was no more than her due, and within the half-hour they were on the road to Brighton. Ellie lay back, supported on cushions, surrounded by rugs and, fortunately, although she was sweating and deathly pale, she slept for most of the journey.

Chapter Twenty-Two

'Blackbirders! Slave-traders! That's what you are.' Judd voiced his suspicions without thinking. 'And that's what you want them for, isn't it, all these leg-irons and neck-braces, locks and chains?' Sweating from his exertions over the makeshift forge on the beach, he confronted the captain of the *Daisy May*. It had been hard, fashioning the metal with such primitive tools and the workmanship had been far below his usual standards. Now he didn't care.

'Wait a minute, blacksmith, before you fly off the handle.' Diedrik held up a hand in warning. 'You should know what we're dealing with here. I suppose you take the popular view that Polynesians are a gentle people who feed on yams and berries and wear grass skirts?'

'I haven't thought about them at all until now, but if slave-trading is your business, I'm not going to be a party to it.' Judd gave a shiver of distaste, reminded of his own experiences inside Melbourne Gaol.

'Oh?' Diedrik said softly. 'But I think you will. You don't really want us to leave you behind, do you? To take your chances on this deserted beach?'

Judd looked around, realising he had no idea where he was. Were they somewhere on the east coast of Australia, or not? His knowledge of geography was poor and, to his inexperienced eye, one stretch of beach looked much like another, some with sands extending as far as the eye could see and others with granite outcrops, tumbling down into the water, huge boulders worn smooth by the pounding of waves and wind-driven sand.

The ship's journey through the Bass Strait had sapped him of all his strength; for it had taken him more than a week to get over his nausea and find his sea legs. He had known terror at the same time. Only a fool would have been unafraid as experienced seamen and novices clung to the rails for dear life as the schooner plunged and bucked through the deepwater menace of waves that reared behind them bigger than houses. Were it not for the Dutchman's seamanship, the ship would have been lost, unable to travel the calmer waters closer to shore for fear of being wrecked on uncharted reefs. Nauseated, Judd had lost all track of time and now his clothes hung on his skinny frame, looking and feeling as if they belonged to somebody else. His muscles felt weak and wasted and it had taken the last of his energy to heat and pound this poor-quality metal to produce the trappings of slavery that Diedrik required. Until now he had been too exhausted, too preoccupied to care. But now, remembering the strong hinges and bolts he had made for the trapdoor which covered the hold, he put it all together and he knew.

'Where are we?' he whispered, looking around him. For some people, the absence of human presence would make it a paradise but to Judd it was only daunting. The tide was out and clean yellow sands stretched in either direction, revealing exotic shells inhabited by living sea-snails which crawled on the shoreline, waiting for the sea to reclaim them. Pelicans, ungainly and awkward out of the water, were hunting them down before they could do so. The ocean beyond was a vivid blue and in the opposite direction, leading uphill from the beach were sand dunes covered in hardy, fleshy ground-cover plants, the only vegetation to grow in such unpromising ground. In the distance was an outcrop of granite boulders stretching down into the sea and trees suggesting primeval forest beyond. Temperate or tropical? Judd wasn't sure. Only the chilling breeze blowing in from the sea made him think they were still on the south-eastern coast of Australia.

Diedrik laughed softly. 'You have no idea, have you? Any more than you know what may be lurking behind those boulders, waiting to pounce on a man left alone. Leave and you'll never get back to civilisation alive and only the hangman awaits you, if you do. You need me, blacksmith, just as much as I need you.'

'The kidnapping of native peoples is no longer allowed. Laws have been passed to protect the islanders, save them from being exploited by people like you.'

'Whose laws? And do you see anyone here to enforce them?' Diedrik made a sweeping gesture, indicating the empty strand. 'I am a Dutchman and my ship sails under the French flag.' He snapped his fingers close to Judd's face. 'I don't give *that* for your British Government or its laws. How much time d'you think the British Navy can waste patrolling this coastline? There are dozens of bays and estuaries where a ship like mine can come and go as she pleases.'

Judd shook his head. 'If I'd known you were involved in this filthy trade . . .'

'Well!' Diedrik sneered. 'For a convicted murderer you have a nice social conscience, Judd.'

'For the last time, Captain, I'm not a murderer.'

'Spare me your pleas of innocence.' Diedrik waved his excuses away. 'They don't impress me a bit.'

Quietly, while they were talking, Diggory Wood had removed the results of Judd's handiwork to the ship. He had returned to see if they were ready to leave, becoming wary when he realised they were locked in argument. 'Everythin' all right here, Cap'n?' he said.

Diedrik answered him although he didn't take his eyes off Judd. 'Strange as it seems, Diggory, Mr Burden's in two minds whether to stay with us not.'

'Oh?'

Judd sensed rather than saw Diggory assume a crouching position ready for a possible attack and he tensed, preparing to defend himself, hoping to see the glint of the seaman's knife before it slid between his ribs.

'All right, then, I'll stay,' he said at last. 'But only because I have no choice.'

Diedrik nodded briefly at Diggory as if calling off a dog. 'Sensible fellow. I thought you'd see it our way.'

But it was with a heavy heart that Judd climbed into the boat and let Diggory row them back to the ship.

*

Tully missed his wife more than he would have believed possible, awaiting her letters with the eagerness of a boy in the first flush of love. He called at the post office to collect them, rather than wait for them to be delivered to the Silver Star. She wrote to him regularly and two weeks later as the hot summer weather abated, giving way to the warm sunny days and fresh winds of March, she told him her health had improved dramatically in Niamh's care. Anxious for news, he tore open the latest letter as soon as he received it, unable to wait until he got home.

My darling, she wrote. *Is it possible you miss me as much as I'm missing you? Niamh is kindness itself but I wish you were here to enjoy the sea breezes with me – you could do with the fresh sea air quite as much as I. It's so lovely and peaceful here after the rush and bustle of the city. You would be amazed to see how much better I am. The sickness has gone, I eat like a horse and I'm already bursting out of my clothes. Yesterday we took a short walk on the beach and I didn't get tired. I've told Niamh I've imposed on her long enough and it's time I went home but she won't hear of it, not until I'm my old self again.*

I think of you almost hourly, my darling, and can't wait to see you. Your own Ellie.

Tully placed the letter in a pocket close to his heart and promised himself to go down to Brighton on Sunday to pay her a surprise visit. He straightened his shoulders as he threw open the doors of the Silver Star, facing his customers with renewed vigour.

On the evening of the same day, when the last customer had gone, he bade an absent-minded good night to Gladys, and went upstairs. He washed himself and shaved – a habit which had become a nightly ritual since his marriage to Ellie – before retiring to their bed which seemed even bigger and lonelier than ever without her. He didn't bother to wear a nightshirt these days. Ellie had laughed at the voluminous old-fashioned garments, persuading him it was better to sleep in the nude.

This particular night he was beset with dreams. He dreamed Ellie was beside him again, curling herself around his back and buttocks, murmuring endearments as she stroked his thighs. He muttered, smiling in his sleep and rolled over towards her, meaning to take her in his arms. Instead, he caught nothing as she seemed to avoid him, slipping beneath the sheet which was their only cover as the night was warm. A moment later she came up almost stealthily between his legs. He groaned as she murmured, stroking him with experienced fingers that knew how to please, before taking his roused penis into her mouth. Instinctively, although still half-asleep, he began moving his hips in time with her rhythm.

But he was a plain man at heart; he liked his sex to be straightforward, regarding anything else as unwholesome. Gently, having no wish to offend her, he wound his hands in her hair and lifted her head away.

'No, Ellie,' he whispered. 'I can't have you abasin' yourself for my pleasure. I want you with me tonight . . .'

Suddenly, he was wide awake, knowing something was wrong. This wasn't Ellie in his bed. How could it be? She was with Niamh. This wasn't Ellie's fine hair he held in his hands; this hair was dark, wiry and strong. His worst fears were confirmed when he looked down the bed to see Gladys lying there, grinning back at him; he could just see the glint of her teeth in the darkness. With a cry of disgust he curled away from her, aiming a kick which was meant to evict her from his bed. His foot connected with her breast, making her grunt in pain but she managed to stay where she was.

'It's all right,' she whispered. 'Beat me, kick me, do what you like with me – I don't care. I'll do anything for you, Tully. All the things that she won't. Jus' tell me what you like – what you want.'

'I want nothing from you, Gladys.' He was so angry he could hardly speak. 'Get out of my bed.'

'Why?' Once more she tickled the inside of his thigh which made him all the more angry as it evoked an automatic response. Shaking with rage now, he seized both her hands in one of his own, taking a handful of her hair in the other and making her cry out as he forced her from the bed.

'Come on, Tully.' She turned back again, thrusting her face into his own. 'Why pretend any more? You know you want me – you always have. An' we're of an age, you an I. I know you only married that girl for her money. You have nothing in common with her. A whore, who's been had by half the officers in the local barracks – I heard her say so.'

302

'If you did, you must have been spying on us – listening at our door.'

'Then you should've been more careful and kept it shut. Know thy enemy, isn't that what they say? I love you, Tully, I always have. You owe me. An' when you hear what I've done for you, I know you'll love me, too'

'My God, woman, you have to be crazy. Get out of this room right now and get out of my life. You can spend the rest of the evening packing your bags. Tomorrow you leave this house – and this time it's for good.'

'Ah no, Tully, you don't mean it.' She smiled at him, her teeth very white and sharp in the darkness. The smile made him shiver, realising he might have spoken more truly than he knew. Gladys might very well be insane. 'I've come too far, I've done too much to give you up now.'

His heart set up a thudding, painful rhythm as he began fearing the worst. 'What, Gladys? Tell me what you've done.'

'My Aunt Sal was the first.' Gladys's eyes filled with tears and her lips worked as she remembered. 'But that was an accident. She kept teasin' me an' I lost my temper. I never meant her to die.'

'And – and if Sal was the first . . .' Tully felt his skin crawl and he drew the sheet around him to cover his nakedness. Small protection against a madwoman. 'Who else have you killed? Not – not Janet?'

'Your wife? Oh, she died of her tumour all right as the doctor said.' Tully closed his eyes in relief but it was short-lived. 'Not that I didn't help it along with a little rat poison in her milk. You should thank me for bringin' her a merciful release from her pain. I was only helpin' her to die a bit quicker. I did it for you.' Tully rubbed his face in his hands, unable to speak. 'Then *she* had to come. That interferin' sister o' yours. Her with the fire in her hair.'

Silently, Tully gave thanks that his sister was safe living miles away in the bush. 'I should have listened to Niamh. I should never have let you come back.' He took the woman by the shoulders and began shaking her. 'And Ellie? What did you do to Ellie, you bitch?' Gladys laughed back at him, relishing even this contact.

'Oh, it was easy when she lost the baby and the doctor

agreed.' Gladys nodded. 'He said that after miscarriage, a woman can often get depressed and go into a decline.'

'I've been a fool. Thank God Niamh arrived in time.'

'Oh yes, Niamh – always the fly in the ointment, the mote in my eye. But they're not here now, are they, any of them? Now there's just you and me.'

'Understand this, Gladys, once and for all: there will never be anything between us. There is no you and me.'

'Don't say never! Don't say that to me.'

'Get out of here, Gladys.' Suddenly, he was exhausted. 'Come on. Just go away and leave me be.'

With a sound that resembled an animal cry of rage, she ran from the room, slamming the door behind her. Cautiously, he got out of bed and pulled on some pants and a shirt. He was still shaking with fear and anger but he felt less vulnerable in his clothes. He started to push the bed forward, meaning to wedge it across the door, but it was solid timber and it took all his strength to move it. Before he could do so Gladys burst into the room again, brandishing his cut-throat razor which was already covered in blood. Blood was spurting from her left wrist, bright red against the white of her nightgown and dripping onto the floor.

'See?' She waved her injured wrist in his face, making him recoil in horror. 'I'm dying now – bleeding to death for you. But I'll take you with me, too. I won't let her have you – no!'

Tully moved quickly. It was easy for him to disarm the woman who was already losing her strength due to loss of blood. All the fight went out of her and she sat listlessly in a chair while he found clean rags to bind up her wound. There was a lot of blood but the injury wasn't quite so serious as it first appeared.

He took the precaution of locking her in her room until morning when he sent for the old doctor who had attended Sally and Janet. Together, they discovered the rat poison, hidden behind the flour on a shelf in the kitchen, and the more damning evidence of the malted milk powder which Gladys had poisoned to feed to Ellie.

'Out of her mind, poor thing.' The doctor shook his head. 'It happens, you know. A widow. Maybe never got over her husband's death. I should've seen it before.'

304

'And you'd have saved us a deal of trouble if you had.' Tully wasn't about to let the old man off so easily.

'What will you do now?' the doctor said, ignoring the criticism. 'Are you going to press charges?'

'What for? We already know what happened and I don't like the thought of disturbing poor Janet's grave. Long as you're sure you can get her committed to an asylum? And give me an assurance she'll never get out?'

It took four attendants to subdue Gladys and a small crowd gathered to see her manhandled into a carriage at the back door. Successful as she had been in concealing the nature of her illness before, she was a madwoman now. Fighting and screaming, with half her clothes torn off, her hair wild and on end, she looked as if she would never be sane again.

It was Sunday morning. Niamh and Ellie were walking along the beach in Brighton, laughing at the antics of Ellie's little dog, a tiny Italian greyhound that Dayman had brought for her; the runt of a litter from the bitch of one of his racing friends. It had been love at first sight between Ellie and the slender, smooth-haired little dog who sensed that his new mistress had been dangerously ill and needed someone like himself to cheer her.

Ellie had lifted the puppy high in the air to look at him, enchanted by his fawn-like brown eyes with their loving expression. 'Symp, I shall call you,' she said at last. 'Short for sympathy. I know we'll be the best of friends.'

'Thank you, Dayman, that was so thoughtful,' Niamh said later when she went to the stables. 'It's so exactly what Ellie needs after a losing her baby – a pet of her own – a little creature to care for and love.'

Dayman smiled and nodded, his face creasing into lines of humour and understanding. Symp's arrival became the turning point in Elinor's fight back to health, setting her firmly on the path to recovery. This morning the dog ran ahead of them, sprightly as a small deer, chasing pebbles if they threw them although, like most of his breed, he didn't care to retrieve.

They walked past the pier and the children shell-collecting, and came to the end of the Bay where a pile of rocks tumbled into the sea. To continue their walk, they would have to hitch up their skirts and climb and they were about to turn back. But, before they could stop him, Symp was up and over, disappearing into the next cove, giving them no choice but to follow, tucking up their skirts and clambering over the rocks to join him.

'Are you sure you're not tired, Ellie?' Niamh said. 'I wouldn't like you to overdo it and have a setback.'

'No, I'm fine,' Ellie assured her. 'Getting stronger each day. All this lovely sea air makes me realise what Tully and I are missing.'

There weren't so many people on this side of the rocks and no houses had been built facing towards the sea. Up on the bluff they could see a sign drooping from a post. Ellie turned her head sideways to read it. It advertised *Land for Sale*, giving the address of an agent although it looked as if it had been hanging there neglected for quite a while.

'Overpriced,' Niamh said, shaking her head. 'Or it would have sold long ago, in a prime position like this.'

'Maybe. But with that view from the headland, they can ask any price they want. Can we take a closer look?'

'Oh Ellie, no. I'm sure you've done enough climbing for one day. We should turn back now.'

But Ellie was already mounting the rough steps leading up to the headland, Symp hard on her heels. By the time Niamh joined her, she was gazing around with a proprietary air and standing on tiptoes to look out to sea.

'I thought so,' she said. 'On a fine day you'll see clear across the Bay to the heads and I can just make out the outline of the city. This would be the most perfect location for a hotel. People could drop in for lunch or even stay overnight. We could offer bed and breakfast – luxury weekends away.'

'Well, somebody could,' Niamh said, reluctant to encourage her. 'But not you. Be realistic, Ellie. Even if Pa was to sell up – which I know he won't, you wouldn't have enough money for such an ambitious project.'

'But I do have money,' Ellie said. 'Lots of it, from my grandparents.' She smiled, remembering. 'Pa was fit to be tied when he found out Granpa had ignored him and left all his money to me.'

'Why did he do that?'

'Because Pa disapproved of my marriage – who knows? Grandpa was always a bloody-minded old cuss and I was his favourite grandchild. Lucky we live here in Victoria where a married woman has the right to own money and property.'

'Yes.' Niamh became thoughtful, remembering it was due to that same progressive law that she was mistress of her own home. 'But Ellie, how much money do you have?'

'I don't know – never bothered to find out. There was nothing I wanted to spend it on until now. What's the name of that agent?' She turned her head sideways again to read the lopsided sign.

'Hold on, Ellie. Shouldn't you talk to Pa before you commit yourself or do anything rash?'

'Why? You have to grab your chances when you see them, and opportunities like this don't come up every day.'

'That notice has been there a long time. Make sure there's no sinister reason why other investors have given it the go-by.'

'Takes a bit of imagination, that's all.' Ellie ran down the steps leading to the beach, Niamh following, surprised to find she was the one out of breath. On the way back they saw a solitary male figure coming towards them. Ellie straightened, tucked up her skirts again and broke into a run, waving her straw hat in greeting. Symp, infected by her excitement, ran barking at her heels.

'Tully! Oh, Tully!' she said, hurling herself into his arms as he lifted her off the ground to swing her around. The dog didn't like it and started nipping his ankles.

'No, no, Symp!' Ellie tried to command the puppy but found she couldn't do so for giggling. 'Naughty dog! Stop that at once.'

Niamh captured the puppy as they greeted each other, laughing.

'It's so good to have you restored to me,' Tully said to his wife, tears of sentiment standing in his eyes. 'Thank you, Niamh,' he clasped his daughter's hand. 'Thank you for taking such good care of her.'

'Oh now, Pa,' she said, making light of it. 'I always told you I'd make a good nurse.'

It was only later, after dinner and in response to Ellie's

repeated enquiries, that he told them about Gladys. He gave them a censored version, of course, seeing no need for either his wife or his daughter to know she had visited him in his bed, inviting the final rejection which pushed her over the edge into madness. Ellie listened, wide-eyed, gasping at each new revelation while Niamh listened in silence, her expression grim.

'You always were too soft-hearted, Pa,' she said when he finished. 'I wouldn't have let her get off so easily. She should have had her day in court and be made to pay.'

'Oh, don't you worry, darlin', she'll pay,' he said gently. 'To be locked up in the asylum for the rest of her days is punishment enough for anyone.'

Incensed and tearful, Niamh wasn't ready to let it go. 'But she'd killed two people already.' She glanced at Ellie. 'Given the chance, she'd have been the death of you, too.'

'Well, she can't hurt anyone now.' Tully shrugged. 'She's in the asylum and it'll be a cold day in hell before they let her get out.'

Ellie changed the subject, bringing it round to the one now nearest her heart – the parcel of land for sale on the bluff. Contrary to Niamh's expectations, instead of rejecting the idea, Tully was cautiously optimistic.

'Oh I know, Niamh,' he said, glancing at his daughter who had stopped in the act of pouring more coffee and was now watching him, wide-eyed. 'I've always said I'd never part with the Silver Star. But times change. The place is full of too many memories now an' not all of them good. Mebbe I wouldn't mind a few of the comforts of modern living an' a place where I could look out on the sea.'

'But there's nothing there, Pa. No foundations, no fences – nothing. Just a rough lump of land on the bluff. You'd have to build everything from the ground up.'

'We'd like that, wouldn't we, darlin'?' He covered his wife's hand with his own and received her answering smile. 'It would really be ours, then. A joint effort. We could have it exactly as we want.' Niamh felt a momentary pang of envy, reminded of the lack of companionship let alone love in her own marriage. 'Old Hanson next door has been at me to sell for years. Wants to knock down the wall between so he can expand.' He paused, glancing at Niamh. 'You wouldn't lose by it, love.

308

We'd make sure you were compensated for your share of the Silver Star.'

'Oh Pa, it's not that at all. I wouldn't need anything if Holly would stop bein' so pig-headed over Noah.' She caught the look that passed quickly between them, becoming defensive. 'What is it, then? What? He's just a baby, for heaven's sake.'

'A baby who doesn't belong to you,' Tully said softly. 'An' before you jump down my throat, I'm not sidin' with Holly. I'm just sayin' that, as a man, I see his point of view. Think it over, darlin'. Is it really worth fallin' out with your husband an' wreckin' your marriage? An' all for the sake of somebody else's child?'

'My marriage was ailing long before Noah came along. I promised Sukie I'd take care of him. He has no one else.' Niamh felt herself getting breathless, choking with unshed tears. 'It was the last thing she asked of me. And, while we're talking of Sukie, there's something else she said, Pa. Something odd I've been meaning to ask you about.'

'Well now.' Tully reached out to pour himself another glass of port, his hand shaking ever so slightly. 'You don't want to take too much notice of that, darlin'. People say all sorts of strange things when they're dyin'. She must've been wandering in her mind.'

'Oh no, she was very clear. She said things would have turned out differently if *you* had been Judd's father-in-law and not Albert. Why, Pa? Why would she say that?'

Tully sighed and passed his hand over his eyes, unable to go on meeting his daughter's honest, questioning gaze. 'Well, I'm not the bravest of men, darlin', you should know that by now. Maggi was always the daredevil, while I . . .' He glanced at his daughter and looked away. 'My sins have always been sins of omission. I went on living with Janet long after I should have done us both a favour and left. I turned a blind eye to the problem of Gladys. And then – then there was Judd.'

'What about him?' Niamh whispered.

Hesitantly, his tongue loosened by the good port, Tully relived the shipwreck and told of Jem's gold which he had used to set himself up in business. 'I was young,' he said. 'An' I wanted to come back to Janet – was afraid I'd lose her if I didn't. I couldn't spare the time to take Jem's money to

309

England.' And at last he told them how he had refused to pay Judd his dues. 'I can't say I'm proud of it.' He concluded with a sigh: 'An' if I could turn back the clock and do things differently, I would. There's no excuse except I was scared and wanted to keep what I had. But if I'd known he was desperate enough to kill a man to get his hands on some money, I'd never—'

'No, my darling,' Ellie interrupted. 'I won't have you blaming yourself for what Sukie's husband's done.' She seized his hand and kissed it, tears standing in her eyes.

Niamh felt suddenly cold. 'So I'm the only one who believes in his innocence. You think he did it – both of you. You actually think he killed poor Uncle Harley.'

'If he didn't do it, who did?' Ellie said gently. 'He had the opportunity. All the evidence was against him.'

'Evidence? Prejudice, you mean!' Niamh stood up and began pacing the room. 'I know him almost as well as I know myself. It's impossible. Judd couldn't kill anyone.'

'He joined forces with Carl to break out of gaol,' Tully reminded her. 'And they murdered one of the guards.'

'I met that man and he was ripe for someone to murder. But Judd didn't do it, I'm sure.' Niamh felt herself getting choked with unshed tears. 'I'm sorry but I can't talk about this any more. I need to be by myself – to go up to bed. You should be in bed too, Ellie. It's not a good idea to stay up late, after being so ill.'

'Niamh, please.' Ellie looked from one to the other, frightened by the rift developing between these two people she loved. 'Don't let the sun go down on an argument. We can't leave it like this.'

'I think we must.' Niamh kissed them both briefly. 'Before we say things we'll all regret.'

Meeting over the breakfast table, sheepish and full of apologies, they blamed their argument on Hollis's port. Radiant after spending a night in her husband's arms, Ellie said it really was time for her to go home.

'I love it here, Niamh, and I can't thank you enough for making me well,' she said. 'But I want to see Granpa's solicitor and find out exactly how much money I have. And then,' she exchanged glances with Tully, 'then I'm going to chase up that agent and make him an offer for that piece of land on the bluff.'

If Niamh was less than effusive, the McDiarmits were too involved in their plans and each other to see it. She waved to them from her doorstep and watched, arms folded, as Dayman drove towards the main road, taking them to the station in her little pony and trap. She turned back to the house, alone again with only her servants and the baby for company. She shivered although the sun was shining through the trees and the morning in early autumn was warm. What isolated her most was the thought that she was the only one who believed in Judd's innocence. Everyone else was convinced of his guilt.

Hollis did get his mortgage but only after a struggle and from the last place he wanted to ask, his own bank. John Westmoreland, the manager, had been an old friend of his father, so Hollis expected a lecture along with the loan. Westmoreland didn't disappoint him.

Grey-aired, grey-suited and somewhat lacking in humour, Westmoreland sat back in his captain's chair at his old-fashioned desk and shuffled the mortgage documents before passing them across the table to Hollis.

'Can't say I like it, me boy. The Oaks has always been free and clear. Never been under encumbrance till now'.

'I know that, Uncle John.' Hollis smiled, trying to contain his patience. 'I promise it won't be for long.'

'And I don't like the idea of sending out papers for your mother to sign. That's not how I conduct business. I'd much rather talk to her in person – make sure she's fully aware. She should know that if your plans go awry and the money is lost, her home is at risk.'

'I'd like that, too, Uncle John ' Hollis lied. 'But she's staying at Lachlan's Holt and I haven't the time.'

The bank manager's frown deepened. 'Then you should make the time. Your father would never—'

'Sadly, Pa can't be here, Uncle John. I have to do the best I can for the family now. I'll tell Mother everything you've told me. I won't let her go into this with her eyes closed.'

'Very well. I'll have to trust that you do. But under protest, you understand. I really would like you to wait.'

311

Hollis bit down sharply on the inside of his lip to stop himself saying something he might regret. 'I'm sorry, Uncle John, but I have to make my move quickly before Horace Ironsides discovers I'm after that land. If he does he'll go in and double the offer to cut me out. That's how valuable that parcel of land's going to be.'

'Maybe. Maybe not. These new ventures always carry an element of financial danger. It's not fair for your mother to risk her home at this time in her life.'

'We'll let *her* be the judge of that, shall we?' Hollis held out his hand. 'The mortgage documents, Uncle John.'

Westmoreland sighed as he passed them across.

Hollis had no intention of explaining anything to Lilias and when he said he was going to forward the papers to Lachlan's Holt, he knew she was already on her way home. What surprised him was that when she arrived and found him waiting for her, she didn't seem pleased to see him.

'So tell me,' she peered at him, sounding almost querulous, 'just how long have you been here? Why aren't you with Niamh at Brighton where you belong?' Then, predictably: 'People will think you've left her. What are my friends going to say?'

'No more than they've already said!' He tried to curb his impatience. 'This is a fine way to greet me, Mother. I thought you'd be pleased to see me?'

'I am. But I'd be much better pleased to see you with your wife.'

Hollis looked at her, trying to assess what was different, what had changed. She seemed refreshed, in control of her emotions and, on the surface at least, recovered from her bereavement. He was shrewd enough to know what she was thinking. A bachelor son was a prize to dangle before her friends who had marriageable daughters. A son separated from his wife was merely a liability.

'I have plans of my own, Holly,' she said. 'I want to redecorate the whole house for a start—'

'Oh no, not again!' he groaned.

'And I shall have card parties as soon as the official period of mourning is over. I might even go on a cruise.'

312

Hollis stared at her. *Official period of mourning* – what was that? Could grief and tears be turned off like a tap and on an appointed day?

'Well, I'm sorry if you think I'll cramp your style. If I'm in the way I'll get out and go to my club.'

'Oh no, you won't,' she snapped. 'You'll only make it worse. People will think you've fallen out with me, too.'

'Whatever I do, I can't please you. What do you want?'

'I've already told you, Holly. Go home to your wife.'

'I can't. Have you forgotten that my father in his wisdom, God rest his soul,' Hollis ground his teeth as if he wished his father anything else but peace in the grave, 'my father left Niamh the house?'

'Yes, but what I *don't* understand is this.' Lilias's perfect eyebrows rose a fraction of an inch. 'You went against everyone's wishes – especially mine – to have her. Now it appears you've changed your mind. You do realise you can't have a divorce? Such a scandal would ruin you.'

'There's no question of any divorce.' He rolled his eyes heavenwards.

'Don't do that, it's irritating. It's time to grow up, Holly and be more responsible. You're not a child any more and Niamh's not a toy you can pick up and discard at will.'

'Spare me the lecture, Mother.'

'If you can't see where your duty lies, then I'll have to tell you. I didn't want you to marry Niamh, I wanted better for you. But now you *have* married her, I'm not all that displeased. She's made of sterner stuff than I thought. She's turned that Briarley Hospital upside down till it's improved out of sight. You wouldn't know the place. Even Sister Kearney is almost human these days.'

'I'm fed up with hearing about Sister Kearney and The Briarley. Niamh never talks about anything else.'

'Go home to her, Holly. Give her some babies of her own and she'll settle down.'

'She has Sukie's baby already. She doesn't want mine.'

'Then that's all the more reason she *should* have a child of her own. Go home and see to it.'

'You talk as if I'm some sort of prize bull.'

'In the marital stakes, I'd say you're no kind of prize at all.'

313

Lilias subjected him to a cool and speculative gaze. At last she shrugged and swept towards the door, unpinning her hat as she went. 'I'm covered in soot from that train journey. I'm going to wash and change.'

'Oh Mother, a moment before you do.' He picked up the papers he had brought home from the bank. 'One or two documents – nothing important. A few papers I need you to sign.'

'Then if they're not important, they can wait.' She waved them away. 'I'll see to them later. Good heavens, Holly, I've only just walked in the door. And you know how I hate signing papers – it gives me a headache.'

'But, Mother, I do need—'

'Well *I* need to change out of these filthy clothes and lie down for a while. I'm getting one of my heads.'

Hollis stared after her as she left the room. In the space of just a few weeks she had changed radically. Where was the mother who smiled and doted on him, denying him nothing? This was a different Lilias – a woman who had something else on her mind – something she wasn't yet ready to share, not even with him. It made him uneasy; he didn't like it at all.

Chapter Twenty-Three

As the vessel sailed north towards more tropical climes, Judd started to enjoy his life as part of a ship's crew. His conscience troubled him only when he saw the empty quarters in the hold and was reminded that they were involved in the notorious recruiting 'trade'.

He admired the strength and seamanship of the kanakas and of Jimi Fiji in particular, whose smattering of English made him their natural leader. They became friends when Judd saw him fishing for yellow fin from the back of the ship and asked Jimi to teach him this skill. Having gained the man's confidence, Judd pressed him further, asking how he came to be part of the ship's crew.

'Doesn't it trouble you, Jimi? To hunt your own kind?'

'Not my people.' Jimi shrugged. 'Not my tribe. One time man catch Jimi – man not from my island. They want to kill Jimi – eat 'im. Then Diedrik come – bang! bang!' He made a pantomime of shooting. 'Jimi belong Diedrik now. Catch many mens for him.'

'I see.' Judd had heard tales of cannibalism in the islands from Carl but it had seemed so monstrous, he didn't believe it. Carl had laughed, telling him about native festivals on the beach where they served *long pig*, embroidering the tale by saying that human flesh didn't taste like pork at all but had more the texture of veal. Judd had taken it as further evidence of Carl's warped sense of humour. But now, hearing Jimi speak of cannibalism so casually, he wasn't so sure.

'And white men, Jimi? They eat white men, too?'

315

'Why not?' Jimi grinned, pointing to his head. 'Get white man's savvy!'

Diedrik, suspicious of Judd's interest in the Fijian, found some chore for the big man, ordering him away.

'No good pressing him, blacksmith. Jimi has no more idea of our position than you do,' Diedrik sniggered, making Judd all the more determined to find out.

But he was no wiser after sneaking a look at the maps when the captain was careless enough to leave his cabin unlocked. The charts and maritime maps meant nothing to him. He knew only that the weather was growing warmer each day and they were cruising north, following the coastline as they sailed towards the equator. Now he wished he had paid attention to geography during his limited time at school.

Melbourne would be going into autumn but here the nights were balmy and warm as the days. The wintry grey of the southern seas had given way to an ocean reflecting the clear, bright blue of a tropical sky. Closer to shore, the waters appeared almost turquoise, reflecting the pale coral sands which lay between rocks and reef.

As they passed through a narrow channel between two islands, the shallows were so clear it was hard to judge the depth of water beneath the ship. Many a time he looked over the side to see huge brain corals apparently inches below the surface and tensed himself for an impact that never came. The ship glided on over coral gardens unharmed. He leaned over the side until he almost fell in, fascinated by this exotic underwater world full of colour; a living thing made up of millions of busy polyps building on the skeletons of their forebears, providing food and shelter for fish and other creatures of the sea.

When he first went to sea, his thoughts had turned often to those he had left behind, worrying and wondering how they would fare in his absence. But as the ship moved away from Victoria, he remembered them less and even his passion for Niamh became less intense. He was leading a different life and she had no place in it, being part of the world he had left behind. A world to which he might never be able to return. He no longer troubled to cut his hair or his beard and Diedrik made fun of his wild appearance, calling him Blackbeard

316

the Pirate. Judd didn't mind; for that's what he felt himself to be. An exile and, albeit unwillingly, a member of a pirate crew.

'Are you quite sure you know what you're doing, Mrs Maitland?' Sister Kearney leaned back and regarded Niamh. She was seated at the desk she had recently inherited from the old matron who had retired. The desk and the high-backed chair that accompanied it were still a novelty to her and she rested her hands on the highly polished arms of the fruitwood chair. She was Matron Kearney now and head of the nursing staff at The Briarley, although Niamh couldn't get out of the habit of calling her 'Sister'. Kearney looked at Niamh's eager face and wished herself young again, if only to have the drive and the energy of this woman.

'Do you know, Sister, that's what you said to me when I first came to you with my sleeves rolled up, ready for work. This time I'll be honest – I *don't* know. But I want to try.'

Sister Kearney leaned forward on her elbows, massaging her temples as if Niamh and her enthusiasms wearied her. 'Think about it, Mrs Maitland. These children come from deprived backgrounds. They don't have nice manners or the first idea how to behave. And you're saying you want to take them into your home?'

'Yes. In some cases their mothers as well. So far as healing goes and the care here, neither you nor the hospital can be faulted –' she paused as Matron Kearney raised her head to give her a direct look, recognising soft soap when she heard it – 'But because of the pressure on beds, you have to send them away too soon. I'm suggesting an alternative – a period of convalescence by the sea.'

'You'll turn your mansion into a convalescent home?'

'It's hardly a mansion, Sister. The Hollies is only a modest suburban home.'

'By your standards, maybe. It'll be as daunting as a palace to some of these folk. Think about it, Mrs Maitland. Is it fair to show them a way of life they can never have?'

'Why not? If these people never know anything but misery and disease, how can they ever raise their sights?'

'Idealistic claptrap.'

317

'Maybe it is. But if you don't want me to do this, why not be honest and say so? Don't tear me down.'

'I'm sorry. I know you mean well, girl. And I'm not unappreciative of what you've achieved so far. But there's a world of difference between a full-time commitment and giving up a few hours of spare time. You'll never be free of it, once you start. You'll be on your feet and busy every moment of the day.'

'I don't mind. I have one child dependent on me already – little Noah. He's only a baby as yet, but I don't want him to grow up coddled and over-indulged because he's a boy alone, raised in a household of women.'

'But won't your husband—?' Matron Kearney broke off, pink spots of colour appearing high on her cheekbones. She knew all wasn't as it should be with the younger Maitlands but she was wary of intruding in anyone's private life.

'My husband is busy and works long hours. He needs to be near his business interests in the city, so it's more convenient for him to stay with his family during the week,' Niamh said smoothly. This was her standard response to such queries but it was also true. Maitland & Maitland had prospered and diversified with Hollis in control. Now, some seven months later, he straddled a business empire comparable to that of Horace Ironsides. He never came to Brighton these days, although he left clothes in the wardrobe to give an impression that he lived there some of the time.

'And if the question isn't too personal, too rude –' Matron Kearney's throat was red now, matching the colour in her cheeks. '– how is the scheme to be funded?' She counted the items off on her fingers. 'Let's say you have enough dormitories, enough linen and beds right now. You'll need a fully-equipped commercial laundry and more privies, let alone food and fuel on a day-to-day basis. Have you an adequate water supply or will you need more tanks? How will your servants feel about taking on extra work?'

Niamh looked thoughtful. She had tested her plans on Becky and Dayman who had received them with enthusiasm but she quailed before raising the subject with Brigid, deciding to wait until she knew the scheme was going ahead.

'Well, I haven't worked it out to the last detail.' She

frowned, trying not to blame the other woman for assuming the role of devil's advocate. 'I wanted to discuss the idea in principle first, to make sure I had your support.' She stood up, getting ready to leave. 'But as you've made it quite plain you don't like the idea . . .'

'On the contrary, Mrs Maitland, I think it's a wonderful idea.' Matron Kearney smiled. Her smiles were rare and always a pleasant surprise, erasing her tense, rather ill-natured expression, transforming her entirely. 'But you must realise what's involved. I don't want you to embark on something you won't be able to finish. In the long run that would do more harm than good.'

'Sister Kearney, my home is half-empty most of the time. It has never been used to its full potential which is a shame and a waste. I want it filled with laughter and the sound of children at play. I don't want my adopted son to grow up alone.'

'I see.'

'You've already shown me that you know what we need. If you can spare the time, would you come to Brighton and give me the benefit of your advice?'

'Yes, Mrs Maitland, I'd like that. I will.'

'Isn't it time you started calling me Niamh?'

'No, indeed, that wouldn't be proper.' Matron Kearney pursed her lips, retreating behind her barriers of starch and formality. 'Whatever next? You'll be wanting to call me Jane.' She opened her diary and turned over the pages, avoiding Niamh's gaze. 'Shall we say this coming Thursday, at two in the afternoon?'

'I'll send my groom to meet you at the station.'

'That won't be necessary, Mrs Maitland. I have my own pony and trap.'

Elinor was agreeably surprised by the amount of money her grandfather had left her. Apart from some shares which were tangled up with her lawyers and not to be touched, she had enough money to buy the land she wanted, engage an architect and start building at once. All this before she needed to touch any of the money from the sale of the Silver Star. As Tully predicted, their neighbour had snapped up the offer and, at Niamh's insistence, he and Ellie had moved in at The Hollies, pending completion of the hotel which could take anything from six months to a year.

But following the visit of Jane Kearney, Niamh seemed depressed and less willing to talk of her plans. It was Ellie who raised the subject over breakfast at The Hollies.

'You've been wandering around with your soul in your eyes since that woman left. What did she say to upset you?'

Niamh sighed. 'Oh, only what I knew already. It's all too expensive and will cost twice as much money as I have.'

'Couldn't you ask Hollis . . .?' Tully began, only to break off cringing as both girls quelled him with a look.

'I shan't even mention it, let alone ask him for money.' Niamh shivered at the thought. 'If he knew I was this desperate, he'd put paid to my plans just to spite me.'

'But Niamh, why didn't you say so before?' Ellie said. 'Money isn't a problem to me. I'm sure I have plenty for everything, including your needs.'

'You might think so now, Ellie,' Niamh said, aware how such projects could escalate, unforeseen expenses running away with cash, 'but the hotel is sure to cost more than the estimate and you'll have to wait six to twelve months for it to realise its potential. Even then you'll have to wait for people to hear about it, for word to get around.'

'Niamh, we owe you everything, Tully and I. If it wasn't for you, I might not be alive to tell the tale.' She passed a morsel of toast to Symp who was under the table.

'Lord, Ellie, you make a fool of that dog,' her husband chided but without any real conviction.

Ellie pulled a face and defied him by offering Symp a whole piece of toast soaked in butter, then went on speaking to Niamh. 'You nursed me back to health. You were there when I found that wonderful plot of land. It was a turning point that gave me a whole new purpose in life. Now I'd like you to realise *your* dreams, as well. Nothing would give me greater pleasure, especially in such a good cause.' Niamh glanced at her father who nodded, waiting for Ellie to go on. 'So we thought, instead of giving you a lump sum for your share of the Silver Star, we'll pay for the alterations to The Hollies, build a new laundry for you and give you a monthly salary to maintain the place as well.'

'Oh Ellie, you've worked it all out.' Niamh felt tears very close to the surface. 'So generous. But I can't possibly accept—'

'You can and you will. Because we won't take no for an answer.'

'How can I ever thank you?'

'You don't need to.' Ellie smiled. 'We're just providing the means. *You're* the one who'll be doing all the hard work.'

Contrary to Niamh's expectations, Hollis offered no objections to her plans. Far from being ill-disposed towards it, he capitalised on her charitable enterprise as it reflected favourably on himself. People assumed he was giving material support and he let them think so. No one outside the family knew he contributed nothing. So far as he was concerned, his wife was suitably occupied. It was Lilias who now gave him cause for concern.

He knew she was protecting a secret but it took him several weeks to find it out. He tackled her when she came home late from the theatre one night, lips bruised as if she'd been soundly kissed, cheeks full of colour and eyes bright and shining like those of a young girl.

'You do you know it's past midnight, Mama?' he greeted her in the hallway. 'Where the hell have you been?'

'To the theatre and dancing, dancing!' she sang, whirling her new red silk cloak around her and taking a few steps in the hall.

'And you've been drinking, haven't you?'

'Only champagne!' She blew him a kiss, refusing to let him spoil her mood.

'Champagne? With whom?'

'*With whom?*' Lilias mocked. 'You're my son, Holly, not my grandfather. I don't have to tell you anything.'

'I gather the person who's been plying you with champagne is no friend of my father's, then? Where did you meet him – at Maggi's?'

'Good lord, no. She never has anyone there but horsy types who stink of the stables – people who've come to buy. No. I met Orlando on the train coming home.'

'Orlando?' Hollis wrinkled his nose, imagining an artistic

type with a full beard and long white hair. 'You let a man speak to you? Pick you up on a train?'

'As it happens, I spoke to him first.'

'How clever of him to let you think so.'

'Don't be so beastly suspicious, Holly. He is Orlando Cavendish, related to the London Cavendishes – you know, the Square. And he's an artist, too—'

'He would be.' Hollis narrowed his eyes.

'– who makes the most wonderful pots with a streaky glaze. I've been to his studio and I've seen his work. It's a French technique, I believe.'

'And what other French techniques has he shown you?'

'Don't be vulgar.' Lilias shivered, coming down to earth now she was no longer under the influence of champagne. 'You must learn to be more respectful when you speak of your new step-papa.'

'Step-papa! Good lord, Mama, I do hope you've done nothing rash?'

'We have exchanged vows, Orlando and I. We are pledged to be married.'

'I think we'd better sit down and discuss this, don't you?' He ushered his mother towards the small parlour they generally used for breakfast. 'I'll ring for some coffee.'

'No you won't. The servants are all in bed. And if I drink coffee at this hour, I won't be able to sleep.'

'I doubt if I'll sleep at all in the wake of such news. Mother, really. It's positively indecent. You've been widowed only a matter of months.'

'Orlando explained all that – he understands these things. And don't look like that!' She frowned as Hollis raised his eyes heavenwards. 'He says it's *because* I was happily married that I'm ready to marry again so soon. It's a compliment to your father. We shall spend half the year in his house in London and the rest of it here. Oh, and he wants me to take the deeds of this house to his lawyer, along with full details of all my income and investments.'

'What?' Hollis snapped. 'Whatever for?'

Lilias sighed. 'To combine them with his own, of course. It's only sensible for us to have the deeds of both our properties put in joint names.'

'Decidedly fishy. What makes you so sure he *has* all this property in London? He could be an adventurer after your own money.'

'Trust you to say so. Trying to spoil it for me.' Lilias produced a scrap of embroidered lace and dabbed at her eyes. 'Anyone would think I was so old and ugly, no one would want me except for my money. I'm not even fifty.'

'I know that, Mama.' Hollis patted her shoulder awkwardly, embarrassed by her tears. 'And a fine-looking woman you are, too. A woman any man of mature years would be proud to call wife.' He paused as a fresh thought occurred to him. 'Just how old is he, this Orlando of yours?' Lilias pursed her lips and gave him a sidelong glance, unwilling to say. 'You might as well tell me. I'll find out anyway.'

Lilias whispered, 'He's twenty-four.'

'Twenty-four? Good God, that's the same age as me.'

'Age doesn't matter when two people are in love.'

'Oh, and what's that? Another pearl from the lips of the ever-resourceful Orlando? I need a drink.' Hollis went to the tantalus, unlocked it and poured himself a large brandy from one of the crystal decanters. He drank it down and refilled it before turning to speak to his mother again. 'I won't give you the deeds of this house nor will I disclose any details of your income and investments – they're too closely allied with mine. And I certainly won't give any information to some shifty lawyer employed by this boyfriend of yours.'

'You can't stop me. The deeds of this house are mine.'

'Afraid not. You gave me Power of Attorney – remember?'

'When? I don't remember doing so. When did I do that?' Lilias sat down heavily, shaken by this news.

'When you came back from Maggi's, remember? You know you never bother to read what I ask you to sign. You say money matters give you a headache.'

'But I didn't mean to do that! People never give Power of Attorney unless they're incapable or out of their minds.'

'Or if they can't be bothered to deal with business matters themselves.'

'But – but, Holly . . . The Oaks – you haven't . . .?'

'Yes. Mortgaged to the eaves, I'm afraid.'

'Oh, no!' Lilias pressed a hand to her throat where a pulse

was beginning to beat irregularly. 'But Holly, this is my home – my security. You know how much it means to me.'

'Don't be so melodramatic, Mama. There s no risk involved here, none at all. Why, I've turned the money around twice over already.'

'Gambling with your heritage, your family home.'

'Is that any worse than your wanting to give it all away to some gigolo you met a few weeks ago?'

'But this is my home. Your father built it for me before we were married. You must go to the bank and pay off that mortgage first thing tomorrow morning.'

'I can't, Mama. The funds are committed elsewhere.'

'Then – then what . . .?' she said in a small voice, plaintive as a child. 'What shall I say to Orlando?'

'I really don't know. And, to be honest, I don't care.'

'I'm worried about Aunt Lil,' Elinor said to Niamh as they dished out a nourishing stew for lunch at The Hollies. Ten children were lining up, ready to take their meal and find a place at the big refectory table which now dominated the kitchen, some waiting more patiently than others. 'No, Tommy, don't push Ian out of the way,' Ellie scolded. 'You have to wait your turn.'

'But I'm hungry, missus!' The little boy gave an exaggerated sigh. 'My belly's growlin' – can't you hear it?'

Occupied with serving the meal, she had no further opportunity to talk about Lilias until the children were seated and quiet for once, heads bowed over their food. Eating was a serious business for little ones like these. It was Niamh who raised the subject of her mother-in-law.

'You were saying about Aunt Lil?'

'I'm worried about her. If anything, she's more wretched than when Uncle Harley died. A few weeks ago she seemed so lively, on top of the world again. Now she's given up on her appearance and seems to have aged overnight.'

'So what do you want me to do? Should I ask her to come and spend some time with us here?'

'I don't think she'd find that very restful.' Ellie gave a wry smile. 'Noisy, convalescent urchins aren't exactly her forte. But even if she won't come, I'm sure she'd appreciate being asked.'

*

324

'And how are you, Ellie?' Lilias asked when they were comfortably settled over afternoon tea. 'I have to say it – marriage appears to suit you. You're positively glowing. How goes the new hotel?'

'Slowly. Everything takes so much longer than I expected. But I didn't come here to talk about myself. I came because we're worried about you, Niamh and I.'

'Oh?' Lilias sniffed. 'I didn't think Niamh had time to worry about anyone now she has her new nursing home.'

'Don't be unkind, Aunt Lil. You should be thankful she has something to occupy her since Hollis neglects her so.'

'You're right, of course.' Lilias stared at the dregs in her teacup. 'My son has changed. He rides roughshod over everyone, these days, even me. Getting the best of Horace Ironsides – that's all he seems to care about.'

'Is it? Tell me about it, Aunt Lil,' Elinor said, realising she was getting close to the heart of the matter. It must be serious, indeed, for Lilias to criticise her son.

Haltingly, ashamed at having been taken in by such a plausible rogue, Lilias told her about Orlando. How he had planned to make sure she was wealthy before he committed himself and how quickly he'd broken it off when he found out her home was mortgaged and her son in control of her finances.

'But that's terrible, Aunt Lil. I'm so sorry,' Elinor said at the end of her aunt's tale.

'Oh, it isn't the loss of the boy – I knew in my heart it was all foolishness.' She gave a shrug and a sheepish smile. 'But it hurt to be ditched with so little ceremony. Serves me right for being a vain old woman, I suppose. I won't make such a stupid mistake again.' She sighed. 'Really, I should be grateful. If it weren't for Orlando's greed, I might never have found out what Holly was up to.' And she went on to tell Elinor how she had trusted her son and how he had slipped in the Power of Attorney with other papers she had to sign in order to give himself a free hand with the Maitland estate.

'But that's monstrous, Aunt Lil. And he shan't get away with it!' Ellie rose, unable to sit still any longer. 'He has no right to risk your security for the sake of his business ventures! I shall have words with him.'

'You can if you like.' Lilias gave a dismissive twitch of one shoulder. 'But I don't think it'll do any good.'

Elinor was in a state of controlled rage when she reached the offices of Maitland & Maitland. She stalked past Miss Johnson and flung open the door of Hollis's office without waiting to be announced.

'Ellie!' He rose to greet her. 'What a nice surprise.'

'You may not think so when you know why I'm here.'

'Please sit down. Can I offer you coffee?'

'Thank you, no. For what I have to say to you, I'd rather stand.'

'That sounds very ominous.' Hollis subsided into his seat, leaning back to regard her, steepling his hands. 'It's Mother, isn't it? What has she told you? She's not been herself at all since Pa died. Haunted by the unreasonable fears that beset a woman of her age.'

'But her fears aren't so unreasonable, are they? She has every right to be frightened while you're playing fast and loose with her finances, gambling with her home.'

'Nonsense. The Oaks has never been at risk and nor is it likely to be. A mortgage is nothing to be afraid of. It's merely a safety net to assure my ongoing credit.'

'Yes. Security against the money your creditors risk.'

'I tell you, there *is* no risk! The first of my estates sold out as soon as it went on the market and we've turned the money around again already.'

'So you *could* have paid off the mortgage before but you chose not to. What about Aunt Lil?'

'If she hadn't made such a fool of herself over Cavendish, she wouldn't have known. It's her own fault for prying into my affairs.'

'Her own affairs, you mean. I'd redeem the mortgage myself if I had the funds. As it is, my money is tied up in the hotel and – and certain other ventures.'

'It's all right, Ellie.' He smiled, noticing her hesitation. 'There's not much escapes me. I know you're giving Niamh financial support, encouraging her to defy me.' He put his nose in the air. 'Some people would call that gross interference – to come between husband and wife.'

326

'And some would say a warm-hearted, generous girl like Niamh deserved a much better husband than you are.'

'Warm-hearted? Generous? Are we speaking of the same woman here? It's no secret, Ellie. Niamh's frigid just like her mother. She doesn't want any man in her bed.'

'Is that so, Holly?' She leaned closer and spoke deliberately, making it impossible for him to avoid her gaze. 'Or is it that you don't want a woman in yours?'

He stood looking at her, breathing heavily, caught out. And when he did find his voice, he spoke softly, unable to look at her. 'You're the only one I ever told, Ellie – what happened to me at that boarding school. And you promised – you promised faithfully never to speak of it again.'

'Because I thought it was over – that marriage to a sweet girl like Niamh would set you straight. But you can't help yourself, can you? I've seen how you stare at strong men when you think no one's watching you.'

'I look, Ellie, that's all. I don't do anything.'

'Oh Holly, I know you don't – being you.' She took his hand but he pulled it away, unwilling to let her mother him.

'All right, Ellie. What is it you want?'

'I want you to sort out your finances at once, redeem The Oaks and give the deeds back to Aunt Lil.'

'Or else?'

'Or nothing. I'm not threatening you, Holly. I just want you to look into your conscience and make sure you do the right thing.'

Chapter Twenty-Four

All through that winter and the following spring, Hollis kept reinvesting his profits although, every time he did so, he remembered Ellie's visit and his conscience troubled him. This time he vowed it would be the last; this time when the profits came in he would pay off the mortgage and use his own funds.

He thought nothing of it when his bank manager sent for him although the messenger told him it was urgent. It was always the same with accountants – forever in a panic over nothing. It was probably just some papers he'd neglected to sign. Reluctant as he had been at first to deal with someone as conservative as John Westmoreland, the association had paid off and they had prospered from it.

But today Westmoreland ushered him into his office without the usual pleasantries and Hollis experienced a feeling that something was amiss. He felt rather like a schoolboy summoned to the headmaster's study.

'Good of you to respond so promptly.' Westmoreland leaned forward to shake his hand. 'Forgive me, Holly, but it's hard to know how to put this without giving offence. I've never questioned your judgement, have I? Never called you to account for the way you've been spending your money?'

'No, John,' Hollis said easily. 'Why should you? The bank's interests are safe with The Oaks for security.'

'Quite so. But I should be derelict in my duty if I didn't pass on my anxieties concerning your latest project.'

'Oh come on, John, don't be such an old woman.' Anxiety made him truculent although he could see the older man didn't like it. 'Everything's run like clockwork before. You know the score. The bank advances the money for my share. I drum up a few extra investors and together we buy out the new releases of land. I do the conveyancing, subdivide and we sell at a handsome profit. What's wrong with that?'

'Nothing, if you'd been as careful and meticulous with your enquiries as you have in the past. But this time you've rushed in without waiting for the surveyors' report. I'm just hoping you haven't made a mistake.'

'You could see how it was, John – we couldn't afford to wait. I had to make my move before Horace Ironsides.'

'Exactly – Ironsides. I'm afraid this ongoing feud with Ironsides will be your undoing.'

'What do you mean?'

The bank manager poured a small glass of water from a carafe and offered it to Hollis who frowned, shaking his head. So Westmoreland sipped it himself, choosing his words with care. 'It's in the interests of everyone for me to have long ears around town. Ironsides was boasting – even laughing about it – how he'd let you think he was after that property, encouraging you to bypass the usual surveys in order to get in first. He intended for you to have it, Hollis. He made sure you snapped up a parcel of barren and windswept plain, while he went after the real prize; the next release on the other side of the river.'

'No, no, that's not true. I have it on the best of authority ...' Hollis faltered, realising suddenly that it *was* true. He closed his eyes, feeling dizzy, clasping his head in his hands. Silently, Westmoreland poured him a glass of water and pushed it across the desk towards him.

'I'm sorry, very sorry to be the bearer of such ill news. Let us hope that forewarned is forearmed. Maybe you can rescue something from all this before it's too late.'

'How?' Hollis snarled. 'It's already too late. The land is bought and paid for. How can we back out now?'

'You could quit it at cost, perhaps?'

'No! My investors would never stand for it. Nor would they trust my judgement again.' He felt the blood drain from his face as the true impact of the situation came home to him. 'That bastard Ironsides. He set me up.'

'I'm afraid he did.' Westmoreland cleared his throat.

'I'll kill him!' Hollis said through gritted teeth. 'That conniving piece of shit, I'll string him from the—'

'Now, Holly, calm down. I know how you feel but you must be discreet. Threats won't help and no one should hear you making them. Not outside these four walls.'

'It's all very well for you, you mealy-mouthed fool! You're not the one who's mortgaged his mother's home.'

'No. And I shall overlook your rudeness this time because I can see you're upset.'

'Oh God, John, I'm sorry . . .'

'Don't apologise, there's no need. But it's futile to go on blaming yourself or me. Put your mind towards salvaging something from this disaster instead. I've told you this in good faith but, at the end of the day, I have to put the bank's interests before your own. We have a month, perhaps, before my superiors start asking questions and I have to tell them how matters stand. After that, I can give you one more month before I have to call in the loan.'

Hollis stared at him, appalled. 'Two months?'

'For anyone else, Holly, it would be two weeks.'

'I – I'll do what I can.' Hollis rose, shook hands automatically and left the room like a man in a daze.

He couldn't go back to the office and look at Miss Johnson's trusting yet anxious gaze and the thought of going home and facing his mother sent a chill of apprehension down his spine. Outside, the skies were growing dark and there was a distant rumble of thunder from the hills. To Hollis it represented the sound of his enemies gathering against him. The wind whistled down the street almost snatching his hat as he stepped out to wave down a cabriolet.

'Quick as you can, driver,' he said. 'Take me down to the wharves.'

In a week or so it would be Christmas again. In a brief moment of respite while the washing was coming to the boil, Niamh walked in the garden, far from happy with what she saw. The seedlings which she had planted with such hope in spring were now wilted, heads drooping and leaves curled, unable to survive in soil which was parched and crying out for rain. This year, the hot weather had arrived early, bringing

330

with it a fresh crop of flies. Absent-mindedly, she took off her hat and flapped it at them, waving them away from her face. If it was as dry as this here on the coast, how would it be at Lachlan's Holt, where it had been arid enough last summer?

This would be a very different Christmas from last year when she had closed up the house to return to the Silver Star. So much had happened since then, so much change. Ellie married to her father. Sukie dead. And now she had Noah, the son she had always longed for, conveniently forgetting he wasn't her own. Shaken by the intensity of her love for him, she hid it by sharing it with the other children who came and went at The Hollies.

Judd she didn't dare think about, or the breathtaking sweetness of that one afternoon; the only time she had allowed herself to give way to her feelings, indulging her passion. Now she had only a memory and an unreliable one at that. Would their love have been strong enough to last a lifetime, to sustain them through illness and old age? She didn't know; their time together had been too short. She had no likeness to remind her and sometimes she panicked, thinking she couldn't recall his features at all. At other times, she remembered him so clearly, she could even imagine a whiff of burnt metal in the air. What would happen if, years later, he came back to find her an old woman, wrinkled and bent? Of course, he would be old, too. Would she know *him*?

The secret of her love had been buried with Sukie. She had never told anyone, not even Ellie, although they were now so close. And she felt guilty when people praised her for her generosity towards Noah. How could she tell them he was her lover's child? And, were it not for an accident of birth, Noah might be her own? That her greatest pleasure in life came from seeing her lover in Noah's eyes. No. It was better to hide her love by sharing it with the other children who needed her care.

This year The Hollies was filled with laughter and the cries of children looking forward to Christmas for the first time in their lives. Dayman had brought in a huge branch of she-oak which was the nearest thing he could find to resemble a fir. Ellie, brushing aside Niamh's protests, had gone out at once to buy candles and pretty glass ornaments to adorn it and now it

331

stood dominating the hallway, decked in its splendour. The children stared at it, open-mouthed, caught up in the magic of this symbol of Christmas. Beneath it, wrapped in coloured paper, was a present for each child.

Although The Hollies had been operational as a convalescent home for less than a year, it was clearly a success. Little invalids who arrived pale and wan, eyes huge and suspicious in wasted faces, soon grew boisterous and cheeky again, nourished by Brigid's good food. Later, as they gained strength, they turned brown as walnuts after playing outside.

Ellie was disappointed in Hollis. Months had passed and he had made no move to redeem The Oaks. She had to face the fact that by mentioning the matter at all, she had probably made things worse for Aunt Lil.

'You're very quiet, Ellie,' Niamh intruded on her thoughts as they worked together, hanging out another line of sheets. 'I thought you'd be jumping out of your skin now the foundations are in. Six months from now, the building could be finished and you'll be moving in.'

Ellie sighed. 'If only everything didn't take so long. And I'm tired of fighting with the architect – it's wearing me out. I know what I want. A solid, comfortable hotel where people can come and relax by the sea. But he wants me to build a showpiece – an Italianate monster!'

'Better not let Aunt Lil hear you say that.'

Ellie shrugged. 'I want a place that's a home, not a monument to his ego. And the builder is almost as bad . . .' Ellie gritted her teeth. 'Every time I complain of his slowness, he comes up with a new excuse. If it's not the weather, it's a shortage of building materials. Last month he just walked off the job to go to the races!'

'Come on, Ellie, be fair. You know everything has to stop for the Melbourne Cup.'

'Yes, but he won't take me seriously – he won't listen to me. If only your father were a bit more forceful.'

Niamh laughed. 'Pa has his faults, Ellie, but no one could accuse him of being forceful.'

'Oh, I know, and that's what I love about him, really. But now it's down tools again. They're taking three weeks off over

332

Christmas! We'll be lucky if the place is finished by this time next year.'

'Patience, Ellie. You'll be surprised how quickly the building will grow now it's started.'

'All I can see is an endless drain on our finances.'

'Oh?' Niamh bit her lip, thinking of Ellie's generous contribution to the upkeep of The Hollies.

'Oh no, I don't mean the money we give you here,' Ellie hastened to reassure her. 'That's a drop in the ocean compared to the expenses of the hotel. I'll feel better when it's up and running, filled with visitors and staff.'

'That's another thing – staff. I remember how hard it was to get people to come here. Nobody wanted to live so far out of town.'

'Then we'll get new chums.' Ellie smiled. 'Migrants make the best servants, anyway. We'll go down to the docks and meet the ships coming in. And with your father's blarney and my smile, they won't have the heart to refuse.'

'Oh, Ellie!' Niamh smiled at her optimism. 'I shall miss you so much when you go.'

'We're not going far – we'll be neighbours, silly. Besides, we'll be under your feet for at least another six months. You may be glad to see the back of us in the end.'

Christmas was an event – a day to remember, the only sour note being when one of the boys tied a tin can to Symp's tail. His laughter alerted Ellie as the little dog ran around the kitchen yelping in terror. She rescued her pet and turned at once on the offender.

'You little beast – it's Christmas Day for goodness' sake! How would you like it if someone frightened you?'

'Sorry, miss.' Suddenly, the boy's lips trembled. 'I was only havin' a bit o' fun. I didnt mean to hurt 'im.'

'Of course you didn't, Pete.' Niamh ruffled the child's hair as, shamed, he fought with his tears and hid his reddened face in her skirts. 'Run along now and wash your hands and face. It's almost time for Christmas dinner.'

'Honestly, Niamh. How is he to learn if you let him off all the time?' Ellie said, comforting Symp who was still shivering in her arms.

'What would you have me do, Ellie? Shall I beat him to teach him a lesson? I think his father did a good enough job already. That's how Pete came to be at The Briarley – with two broken legs.'

'Oh.' Ellie's expression softened. 'I didn't know.'

'I did warn you, Ellie, before you came here. These children aren't the little nursery-school angels you're used to. The problem is that when they've been badly treated, they tend to pass it on. Symp is altogether too trusting – an easy target.'

'Right, then. I won't let him out of my sight.'

'No need to go overboard. Just be aware, that's all.'

Everyone was seated at the refectory table in the kitchen. The red candles in honour of Christmas had been set alight, Niamh had said grace while the children fidgeted and Tully was preparing to carve the turkey when a carriage came clattering up to the back door. Dayman rose and left his place immediately to take charge of it while the children looked at each other and groaned in unison, afraid the longed-for Christmas dinner was going to be delayed.

'You carry on here,' Niamh said, pressing a hand on her father's shoulder. 'I'll go and see who it is.'

She couldn't have been more surprised if the Governor of Victoria himself had driven up unannounced. Her visitor was none other than Lilias accompanied by Hollis. Having seen neither of them for over six months, she was shocked to see them so changed. Hollis kept glancing about, a haunted expression on his face, and his mother appeared to have aged overnight. She started complaining at once after greeting Niamh with a peck on the cheek.

'You should see to that driveway, Hollis. It's a disgrace. All potholes and stones. My poor bones are quite shaken up. I shan't be myself for the rest of the week.'

'Sorry, Niamh,' he whispered under his breath. 'This wasn't my idea.'

'Families should be together on Christmas Day.' Lilias overheard him. 'If I don't make you keep up appearances, who will? We must keep the gossips at bay.'

'Come in, Aunt Lil,' Niamh grinned, thinking nothing had changed much, after all. 'You're just in time for lunch.'

'Good.' Lilias smiled at last. 'Elinor's been singing the praises of your cook.'

But she stopped on the threshold, daunted by the noise. 'Good heavens, what bedlam! I thought these children were supposed to be sick, Niamh?'

'They're not the poor little scraps you see at the hospital, Aunt Lil. Most of them are well now – but we didn't have the heart to throw them out before Christmas.'

'You're generous to a fault, isn't she, Holly?'

Hollis shrugged, refusing to be drawn into it. Niamh was sure this was the last place on earth he wanted to be. He flinched at the sounds of childish laughter and high-pitched chatter. Although, when the children saw there were strangers among them, a lot of the noise died down.

Tully waved a greeting, standing to carve more turkey for the children, who were already eating it with their eyes.

'Will you eat with us here in the kitchen, Aunt Lil?' Niamh said. 'Or would you prefer to be more private and have your lunch in the parlour on a tray?'

'Oh yes, please. I think we'll settle for the tray,' Lilias said, looking at runny noses and sticky hands, imagining them on her skirts. She was no more enthused at the idea of sharing a bench with the children than they were to have her. Niamh suppressed a smile, sensing rather than hearing a concerted sigh of relief from the children as the adults retreated, leaving them to continue their Christmas lunch.

Chapter Twenty-Five

Lilias was spending New Year's Eve by herself. She didn't mind this at first because she expected Hollis to be back before midnight to join her and see in the New Year. But when midnight chimed and she heard a muffled cheer from the servants, celebrating in the kitchen below, she realised he wasn't going to be there. Last year's New Year's Eve had been very different. She had been among people who loved her – Callum, her brother and Harley, dear Harley, had still been alive. Now, as a widow, she was no longer so acceptable socially, ignored by the same people who had courted her attention before. Tears of self-pity stung her eyes as she poured herself a large glass of port from a crystal decanter. She didn't touch the bottle of champagne she was keeping to share with Hollis.

'Happy New Year to you, Lilias!' She spoke up bravely as if she were talking to a room full of people, and raised the glass to her reflection in the mirror over the mantel. The gas-lights revealed all too clearly the disfiguring lines of sorrow and discontent that now scored her face. Neglect had taken its toll. Enjoying the warm feeling given by the port, she poured herself another, still talking to herself. 'You do realise you're well on the road to becoming a closet tippler, Lilias, drinking alone?'

Too restless to go to bed, she decided to wait up for Hollis. By one o'clock she was angry, by two o'clock she was in tears and by the time the clock struck three, she was in a lather of anxiety. Closing her eyes, she said a small prayer of thanks when she heard a carriage draw up outside.

It took Hollis a long time to let himself in and she heard

336

him curse, beginning to pound at the door. He must have mislaid his key. Quickly, she ran down the stairs to meet him. If he was coming home drunk from his revels, she didn't want the servants to see it. He almost collided with her as she opened the door and she took a step backwards at the sight of him, her hand at her throat. He came in shambling and awkward, his clothes torn and covered in filth, his hair matted and hanging over his eyes. He smelled strongly of sweat that wasn't his own and was bleeding from the mouth and the nose.

'Well, well, Mother,' he said, leaning against the doorpost to stop himself falling, and smiling at her through the blood on his teeth. 'Why aren't you abed? It's a long time since you've waited up for me.'

'Good God, Holly, what's happened? Have you been in a fight?'

'A fight? You could say that. I went out to fight the world an' I lost. Some people –' he belched gently '– some people would say I got no more than I deserved.'

'Here, let me help you.' She took a step forward until he stopped her, shaking his head.

'No help for us now, Mother. We're ruined. Just like you said. All the glory days – this monument to my father's work, this solid symbol of his wealth – all gone!' He made a sweeping gesture to include not just the hall but the whole house. 'D'you hear me? We're ruined. This isn't your home any more. I've lost The Oaks.' He stood there swaying, waiting for her to fly into a rage, screaming and slapping his face. That's what the old Lilias would have done. This one just stood there, calmly waiting for him to go on. 'Well? Have you nothing to say? Don't you want to rant and rave at me? Tell me what a fool I've been?'

'Would it help, if I did? You still haven't told me what happened to you. Are you drunk?'

'Oh, I'm drunk all right – among other things. I went to a pub on the wharf and got splendidly drunk. Saw the New Year in with some sailors. Then – then we went outside and things got a bit boisterous.' He glanced at her to see how she was taking it. 'I don't remember too much after that.'

'I see.'

'Do you? I wish I did. You can't see much with your hands held behind your back an' your face in the mud.'

'Oh, Holly,' Lilias whispered. She felt bone weary and sick at heart for him. Whatever had happened, whatever he'd done, he was still her son. 'And if you're trying to shock me, you'll be disappointed. Come and sit down before you fall down and let me see where you're hurt.'

'No!' Once more he held up his hands, warding her off. 'I can't let you touch me. I must stink of the fleshpots.'

'D'you think I care about that?' Lilias embraced him carefully as she would a nervous animal, pressing her forehead against his own. 'If anyone failed you, Holly, I did. Showing off with my big house and my parties, more concerned with the vanities than with my own husband and son. I didn't see you as a person, just as an adjunct to my success. I wanted you married well and for people to praise you, just to bring glory to me. If your marks at school were all right, then you had to be all right, too. I looked no further than that.'

He stared at her, sobered by this sudden change in her values. Was this really his mother? She who had made such a god of keeping up appearances before? She couldn't have heard him. She hadn't understood the extent of their plight.

'Didn't you hear me, Mother? I've lost everything, including this house – the home that means so much to you.'

'Well, I've decided it doesn't. Not any more. What is it for me without your father? A shell – a showpiece, not a home. I took you for granted – you and your father – but I'm not going to make that mistake any more.'

He whispered, closing his eyes. 'But you don't know the half of it, Mother. The things that I've done.'

'And I don't *want* to know, Holly. Let them lie. Come upstairs to my room and I'll clean you up. We'll put some salve on your wounds and you can sleep in my bed. I'll sleep in your father's old dressing-room. Then, in the morning, when you're sober, we'll look at it all again. Things may not be quite as hopeless as they seem.'

'Oh yes, they are. Westmoreland has given me as long as he could but time's running out. We have ninety days from today to vacate this house. After that it will have to be sold at auction to cover my debts.'

338

'Three months . . . A lot can happen in that time. And Holly, there's one thing more. I want your promise on this and then we need never speak of it again.'

'What?' He shivered, having a good idea what she'd say.

'You must stop going to these dangerous places; these bars and brothels at the wharf. You could be stabbed for as little as half a crown and left to die in the street.'

'Maybe that's what I wanted. So I wouldn't have to face you and tell you what I've done.'

'And we'll have no more talk like that,' she said briskly, drawing him towards the stairs. He was limping now, getting stiff. 'Come along. I want to bathe you and get you to bed.'

'Lord, Mother. You haven't bathed me since I was ten years old.'

'Then –' she put her arm around him to support him as they went up the stairs 'then maybe it's time I did.'

'I'm sorry, madam.' Becky looked at Niamh with anxious eyes. She had chosen this moment to catch Niamh alone, while Ellie and the children had gone to the beach. Brigid was upstairs, taking a nap. 'I can't say I haven't enjoyed it here, 'cos I have. An' I loved lookin' after Noah. But I've been shut away from everythin' for more'n twelve months now an' I – I can't –' She broke off, twisting a limp handkerchief in her hands.

'You can't live without a man in your life?' Niamh finished the sentence for her.

Becky relaxed, her expression clearing. 'Oh madam, I knew you'd understand.'

Niamh gave her a wry smile. 'I'm not at all sure I do. But you must do what's best for you, Becky. I can't order your life. You were there for me when I needed you and I'll be eternally grateful. You've been a godsend to Noah and I know he'll miss you. So will Brigid. So will I,' she added late and rather as an afterthought.

'Oh well, that's settled then.' Becky shrugged. Having obtained her freedom more easily than she expected, she looked vaguely wistful as if she hoped Niamh would beg her to stay. 'It's not that I don't love kids – I do. But I can't give up everythin' for them.'

'Becky, it's all right. You don't have to explain.'

339

'It's just – I can't live like a nun, like you do!'

Niamh thought about this for a moment, taken aback. 'And is that how you see me, Becky? As a saintly do-gooder whose feet don't quite touch the ground?'

'No, o' course not,' Becky grinned. 'But I can't let life keep passin' me by. So I have to go.'

Noah wasn't as dismayed by Becky's departure as most people feared. Maybe he sensed that although she had been the centre of his universe, the mainstay of comfort and food for as long as he could remember, there was always a part of her that remained uncommitted, detached. He never called her 'Mumma', reserving this name for Niamh. Diverted and spoiled by the other children, he had enough to occupy his infant mind without crying for Becky. If she could have seen how little he missed her, she might have been miffed. During the first week of her absence, he asked for her and cried when she couldn't be found but with Niamh to comfort him, to read him a story and tuck him in bed at night, he was quite happy. And, after a while, he forgot her entirely.

Instead of returning to the coast of Australia, bringing kanakas to Queensland, Diedrik traded between the islands. He developed a pattern of gathering 'recruits' in the Solomons and delivering them to plantations in Vanuatu, Fiji and New Caledonia because he could do this quickly and turn the ship around. Some trips went better than others. Sometimes the men were quiescent, almost eager to escape from the restrictions imposed by their tribal elders. But there were also those who went unwillingly, snapping their teeth at their captors and looking so feral that even Judd was grateful for the chains that restrained them and the heavy hinges and bolts on the trapdoor which kept these wild men in the hold.

'Never forget,' Diedrik warned Carl and Judd. 'They were raised to be warriors, head-hunters. And don't make the mistake of thinking they're stupid just because they don't speak the same language as you do.'

Once or twice when they were in port, Judd considered jumping ship and leaving but he decided he would be no better off, stranded on some island in the middle of the Pacific where the next captain he joined might be even more of a despot. Diedrik kept a tight ship and transported no women, dealing only in brawn. In comparison with other ships that reeked of the vomit and dysentery of their human cargo, the hold of the *Daisy May* was kept relatively clean, her 'recruits' always given the same food as the crew. Diedrik never starved his kanakas into submission nor was he unnecessarily cruel. While Judd came grudgingly to admire Diedrik for this, at the same time he realised he was merely protecting his investment; Diedrik would have taken just as much care of a cargo of fruit trees or prime cattle.

But on returning to the Solomons yet again, everything went horribly wrong. One of Jimi Fiji's kanakas was seized while diving for fish just off the shore. And when the crew of the *Daisy May* tried to rescue him, they were driven back by a salvo of spears and arrows from the warriors who had taken him. They could only watch in horror as the islanders disembowelled their unfortunate crew member while he was still alive and screaming, bound him hand and foot to a pole and carried him off to form part of a cannibal feast.

The only other casualty was Carl Bradley, who took an arrow in the thigh. It was Jimi Fiji who pulled it out, sniffing it cautiously and then wrinkling his nose.

'What is it?' Carl snapped.

Jimi shrugged and tossed the arrow overboard, careful not to touch the bloodied point of it as he did so.

'Poisoned, isn't it?' Carl murmured, leaning back and resting his arms across his eyes. 'Sweet Christ, what a way to die.'

'Buck up, Carl, s'only a flesh wound.' Diggory poked him in the ribs, trying to cheer him. 'Bet you've had worse scratches from whores on a Saturday night.'

'Shut up, you idiot!' Carl opened his eyes to glare at him. 'You know as well as I do – arrows that stink like that will be poisoned. Dipped in the liquid of festering bodies. Even a scratch can lead to a poisoning of the blood.'

He was right. Two days later he died in agony from convulsions brought on by tetanus. Nothing could be done to save him.

Judd had never liked Carl. He had been the worst type of criminal, an unscrupulous adventurer who lived only for the moment, taking what he wanted without remorse. But in spite of all this he felt sorry for the young man and his wasted life. Nobody deserved such a painful, untimely end.

Diedrik, with his usual Dutch stoicism, seemed unaffected. He gave Carl a hasty funeral, reciting such scraps of religious jargon he could remember. Then he ordered the body thrown to the sharks and told Diggory to set sail for the Malo Passage.

The summer continued dry and hot with no prospect of relief. One afternoon in February when it was particularly oppressive, the cicadas starting up one after another, drilling their relentless rhythm through Maggi's head, she came in from the stables to find her husband seated at the kitchen table, his head in his hands.

'You're back early,' she said. 'I didn't expect you till supper time.'

Wordlessly, he shook his head.

'Come on, love.' She dropped a kiss on top of his head. 'We've seen it all before. This weather can't go on for ever – it's just too hot. Sooner or later it has to break.'

'Dammit all, Maggi. You've said the same thing every night for the past two weeks.' He raised his head to glare at her but she didn't take it amiss. She knew his frustration and anger was directed not so much at herself but the weather. 'The dams are empty – nothing but a few inches of mud and I'm sick of looking at it, that's all. Sick to death of burying dead sheep!'

'Sure'n things have been as bad as this before. We're better off than some. There's the money from the sale of my horses – more'n I hoped for. Soon as we get into March the weather will ease. Then around Easter I'll go down to Melbourne an' pick out a few likely foals . . .'

'This is a sheep station, Maggi. Your horses won't ever amount to more than a hobby.'

'A hobby, is it?' Her own temper flared. 'Be a fine thing, indeed, if we was relyin' on nothin' but wool for these last two seasons. We'd never have kept the boys at that school.' Having had little in the way of formal learning herself, Maggi was determined her boys should not be similarly disadvantaged. They were having the best education their parents could afford.

342

'That's all you care about, isn't it – your horses and the boys' education. I'm losing sheep every day and we'll be out of water ourselves in less than a week. The whole place is going to rack and ruin, shrivelling up in the heat.'

'The weather will break, love, I know it. You've got that pinched look around the eyes. You always get a bad headache before a storm.'

But later that evening, in spite of Maggi's predictions, the storm didn't come. She lay in bed, too anxious to sleep while Callum lay on his back alongside, arms flung wide, snoring gently.

A sound at the stables made her sit up; some of the horses were restless. She crept out of bed, opened the window wide and leaned out to listen. The night was still, velvety dark and warm with little difference in the temperature, inside or out. As she did so, there was a distant rumble and a flash of forked lightning, followed by a distinct smell of ozone. Maggi sniffed the air, hoping she was mistaken. An electrical storm without rain would be worse than no storm at all. It might even start a fire.

There was a louder rumble, followed by a double flash of forked lightning. The horses were whinnying now, spooked by the noise of the storm which was coming closer.

She pulled on her clothes, trying not to wake Callum but he woke up anyway, groaning and rubbing his eyes in the darkness.

'What is it? Wassamatter?' he said, still half-asleep.

'The storm's disturbing the horses. I have to see—'

'I'll go with you,' he said, swinging his long legs out of bed.

'Catch me up,' she said shortly, too anxious to wait.

Down at the stables some of the horses were kicking their stalls, angry at being restrained when they wanted to run from the sounds that were frightening them, and coming closer. Maggi and Callum were checking each horse in turn, trying to pacify them, when there was a deafening clap of thunder right over their heads.

Outside they heard Patrick Hegarty's voice hoarse with dread: 'The house! The house has been struck by lightning. Molly! Make sure Callum and Maggi are out!'

'It's all right, Paddy, we're here,' Maggi called, coming out of the stables to join him. Molly was with him, looking like an ageing Christmas angel with her flowing grey hair and voluminous nightgown.

In a very short time the homestead became an inferno. With no water to douse it, the fire took hold and they could only stare at it, expecting to lose everything.

'Ah dear God,' Molly whispered. 'Let it rain.'

The rain came on the instant, as if in direct answer to her prayers. It started with great drops that splashed on their upturned faces, gathering speed until it had all the force of a tropical downpour. The farm buildings, the stables, the quarters set aside for the shearers, the laundry, the kitchen block were all untouched. Only the homestead was destroyed. With the roof gone, the damage commenced by the fire was completed by the rain.

'Oh, Callum.' Maggi put an arm round her husband as she looked at it. 'So many years. So many memories. All your mother's things.'

'Mother didn't care so much for material things,' Callum said unsteadily. 'She'd rather see everyone safe as I would. Thank God the boys are away at school. Ah well, it's an ill wind.' He was thoughtfully, rubbing his chin. 'I've been wanting to build a new place for years and you've always talked me out of it. No help for it now.'

'Why can't we make do with a cottage and extend the stables?'

'We've already extended the stables. For the first time in our lives, we'll have the chance to modernise, to live in comfort. Forget the stables and think of our sons for once. They're going to inherit it one day – they won't want to live in a hovel.'

'Who says they'll want to live here at all?'

'But of course they will!'

'Well, I'm not going to argue about it – not on an empty stomach.' Maggi strode away towards the kitchen block.

'That's right. Dodge the issue, as usual.' Callum ran after her, catching her up.

The Hegartys exchanged knowing glances. The question of expansion was an old bone of contention between the Mac-Gregors and unlikely to be resolved overnight.

*

344

The Malo Passage and the island of Malekula . . . what an eye-opener that was for Judd. Everything an island paradise was supposed to be, the islanders welcoming and hospitable. A place where white men had amassed fortunes at their plant-ations on nearby Tanna and the local chiefs had grown fat and lazy, sharing the profits. Diedrik was greeted and escorted from his ship like visiting royalty, a pig roast laid on in his honour.

And this was where Judd forgot all his good resolutions. This was where he met Lalia. Until now, he had avoided the island women, telling himself he had enough complications in his life with the two women at home without adding more. Also he thought it unfair to take advantage of girls who were naive and trusting as children, running around in grass skirts and no other clothes. Until he met Lalia. Lalia, who made him forget all his self-imposed rules. He saw her and he wanted her. It was as simple as that.

She was somewhere between sixteen and eighteen, twenty at most. She wore her hair oiled, straight and it hung down her back to her waist. She had good bones, good teeth and wore only the briefest of calico skirts, sufficient to hide her sex. Her complexion was dusky rather than dark and he was fascinated by the coffee-coloured curve of her lips.

Instead of crowding around the seamen with all the other girls, she had eyes only for Judd and he felt his heart skip a beat as he stared back, wanting her. She was sweet and succu-lent, fresh as the newly plucked hibiscus she wore in her hair. When she was sure she had his attention, she smiled, stepping forward to offer him drink in a coconut shell. Gazing into her eyes, he drank deeply, realising too late that he should have sipped it to find out what it was.

'From coconut,' she smiled, pointing up at the palm trees where he could see the still-ripening nuts. 'Is good. Make a man big – strong.' And she looked at him under her lashes, making him wonder what sort of strength she meant. He decided she was too young, too innocent surely, to mean what he thought. But it did make him drunk and he had no will to resist when she led him away from the party and over the dunes, taking the narrow track which led to another beach. Just as suddenly the potion took effect and he found he had all

345

the strength he needed; so much so, he could hardly walk. The sea seemed to roar in his ears as they emerged from the bushes onto a small but deserted beach.

Belatedly, he remembered advice from Carl: *Don't be caught by false modesty – don't let a girl lead you off. If you want her, have her, but don't be afraid to do it in front of everyone else.'*

Was this where he would die then? Was the girl a decoy, leading him into a trap? Would some young warrior leap from the bushes, waving a tomahawk, ready to finish him off?

But Lalia had no such intention. She let him kiss her, opening to him like an exotic, sweet-smelling tropical flower and making him realise he'd been without a woman too long. And when he pushed her down against the cool white sands to make love to her, she resisted for only a moment, holding him off with a hand against his chest.

'Please – be careful with Lalia,' she whispered, eyes wide. 'First time.'

He nodded, too breathless to speak, teased past the point of endurance as he pressed himself against her, moulding her body to his. What with the drink and the months of frustration, his need of her was too great for him to be gentle but he soon realised the small cries in his ear were not those of discomfort but of passion and delight. After the sex, they rolled over and over, laughingly entwined and she tongued his ear, nibbling the lobe and teasing him until he was roused again. They made love half-submerged in the warm sea and on the sands again until Judd fell into an exhausted sleep.

At daybreak, he had to run all the way to catch up with the *Daisy May*. Diedrik was preparing to sail without him. Lalia ran too, but she couldn't keep up with him. He didn't say goodbye and he didn't expect to see her again.

To his shame, as the ship starting moving, she arrived alongside in a canoe, begging to be taken aboard.

'You! My lovely man!' she called out to him. 'Take Lalia with you. She will be good wife for you!'

'Lalia, go home,' he told her. 'I can't take you with me. I'm married. I have a wife already.'

'Have two!' she cried, imploring him. Judd shook his head, feeling like a brute when she burst into noisy tears. As yet there wasn't much wind to fill the sails and the ship moved only sluggishly through the water, enabling her to keep up with them in her canoe. Finally, Diedrik put a stop to it by ordering Jimi Fiji to throw a rock through the fragile craft, sending it to the bottom.

'No! No!' Judd cried as he saw it sinking, leaving the girl treading water, her hair spreading about her like an Ondine in the water. 'She'll drown!'

'Drown? Not she!' Diedrik gave a snort of laughter. 'She can swim better than you or I. I've seen her pull that stunt a dozen times. Little whore.'

'She's not a whore – or she wasn't till I made her one. I took her virginity only last night.'

This time Diedrik laughed harder than ever, wiping tears of mirth from his eyes. 'Took you in, did she? She must have given away her virginity more times than you've had hot dinners. Where d'you think she got those magnificent tits? By keeping them to herself?'

'But she was afraid of me – she was shy.'

'Part of the act, old son. How d'you think she learned to speak English so well? From other sailors, of course. You'll be lucky if she hasn't passed on the pox.'

The girl gave one last regretful wave before turning and swimming strongly for the shore. At the time Judd felt like taking a swing at Diedrik and bloodying his nose but when he thought about it later, once he had cooled off, he admitted he had been duped. Lalia wanted a husband and meant to get one the only way she knew how.

Over the next few weeks he examined himself daily, looking for sores, greatly relieved when they didn't develop. But this experience made him wary. He never accepted liquor from any islanders nor did he succumb to the wiles of their women again.

Chapter Twenty-Six

Once more Lilias was sitting up late at night waiting for Hollis to come home. A week from now, at the end of March, The Oaks and everything of value inside it was to be sold. Most of the furniture and antiques had already been inventoried. Only her clothes and most intimate possessions were to be saved. Fortunately, with the help of Agnes, her loyal servant and friend, she had managed to hide and keep a few of her favourite jewels. Ellen and most of the household servants were gone and only Agnes remained. Agnes who wouldn't allow herself to be dismissed.

'I couldn't start with anyone else, madam, not at my time of life,' she said in response to Lilias's tears. 'Whatever lies ahead of us, my place is with you.'

'But Agnes, I can't pay you. I don't even know what I'll do for money myself.'

'Well, if you think I've put up with you and your foibles over the years just for the money ...' Agnes gave a wry smile. 'Something'll turn up, madam. It always does.'

And somehow Lilias knew that it would, although she had no firm plans. Oddly, this didn't concern her as much as it should, although the date of departure loomed. She considered her options, remembering the heated discussion with Hollis which had taken place after a meagre dinner earlier that evening. Agnes was no great shakes as a cook.

'It's not just a question of where we're to live, Mama, but what I'll be able to do.'

'Oh Holly, you'll do what you've always done.' She thought

this the least of their worries. 'You'll take care of your father's business.'

'Hah! If there's any business left to take care of. Who's going to trust me after this débâcle, when everyone knows I've had to sell my own mother's home from under her in order to settle my debts?'

'No shame in settling your debts, Holly. It's the honourable thing to do. No one should blame you for that.'

'They shouldn't but they will,' he said, not without bitterness.

'But we have to make up our minds where to go. If it wasn't for the disaster at Lachlan's Holt, I could have gone to Maggi and you could have stayed at your club.'

'Mother, you don't understand. I'm no longer welcome there – no longer a member of *any* club.'

'All right!' She was losing patience herself. 'But will you stop making objections and tell me what *can* be done. I can't be a burden to Maggi.' She gave a delicate shiver. 'She and Callum are slumming it in the shearer's quarters as it is. We shall have to go to The Hollies. Niamh's a sensible girl and not at all the sort to bear a grudge.'

'No, Mother!' He pushed his chair from the table and stood up. 'I've sunk my pride far enough. I'd rather die than go begging to Niamh, cap in hand.'

'She's still your wife, Holly. She wouldn't want to see us destitute and with nowhere to go.'

'Besides, she has a full house already with her father and Ellie still there.'

'I know it'll be noisy and crowded, not at all what we're used to, but . . .' Lilias broke off with sigh that was almost a sob. 'I just don't know what else we can do.'

Hollis stared at her, breathing deeply, his expression giving her no clue as to his thoughts. 'All right,' he said at last. 'Maybe that is the best solution – for you. Send Agnes down to Brighton with your bags. You can put up at an hotel till she's settled in.'

'But what will *you* do?'

He didn't answer the question but gave her a quick buss on the cheek on his way to the stairs. 'I'm going out for a while. Don't wait up.'

'Oh Holly, don't go. I have a bad feeling about it. I don't think you should go drinking, not in this mood.' But he didn't wait to hear what she had to say. Some ten minutes later she heard the front door slam. He had left without saying goodbye.

And she had been sitting here for hours with the lamps turned low, watching the hands of the grandfather clock creep around to strike midnight, the hour of one and then two. She imagined Hollis dirty and bleeding as he came home before, this time left to die in the street. At half-past two, she shed a few tears and was exhausted enough to doze, only to be woken almost at once by a loud hammering at the front door.

She reached it at exactly the same time as Agnes, who had thrown on a robe to cover her nightgown and stood there, eyes wide with fright.

'D'you think we should open it, madam?' she whispered. 'Two women alone, an' at this time o' night?'

'Don't be silly, Agnes.' Bravely, Lilias threw the door wide to reveal two men standing on the doorstep, pale and grim-faced. They snatched off their hats immediately as a mark of respect as one stepped forward to speak.

'Is this the home of Mr Hollis Maitland?'

'I am Lilias Maitland,' Lilias answered them. 'Hollis is my son.'

'Well, I'm sorry, madam – there's no way to put this nicely – your son has met with an accident.'

'Is he badly hurt?' Lilias pressed a hand to her throat. 'Where is he?'

'It was dark, you see. He must've missed his footing and tumbled into the water when he an' his friends left the pub. They were all too drunk to be sensible an' by the time they got Mr Maitland out of the water, he'd drowned.' The man glanced at his companion, wondering how to proceed in the face of Lilias's silence. 'So perhaps, if there's a gentleman in the house, maybe he could accompany us – to identify the body.'

'I am a widow.' Lilias spoke hoarsely. 'There is no one else.'

On her return, shattered by the experience of identifying her son's bruised and waterlogged body and wishing she'd let Agnes go with her, Lilias crawled into bed with her clothes on.

Tomorrow it would take all her courage to pass on this news, let alone go into Hollis's room to go through his clothes and effects.

His room smelled of the expensive pomade he used on his hair and was so exactly as he left it, she was moved to tears. She ignored the slim envelope leaning against the clock until she saw it was addressed to herself.

Dearest Mother, he wrote. *You of all people must know what a coward I am – too much of a coward to try killing myself. I'd probably botch it anyway, as I've botched everything else. So I'm going to dice with Death instead, in the hope that he'll take me. If you're reading this letter you'll know he already has.*

Don't grieve, Mother, and please don't be angry with me. This is what I want. I can see no other way. I can't live with the guilt of what I have done.

'Oh Holly, Holly, why didn't you tell me?' Lilias whispered, her eyes prickling with unshed tears. 'We could have worked it out together. Nothing could be so bad.'

You've forgiven me so much already. For wrecking my marriage – the fault was all mine although I let you think otherwise. For losing The Oaks. You even forgave me my senseless pride. And I could have lived with that – all of it – but for one thing more. I leave this – my confession – in your hands. Do as you like with it. You be the judge.

I committed a crime. A crime so reprehensible I find it hard to believe I was capable of it. I did it because I hated Judd Burden – with a hate so irrational, so fierce, it consumed me and coloured the whole of my life. Firstly, I hated him because he was everything I wasn't and secondly because he loved Niamh – the only woman I ever tried to love. But I hated him most for being the unwitting cause of Pa's death. So when I saw the chance to harm him, I seized it with both hands.

But now – now I've had these past twelve months to consider and brood on it, a horrible thought keeps coming back to me and it won't go away. I might have killed Pa myself.

Lilias closed her eyes and took a deep breath to steady herself before she could read on.

As Miss Johnson so rightly witnessed, I was the next person to go into Pa's office after Judd Burden left. She had already told me she heard voices raised in argument. That's what gave me the idea. There's no excuse for what I did but I was angry with Pa for taking Judd Burden's part, for making me look small before my colleagues and friends.

I found Pa collapsed at his desk, blue to the lips, the pill box in front of him that he had been trying to open. He had suffered another heart attack, a fatal one this time. The body was warm but there was no pulse. He wasn't breathing and I was sure he was, dead.

If I'd thought about it, I couldn't have done it. But I wasn't thinking of Pa, only of Burden and my revenge. Quietly, so Miss Johnson wouldn't hear, I dragged Pa's body across the room and positioned it over the fender, half in the fireplace. Then I took up the poker and struck him once on the back of the head. You won't believe it, I know, but I did it myself. I wanted Judd Burden punished for causing Pa's death.

Lilias gasped but she read on, dreading what would follow.

The very thought of it fills me with horror now. Horror and self-disgust. But I wiped the marks of my hands from the poker, I tidied the desk and cleaned his seat to remove any evidence that he died there.

But lately I've been haunted – so much that I can't sleep and can't look at myself without loathing. Nor can I live with the burden of your forgiveness – although I doubt even you will be able to forgive this. Death, when it comes, will be both a blessing and a relief.

Never doubt that I loved you, Mother. You and Pa. But I don't think we'll meet again in this world or the next.

Your loving son Hollis.

Lilias re-read the letter several times to be sure there was no mistake. Her son's death had been recorded as misadventure, an accident – that was the official view. No point in muddying the waters with his confession now. Judd Burden had escaped the gallows and Hollis was dead. Justice had already been served. She folded the note until it was small and tucked it into the cleft of her bosom, intending to destroy it later on. No one but herself need know it had ever existed.

'Oh Aunt Lil, you're not out here again!' Lilias was missing and Niamh had known exactly where to find her; seated on the rustic bench built around the old gum tree. From this position she could overlook the small family plot where two people lay buried, Sukie Burden and Hollis. 'You really mustn't sit out here in the cold, staring at his grave all the time.' She shivered herself, having come out wearing only a light shawl. 'You'll catch your death.'

'Would it matter so much if I did?' Lilias whispered. 'This is my fault – all of it – because I was a bad mother. I should have seen it coming. I should've known how desperate he was. Oh Niamh, if only—'

'Stop it, Aunt Lil. You *have* to stop blaming yourself. There's nothing you could have done.' Niamh put forward the same arguments she had offered since Hollis's death but it seemed that nothing would shake Lilias out of this endless spiral of remorse. 'Hollis was his own man and he'd take advice from no one, not even Uncle Harley. You can't go on feeling responsible.'

'But I do.' Lilias was lost in her own train of thought. 'All I cared about was my house and giving parties for my friends. But now the house is gone, the friends are gone and I don't care. I'd give it up all over again if only I could have my husband and son alive and with me again.'

'Oh, Aunt Lil.' Niamh crouched beside her, taking her aunt's bloodless hands and rubbing them, trying to warm them in her own. 'That's like crying for the moon. We have to look to the future now, you and I.'

'You can look to the future – you're young,' Lilias grated, her face ravaged with misery as she glared at her niece. 'You'll get over it and make a new life. I can't.'

'But you don't even try!' Niamh said, taking advantage of even this glint of anger to shake Lilias out of her apathy. 'There is work to be done here. Work that you introduced me to – remember? Work that you started.'

'You suggest healing through work, Niamh. I wish it were so easy.'

'I didn't say it would be easy. But somehow you have to try to make a new start.'

'Mumma! Mumma! Aunt Lil!' The back door opened and Noah came running towards them, unsteady on infant legs. Lilias turned towards him, frowning at the interruption.

'I can't have him calling me "Aunt", Niamh,' she snapped. 'I'm nothing to him.'

'Oh, but you are!' Niamh laughed, catching the little boy in her arms to receive a hug and a moist kiss on the cheek. 'Noah loves everyone. Don't you, sweetheart?' She turned, smiling at Lilias. 'You can be his nan if you like. Nana Lil.'

'Nana Lil! Nana Lil!' The little boy shrieked with delight, stretching towards Lilias, expecting her to take him into her arms. He had a winning smile which he used to full advantage to melt female hearts. Most people found him irresistible. Stiff and disapproving, Lilias received him with a nervous smile. She wasn't used to handling young children. Hollis had been largely raised by a nurse.

'Pretty lady! Pretty hair!' the little boy cried, catching hold of a strand that had come loose and settling himself more comfortably in her arms, making Lilias open her eyes in surprise. 'Story! Tell me a story!'

Lilias glanced towards Niamh, wanting to pass him back but Niamh danced out of reach, avoiding it.

'A story? Well now, let's see.' Lilias thought for a moment. 'There's one my mother used to tell me. It goes like this. Once upon a time there were three bears—'

'Koala?' Noah cried, pointing up at the trees.

'No no, not koalas. These were big, brown bears and they lived in a house like we do – Father Bear, Mother Bear and also Baby Bear.'

'Like me! Like me!' Noah jigged in her arms.

'Not a bit. Baby Bear didn't shout or wriggle. Now keep still or I'll put you down and I won't tell you the rest.' She sat down on the bench again, the child in her lap.

This was the turning point for Lilias; the way back from her sorrow. The company of this little boy and the love which he gave without stinting brought her back from the precipice, saving her from wallowing in misery and self-recrimination. Soon she was able to relate to the other children as well, becoming an honorary grandmother who was loved by all of them.

Niamh breathed a sigh of relief and gave thanks to a benevolent deity for providing Lilias with a whole new purpose in life.

*

354

Elinor made sure that the official opening of The Star Hotel was eagerly awaited by Melbourne society and as much of a gala occasion as she had promised. No expense had been spared, on either the hotel or herself. Tonight she was dressed in cherry red silk and with matching silk flowers caught in her hair. Long kid gloves concealed hands which had done a lot more of the real work towards getting the hotel ready on time than most people suspected.

The look of startled admiration on her husband's face was enough to assure her she had chosen well. 'My God, you look lovely, Ellie,' he whispered. 'I'm tempted to lock all the doors and keep you here all to myself.'

'Now that wouldn't do,' she laughed, giving him a quick kiss, careful not to let him pull her into his arms and ruin her grooming. 'We must be ready to greet our guests and see the hotel come to life.'

They meandered through the rooms, checking that all was in readiness on their way down. Opulent vases of flowers stood before the mirrors on every landing and the whole place smelled of new carpet and recently dried paint.

Ellie's battles with the architect had paid off. Outside, it was an impressive three-storeyed building surrounded by verandahs and balconies trimmed with iron lace, and inside it was warm and welcoming.

A coach entrance had been built to one side with facilities for horses to be watered, stabled and groomed.

No expense had been spared on the fittings within. Ignoring Tully's protests about her extravagance, Ellie had gone ahead. And now, seeing the rooms completed with rich red cedar around the doors, the fireplaces and the bars, he had to admit she was right. A beautiful panel of coloured leadlight was visible from the entrance hall above the first flight of stairs. Marble shone and brass rails glittered in all the bars. Souvenirs, pictures and even the old brass spittoons from the old Silver Star had found a new home in Tully's honky-tonk bar, living in harmony with his upright piano. Even the old mirrors had been carefully taken down and transferred to the new hotel without mishap.

Staff had been poached or otherwise acquired by paying them over the odds. Now it remained only to see if Ellie's investment would pay off.

As the guests arrived, the rooms came to life, filled with the buzz of enthusiastic conversation. Ellie drifted around, greeting friends from both far and near. Even the Governor of Victoria had been persuaded to attend; an inhibiting presence, stiff and formal in full regalia, a worthy representative of his Queen. Luckily, he stayed long enough only for the press to note he was there and he left early to take in another engagement elsewhere.

Nobody mourned his departure. His host and hostess escorted him to his carriage and waved him away. Going back up the stairs to rejoin the party, Ellie grinned, squeezing her husband's arm. Now everyone could begin to enjoy themselves; now the real festivities could begin.

'We *will* be successful, I know it,' she assured him. 'The culmination of all our planning and hard work.'

He smiled back at her, knowing he would never have embarked on something so ambitious alone. Without her, he would surely have ended his days at the Silver Star. Tonight she was so full of happiness and pride, it made his heart hurt to look at her. What had he ever done to deserve such good luck?

Tonight he too was resplendent in the suit he had worn to Niamh's wedding. Happiness and contentment had added a little weight to his frame and, now the Governor had departed and there was less need to be formal, he unfastened the bottom couple of buttons of his waistcoat in order to ease the strain.

A round of cheers and applause greeted their return to the salon and somebody called out, 'Come on, Tully! Let's hear this new piano of yours. Give us a tune.'

He sat down and tried out a few experimental chords. 'What would you like?' he said.

'Maureen can sing it.' Someone pushed forward a daughter, plump and blushing, unable to assert herself and resist. 'Give us *The Black Velvet Band*.'

Tully's smile faltered a little although he played the introduction almost without thinking. It was one of Maggi's songs. She should have been here tonight to celebrate with them but she and Callum were still coping with the aftermath of the fire and the building of their new house, which she complained was going to be too grand for her.

Maureen was no diva. She stumbled her way through the song, forgot the words and was grateful when Tully rescued her by adding his voice to her own. He kissed her hand when they finished, making her blush even more, and nobody asked for an encore.

The festivities continued until long after midnight and later, lying in bed, Ellie voiced the question that was foremost in both their minds.

'They came tonight as our guests and because it was free. Do you think they liked it enough to come again when they have to pay?'

'Oh, I think so, my darlin', especially when summer's here and its hot. Who can resist a cool beer and a breeze from the sea?' Tully drew her into the protective circle of his arms, kissing her gently and without passion this time. They were both too exhausted to make love. 'But only time will tell.'

Chapter Twenty-Seven

Eighteen months were to pass before Judd saw the coast of North Queensland for the first time. Weary of the whole sorry business of the recruiting 'trade', he promised himself he would leave the ship as soon as she touched Australian shores and take his chances with the law.

The opportunity didn't arise until Diedrik was scared out of New Caledonia by a new crop of French officials sent in to replace the old ones who had grown lazy, tolerant and too easy to bribe. These new men were young, ambitious and anxious to make a name for themselves, their wits not yet dulled by alcohol and the enervating heat of the tropics. They denounced Diedrik's papers as forgeries and informed him he had no right to be sailing under the French flag. And worse, they were threatening to impound the ship while the matter was fully investigated.

So Diedrik didn't wait. He set sail immediately, heading due west for Mackay on the North Queensland coast.

'The French officials are wise to us,' he said, for once informing the crew of his plans. 'We'll have to refit the ship, register her in Australia and go legal. And it's no use moaning about it, Digs,' he said, seeing the mate looking pained. 'We've had a good trot. One way or another, we knew it would come to this in the end.'

'But goin' legal – isn't that a bit drastic?' Diggory was unconvinced. 'Those nosy Government agents jumpin' all over us – the whole bit?'

'That's right. Nosy Government agents – the whole bit.' Diedrik nodded. 'Cheer up, Diggory. It won't be for ever.

There's always a new angle, always a new way to get the best of these plodding Government men.'

'If you say so, Cap'n,' Diggory sighed.

They stayed in Mackay for six weeks while the ship was hauled out of the water, to be scraped, painted and refitted to Diedrik's satisfaction. During this time Judd explored the thriving town of Mackay, deciding he liked it. Small but affluent, it prospered because of its sugar plantations and the mills which refined the cane. A sickly smell filled the air while the cane was being harvested and crushed. A smell which was curiously tropical and permeated everything.

The main street was long and wide with an impressive array of hotels for a town of its size, some built of wood and cast iron in a raffish Colonial style while others were of solid brick confirming an English presence. Common to all were the wide balconies on the upper floors and the verandahs below which covered the street and provided shade. Judd was pleased to see that almost all made lavish use of iron lace. Inside, high ceilings kept the rooms cool.

Horse-drawn transport was much in evidence and Mackay boasted a fine race-track which drew visitors from the surrounding countryside. Judd loved the place and, after spending more than two years in the tropics, was acclimatised to the heat. For the first time since his escape, he began to visualise a future, a new life. Maybe he could bring Sukie and their son to settle here. There was always work for a smith and in time, perhaps, he could take up his old craft. But he dismissed that idea. His work was distinctive and someone, even this far from Melbourne, might recognise it and report him.

But when it was time to return to the ship, displaying her new name of *Island Princess* in shining gold letters, his footsteps slowed. What was he doing here? He didn't want to go to the islands again. He had a son growing up, living hundreds of miles away on the other side of the country. Suddenly, desperately, Judd wanted to see him. The ties of parenthood were stronger than he supposed.

Diedrik laughed in his face, when he said why he was leaving. 'You're going back to Melbourne to look at your son – whatever for? Aren't the island women pretty enough? They'll give you all the sons you want. Don't be a fool, Judd. Get aboard.'

'I must see Carl's parents, as well. They were good to me once. They'll want to know how their son died.'

'Will they?' Diedrik sneered. 'They're more likely to thank the good Lord they've seen the last of him. Stay with us, Judd. New vistas are opening . . .'

'I don't think so, Captain. The recruiting trade's had its day. And, if it hasn't, I'm tired of it – tired of deceiving people, pretending to take them onto a better life when we're really selling them off into three-year contracts of near-slavery.'

'Are these people slaves?' Diedrik pointed to a party of brightly dressed, well-fed islanders, arms linked and singing as they went on their way to a pig roast. 'No. They were slaves when we rescued them. Slaves to their chiefs in the islands, living from hand to mouth without so much as a loincloth to call their own. D'you know that most of them want to stay when they've done their time here?'

'I still say it was wrong to take them. Wrong for the white man to interfere.'

'Too late now. Can't halt progress.' Diedrik shrugged. 'I'm not here to change the world but to make me a living.'

'Yes. And, talking of money, if you can see your way clear to paying me, I'll be on my way.'

'You expect me to *pay* you?' Diedrik found this amusing. 'No, you're the one who should be paying *me* for your passage. A man on the run from the law.'

'I haven't killed anyone. But if I stay away, I'll never be able to prove it.'

'Don't even try. You were found guilty. Return and they'll string you up first an' ask questions afterwards.'

'That's a chance I'll have to take.'

'I shall be plying between here and the islands. You'll have to work your way north if you change your mind . . .'

'I won't.'

'Don't be so sure. Things change while you're away, people most of all. Take it from one who knows – you can never go back.'

But Judd wouldn't listen. He collected his belongings into a seaman's bag, said his farewells to Jimi Fiji and Diggory and, with a last jaunty salute, sprang ashore.

Diedrik called after him: 'You there! Judd Burden!'

He stopped in mid-stride. He should have known the big Dutchman wouldn't let him go so easily. Slowly he turned to face Diedrik who had followed him onto the wharf and now stood challenging him, holding a pistol at arm's length aimed directly at his heart.

'Not a word about the activities of the *Daisy May*.'

'A ship that never existed?' Judd shrugged and raised his hand in a gesture of peace and farewell as he turned away. Diedrik was a hard man but he wasn't a murderer; he wouldn't shoot him in the back. 'So long, Cap'n!'

As he walked back towards the town his heart lifted. He was his own man again, beholden to no one. All he had to do now was work his way south.

He was so thin that Niamh didn't recognise him. Not from a distance, anyway. She saw only a tall, spare man dressed in country clothes; the practical clothes of a stockman, a wide-brimmed hat pulled forward to shield his face. He wore a thick cotton shirt, corded breeches tucked into the tough, high-heeled boots of a horseman which added inches to his height. He was carrying a jacket hooked on one finger and slung over his shoulder as he examined the headstones of the graves in the family plot. She wondered why this was always so, why each visitor who came to The Hollies for the first time seemed drawn to inspect the graveyard.

With Noah in her arms she hurried towards him, believing him to be the father of one of her convalescents. But, before she could draw breath to ask him his business, he took off his hat as a mark of respect and she knew him. She would have known him anywhere as soon as she saw the sunlight on his hair; thick hair inherited from his Spanish forebears, dark and without a trace of grey.

'Judd. Oh, Judd!' She felt as if she could hardly breathe. 'Is it really you?'

'Well, it isn't my ghost,' he said with a wry smile.

'But you're so much thinner, and – and so . . .'

'Sunburned,' he said shortly, turning back to look at the two graves. 'Niamh, what happened here?'

She remembered with a jolt that he'd never been told

361

about Sukie. 'Oh Judd, I'm so sorry you had to find out this way.'

He looked at her and he too saw change. The young girl he had loved was still there but another dimension had been added. She had confidence that hadn't been there before and she was a mother used to carrying a child in her arms, as now. He should have known she would have children. He could hear them now, voices piping in the distance, carrying on the still, afternoon air. Many children. Were they all her own? Her figure didn't show it; she was slender as ever. And, as always, her clothes were practical, of quality yet plain. Shy in the presence of a stranger, her little boy watched him from the safety of his position curled into her neck, a thumb in his mouth.

'I went to see Daisy – Daisy Bradley. We had a lot to talk about. I told her how we lost Carl and she wept – said she was sorry for thinking the worst of me. And then she told me about Sukie – how she died.'

'It was some time ago – over two years. Oh Judd, if only I'd known where to write, where to reach you, I would have sent word.'

'Niamh, I know. I don't reproach you for anything. If anyone should feel guilty about Sukie, it's me.' He faltered, ashamed to tell her the truth of his feelings for Sukie. Sorry as he was to hear of her death, it had been a release from his obligations, a relief. His love for Sukie had never been more than affection, strengthened by the fact that she had given him a son. He had never loved her with the same intensity, the same passion she'd shown to him. 'And Daisy told me also that my son is alive.'

Niamh stared at him, unconsciously tightening her grip on Noah who started to whine and squirm in her arms.

'Mumma! Mumma, you're squeezing me!' he complained.

You can't have him, he's mine! was her first thought.

Sensing her change of mood, Judd stared at her, unable to fathom this hostility. She had believed in his innocence wholeheartedly before, so why had she changed? He had expected that she, of all people, would be pleased to see him. But everything had changed, including her opinion of him. Diedrik had been right. *You can never go back.*

'And how did your husband . . .' He didn't complete the sentence, glancing at Hollis's grave.

'It was an accident.' She didn't want to explain it. 'He drowned.'

'And left you a widow, with a son?' He turned his head on one side, looking at Noah.

She almost lied to him. Why not let him think so? She could say that Daisy was mistaken and his own son had died. There had been an epidemic of measles last year, a terrible time, and many children had not survived. But she had loved him once, loved him to desperation. And although she had buried it deeply, a part of her loved him still. So she owned up to the truth although the words almost choked her.

'He calls me Mumma but this boy is your son, Judd. I have no children of my own.'

'Oh!' Judd took a step forward, wanting to look more closely but Noah turned away, clinging tightly to Niamh.

'Judd, if – if you want to be a father to Noah . . .'

'Of course I do! Why else d'you think I'm here?'

'Nothing's changed. You are still a condemned man.' He recoiled, injured by her words. 'A child needs stability and you can't be a proper father if you keep drifting in and out of his life.'

'Since when did you get to be such an expert?' Her attitude angered him and he wanted to hurt in return. 'A woman who has no child of her own?'

'Since I turned my house into a convalescent home for sick children. This is my work, Judd. It's what I do.'

So engrossed had they been in each other that they didn't hear Lilias until she spoke up behind them, making them start.

'Niamh! Brigid needs to know if you want the children to have rice custard today or if you'd prefer a bakewell tart that we can cut into pieces and take to the beach?'

'Bakewell tart,' Niamh said without looking at her.

Lilias nodded and was about to go when she sensed the atmosphere of tension between Niamh and this man. He seemed vaguely familiar although she hadn't yet placed him.

'And this is?' she said, prompting an introduction.

'Judd Burden,' Niamh said without thinking. Lost in the

turmoil of her own thoughts, she hadn't considered the effect such an announcement would have on Lilias, who clasped her hands to her mouth and took a step backwards, looking at him as if she were seeing a ghost.

'Oh no, not *that* Judd Burden?' she whispered, backing away. 'I want you to wait here, both of you. Wait for me here.' And she ran awkwardly towards the house, almost stumbling in her haste.

'I'd better go,' Judd sighed, realising that Lilias would see him as a desperado. 'I expect she's gone to send someone to raise the alarm.'

'Yes. Yes, maybe you should,' Niamh said, so choked by conflicting emotions, she could hardly speak. Noah burrowed into her shoulder, hiding his face, and she did nothing to encourage him to get over his shyness. 'You do see, don't you, Judd? What sort of a life would this child have with you always looking over your shoulder to see if the troopers were gaining on you.'

'It wouldn't have to be that way. There's a place up north on the coast, a nice little town called Mackay. They grow sugar there. It's much warmer than here.' He made the point by pulling on his coat and shivering against the cool of the afternoon. Most people would have called it a mild winter but Judd was unused to feeling cold. 'We could make a new start up there.'

'With murder still hanging over your head?' Niamh tightened her grip on the child.

'Niamh, I didn't do it. I didn't kill Harley Maitland. I expected you of all people to go on believing that.'

'I do. But you killed a man when you broke out of gaol – you and Carl.'

'Everyone knows it was Carl – even Daisy and Matthew. You can't think I approved?'

'I don't know what to think any more.' Niamh was close to tears. 'But I can't let you take him. I won't let you take Noah away from me.'

'Oh, Niamh!' He took a step towards her, coming into her space and crowding her, reminding her of the love they had once shared. At once she was assailed with that smell of musk and hot metal; the familiarity of it made her feel dizzy,

364

overwhelming her so that she closed her eyes. He misinterpreted that, as well.

'You loathe me so much you can't bear to look at me?'

She stood there hugging his child and shaking her head, too wretched to speak.

'It's those two in the graveyard, isn't it?' He was as miserable as she was. 'Your husband and my wife. They stand between us more effectively than ever they did when they were alive. And they're dead because they loved us and we couldn't love them enough.'

'It wasn't like that, Judd. Not at all. Sukie loved you, I know. But Hollis – Hollis never loved me.'

'Then why on earth did he—'

'Pride. It was nothing but pride with Hollis all along. He never loved me for myself, just the idea of me. All he ever cared about was getting the best of a man called Horace Ironsides. Ironsides outwitted him in the end and it finished him. If you must know, men were always much more important than women in my husband's life.'

'She's right, you know.' Lilias had returned and was listening to what Niamh said. 'I have something for you. I promised myself that no one should see it and once I almost destroyed it but I couldn't – my son's last words.'

'Aunt Lil!' Niamh stared at her. 'But you always told us there was nothing – that Hollis left no word?'

'Because it was private, wasn't it? Written to me.' Lilias rounded on her, tears standing in her eyes. 'And if you think it's easy for me to give it up now – well, it isn't. I give it only because it has a bearing on this man's life. Go on, take it, young man. Take it before I change my mind.'

Roughly, she thrust the paper at Judd. 'I hid it to save my son's reputation but you must use it to set the record straight.' She held out her arms for Noah who transferred to her at once, bored with all this adult conversation. 'Poor little boy,' she said softly. 'Are you tired?' The child nodded, yawning even more widely. 'Come to me, then. Nana Lil's going to see you safely to bed.'

'Nana Lil?' Judd repeated. The child didn't spare him a second glance and he realised, watching them leave, that he hadn't been allowed even to touch his own son.

'Don't you want to read it?' Niamh offered Hollis's note. 'It obviously cost her a lot to give it up.'

Together they read Hollis's words. Quickly once, and more slowly the second time, so as to take it all in.

'Do you think,' he said at last, 'that Mrs Maitland would come with me to back this up?'

'What?' Niamh said, almost in a daze. She pictured Hollis and how he must have felt as the doubts came creeping in, finally convincing himself that his father had been alive when he struck him over the head. And poor Lilias, carrying the burden of this knowledge alone for so long. The knowledge that Hollis had mutilated his father's body in order to implicate Judd. 'I don't think you can ask her to do any more. I'll go with you to the authorities, if you like. He was my husband, after all.'

In less than a week Judd was clear of all charges, even complicity in the murder of Gusto Rancio in the Melbourne Gaol. He returned to The Hollies, where Niamh greeted him in the kitchen with a wary smile.

'Oh, what a pity! You've just missed them,' she said, smiling a little too brightly. 'Aunt Lilias and the children have gone for a walk on the beach.'

'Then I'll catch up with them there.'

He gave her a jaunty salute and left immediately, leaving her feeling as if her authority were about to be undermined. Resisting the temptation to follow and see their reunion for herself, she waited impatiently for their return.

The children arrived pink and glowing from their games on the beach, Noah perched high on his father's shoulders, crowing with delight. In no time at all he had accepted Judd and was no longer shy. Even Lilias looked years younger and had a new sparkle in her eye. *He's just like the Pied Piper with that fatal charm of his*, Niamh thought. *He has them all eating out of his hand.*

'I hope he's not over-excited,' she said, holding her arms out for Noah. 'He's only little and needs his rest.'

'He needs to enjoy himself, too.' Judd's smile faded. 'Do you always have to put such a dampener on things?'

Tactfully, Lilias retrieved Noah and with the help of the

366

younger mothers, bore the children away to take baths and showers to wash away the salt and the sand before they sat down to high tea.

Judd and Niamh stood alone in the kitchen staring at each other, locked in a silent battle of wills.

'Niamh, walk with me,' he said at last. It wasn't a request but a demand. 'I shall be leaving soon, and before I go, I think we need to talk.'

'If this is about Noah, I don't want—'

'Yes, it is about Noah. And everything else. Bring a shawl, too. There's a cool breeze getting up.'

'A breeze? I hope you haven't let him catch cold!'

'Will you stop worrying about the boy? He's the healthiest, sturdiest child I've seen in a long while.'

Upstairs, while she was fetching her shawl, she tried to address the situation calmly, wondering why her feelings were in such a turmoil. Wasn't this the moment she'd longed for, for both of them to be free? But would they ever be free of those feelings of guilt? That it was their fault that their partners were both dead . . . Such thoughts would keep them apart more surely than if Hollis and Sukie were still alive. He'd been away too long, among people and places she didn't know; places she'd never heard of. And he'd come back a stranger. Someone capable of robbing her of the most precious thing in her life; her adopted son.

She took a quick glance in the mirror, patting her hair into shape, admitting that she, too, had changed. She looked pinched and anxious, a little like Janet, her mother, her hair drawn back too severely to flatter her face.

As if by tacit agreement, they walked in silence, taking one of the paths that led to the beach. Gulls wheeled overhead, mournful and plaintive in winter when there was less for them to scavenge on the beach. To Niamh, their cries were an echo of her own misgivings.

She could see at once where he was leading her; that same little beach they had found when the balloon came down on the bluff. That afternoon when they had walked and talked for hours without heeding the time. That, too, reminded her her how little they knew of each other. How little time they had spent together. Two stolen afternoons.

He came to a piece of driftwood; a tree washed up on the shore by the wild, winter seas. And he perched on it, his long legs stretched out in front of him, crossed at the ankles. Taking her hands in his own, he pulled her down beside him, staring into her face as he tried to reach her and read her mood. Embarrassed to be the subject of such close scrutiny, she pulled free and shielded her eyes with one hand, pretending to be looking at something far out on the Bay. The intensity of his gaze set the blood pounding through her veins, waking her heart that had been too long asleep. Biting her lips, she fought it, unwilling to be reminded of the past.

'You do know that Noah has inherited Albert's house?' he said. 'The foundry's gone, of course but the house is there.'

'Ah yes,' she said, not without bitterness. 'And I suppose you can't wait to get your hands on it.'

'I don't want it,' he said, amazed that she should think that of him. 'Daisy and Matthew have a tenant in. But it seems Albert had a premonition that something might happen and he hid my master templates, my moulds, in the wine cellar. Anyway, that's where Matthew found them.'

'So what will you do now? Set up in business again?'

'Not here, no. I can't take the cold any more, not now I'm used to more tropical climes. I was thinking of trying my luck in Mackay. I had hoped to take my family with me.'

'You're not taking Noah. Sukie left him to me.'

'No, Niamh, that's not true. I think she asked you to keep him for me. She left him to both of us.'

'How would you know?' She glared at him. 'You weren't there.'

He narrowed his eyes to look at her. 'Niamh, what's happened to you?' he said at last. 'What did I ever do to make you think so ill of me?'

'Nothing,' she said, her voice snatched away in the breeze. 'Nothing at all.'

'You've changed.'

'And you think you haven't? Consorting with pirates and cannibals, transporting islanders? And you tell me you haven't changed?'

'Not as much as you. You want my child because you're too selfish to share your life with a man or bear a child of your

368

own. Oh, you've changed all right. You're like a crabbed, mean-spirited old maid.'

'Mean-spirited?' She turned on him, unable to bear the insults any longer. 'You call me selfish and mean-spirited? After all I've done – all I do – for the sick children of this town?'

'Yes. Because you don't have the guts to remarry and live a life of your own.'

'How dare you say that to me!'

'Good, I've made you angry. Much better than all that controlled apathy as if your heart consisted of frozen stone.'

'You bring me nothing but trouble, Judd Burden. You always have.' Great sobs started shaking her. 'And now you want to take my son away from me. You want my Noah.'

'I want you, too. I always have,' he said softly.

'A crabbed, mean-spirited old maid?'

'Ssh!' he said, letting her cry against his shoulder. 'I shouldn't have said that.'

He took a clean handkerchief from his pocket and let her wipe her tears and blow her nose. Then he kissed her lips very carefully and gently, as if embracing a child. She let go a long, shuddering breath and looked up at him.

'But it's hopeless, isn't it? You want to make a new life hundreds of miles away up north and I must stay here.'

'Why?'

'For the children, of course. For my work, my . . .'

This time his kiss wasn't gentle at all and she tensed in his arms. He refused to loose his hold and stop kissing her until he felt her relax and respond.

'I'll show you how much you're needed here,' he said. 'Who's looking after the children now? Who's bathing them now?'

'Lilias, of course. Lilias and their mothers.'

'Who cooks for the children?'

'Brigid,' she said. 'So what? Where is this leading?'

'And the washing? Who does the washing each day?'

'I do!' she said, triumphant at last. 'So you see I am indispensable.'

'Well, you're wrong,' he said. 'You've just shown me. You do nothing that couldn't be done by a laundry maid.'

'Judd . . .'

'You'll make me sorry I didn't marry a woman from the islands. At least they smile all the time and try to please a man instead of coming up with all these silly objections.'

'Silly objections? But this is my life – my work!'

'I told you – nobody's indispensable. And I need you now.'

'Certainly you do. But not for myself – to be a mother to Noah.'

'All right,' he shrugged. 'If you won't marry me, I'll just have to marry somebody else.'

'You wouldn't dare.' She flung herself into his arms and kissed him soundly. 'If I ever see you so much as glance at another woman . . .'

'You'll what?' he said, loving it, knowing he had her now.

'I'll drown you in one of your own fountains.'

Laughing, they held hands and started running against the wind, as carefree as they'd been on that summer afternoon so long ago. The clouds had rolled away and the sun had come out, smiling on the pledge they had made. They were young and strong, unafraid of hard work and could see nothing ahead of them but good fortune and smiles. Life would be kind to them now.